ANVIL OF NECESSITY

Stuart Slade

Dedication

This book is respectfully dedicated to the memory of
General Ivan Cherniakhovskii

Acknowledgements

Anvil of Necessity could not have been written without the very generous help of a large number of people who contributed their time, input and efforts into confirming the technical details of the story. Some of these generous souls I know personally, others I know only via the internet as the collective membership of "The Board" yet their communal wisdom and vast store of knowledge, freely contributed, has been truly irreplaceable. In particular, I would like to acknowledge the assistance of Shane Rogers who provided much valuable insight into South East Asian and Australian politics and history.

A particular note of thanks is due to Ryan Crierie who willingly donated his time and great expertise in producing the artwork used for the cover of this book.

I must also express a particular debt of gratitude to my wife Josefa for without her kind forbearance, patient support and unstintingly generous assistance, this novel would have remained nothing more than a vague idea floating in the back of my mind.

Caveat

Anvil of Necessity is a work of fiction, set in an alternate universe. All the characters appearing in this book are fictional and any resemblance to any person, living or dead is purely coincidental. Although some names of historical characters appear, they do not necessarily represent the same people we know in our reality.

Copyright Notice

Contents

Part One - Anvil

Chapter One
World after War

Wallsend, Tyneside, UK

"Good simple, solid grub, that's what I like. Not this foreign mucked-about stuff." John McMullen's voice took up a sneering overtone. "Ree-Zot-Ow. Rah-vee-owli. Spar-get-ee. What's wrong with foreigners, why can't they eat honest meat-and-two-veg like normal people? Nah, they've got to muck around with everything."

"I'm sorry luv, but its all the shops have. I searched all day but there aren't potatoes to be had for love nor money. Tried everywhere I did. Even went down to the corner." Maisie McMullen used the euphemism for the black market with the ease of long habit. "They didn't have none either, not for any price. Had some fish they said was cod from the Atlantic but it looked like herring to me. Didn't want to chance it. But the grocer had this risotto stuff, it was only one point for the box, and I thought it would be best. Looks a bit like potato don't you think?" She tried to smile bravely but tears were trickling down her cheeks.

McMullen looked at his wife crying, guilt at his outburst coiling around inside him. He hadn't been fair, she was doing her best to keep their home looking nice and trying to see they got as close to being well-fed as the scanty food rations would allow. It wasn't her fault there was so little food available and what there was didn't count as honest food for a British stomach. It was the damned Yanks who were responsible, what with them dropping their atom bombs on everybody. "Aye Maisie love. It does look a bit like a good mashed spud doesn't it? And it's pretty tasty when you get used to it. You've done us proud love, I don't know how you keep food on the table honest I don't."

7

And that was the truth. The crops had failed in 1947, they'd started the year strong enough, but come harvest season, the ears of wheat withered and the fruit on the trees had shriveled. And the eggs, McMullen's stomach turned at the thought of what the eggs had been like. Even in the worst years of the war, the ration of an egg a week for each adult and one extra for each child under five had been maintained. Now, eggs had gone completely, only the dried egg ration, one packet per month per adult, was available.

Then, the winter had been terrible, it had started snowing in mid-November and hadn't stopped until March. The streets had been blocked up, what little transport was left had come to a halt. Coal was already rationed, then power had been cut as well. The gasworks had shut down, it had only been kept working by a miracle after the Yanks had bombed it, so the snow had just finished the job their Corsairs and Skyraiders had started. Old Missus Archer, they'd as good as killed her. Two wars she'd survived, then she'd frozen to death, alone in her house. She'd just been one of thousands.

Still, the winter hadn't been all bad. The government had kept conscription running, but instead of putting the men into the armed forces, they'd formed them into shovel-gangs to dig the streets clear. That had at least been work of a sort and it had brought money into the house. Other conscripts had been sent into the mines, trying to get them up and running again, while more had been set to work on the railways. Nobody admitted it but it was the hard cases, collaborators and black marketeers, who'd been sent to work on the railways. It was dangerous work, the Yanks had dropped delayed-action bombs on the railway lines and a lot of them hadn't gone off.

The worst had been down south in Clapham. When the work teams had gone in to try and get the big junction there back into operation, one of them set off a 2,000 pounder. Killed more than two dozen it had. It wasn't just the danger, though, that made clearing the railways a job to be feared. In their relentless bombing of the railway system, the Yanks had found trains had started to hide in the tunnels so they'd drop their rocket-powered bombs on one end to cave the exit in, then toss some jellygas tanks in the other. Nobody got out alive from that death-trap and nobody who saw what the inside of the tunnels looked like afterwards ever forgot it.

Spring had come, such as it was, the snow melted and the work gangs were moved to other tasks; clearing bombsites, removing wreckage, trying to repair what could be repaired. McMullen had been working on clearing bombsites and learned the arts of that task well. It wasn't just a case of shifting the rubble out of the way, each piece had to be inspected for its salvage value. Intact or superficially damaged bricks had to be put carefully to one side for re-use, metal piping sorted and stacked for recovery. Also, the unending vigilance for unexploded bombs and rockets was critical. Every man had a whistle, if he saw something that looked like a UXB, he'd blow it and work would come to a halt. Then a bomb disposal team would come, check it and if it was a danger, either defuse it or blow it up on site.

Everybody had thought that when the spring came, the famine would be over. McMullen had drawn his seed ration from the Government office, gone to his allotment and planted them. He'd been there every evening, tending his little plot of land and babying his crops. Only, they'd come up sick and yellow, then died in the ground. He'd cursed his ineptness, tearing at himself with the accusation that he'd done something wrong to ruin his crop, but then he'd seen that the same had happened all over. It wasn't just his little patch, or the allotment area it was in, but the whole city. Then, on the radio, increasingly grave voices had revealed it wasn't just the whole of the country, the crops had failed across Europe. The winter of 1947/48 had consumed the last food reserves of the war-ravaged continent and there was nothing left. The voices on the radio didn't say so but people in the street knew the truth, it was the damned Yanks and their atom bombs that had caused the disaster.

Now, Britain and France and all the others were depending on charity for their survival. Canada and Australia were sending wheat and meat over. So were the Yanks, conscience money probably, McMullen thought. They thought they could buy their way out of anything. Spain and Italy had also joined in, shipping in as much food as they could to stave off the impending catastrophe. The coming winter was going to be another bad one, McMullen could feel it in his bones. It was still August but he could feel a chill in the air already. Another bad winter to knock a defeated Europe flat on its back again.

He finished off his supper and polished the plate with the last of his three slices of bread. "That wasn't bad Maisie, not so bad at all. Only a point you say? Well, perhaps them foreigners have something

9

after all. Now, I got some good news for us." He'd been bursting to tell his wife ever since he'd got back from his clearance detail. "The yard is opening up again. They're taking on workers and I start next week. I'll be a riveter again for a while. I'm back in a real job at last."

Maisie McMullen forgot her depression and her face lit up. "Oh John. That's wonderful. How long's it for?"

"Couple of years at least the Union reckon. Two cruisers are coming in for a complete refit. Spent the war in Australia so they say, now they're off to South Africa. Here's the thing though. After that, the Navy's giving the yard a contract to build a submarine. Only that's a welding job there days so there are some coming over from Canadian Vickers to train us in welding. Union's got something to say about that. Welding's a riveter's job, stands to reason, but the steelworkers are claiming its their people who should be getting it. Union says could go to a strike in the end. Still, that's two years down the line they reckon.

His wife cleared the plates off the table. She had a surprise for her husband. When she'd picked up their weekly eight ounce bacon ration from the butcher, he'd told her there would be some sausages in tomorrow and she'd asked him to put three aside for her. Two points each. She'd also got a packet of the new instant mashed potato the Americans were sending over, just add boiling water the packet said. So tomorrow, her husband could have bangers and mash for his supper. That made ten points she'd spent this week, they still had six left and it was Thursday already.

Submarine Bunker, Faslane, UK

This was probably his favorite view, of all the spectacular sites in the great concrete bunker, this was the one that was truly awe-inspiring. After coming down in the lift and stepping out onto the gallery, he could see the whole of the left-hand bay containing the submarine trots stretched out beneath him. The right hand bay, the other side of the thick blast wall, had a problem. The roof of the bunker was massive, 30 feet of reinforced concrete topped with a further six inches as a fuse initiator. The Americans hadn't been able to drive a bomb though it, although the pockmarks in the top and the cracks showed how hard they'd tried. Then, one day, their Skyraiders had dropped a strange bomb, one that bounced across the surface of the water. Fortunately for the occupants of the right hand bay, the steel doors had been closed and they'd kept the strange bomb out but the blast had jammed the doors in place. The Germans had built the bunker so strongly, it was proving the devil's work to free them. Meanwhile, there were six perfectly intact Type XXIC U-boats in there, unable to get out.

All six spots in the operational bay were occupied, the first four by U-class submarines, the two furthest away by X-class boats. Commander Robert Fox could recite their names without prompting. *Ursula*, she was charging batteries, a plume of spray and steam was rising from the exhausts built into her after casing, only to be snatched up by the ventilation hood and carried away, outside the bunker. Then there was *Undaunted,* the last time Fox had seen her, he was limping into Churchill with her saddle tanks battered in where a German destroyer had placed its depth charges almost, but not quite, accurately enough to do for her. Next to her was *Unbroken*, the little submarine that had pushed right into the Kattegat and put four torpedoes into the German cruiser *Prinz Eugen* before getting back to Churchill with her fuel tanks dry. Finally *Upstart* was destoring, she'd just come back from a training and monitoring patrol in the North Sea.

The Royal Navy had retained the U-class because they were largely British-equipped and were riveted. The later V-class had been divided out between the Commonwealth navies; they had American-supplied equipment and engines, ones that would cost hard currency to support. Anyway, the V-class were largely welded and it would take time to teach the British shipyard workers how to weld ships.

Right at the end of the line were two larger submarines, ones that overlapped the diminutive U class at both ends. A new class, one that incorporated all the lessons of the War. Derived from the U-class certainly, but radically different. Smooth, streamlined and as fast as a thief underwater. They'd been designed with a complete outer casing, not the saddletank design the British had used for so long. Still had four tubes forward but an extra set of reloads and two short tubes aft for the new anti-escort torpedoes. No gun, that was the big difference. No guns at all. *Xanadu* was the lead ship of the class, she'd made one patrol before the war had ended. Next to her, was Fox's new command, HMS *Xena*. New ship, just delivered from Canadian Vickers.

A command that he'd never expected to get. Fox had finished the war as a Lieutenant Commander with a splendid war record and, due to a complete inability to say the right thing to the right person at the right time, looked like finishing his career in the Navy as a Lieutenant-Commander with a splendid war record. In fact, by all rights, his career was already over. He had been passed over for promotion six months after the war had ended and had already started to look for a career outside the Navy. The problem was that the naval officers preferred choice for a post-military career, farming, wasn't practical in a Europe where crops just wouldn't grow and livestock died.

Then, during a particularly onerous meeting in Whitehall, a French Navy representative had started a long lecture on how the RN was going to have to learn to take orders from its betters, ones who hadn't run away to America but had stayed in Europe to make the best they could of things. The diatribe had been interrupted by Fox's fist breaking the Frenchman's nose. The resulting court martial had found him guilty (with extenuating circumstances) of 'Conduct Unbecoming' and sentenced him to a year's loss of seniority. That had put him back in the promotion zone and he'd been made Commander on the next list. Now he had command of HMS *Xena*. As he mounted the narrow gangway, he got the strange feeling that he was coming home at last.

Xena's wardroom was typical of a war-built submarine, everything done to save time and simplify construction. A central table flanked by seats that could be converted into bunks. A small bookcase, a barometer and a clock and a profusion of piping and ducts, punctuated by valve handwheels. It looked hideous but was severely practical. Exposed piping could be reached and fixed when depth-charging caused it to spring a leak, easy-to-access valves could be shut quickly when blasted open by near-misses. His officers were assembled, waiting for him.

"About time the bar was opened." Fox said.

The wardroom noted the remark, the Captain's policy about the bar was vital for the happy running of the ship.

"Here's to us. Now that we're together for the first time, I want to make a few points about what I hope to achieve in our first commission. I won't be speaking in this rather pompous manner again, but we have a big task ahead of us. It's been almost ten years since the Royal Navy has been operating on a peacetime footing and we are all out of practice in that regard. The way we will have to do things from now on is likely to be quite different from anything we've been used to. It's not just a matter of going back to 1938, because we aren't in that world any more.

"The Americans changed everything when their bombers took Germany out and we're not certain what the new world is going to look like. I needn't add we're not the same Navy any more either, you all know that. So to a large extent, we'll be making the rules up as we go along and writing the book as we do so. That's a hell of a privilege, and its one hell of a responsibility. In a very real sense, the navy for the next twenty years is going to be what we make of it in the next three or four.

"A lot of people out there are saying that we don't have a role, that Navies and Armies are obsolete and that all a country needs is a giant fleet of bombers. Well, I think they're wrong. They didn't look and see that it was the Navy that kicked the doors open for SAC's B-36s, they didn't look and see that it was the armies in Russia that bought the time to built those bombers. They didn't see that it was us, the Canadians and the British, who kept the convoys running to Archangel and Murmansk, who took the war into the German's backyard, the Channel, the North Sea and the Arctic. They don't see any of that, so we're going to have to show them.

"That's a big job for us and there aren't many of us to do it. You saw the boats here when you came in. Well, apart from a handful of destroyers, that's it. The rest of the fleet is laid up, the Government can't afford to pay the crews, even at conscript rates. The eyes of the whole fleet are on us to set an example, to show the country and the rest of the world that we are still *the* navy. I think, with a bit of luck, we can do that and we should have a very good commission."

The Wardroom picked up their glasses again. Fair enough, they said to themselves.

Chulachomklao Military Academy, Bangkok, Thailand

This was the part that Sergeant Major (First Class) Manop Patmastana had been dreading. The first parade of new officer cadets and the first one under the new rules. The cadets were drawn up by size, tallest at the right, shortest at the left. As Manop walked down the line, he was filled with a growing sense of impending doom. It wasn't the uniforms, quite.

The Army, as was traditional, issued its uniforms in two sizes. Too large and too small, and left the individual cadets to make them fit. The results of giving this task to young men who had never handled a needle and thread before was painfully obvious. Hems and seams were uneven, pants legs were different lengths, threads were hanging down and, if Manop had looked, he was in no doubt he would see wounds where needles had been driven into fingertips. Idly, he wondered how many of the cadets had sewn themselves to their uniforms the night before. He relieved himself by screaming insults and abuse at the more obvious examples of ineptitude. Then he came to the part he was dreading.

The last four cadets were a striking contrast to the rest. The uniforms for example, the alterations might not be professional-grade but they were neat and serviceable. Alterations that showed a disturbing level of familiarity with the art of sewing things. They'd even let the chest of their jackets out slightly, and taken in the waist. Sergeant Major Manop looked at the back with interest. His guess had been correct, they hadn't got that right; pants intended for male soldiers didn't quite fit female rear ends. He leaned forward so his face was barely more than a few centimeters from that of the tallest of the female cadets then let loose with his best parade ground bellow.

"May the Lord Buddha have mercy on us. Who are you and what are YOU doing here?"

The woman's expression didn't change. "Officer Cadet Sirisoon Chandrapa na Ayuthya Sergeant Major. Special Entry Cadet, Sergeant Major."

Manop swore under his breath, he'd been hoping she would get flustered and call him 'sir" which would give him an excuse to scream more insults. "Officer cadet? You call yourself an officer cadet? Only soldiers can be officers. You're not a soldier are you?"

"Not yet, Sergeant Major."

"Not yet? Not ever. Women can't be soldiers cadet. Soldiering is man's work. You're not going to be a soldier, cadet, you're taking up the space of somebody who could be. Do you know what a water lily is cadet?"

"Yes, Sergeant Major."

"Then you know it is very beautiful to look at, smells nice and is decorative. And it is also a useless parasite. No good to anybody. So you four are this company's water lilies. What are you?"

"Water lilies Sergeant Major."

"Good." Manop started to turn away when he heard behind him.

"Very *militant* water lilies."

His face never changed, he was of the firm belief that if he smiled on parade, his face would crack. But underneath his scowl, his sense of doom and foreboding faded slightly. One at least of these, these *aberrations*, was ready to stand up for herself. Perhaps there was hope for the Army after all.

Flight Deck B-36H "Texan Lady", 42,500 feet over the North Atlantic

"Coming through Sir."

Colonel Bob Dedmon pushed the nose of *Texan Lady* into a slight dive and was rewarded with an ascending "wheee" noise form the bomb bay tunnel. Then, the hatch opened and two hands emerged holding a tray. Sergeant King took it and held it while Smith extracted himself from trolley. Eventually, he made it up to the flight deck, retrieving his tray on the way.

"Here you are Sirs. Two coffees, black with sugar. Two steak sandwiches, ketchup and mayo. Yours has Swiss cheese on it, Major Clancy.

There was something about a steak sandwich that was unique when it was cooked over 40,000 feet up. Everybody knew it. Now, the war was over and the B-36s had a proper galley again, the weight had

15

cut their maximum ceiling by 1,000 feet or more but now, in peacetime, that didn't matter so much. The galley was small but it made two-day missions much more comfortable. It took a long time to fly 10,000 miles at 250 miles per hour. Dedmon bit into his sandwich.

"Good, very good. Thank you Smith."

"Uomph thmadms yuus."

"I think that's mouth-full-Clancy-ese for 'thank you' as well. How's it going back there Smith."

"Pretty good Sir, The electronic pit is just getting their new gear set up now. The new coffee machine has been working just fine as well."

"Glad to see we have our priorities in the right order. Want a helping hand getting back?"

"Please Sir." Dedmon waited until Smith was back in his trolley then angled *Texan Lady* back into a shallow climb. The angle sent Smith back down the tunnel, removing the necessity of pulling himself through hand over hand.

"Bomb-Nav station? How we doing?"

"About four hours to feet dry sir. We'll be crossing the British coast just south of Glasgow, then heading over the North Sea, across the Baltic and doing the feet dry thing again over Petrograd. Then on to Moscow and landing at Sheremetevo. Weapons embarked are unarmed sir. Three Mark Fours and a Mark Five. We can arm them any time you say so. Engines are behaving themselves Sir. Even Number Six." That was the engine that had been replaced after *Texan Lady* had been damaged during The Big One. It had never quite worked as well as the other five piston engines.

"What we going to do in Russia Sir?" Dedmon stretched in his seat, it was going to be a long flight. Phil Clancy was a new member of the crew, replacing Major Pico who'd left to help form NORAD. Clancy had still to get used to the idea that the B-36 could go anywhere it wanted, any time it wanted, and there was nothing anybody could do about it.

"Just routine. We go there with *Barbie Doll* and *Sixth Crew Member* and stay for a few days. The Russians will ask us to fly around a bit, maybe overfly an area where the Germans are still holding out. In theory, if the Germans use gas again, we could do a laydown on them but that's fairly unlikely now. In a week or so, we fly home, another hometown takes over, then we go to Nevada. There's some sort of exercise due to happen down there.

Office of Sir Martyn Sharpe, British Viceroy to India, New Delhi

"Have you read the latest report Sir Eric? It just came in this morning, the Air Force has lost another one. Same story as all the others, the aircraft broke up in mid-air. We can't carry on like this, it's the fifth one we've lost this month. I've issued orders to ground the whole fleet until the problem is sorted out. Its bad, but we can swallow it for a while, the Ostrich squadrons can carry the load until we get this sorted out. Is there any word on the investigations? I suppose the real question we must ask is whether the Hornet will be affected the same way."

Sir Eric Haohoa thought carefully for a few seconds. There was a good reason why the post of Cabinet Secretary also contained the administration of the intelligence services within its remit. Both required the ability to distinguish what the important issues really were, as distinct from those that everybody thought were significant. Related to that was the skill in answering questions in the order the questioner needed, not in the order they were asked. This was one of those times.

"Sir Martyn, the investigation into the Mosquito crashes has reached some tentative conclusions. It is too early to make these public yet but the Accident Investigations Board thinks they have a handle on the problem. It's the glue, Sir Martyn. When de Havilland's originally designed the Mosquito, they used phenolic resins for the wooden structural members and the plywood composite skinning. That's all well and good, but they elected to use Casein as the glue in the joints between the structural members. Questioned on that issue, Sir Geoffrey said that it was partly a matter of economy, partly a matter of it being easy to work with and partly the fact that it has gap-filling properties that made allowance for manufacturing tolerances.

"That probably made a lot of sense in Europe where its cold and relatively dry and it was satisfactory in Canada where it was colder and drier, but out here, its a problem. Casein is basically just stiff cheese and the heat and humidity here is causing it to go moldy and lose strength. Also, its not waterproof and the wood in the airframe is getting waterlogged. That's particularly bad in the lower wing surfaces and it seems as if the break-ups with the lower wing surfaces disintegrating and their joints failing.

"This is hitting us in a few ways. One of them is very strange and ironic. We may not be a heavily industrialized country yet but we are a nation of carpenters and woodworkers. The components here are made to a much higher standard than de Havilland achieved elsewhere and their fit is much better. In industrial terms, we can work wood to much finer tolerances than the designers anticipated. So, there is less glue in the joints. That's good and bad of course, there is less glue in the joints to provide strength but we don't need the gap-filling character of Casein. Any adhesive that has the required strength will do. Another problem is unique to us. Casein is a milk product. A cow's milk product. We have serious problems getting Hindu workers to handle it. So de Havilland's recruited the assembly workers from Moslems."

Sir Martyn looked up very sharply. "Sabotage?"

"Not as far as we can tell, more like they don't take as much care as one might expect of a more dedicated workforce. There may be some outright examples of sabotage but we haven't been able to find any. In any case, shifting to another type of glue will solve that problem as well. But, speaking of competence." Sir Eric gathered his thoughts for a second. Getting de Havilland and Folland to set up shop in India had been a major coup for Sir Martyn, most of the other major aviation designers had gone to Canada or Australia. Being a bearer of bad news was a chancy profession at best. "We've been having a quiet word with some of the other aviation companies and de Havilland do not have a good reputation within the industry. Or rather they have a reputation for cutting corners and taking chances that other designers view with alarm. I think we may have an example here. It's not that anybody decided to use Casein as a glue in the Mosquito, its that nobody decided not to. De Havilland used it before so they used it again without considering the different circumstances.

"As to its effects, Sir Martyn, this may not be as severe as you fear. If these preliminary findings hold true, we will have to inspect all the in-service Mosquitos, find those that have deteriorated and scrap them. We can salvage their engines and guns, those are not affected by the problems and they represent the greatest burden on foreign exchange. We have Ostriches in store we can use to replace them. Our light bomber crews prefer them anyway. It may be much slower but it has greater firepower and its Pratt air-cooled engines are much less vulnerable to ground fire than the liquid-cooled Allisons in the Mosquito.   And the Ostrich is heavily armored of course.   The Russians didn't call it the Australian Sturmovik for nothing."

Both men laughed. The way the name 'Australian Sturmovik' had passed through two languages, three accents and four countries to become "Ostrich" was fast becoming an aircraft industry legend. But then, again, so were the Australian-built Beaufighters. The Australians had taken the basic Beaufighter design from Bristol, cleaned it up and replaced the unavailable 1,600 horsepower Hercules radials with 2,250 horsepower Pratt and Whitney R-2800s.   Then, they'd replaced the original four Hispano 20mm cannon with the same number of Russian 23mm Volkov-Yartsev guns and put six American .50 caliber Brownings in the wings in place of the old .303s. With 2,000 pounds of bombs under its now-armored belly and eight 90 pound rockets under its wings, the Ostrich had proved a devastating close support machine. With the whole Mosquito project in growing jeopardy, it looked like the Indian Air Force would be using it for a long time yet.

"Fortunately, the Hornet won't be affected. It has metal lower wing panels and it is being built using a combination of phenolic resins and resorcinol glues that are not subject to water damage. We need to downplay the fact it's based on Mosquito experience of course. As to the Mosquitos themselves? We have to decide whether we wish to continue with them. We can change the glues and perhaps the wing paneling easily enough but repairing the aircraft's reputation may be a lot harder. Then, of course, there is the jet problem."

"Or should we just bite the bullet and admit we got it wrong?" Sir Martyn tapped his teeth with the butt end of his pen. "The Mosquito seemed sound enough a few years back but now it isn't fast enough or high-flying enough to avoid fighters. We could drop the aircraft completely and just concentrate on building the Hornet. The

Americans are offering surplus B-27 Super-Marauders at very low cost. Really, we should be looking at buying jets but the fuel......."

He sighed. Jets had made most piston-engined aircraft obsolete. The problem was that the world's oil refineries were geared up to produce gasoline, not jet fuel, and there was a worldwide shortage of the latter. A shortage not made any better by the Americans buying up what supplies were available. There wasn't a single oil refinery in India that could produce jet fuel, if the Indian Air Force went to jets, every drop of fuel they burned would have to be imported. Sir Martyn's economic experts were predicting it would be a decade at least before jet fuel was available in adequate supplies. Until then, nations would have to go on flying large numbers of piston-engined aircraft despite their vulnerability. That was why India was developing the Hornet, piston-engined certainly but about the best anybody could come up with.

"Low cost indeed Sir Martyn. They are offering B-27s at a cost that is barely more than the amount we pay for a pair of Allison engines for a Mosquito. Sometimes I think they are using their huge supply of surplus aircraft to crush everybody else's aircraft industry before it can get off the ground."

"I'm sure that has figured in their planning. In fact I think we can be certain it has. If The Big One proved anything, it is that the Americans do not play games where their interests are concerned. As for de Havilland, I have heard much the same as you from different sources. Originally, we had planned on allowing the new company a free hand but this Mosquito business gives me cause to question that decision. I think the time may have come for the Indian Government to take a stake in de Havilland (India)."

Chapter Two
World Still At War

Headquarters, Army Group Vistula, Riga, "The Baltic Gallery"

The timing of the message had been purely happenstance but it was making a valuable point nevertheless. An intelligence report, adding one more pin to a map where the horde of red made the addition difficult. There were so many hostile units that there was literally not enough space on the map for them all. Opposing them, the scattered line of blue pins looked desperately thin. Yet, the red mass was increasing every day as more units arrived from the Kola Peninsula. The surrender of Finland had allowed the Russian/Canadian Army that had held the peninsula for five long years to split. The Canadians were going home, the Russians were moving to liberate the Baltic provinces.

"And now, given the situation we see before us, how do you suggest we go about securing the territory we presently occupy against the attack that is building up?"

The Field Marshal's staff had heard the dangerously silky tone in their master's voice and quickly found excuses to be anywhere else. That tone meant some unfortunate had said something extraordinarily stupid and was about to get a lesson in the military arts. If the recipient was wise, he would say nothing and listen for the speaker was an acknowledged master of the art of war. The commander of Army Group Vistula was Field Marshal Erwin Rommel.

The listener waffled with a few aimless comments about moral ascendancy and the German warrior-spirit. Eventually, Rommel cut him of impatiently. "Yes, yes, yes. All very good and it sounds most impressive. But do you know our troops will fight at all? I cannot be sure of that and I have taken pains to make sure we do not put the matter to the test. In case you have not noticed, Germany has been destroyed. The men here have nothing left to live for, that is true, but equally, they have nothing left to die for. Your SS troopers may be determined to leave the world in a blaze of revenge-filled glory but my Landsers are not so sure on the matter. And, just remember, we have tens of thousands of civilians here as well. We must think of them as well. The last thing we want is what happened to Germany being repeated on us."

"But the Americans are leaving, they are going home."

"Really? Then explain this." Rommel produced a copy of Life magazine, dated the week before. Its cover story was how Russia and America were working together to rebuild Eastern Europe. One of the pictures was of Sheremetevo airfield, a big airfield on the outskirts of Moscow. The story was of how the airbase, once a major military facility, was being converted into an international airport, but the photographs showed the line of B-36 bombers parked by the runways. The SS General stared at the pictures, his stomach involuntarily curling at the sight of the bombers that had wiped a country from the map. Rommel watched his expression, then changed his tone.

"The American Army is going home, yes. So are the Australians, so are the Canadians. A good guest knows when it is time to leave. But the Americans have left their bombers and it is fair to guess that those bombers will not be dropping flowers on us. That is the American doctrine now. They do not fight their enemies any more, they just destroy them."

"The problem with fighting the Americans is that they do not know what their doctrine is and those that do feel no obligation to obey it." The general smirked as he repeated the quotation.

"General, that sounds very fine when you repeat it in an admiring salon filled with civilians. But we are professionals. The Americans know exactly what their doctrine is and they apply it consistently and ruthlessly. It is called overwhelming force. They applied it before they brought nuclear weapons into the world and they continue to apply it now. You remember the battles along the Volga bend? How our attacks were smothered under a mass of American machines? How their fighter-bombers crushed every attempt we made to move, saturating our rear areas with fire and death? From what I have heard, it was even worse in France and England.

"Remember how their artillery followed every move we made, their massed battalions of guns pointed with the unerring precision of a sniper, switching from target to target with the delicacy of a ballet dancer? The Americans fight our blood and flesh with their machines and, win or lose, we lose. Their bombers sitting on a Russian airfield tell us all we can look forward to is more of the same. Overwhelming force, applied against a helpless enemy that cannot even pretend to defend itself. If, General, you look for a slogan to apply to our situation, I would recommend a different one. 'When rape is inevitable, the only thing left is to lie back and enjoy it.' We're going to get raped, General." Rommel gestured at the situation map again. "And it is inevitable. If we have no choice but to fight then fight we will, if we can and for as long as we can. But if an agreement is possible, then we should lie back and enjoy it. However much it hurts."

The SS General looked at the chart as well. Beneath the bombast, he was an intelligent, some said brilliant, man and knew a hopeless situation when he saw one. If Army Group Vistula stayed where it was, it would be crushed. If it tried to break out, it would be massacred. And if it broke out, where would it go? What would it do?. Poland was an independent country again, crossing that country would mean an act of war. Or would it? The General was no longer sure of exactly what the status of Army Group Vistula was. The SS had never particularly studied the rules of war. "Is an agreement possible?"

Rommel nodded. "It may well be, yes. The last orders we received from Germany were from President Goering. They ordered us to cease all offensive operations, take only the minimum actions necessary for self defense. That we have done. Germany was surrendering unconditionally and, as an element of the German armed forces, that applied to us. There is another factor though. Under international law, an offer of surrender is only valid when there are forces capable of and competent to accept the surrender available. One of the reasons why we have withdrawn from the Petrograd front was that by doing so, we avoided being in contact with any forces competent and capable of accepting our surrender. We made sure we couldn't surrender because we carefully avoided meeting anybody we could surrender to. That bought us time but we've run out of it. We can't retreat any more, we are pinned against the coast. We are under orders to surrender and the Russians know it. Don't deceive yourself General, so do our men.

"However, surrendering a force like this requires organization and negotiation. The Russian commander, what's his name ... Rokossovski .... knows that as well. He wants a meeting so we can make the arrangements to surrender our forces. That meeting will be our chance to see what we can negotiate. We have a few cards we can play. Russia has been bled white, they'll want to avoid casualties if they possibly can and we are in Russian soil, they will not want the Americans dropping hellburners on us if it can be avoided. If we can make an agreement out of that, get our people treated decently, then its the best we can achieve. If not.."

"We fight"

"Exactly. But remember this, our country has capitulated and we are under orders to surrender. If we fight, we do so as lawless brigands and bandits. And that, General Skorzeny, means we would have no right to expect mercy from anybody."

Khabarovsk, Siberia, Russia

The bands had been practicing their display for weeks and had got it down perfectly. The two, one Russian, one American, stood side by side on the parade ground belting out a long series of military marches. The spectacle was that only one band was playing at a time, they were switching program between them, never missing a beat with the transitions. Unless the spectators looked, there was no way to tell which was playing at any given time. Few thought to do so, it didn't really matter who was playing and, anyway, the spectacle in front was too, well, spectacular.

The American units were drawn up in front of the parade stand. One by one, the color bearer of each was stepping forward and the regimental color was dipped and cased. Then, carrying the furled color, the bearer stepped back while the Russian units opposite held their salute. The ceremony was marking the end of an era. The 84th Infantry Division was going home, and with it FUSAG-Russia, the First United States Army Group Russia was standing down. The men would be leaving by the big C-99 transports that had brought them, their equipment, the tanks, armored personnel carriers, artillery, trucks, would stay, donated to the Russians. A generous gesture, one not entirely prompted by the truth that it would cost more than the equipment was worth to ship it home. But, the men were going home, after five years away. First in, first out was fair enough but not too much of a sacrifice for the others. SUSAG-Russia would be following within months.

Some of the crowd were watching the figures on the parade stand. Two figures in particular, the dour, glowering figure of President Zhukov and, next to him, the dashing General Patton. Thunder and Lightning the Germans had called the pair and they had never worked out which they feared the most. Fighting Zhukov was a grim death-grapple with an enemy who never gave up and never gave in. Once battle was joined it went on until exhaustion prevented its continuing any longer. Fighting Patton was a different matter entirely, an exchange of maneuvers, a slashing exchange of blows, of American units that could mysteriously chance their facing through 90 degrees overnight, who would turn up hundreds of kilometers from where they were supposed to be.

Colonel Yvegeni Valerin was one of those who watched the Generals, not the parade. One of Zhukov's staff officers, it was his job to sort through the vast mountain of equipment that the Americans were leaving behind. Some of it was destined for the units reclaiming the captured territories in the West. The armored personnel carriers for example, they were proving a major revolution in fighting the groups of bandits that infested the area between Moscow and the pre-war frontier. Then there was the task of patrolling the new borders, making sure that the soil of Mother Russia was protected again. The American armored cars were good for that. And the artillery, Valerin was a good Russian soldier and a good Russian soldier never threw artillery away. Something the Germans had learned to their cost when the Russian Army lined their guns up wheel-to-wheel and blasted holes in the German positions by sheer weight of steel. Then there were the trucks. The scale of issue of motor transport in an American unit had stunned the Russians. Even in an infantry division, it seemed that nobody in the American Army walked.

But the American tanks? The M-26 in all its versions was hopelessly obsolete. It even had a gasoline engine, something the

Russians and the Germans had dumped early on in the war. The later M-46 had a diesel engine and a new 90mm gun, one that outperformed both the German 88mm and the Russian 100mm. Well, the early versions of the 100 anyway, the Americans had sat down with the Russian designers, shown them a few tricks and some new ammunition concepts and the 100 had suddenly become a feared tank-killer. In exchange, the Russians had taken a look at the layout and armor on the M-46, shuddered and started to show the Americans a few tricks and the concept of sloping armor plate. The full result of the co-operation wasn't available yet, but would be soon. The American's new M-48 was much more Russian than the Americans liked to admit while the new Russian T-54 was much more American than the Russians liked to concede.

No, the American tanks and so much else of the donated equipment would be scrapped, its metal going into the blast furnaces that fed the huge armament industries around Khabarovsk. When Valerin had arrived here, back in 1942, it had been a small Siberian town, a backwater noted only for its vast railway marshaling yard. However, that yard had made it suitable for relocation of the industries that had been evacuated from the west and provide homes for the refugees who had fled from the Germans.

Then, the Americans had started to arrive, a trickle at first, then an ever-growing tide. When the Americans had arrived, they built things. Like a runway so large everybody else thought they were joking -- until the first of the six-engined C-99 transports had started to land. They'd been landing steadily ever since, an Air Bridge the Americans called it, pouring men and equipment directly from American factories into the Armies fighting in Russia. The heavy stuff had come by sea, landing in the port of Vladivostok but the men and the priority equipment had come by air.

The Americans had done more than just build an airstrip. They'd started building factories so that they wouldn't have to fly common articles from America. They'd started to build oil refineries so they wouldn't have to ship refined oil products in. Their "production engineers" had gone around the Russian built factories and suggested changes, a few things here, a few there. And Russian production had soared. Now Khabarovsk and dozens of towns like it in what had once been the wilderness of Siberia had become thriving industrial centers. Lately, the Americans were speaking of something else. Oil. Their petroleum explorers had come to Siberia and looked around, then got very excited. Siberia was oil-rich. Getting at it was going to be a problem but where there was a will there was a way.

Now, the Americans were going home. A wise decision. They had done their share, they had helped Russian hold the line against the onslaught from Germany. But, Germany had been defeated and now, Russia had to be recovered by Russians. Only there was something else happening. With Russia-in-the-west occupied, Russia-in-the-east had become an economic powerhouse in its own right. And now Japan, freshly installed along its recently-conquered Chinese border was eyeing that powerhouse.

Flight Deck B-36H "Texan Lady", Final Approach, Sheremetevo Airbase, Russia

"One-Three-Five...............One Three Zero............One Two Five ....One Two Zero......... One One Five"

There was a lurch and the wheels screamed suddenly. "On the ground. Engines one to six, full reverse power. Argus, you missed ETA by 45 seconds. That's five bucks you owe the crew welfare fund."

"First time in six months Sir." His words were nearly drowned out by the roar as the six piston engines went into full reverse power, slowing the big bomber down. As it reached the start of the turn-offs to the taxiways, three jeeps came out from the side, one had a big "Follow Me" sign on its back, the others were armed with machineguns and took station either side of *Texan Lady*.

"Hey, look over there Sir. I didn't know the boss was going to be here." Major Clancy was pointing at the side of the runway where General Tibbett's B-36, *Enola Gay* was parked in the dispersal area with her Hometown mates *Bocks Car* and *The Great Artiste*. Altogether, over a dozen B-36s were in dispersal, the whole area surrounded by barbed wire and guarded by Russian troops. He gestured at the wire, the guards and the two jeeps keeping station on the taxying bomber. "Those don't look too friendly."

"Don't get the wrong idea. Moscow's been back in Russian hands for six months now and they're still a lot of hold-outs, deserters, bandits, you name it, loose out here. And you saw what's left of the city as we came in. There are people here who would kill for what we have in our galley. All this stuff's here to protect us, not to keep us in. This is your first trip to Russia isn't it Phil?"

"Yes Sir."

"OK. You got the standard briefing then. Remember it. Few extra words of advice. When we get out, there'll be Russians meeting us with bread, salt and vodka. Take it, its a traditional welcome. All these people have got left is their pride and making us feel welcome is a big part of that. Something else to remember, these are just about the only people in the world who actually like us at the moment."

The conversation broke off as Dedmon turned *Texan Lady* off the runway, onto the taxiway to the dispersal apron. They were passing a long line of Russian fighters, mostly piston-engined Lavochkin 9s and 11s but also a handful of the Yakovlev jets, a strange looking aircraft with its single jet engine hanging under the nose. Clancy searched his memory. Yak-17s, that was the designation.

He waved at the fighters. "They any good Sir?"

"The Lavochkins? Damned good for piston-engined birds. They'll take down a German Ta-152 nicely, especially at low altitude. Against a B-36, they run out of steam 20,000 feet below us. The Yak jets are good little dogfighters, at least as good as the F-80, but they've got dreadfully short range. They top out just over 40,000 feet but they use so much fuel getting there, all they can do is go straight back down again. The Russians have the same problems the Germans had. They've hit the maximum power they can get out of a jet engine without some pretty advanced metallurgy and they don't have it. I hear our guys are working with them on that."

"Sir, what did you mean these are the only people in the world who like us? We finished off the Nazis, didn't we?"

"Yeah, but the way we did it doesn't sit too well with an awful lot of people. Nobody's ever destroyed a whole country like that before and people are having a job getting their minds around it. At first people were happy enough to see the war was over, or so they thought, but its a year later now and they're looking at what we did to Germany and having second thoughts about it. And about us."

"Don't they know what the Germans did? Are they insane, have they forgotten all of that?"

"For most of them, its second or third hand or even more remote. Just stories and old stories at that. Film of the destroyed cities in Germany is first hand and it's a new story, something they see today. And we have all the old questions coming up. Why should people at home be destroyed instead of the soldiers at the front? Why should people be killed when its their leaders who were responsible? All that stuff. The reality of what happened here is far away from them. The destroyed cities in Germany are on their cinema screens every week. So we ain't the world's most popular people right now. Whoops."

Dedmon saw the "Follow Me" jeep break right and steered after it. He frowned for a second, he'd been late catching the change in direction and it seemed, just for a brief second, that *Texan Lady* had anticipated him, started the turn on her own before his own control inputs took effect. Imagination of course.

"Here, its different. The Russians know the Germans did, first hand, and they're still uncovering the worst of it. There isn't a family in Russia that hasn't lost members, some by the dozen. Did you know the Germans deliberately starved a million and a half Russian PoWs to death in 1941 alone? And that went on for six years.

"Take a look of those fighters. The one at the end there, Yellow-32. Painted on its nose. *For Maritsa.* Don't know who Maritsa was, might be his mother, his sister, his wife, daughter, whoever. But she was part of his family, she's dead and the Germans killed her. So every time that pilot kills a German he does it 'for Maritsa'. Every one of those fighters has its own dedication. God knows what would have happened if the Russian Army had made it to Germany, with all the rage and hatred that has built up, they would have slaughtered everything in sight. It would have been a bloodbath.

"So of all people, the Russians understand what we did and why. And they honor us for it. They also remember something else, when they were fighting the Germans alone, we were the ones who came to help them. Oh, you and I know that there were other reasons for that and the Australians and Canadians were there as well, but to the Russians, we were what they saw. They reckon they owe us and anything they can do for us helps to pay off that debt. So, if you're offered anything as a gift, take it. And honor it. Just remember who gave it to you and a day or so later invite him on board for a sandwich.

"The only secrets we have here are in the bomb bay so there's nothing to worry about. And your guest will tell his grandchildren about the day he ate a sandwich on board the bomber that killed Berlin."

Submarine Bunker, Faslane, UK

"Thank you for coming, Commander. How are you settling into *Xena*?"

"Very well Sir. She's a world different from the U-class or even the Vs of course. If we'd had them back in '45...."

"Indeed. Still, we've got them now. A few at any rate. You ready for sea, Commander?"

"Sir. We've finished loading stores. Only four Mark Eights and a pair of the new anti-escort fish though. No reloads at all."

"You won't be needing those. You'll be taking a boffin out for a ramble through the North Sea." Commander Fox's face was suddenly seized by an expression of almost incoherent panic. Dark indeed were the tales of submarine commanders who had been assigned the task of taking boffins out on a ramble to gather information for their strange investigations. Some commanders so afflicted had never been quite the same afterwards, prone to inexplicable panic attacks and waking whimpering in the middle of the night. Fox himself remembered one such creature arriving for research purposes with seventeen trunkloads of instruments to be installed in *Untiring*. Then, twenty minutes before setting sail, demanding that three six inch diameter holes be drilled in the pressure hull. FOSM looked at him with a combination of amusement and sympathy. "Robert, you'd better join us in the Conference Room."

The 'Conference Room' had once been the old German operations center and it still had a vaguely Teutonic air about it. Fox

30

could imagine the Kriegsmarine officers looking at the situation displays of the North Sea, the Arctic and the Northern Approaches while blonde German women auxiliaries moved the counters on the tables and brought the messages in from the U-boats. The Royal Navy had a similar operations center in Churchill, or had, it had been handed over to the Canadians now. Here, the operations table had been covered over with a cloth and there were charts scattered over it. Beside them, a character Fox thought of as being a typical scientific-looking fellow, was reading some sheets of data, his expression grim. Fox didn't like it when scientific-looking fellows had grim expressions. It usually meant nausea for somebody.

"Doctor Swamphen, I would like you to meet Commander Fox of *Xena*. He'll be taking you out on your next trip. Robert, Doctor Swamphen from the Admiralty Underwater Weapons Research Establishment."

"Doctor, pleased to meet you. Will you be bringing much in the way of equipment?" Fox's voice was so plaintive that his companions were hard put to stop laughing.

"Just that." Swamphen pointed to a small carpet bag sitting on one of the stools. "And some equipment for taking water and bottom samples. Nothing that won't fit into a standard suitcase. Sorry about that, I've been spoiled I'm afraid. My last trip was on an American fleet boat. Harrowing trip, the ice cream machine only served six flavors. Crew nearly mutinied." This time everybody in the room did laugh. The luxuries of the big American submarines were notorious. Still, the way things had worked out, it was the small U and V class boats that had done the really vital stuff. So much so, the Americans had bought V class boats from Canadian Vickers to replace their old S class. Fox felt himself warming to this strange scientist.

"You are familiar with these of course?" 'These' were charts of the North Sea. Fox wasn't just familar with them, he could have drawn them in his sleep and the Admiralty cartographer wouldn't have been able to tell the difference between the original and Fox's rendition. Swamphen looked rueful. "Well, they're pretty good, the Navy's spent a lot of time drawing them and keeping them up to date. Inshore, they're fine and the coverage of the North Sea is pretty good. Outside those limits, we hardly know what is out there. The soundings are tens, perhaps hundreds of miles apart and we have no idea what's between them. Submarines are getting faster every year now, you mark my words, one day, somebody's going to plow straight into an underwater mountain nobody even guessed was there. That's one thing we've got to look at. We need better charts.

"That's one thing we're going to be doing. We need to know in detail what the seabed looks like and we need to know how the sea behaves. We've made a start, and to be honest, the answers are frightening. We know far less than we thought and most of what we did know is wrong. Commander Fox, everybody is talking about the next great step in ASW. They Type XXIs gave us a scare but we coped with it. Just. Mostly because we knew what the XXI was like and what it could do long before it entered service."

And there, Swamphen thought to himself, we have to leave that little subject. Most of the Type XXI data had come via an organization called "The Red Orchestra" in Geneva and their activities had been very secret indeed. "We mined the Type XXIs into their ports, we nailed them as they came out of port, we nailed them when they tried to make their attacks, we harassed them on the way home and the mines were still there when they reached their home ports. Aircraft, helicopters, the fast destroyers fitted with ahead-throwing mortars, they kept the XXIs in check. Few of them managed to get to make a third patrol. Only you and I know the XXI is already obsolete. It did 17.5 knots underwater, your *Xena* does, what, 20? And the XXI was noisy, once we knew what to listen for, we could hear it coming a long way off. The next generation of boats will address that, we've already got some design ideas in that direction.

"So we've got to find ways of picking up the boats between leaving port and the time they reach a convoy. And we've got to find a way of detecting boats that are a lot quieter than the ones we have now." Again, Swamphen decided this was a good time to keep quiet. There were rumors the Americans had some really innovative ideas coming up, ones being developed by a man called Rickover. Ones that could flush everything down the pan. He picked up again smoothly. "To do that, we need to know much, much more about the how the sea works, how the water and current patterns interact. We started to study that and in doing so we learned something rather worrying. Charles, old fellow, could you pull back that cover please."

Fox was charmed to hear the august Flag Officer Submarines being addressed as 'Charles, old fellow.' He was definitely beginning to like this scientist. Then he caught his breath. What had once been a flat operations display was now a contoured map of the countryside somewhere. It was vaguely familiar despite being painted an odd shade of blue. The moors behind Dartmouth perhaps? Then it clicked. He wasn't looking at the countryside at all, he was looking at a model of the seabed at the southern end of the North Sea. Somebody had painstakingly cut plywood sheets to the shape of the depth contour lines and assembled them into this model. It was fascinating, for all his familiarity with the charts, this model expressed the information in a revolutionary way.

"Great isn't it? We got the idea from a rather creepy bunch of Americans. They make three-dimensional models of everything, you should see the ones they made of German cities. Before they flattened the originals of course. One of the things we'll be doing, Commander Fox...."

"Robert" said Fox, his eyes glued on the model.

"Thank you Robert. One of the things we'll be doing is taking extra measurements to fill in the gaps here and refine this model. However, in getting this far we've discovered something rather worrying. You see this valley coming up the middle of the model? Well, a few thousand years ago, when the North Sea was still a flat plain between Britain and the Netherlands, that was the river Rhine. The Thames comes in here, it was a tributary of the Rhine back then and the river reached the sea up between Scotland and the Orkneys. Well, guess what. We think, we're pretty certain, there's still fresh water flowing down there. Fresh water doesn't mix with the salt water as much as you might think, the densities prevent it. That water is flowing from the Rhine's source, all the way under the North Sea, all the way to the Atlantic. At least, we think it is."

"Uh-oh" FOSM was quick on the uptake. "All the way through Germany."

"Exactly Charles. When the Americans, uhh 'took out' Germany to use their rather delightful phrase, they dropped radioactive contamination all over the place. The worst hit was the water. The fallout fell into it and formed a slimy skin on the surface. A skin that was severely radioactive, chemically poisonous and corrosive. Anybody who got it on their skin found nothing could wash it off and it burned them alive, from the outside in by chemicals, poison and radiation. If anybody swallowed it, they burned from the inside out as well as the outside in. That alone killed tens of thousands, the ones who thought the water would shelter them from the fires.

"We never thought it was a problem; the radiation from that scum is severe but it was short-lived. More than 90 percent of it had gone within 12 hours. What we didn't realize was how chemically poisonous it was. It degraded alright but it was collected in the mud of the river bed. A mixture of heavy metals and long-lived radioactive fallout combined with the mud to make a contaminated sludge."

"And that river mud is now being swept towards the sea?" Fox was beginning to appreciate the problem as well.

"Exactly. The light stuff comes down first, the heavy stuff follows more slowly, but its all coming down the rivers. Not just the Rhine but that's the one that worries us. Look at this." Swamphen took an overlay out of his case and put it on the model. "You remember last year, there was some contaminated Herring from the North Sea sold on the black market. A dozen people died, lot more got sick? That was heavy metal poisoning, so we decided to have a look. We took water and seabed samples and found this area was being contaminated."

The overlay was an orange film. Swamphen positioned it carefully. It showed a finger reaching out from the mouth of the Rhine into the North Sea. "Then six months later, we measured again and found this." Another overlay. The original area was now a brighter, deeper red and the area covered was noticeably larger. It was spreading along the valley where the Rhine ran under the North Sea. "Obviously, we need to look again and monitor the contamination. See how much comes down and how far it spreads. If it continues to spread at this rate, the North Sea fisheries may be permanently destroyed."

The red patch of contamination glowered at the audience from the dark blue of the seabed model. Fox's voice was quiet in the room. "Do you think the Americans knew this would happen?"

"I very much doubt it. I don't think the Americans knew a quarter of what would happen when they planned the attack. Oh, they knew the initial results alright, but I think nearly all the long-term effects escaped them completely. In fairness, nobody could know all the aspects of what would happen in a nuclear until somebody tried one. I wouldn't say they experimented on Germany, just that it was a case of learning on the job as it were.

"When I was over there, one of their spooky nuclear planners told me that nuclear weapons weren't just big bombs, they were an entirely new class of weapon. Something unique in history. I think they knew the words but they didn't understand the full impact of them. We've got to find out just how bad these unexpected effects are."

There was another long silence as the model cast its spell over the three men. Eventually Swamphen sighed. "You know the really ironic thing? All the studies we're doing on the seabed? Some of the American oil people saw them and got quite excited. They say there may be oil down there under the North Sea. Ironic isn't it. For most of this century, British policy has been orientated around getting oil from the Middle East. Now we may have an oilfield right on our doorstep. And if this contamination problem gets really bad, we may be unable to touch it.

Chapter Three
World Going To War

Wallsend, Tyneside, UK

The riveters were the infantry of a shipyard. Like the infantry, their job appeared simple yet was really very difficult, there were thousands of them, and without them nothing of any significance could be achieved. Like the infantry, their day started early. John McMullen had got out of bed just after five, dressed in his woolen linings and trousers, his two-piece overalls and the inevitable muffler and cap. His wife had risen with him and adjusted his cap with the pride of a wife, seeing her man off on his first day back at a real job. It was still before dawn when he set out, guided by the widely spaced street lights, still gas in this part of town. As he walked down the street, more men came out of their homes, thickening the growing crowd that was drawn by brighter lights than those on the street. Lights shining through painted glass windows that drew the shipyard men down to their bars.

The pubs clustered around the yard gates were allowed to open at six, and what followed was as fine an example of industrial precision as any shipyard could hope to achieve. The doors of the pubs opened at six on the dot to reveal the long tables. Once, before the grim war and even worse peace, the tables had been loaded with cups of good strong tea and coffee, thick with milk and sugar, and beside them nips of rum or whisky. Now, there was only tea, weak, unsweetened and black while the nips were, well, the only way to describe it was 'something'. Home brew probably, the product of a still somewhere it was better not to ask about.

The men poured in and had just the time for a cup and a nip to scald their lips and throats before heading out again, their debt chalked up on the slates that hung behind the bar. McMullen wiped his lips on his sleeve as he left, running across the road before the yard gates locked at five past six. Woe betide the man who arrived after that time for his job would be lost, his place would be taken by another man who was already waiting in line for the chance. Then, the unlucky worker would be left with nothing but a cold walk home with empty pockets to meet an angry wife.

The two cruisers had arrived on Friday, warped in from the yard basin and tied up alongside the refit dock. *Belfast* and *Edinburgh*. Those were their names now but that wouldn't be for long. Their new nameplates were already waiting. *Capetown* and *Pretoria*. McMullen was on the *Edinburgh* work gang, an easier job than *Belfast* but more to do. *Belfast,* soon to become *Capetown*, had been mined early in the war, her back broken by a magnetic mine. She'd barely been repaired in time to make the run to Canada but at least she'd received some modernization while in the repair yard. The problem was there was heavy structural repairs, left unfinished from her mining, to be made inside the hull. *Edinburgh* hadn't been damaged so she was spared that, but she hadn't been modernized either so there was more minor work to be done before she would set sail as *Pretoria*.

'McMullen!" The gang foreman yelled and pointed at two plates waiting to be riveted. By the look of them, they would form part of a new deckhouse. It would be built down here, then swung up to wherever it had to go. Nearby a fire was already burning fiercely, the rivet-heaters working their bellows and turning the lengths of steel in the fires. Glowing red hot they were yet not quite ready for use. Only when they turned white would they be thrown to the rivet catchers who would catch them in tins and ready them for insertion. Every so often a 'prentice would forget himself and try to catch a rivet in his bare hand. Then there would be a dreadful scream. For those working up top, the result of seizing white-hot steel in a bare hand was almost always a fall and a death. For those on the quay side, it was just a hand burned and crippled beyond use.

The steel plates weren't quite aligned properly, the holes drilled in them didn't quite match. It would have been the work of a second to shift them into line but the riveting gang were riveters and thus members of the Boilermaker's Union. Shifting steel plates was a job for a member of the Steelworkers Union and the start of riveting would have to wait until a couple of steelmen turned up to adjust the job. McMullen was lucky. As the siren went at quarter past the hour, two steelmen shifted the plates into line and there was a clang as a rivet landed in the cup.

As McMullen swung his hammer back he saw what appeared to be a snowstorm overhead, a cloud of white-hot rivets being thrown through the air to the men working on the gantries that surrounded the cruiser. Even as the howl of the siren faded, the deafening noise of a day's work at the shipyard started.

McMullen took his first swing. This was the critical bit. If the hammer didn't strike square, if the timing was slightly off, then the rivet would be distorted or loose. Not far behind the riveting gang was the check-man. He'd look at each rivet, inspecting it for tightness and accuracy. If it passed, he would take his white chalk and make his check-mark, a white tick across the rivet, a short down-stroke left to right then a long upstroke. If the rivet was suspect, it got an angry red cross. Then, that rivet would have to be drilled out and replaced, The system was simple. The riveting gang got paid for each white tick but fined double that amount for each red cross. Good riveters did well, bad ones didn't last long.

It was the rhythm that was important. A good team would have its rivets caught and in place before the riveter himself took his swing. A really good riveter didn't need the check-man to tell him whether the rivet was sound, he could feel it by the vibration in the hammer when it struck metal. Once the yard had used pneumatic hammers to drive the rivets home but that equipment had long gone. Taken to Germany for the shipyards there and then turned to radioactive slag by the Yanks with their atom bombs. So it was back to manual hammering. McMullen felt the good strikes all morning so when the siren went for tea-break, he wasn't surprised to see the line of white ticks behind him. Not a red cross in sight.

It was 15 minutes for a cup of tea, then back to the quayside. By the time the noon siren went, they had reached the end of the first long line and started the short side. Looked like the structure they were building would fit crosswise on the ship somehow. Didn't matter of course, what did was that there wasn't a red chalk mark in sight.

Thirty minutes for lunch. Tea and a wad. Or what had been a wad once, before the war. Then it had been a thick sandwich, two slabs of bread stuffed with fresh-fried bacon or ham. Came out the wage of course but few had complained about it. Well, no more than any good workmen complained about anything the bosses did.

But now the wads were thin and sparse things. Off the ration, that was the one good thing about them. But the bread was skimpy and where it had once been dripping with melted fat and butter, now the margarine was scraped thin and the sandwich was filled with strange things. Whale meat was one, some sort of nutty paste was another. No bacon in sight. Hardly food to fill a working man's stomach. Even a good union man like McMullen couldn't bring himself to blame the bosses, they were doing the best they could. The thin tea and meager wads, that was the Yank's fault. Dropping their atom bombs on everybody.

30 minutes on the dot. The men had been exchanging ribald jokes, traditional ones between the Unions, between the men who worked on the gantries and them as worked on the ground, between the veterans and the 'prentices. Then the siren went again and the joking stopped, drowned out by the roar and crash of the hammers, the pounding of the engines and the rattling of the cranes.

Five o clock, 11 hours on the job. Ten hours work. McMullen got his ticket from the check-man, taking pride in its totals. All white approvals, not a red cross all day. He went to the tally-office and handed it in. There was a stranger there, a big man with a reddened skin who looked at the ticket and nodded.

"This your gang McMullen?" The accent was thick and heavy, sounding as if the man had a bad cold. Sounded Dutch or German. Its shipyards had made Tyneside a surprisingly cosmopolitan city and McMullen pegged the accent immediately. South African. McMullen nodded and the man reached into a bag in the tally-office and gave each member of the gang a small envelope. McMullen's fingers accurately gauged the contents. A two-bob bit.

"Gift from South Africa, bonus for a good job. Every gang has a day without rejects, gets the same. Every day without rejects gets you a bonus. Our Republic thanks you McMullen."

McMullen left the factory gates fingering the coin. He didn't see the South African watch him leave, then note his name down in a small book. He was too busy rejoicing in his unexpected fortune. A bonus paid daily? Generous one too. By the time he got home, McMullen had already decided to give the first one to his wife, and make sure she spent it on herself. The smell of sausages cooking and the sight of mashed potato just confirmed that decision. A day's real work and a solid British supper. It had been a good day.

Chulachomklao Military Academy, Bangkok, Thailand

The officer cadets were sitting in ranks in the lecture theater. They'd spent the last couple of days being run from one place to another, learning the layout of the college, where they had to go and when they had to be there. Learning their place in the world which, as everybody took pains to remind them, was at the bottom of everything else.

Today, though, was a little different. Today they were, in a small way, in charge of their own destinies. Today they would be determining the course of their military careers. On the desk in front of them was a pad of forms several pages thick. It had to be filled out, completely and accurately. Right at the end, on the last page was a block where the cadets had to enter their choice for their selected army careers. Their Military Occupational Specialty or MOS.

"Cadets. Today you will be selecting the particular direction your army career will be taking. You will fill out the forms in front of you and enter the code for the military specialty which you want to follow. You will then be assigned to the studies appropriate to that MOS. Each of you has one of these." The instructor picked up a book, almost three centimeters thick. "This contains all the MOS codes. Find the one that applies to your desired career and enter it on the last page. If you can't find the code or you have another problem, enter MOS 11B. It's a general course and we'll sort you out later."

The attendants started to hand out the thick books while the cadets filled in the forms. The experienced cadets, the ones who had relatives already in the service had been tipped off and had been told their desired MOS code earlier. The far-sighted had also found their desired code out in advance. The cynical put down a code at random, any code other then 11B (as a result one delighted cadet found himself in Public Relations, two more became rural development specialists and one took up a short but very exciting career in explosive ordnance disposal).

As the attendants started to collect the books and forms, far too early for anybody else to look through the reference book properly, most of the Cadets put themselves down for MOS 11B.

A few hours later, in the Commandant's office, the staff were going through the forms with satisfaction. It had worked again. The Commandant looked at the Instructor with a slightly pained air. "A *general* course Tawat?"

"Well Sir, some of them may end up as Generals." A ripple of laughter spread across the room.

"Tell me Tawat, doesn't your conscience ever trouble you about this?"

The instructor looked thoughtful for a second. "No sir. Anyway, out of 100 cadets we have 84 volunteers for the infantry. It never fails to inspire me Sir how the Cadets always choose to serve in the infantry. Selfless of them."

A ripple of laughter spread around the office again. However, the instructor was suddenly afflicted by a strange, troubling sensation of disaster. His ghost-guardian was warning him of something, he thought. He was making a mistake. Superstitiously, he quietly felt the Buddha amulet around his neck and was eased by the act of touching the image. Nothing could be that wrong, could it? Of course not.

As a matter of fact he was wrong. Everything was very wrong indeed. The years of bad karma earned by tricking poor innocent cadets into signing up for the infantry had suddenly come home to haunt him. His ghost-guardian had tried to warn him but failed.

The eternal balance of good and evil, of honesty and guilt, of rewards and punishment was just about to be evened out. In doing so, the Army's carefully-planned introduction of women officers to take over secretarial and office work in the military headquarters and administrative departments had run hard onto the shoals of unexpected hazards. For, unnoticed in the pile of forms that represented all those who had signed up for Military Occupational Specialty 11B (Leg Infantry) were those submitted by all four female Cadets.

He didn't know which frightened him most. The sheer mass of forces that were being assembled or the fact that the Russians hadn't cared how much he saw of them. They'd just met his Kubelwagen at the agreed spot and he'd got into the jeep to be brought here. In doing so, the Russians had driven him right through their lines. And what lines they had been, a horde of tanks, T-44s, some with 85mm guns, some with the new 100mms. Older T-34-85s. The SU-100 tank destroyers with their cross-hull rangefinders. Armored personnel carriers for the infantry, some with the stains on the paint where the American markings had been scrubbed off and replaced by Russian.

Oh yes, the Americans might be going home but their machines were still here. And, always, where the Russian Army went, so did its God of War. Artillery. The guns were ranks deep, parked wheel-to-wheel. The Russians didn't use artillery with the deftness and precision of the Americans, they just used it in such volume, with so many numbers that they crushed everything within range. Field Marshal Erwin Rommel hated the Russian artillery.

The headquarters was a wooden building, more than a lean-to, less than a mansion. Probably the home of a well-off farmer or woodsman. The Russians took him inside and his eyes took a second to adjust to the dimmer light inside. There was no mistaking the figure that sat behind the desk. Handsome, remarkably so and exuding a magnetic charm. Marshal of Russia Konstantin Rokossovsky was reputed to be irresistibly attractive to women. Rommel had heard that once Beria had tried to frame him by sending Stalin a long list of Rokossovsky's sexual exploits. When Beria had received his orders from Stalin, they consisted of two words "Envy Him." Now when Rokossovsky saw the German entering he stood up.

"Marshal Konstantin Rokossovsky. Commander, Second Karelian Front, Russian Army."

Rommel was startled, he had expected to be treated with coldness at best, open rudeness was more likely. Proper military courtesy was unexpected and, instinctively, he responded in kind. "Field Marshal Erwin Rommel. Commander, Army Group Vistula. German Army."

Rokossovsky gestured to a seat. When both men were comfortable, he stared at the German intently. "German Army you say? Not President of the independent state of East Arselick?"

Rommel stared back. "Marshal, I am a German soldier, not a bandit. And I am still an officer in the German Army."

Rokossovsky gave a single curt jerk of his head. "Then as a German officer you are aware that you are under orders to surrender unconditionally?"

Rommel said nothing but took his pistol out of its holster. He could feel a couple of the guards tense but he continued to move slowly, dropping the magazine and racking the toggle so that the round in the chamber ejected and the action stayed open. He glanced quickly to check the chamber was empty and laid the pistol on the table in front of the Russian Marshal. The room was still and silent.

Rokossovsky picked the P'08 up and looked at it. "Engraved with your name I see. I will add it to my collection."

"To the winner, the spoils Marshal." There was a movement beside them and a Russian woman placed two bottles on the table, one vodka, one schnapps and two small glasses. She poured the drinks and stepped back into the shadows. Before she did, Rommel caught the glance she had exchanged with Rokossovsky. Obviously one of his lady friends.

"To peace." The glasses touched. Then Rommel caught his breath. This was going to be the hard part.

"As ordered I surrender Army Group Vistula to you - unconditionally. But Unconditional surrender is one thing, the method by why we reach that end is something else. Marshal Rokossovsky. There has been too much killing already, let us not waste more lives on a war that has ended. We owe it to the men who fought for us that we arrange this surrender so that as few lives as possible are lost. But to achieve that, my men must have something to surrender for, a real hope of going home."

"What makes you think they have a home to return to? You know what the Americans did to Germany?"

"I have heard the destruction is terrible, unimaginable."

"No more than you deserve German. No more than you deserve. But there are....... options. For those who deserve them."

Rommel looked at the Russian, waiting to hear the rest. Beneath his charm, Rokossovsky was a Russian general, he reminded himself never to forget that.

"For those who surrendered in accordance with their orders there are indeed .... options. The question is who deserves to be given that privilege and who does not?"

Rommel listened carefully. He saw now the trap this Russian had laid for him when he had first entered and how he had escaped it. This would take care. "Marshal, perhaps we can establish where we agree. In complex matters like this, there is white and black we can agree upon. Then we can make a list of all the areas that have gray within them and take that list away to think upon. Perhaps when we meet again, some of those areas may have a solution. With patience, all of them."

"Very well. I will start with a white issue. We have a policy for German PoWs. Those who are without blame, those who just served as any soldier served, they may seek refuge where they can find it. Norway and Sweden will take them in. So will Finland, and the Netherlands, Denmark and Britain. Or they may go home to Germany and try to rebuild what is left there. We will assume that those soldiers against whom we have no information are innocent of wrong doing. But the solders only, Officers and non-commissioned officers we must hold for further investigation. But for this white I demand a black. There are those who have committed the gravest of crimes against the Russian people. The partizanjaegers, the Einsatzkommandos and Einsatzgruppen, the scum of that kind. The ones are mad dogs and who will be put down the same way as a mad dog."

Rommel allowed himself to relax slightly. A start had been made, a good start, better than he had hoped. "Marshal Rokossovsky, there is not a man who wears the gray of the Wehrmacht who will deny you your black. Or fail to help you find those you seek. But I must warn you that the people you wish are outside the Army chain of command. Even the SS units that are part of Vistula are technically outside my chain of command."

"You say you cannot enforce any agreement you make? Then why do we hold this meeting?"

"To find a way that we can enforce the agreement we make. Marshal Rokossovsky I could lie to you and claim that any agreement we make will be easy to enforce. I will not do that. We have a problem and we owe it to the men who have served us so well to solve it as best we can. But it is a problem indeed. The SS, they are the heart of that problem. If they choose to fight, there are no orders I can give to stop them."

"Field Marshal Rommel. The Red Cross will be here tomorrow with information on the numbers of your soldiers various countries are prepared to take as refugees. Once we have those numbers we can arrange the surrender of the first of your units. They can send messages back when they reach their destinations, that will ease the doubts of the rest of your men. But, for the SS, if all else fails.." Rokossovsky reached into his case and picked out a picture taken from a bomber called *Roxanne*, one of a mushroom cloud rising skywards, a B-36 making its escape in the background.

Rommel looked at it sadly. "Yes, there is always that. Let us pray to God we can avoid it."

"Amen" said Marshal Konstantin Rokossovsky

Aft Compartment, B-36H "Texan Lady", Sheremetevo Airbase, Russia

"Now this is a cultured way to go to war. *Texan Lady* went to Berlin like this?" The question came out mixed up with a steak sandwich, Swiss cheese and coffee. The coffee was good but the steak sandwiches just didn't taste the same cooked at ground level. Guards-Colonel Aleksandr Pokryshkin hadn't had the privilege of a high-altitude sandwich yet. And wouldn't, not unless he had a ride in a B-36 for his MiG interceptors were austere even by fighter standards. This flying hotel in the rear compartment of the B-36 was an amazement for him.

"No Sir," technically Dedmon and Pokryshkin were equal in rank but the Russian's "Guard's" prefix was a tie-breaker. Getting that, being the commander of a Guard's Fighter Regiment, indicated something very special indeed. "*Texan Lady* is currently a B-36H-30 Featherweight IVP. What that all means is she is stripped down for minimum weight. They even took away our ability to carry conventional bombs. All the racks and wiring were taken out when we converted from Featherweight III to IV configuration. Taking the wiring out alone saved 800 pounds.

"The P, though, indicates an aircraft in peacetime standard. That gives us back our galley here, the bunks we're sitting on, a coffee machine and a few other luxuries. When we go to war again, all that comes out and we go from IVP back to IV status. Takes about twenty minutes to do the job. All the amenities on board are palletized you see, we just lift them straight out. When we went to Berlin, we ate Army emergency rations, drank coffee from thermos flasks, slept on the deck back here in sleeping bags and the comfort station was a bucket."

"How high do you fly Colonel? We heard you made your bombing run from over 50,000 feet. How did you hit something from so high?"

Dedmon hesitated for a second. What the hell, he'd been told to hide nothing, or more, precisely, he'd been advised that what he shouldn't tell, he didn't know. "Bombing's done by radar these days. We don't even train for visual bombing any more. Normally we cruise between 37,500 and 42,500 feet, that's primarily to reduce the fatigue on the fuselage from pressurization cycles.

"On paper, the service ceiling of a H-30 Featherweight III, that was our configuration when we went to Berlin, was 48,500 feet. Truth is though, that's service ceiling, defined as when our rate of climb drops to 200 feet per minute. In reality, we did the run to Berlin at 52,500 feet, we were maxed out at that point *Texan Lady* was giving us all we could ask from her. As a Featherweight IV I guess we could get to 54,000 easy. The RB-36s go higher but you'd have to talk to one of their crews about that. The Recon Rats don't talk much to the Bomber Barons. What are you flying now Sir?"

Pokryshkin was licking the grease off his fingers. "We are converting to MiG-9 jet fighters right now. Once we are operational on them we will make our first foreign deployment. Then, we are to be the air defense regiment for Moscow. We do not think the fascists will be foolish enough to try an attack on Moscow. Mostly they are trying to save their skins. Some are negotiating, some trying to fight us off. But, in truth, who knows what the fascist beasts may do in their madness? So we must always be on our guard. Over Archangel, we never had to worry about high altitudes. For us to fly as high as 5,000 meters was unusual. There, our Lavochkins were the equal of anything the fascists had. But now, the world has changed has it not?"

Dedmon was quiet. The history of the war on the Eastern front was studded with the names of sieges. The ones everybody knew, Sevastopol, Stalingrad, Petrograd, Moscow, and the ones only the historians and the military professionals remembered. Nizhny Novgorod, Smolensk, Kursk, Kiev, so many others that the American Navy had named an entire class of aircraft carriers in their honor. But of them all, there was one that had a chilling horror clinging to it, a cold that froze the bones, like the frigid fog that had shrouded the city during its calvary. Archangel.

The great port-city on the Arctic circle that had marked both the northern end of the Russian front and the furthest edge of the German tide. Stalingrad had held for 150 days before falling, Moscow for 180. The street fighting in Archangel had lasted for 650 days and not one of those had been any the less ferocious than the worst of those in the other cities.

"Yes sir, its changed, and I hope for the better. Our nations should never have to pay such a price again. Perhaps when the world understands what Germany brought upon itself, it may decide that its time to find better ways to live."

"I doubt it Colonel. In Russia we have a saying. 'The beast never dies, it only sleeps.' The world will learn for a moment but then it will forget. Perhaps this.." He was interrupted by a rumble in the communications tunnel that stretched for 80 feet through *Texan Lady's* bomb bay. The hatch opened and a boy started to clamber out, discreetly helped by Major Clancy. Pokryshkin beamed as he saw the delighted smile on his son's face.

"How did you like our cockpit son?"

"Very good Sir. Thank you. Sir." The boy spoke good English although it was labored. Dedmon guessed his parents had taught him a few polite phrases and responses and rehearsed him in them.

"Would you like another hamburger?"

"Very good Sir. Thank you. Sir." Yup Dedmon thought, carefully taught some polite phrases. In the background, he could smell Smith starting to cook another hamburger for the kid. The aft compartment had a warm, comforting air to it, reminded Dedmon of the local diner back home.

"What would your son like to be when he grows up?"

Pokryshkin translated the phrase into Russian. His son said something before grabbing his hamburger and eating. "He says he wants to be a fighter pilot. He apologized, but said that bomber pilots could kill more Germans but fighters protected the Rodina. Mother Russia." He paused for a second and looked over to his wife who had been sitting quietly in a corner while the men spoke. Now she had tears on her cheeks. "We spoke of change in the world Colonel Dedmon? Now, here today, we have seen a small but important change. For many years we did not dare say 'when' our children grow up here in Russia. We said 'if' they grow up. Now, at last we can say 'when' again."

Suddenly Dedmon's mind came to a screeching halt. "Foreign deployment Sir? May I ask where you'll be you going?"

Pokryshkin grinned. "Nevada!"

Russian-Japanese Border south of Khabarovsk, Siberia, Russia

Sometimes, one could see a mistake coming and do nothing to avoid it. That time was coming fast. Soon, the border would be making a sharp turn northwards and the formation of Russian aircraft would make a terrible mistake and miss that change. They would then fly accidentally into Chinese - now Japanese - airspace. Ooops. Navigational error. Apologies all round. There were five aircraft in the group. One, an RF-63F Kingcobra was below them, its cameras ready to start turning. A thousand or so feet higher and behind the photorecon bird were its escorts. A flight of four Yak-15 jets, their pilots craning their heads around in their seats, watching for interceptors. They were being screened by radars, certainly from the Russian side and those radars were supposed to warn them of an impending attack. The Yak pilots trusted those radars just about as much as they trusted German promises.

They were also being tracked by Japanese radars and the Russian pilot's eyes gave them warning of the attack only a split second after their ground radars sent the message to their ears. Japanese interceptors closing from five o'clock high, estimated speed 800-kay. That meant Kendras. The Nakajima-built equivalent of the German Me-262.

The Japanese had been very reticent about making public their aircraft designations so the Americans had come up with a naming system. Women's names for fighters, men's for bombers. Much easier than remembering some foreign names and numbers. Senior Lieutenant Paul Lazaruski watched the Japanese fighters streaking in, carefully waiting his moment. Once, he'd done what many would consider impossible, he'd shot down a Me-262 with his old P-39Q. He'd seen it flying below him, limping for home after one of its jets had exploded, he'd dived on it and shot the cripple down with a careful burst of 37mm into its cockpit. The feat had got him a medal but it was pure luck. Now, he was flying a better match for the twin-engined jet.

"BREAK! BREAK! BREAK!" He and his wingman yanked their Yaks around to the right, the other pair of Yaks breaking left. The Americans, with their elegant turn of phrase, had once remarked that the Japanese pilots didn't do teamwork. Their fighter pilots looked on themselves as the modern samurai, seeking to engage their enemies in a one-on-one duel to the death. The American and Russian veterans knew teamwork was everything, they fought in pairs and if that meant winning a fight by shooting their opponent in the back, so be it. Winning trumped fairness, life trumped death.

That was happening now, the Yaks had split, opening a gap between them. The Kendras were diving into the formation, each Japanese pilot picking a target. Only, they weren't coordinating properly. Also, the Yak-15 was just a Yak-3 whose piston engine had been replaced by a jet. It still had the thick wings of a piston-engined fighter. That cost it in speed, it was 80 kays slower than the Kendra but those thick, high-lift wings meant it could turn tighter, much tighter.

The Yak was in a clawing turn, standing on its right wingtip, its throttles rammed all the way forward for maximum power, Lazaruski hauling the stick back into his stomach. Despite the power from the jet hanging under its nose, the Yak was shuddering on the edge of a stall, its controls vibrating. Despite his American-supplied g-suit, Lazaruski's eyes were blacking out as centrifugal force drove his blood from his brain.

Only the Kendra was going 80 kays faster and speed translated into centrifugal force and that translated into weight and that meant the loading on the wings was greater and that meant its turning circle, greater than the Yak's to start with, was too large. In his mirror, Lazaruski saw the Kendra drifting off to his left, trying and failing to follow his turn. He slammed the stick over and the Yak, bless its thick, drag-inducing high-lift wings rolled sharply. In his vision black was replaced by red as negative g replaced positive. Lazaruski came hammering around the reverse curve, his nose swinging towards the Kendra a few hundred feet away.

The Japanese pilot had seen what was happening and was trying to reverse his turn but speed and wing-loading were against him. His first turn had bled off too much energy, too much speed, loaded his wings too highly. He was starting to reverse his turn but Lazaruski had started first, he was there first, and being first meant far more than all the aerobatic skills in the world. Because his nose was swinging across, catching the Kendra, pinned like a specimen fly to paper by a needle made of speed and centrifugal force and weight.

Lazaruski's thumb stroked the firing button on his control column, gently, so gently, as gently as dew forming on the morning grass. His twin 23mm cannon roared, spewing a line of invisible shells towards the Kendra. Invisible for no hardened veteran pilot used tracer. The first sign of his burst was the bright flash of hits on the Kendra's nose then along the side of its fuselage. Its bubble canopy exploded from the hits and Lazaruski saw the pilot jerk in his seat.

He knew what would happen next, had seen it so many times. The pilot's hands jerked back, towards his wounded body, yanking the control column with them. The Kendra reared, loading its wings and snapping into a near-vertical climb. As it passed through its critical angle of attack, its left wing stalled out and it snapped over onto its back before dropping into a tight spin. Lazaruski was onto it like a wolf onto prey, bring his twin 23mm guns to bear.

"BREAK LEFT! BREAK LEFT!"

Instinctively he left his kill as his wingman screamed the warning. He was already in a left turn as the bright red tracers started to sweep past his aircraft. The second Kendra was coming at him hard and fast and was hosing him with his paired 20mm and 30mm guns. Lazaruski continued his bank, racking the little Yak around and turning his turn into a barrel roll that took him around the stream of fire. Veteran pilots never used tracer, the Japanese pilots were skilled, in technical terms probably the best in the world, but they weren't veterans.

As his roll bottomed out, Lazaruski slammed the nose down and started to dive away. He could almost read the second Kendra pilot's mind, the prey was getting away. But the Kendra was heavier, more than twice as heavy, and that meant it picked up speed faster in a dive. The Japanese pilot knew that as the Yak accelerated away, the speed difference between the two aircraft would diminish and then be reversed and it would be the Kendra that would close on the Yak. It would just take time.

The Japanese pilots saw themselves as samurai, fighting duels, one on one, honorable victory for one, honorable death for the other. The Russians were killers whose goal was to see they lived and their enemies died. As Lazaruski came out of his roll and extended, the Kendra dived after him. The Japanese pilot never saw Lazaruski's wingman finish his turn and swing onto the tail of the Kendra as it swept past in pursuit of its prey.

The wingman's guns hammered out the finale, a tracerless, invisible finale befitting an assassin. The torrent of 23mm shells slashed into the Kendra's wings, belly, fuel tanks, engines, shredding them, slashing fuel lines and causing a black-red sheet of flame to erupt from the stricken fighter. The Japanese pilot bailed out, his clothes and his parachute already aflame.

Lazaruski pulled out of his dive and swept around, looking at the hurtling fireball that had once been a fighter. No way was the parachute going to save anybody's life now. Below, he saw a mushroom as the fighter's wreck spun into the ground and, he thought, not far away the puff as a burning body hit the ground.

It was over. Of the three Kendras, one was dead, a second limping away streaming black smoke and a third was covering it. The Kendra was as short-legged as the Yak-15 and both aircraft were running dangerously low on fuel. Far too low to continue fighting. Below him, the RF-63 was already running home, its precious film safe in its belly. The four Yaks formed up and followed the Kingcobra.

An easy fight, Lazaruski thought. The Japanese pilots were superb, well trained and their aircraft were excellent. Only they'd spent years fighting Chinese peasants who had only a few hours in their aircraft before being thrown into battle. Today, the Japanese had met the fighter pilots who had survived seven years of war against the Luftwaffe's Experten. It wasn't the same thing, wasn't the same thing at all.

Reconnaissance and Intelligence Center, Khabarovsk

The Air Force lieutenant burst into the center with a broad grin on his face that told Colonel Yvegeni Valerin all he needed to know.

"We have our pictures?"

"Yes, Gospodin Colonel. The Kingcobra got back safely and its pictures were good. I hear the Japanese are already screaming with anger and threatening dire consequences. The escorting Yaks shot down one of their fighters and damaged another, Sir. I understand they will be making a formal complaint and we will, of course be making a full investigation of the regrettable error in navigation. It will, of course, be a thorough inquiry. I understand Chairman Shayvin of the Khabarovsk Military Region will be conducting it himself."

Everybody in the room laughed. Few of its characteristics had survived the quiet death of Communism after Zhukov had become

President but one that had was a remarkable skill for making bureaucratic activity a substitute for achievement. Even amongst the most pettifogging of the bureaucrats, Chairman Iosef Shayvin was legendary. It was whispered that he had even left his grandmother behind to be taken away by the Germans because the old lady hadn't filed her travel application in triplicate. The Japanese were about to find out just how bureaucratic an inquiry could get.

The young lieutenant spread the pictures out on the table. "I'm afraid they ask more questions that they answer Sir."

Valerin took the stereoscopic viewer and started to look at the pictures. What had appeared flat pictures now took on a three-dimensional life of their own. The first pictures were of what appeared to be an infantry camp close to the border. "How many men do you think are based here Lieutenant?"

"Military Sir? None Sir. That camp is abandoned."

"How do you know? I can see tracks all over the place."

"Yes Sir, but look. They're all around the field boundaries, never across them. That's farmers avoiding trampling their crops. If you look at these pictures Sir, these are of an active Army base. You can see where the soldiers have ignored the field boundaries and trod down the crops."

"Could they be bluffing us? Acting like farmers to hide their base?" A Russian officer might well think of that. It was hammered into them from the first days of their training. The three principles of warfare. Maskirovka, Maskirovka, Maskirovka. Deception, deception, deception. Never be straightforward when one can be devious. Never be open when one can deceive. Never do the obvious when an alternative exists. Misdirect, misdirect, misdirect.

"I don't think so Sir. Take a look at these shots, see how the trucks are parked to use the shadows and the terrain to make them less obvious. The Japanese are good sir, they know their business. They're doing things by the book on the bases we think are occupied. I think its genuine, they're pulling back a lot of their troops."

"How many of the frontier bases have been abandoned?"

"From these photographs and the ones taken earlier, about a third. The problem is sir, now we're running into those other questions that I mentioned. We have coverage of only a very limited area of the border in length and an even more limited area in depth. Also, the reconnaissance aircraft we have, well their cameras aren't very good. They can't be, the RF-63 just isn't big enough to carry a good camera and it doesn't have the range to get very far along the front or the speed to get very deep. We could send an RB-27, they've got the range but they're well within the intercept envelope of a Kendra, even more so of a Layla. By the time they get deep enough, to see something, there'll be fighters all over them. We can get away with one border incident, not two."

Valerin stared at the pictures. They were telling him the answers to the questions he had asked but not what he needed to know. The Japanese were thinning their border troops out. Did that mean they were confident the border was peaceful and they could send them to places where the need was greater? The Japanese-Chinese war was winding down now, the Japanese had everything of value, just a few Chinese holding out in the more remote areas.

Or did it mean that the Japanese were concentrating their troops ready for an incursion or even a full-blooded invasion. Eastern Russia was the powerhouse that was fueling the liberation of Western Russia. Another war here could be a disaster. Or were the Japanese pulling back, afraid of a Russian strike and so keeping a thin border screen while establishing a strong reserve? The pictures didn't tell him.

"Nikita Sergeyevich, have the organs of state anything to say that can help us?"

Khrushchev shook his head. In the old days, when it was Chinese across the border, the "organs of state" had known everything that moved. But then the Japanese had arrived and with the Kempeitai. Now those who might have spoken were too terrified to whisper.

"We must have more information. If the Japanese are going to attack, we must pre-empt them. We have no aircraft that can get pictures to help us? That can get far enough behind their lines to tell us what is going on? And do so in safety?"

The air force lieutenant shook his head. "We have no such aircraft. But there is one that can do just that."

Chulachomklao Military Academy, Bangkok, Thailand

"I hate him. He's horrible."

"Why?" Officer Cadet Sirisoon Chandrapa na Ayuthya squinted down the barrel of her Mauser. Bright shiny bore. Her hands moved quickly as she pressed the retention plunger in and screwed the firing pin assembly back into the bolt. As far as she could see, every last drop and fragment of cosmoline had been cleaned out of the rifle. She quickly wiped some excess oil off with a fragment of rag, then slid the bolt into place. Rifle reassembled. She quickly slid her bayonet out of its scabbard and checked that as well. 20 centimeters of steel, razor sharp on one edge, the first four centimeters sharpened on the other, the rest a vicious-looking sawback. Ten years earlier, the German instructors that had founded the modern Thai Army had been horrified by that sawback. During the First World War, accusations of barbarity had made them grind their sawbacks off. No answer yet. "Why do you hate him?"

"He's always picking on us, making fun of us."

"Of course he is, its his job. If we can't take pressure here, how can we take it outside?" She clicked her bayonet back into the scabbard. "And we're strangers here, this is their club and we're forcing our way into it. You were in university weren't you? You were in a sorority? How would you have felt if the university authorities had ordered your sorority to accept members you didn't want? You wouldn't have liked it would you? And you'd have taken it out on them. Hazed them far worse than the ones you'd chosen."

"But it's not fair. And he makes it so personal."

"Whoever said life was fair? War is personal, when somebody tries to kill you, its very personal. And we're officer cadets, out there we'll be taking responsibility for other people. Sergeant Major Manop is part of a system that is trying to weed out the one's who aren't able to do that. For their own good as well as for everybody else's. So don't sit there and sulk saying you hate him. Beat him by not giving him an excuse to throw you out." She slung her rifle over her shoulder. "Now wish me luck, I'm going into the tiger's den."

She slapped the crude wooden partition twice with her hand, waited a few seconds then stepped through the hanging curtain into the main part of the barracks. Some of the men there stared at her resentfully, a few more mentally undressed her. One just went through the motions of doing so. Hmm, she thought, I wonder if the others have guessed about you yet. Other end of the barracks, she stopped in front of the Sergeant-Major's door and knocked respectfully. Sergeant Major Manop opened it.

"Officer Cadet Sirisoon Chandrapa na Ayuthya requests the Sergeant Major inspect Rifle, 7.92 millimeter Mauser Type Kar98k serial number 338250 Sergeant Major."

Manop took the rifle and went to the table in the middle of the barracks. "This should be good, boys. Women like cleaning things don't they?" There was a swell of laughter around the room at the sally. One of the good things about being a Sergeant Major was that the cadets all appreciated his little jokes. His hands moved quickly and expertly as he stripped the rifle down, inspecting each part as he took it down. Then, he produced a pull through and a strip of white silk.

Sirisoon gulped, her rags had been cotton, that piece of silk would attract every scrap of dirt in the bore. She held her breath as Manop pulled the silk rag through the barrel. To her relief, it came out white, just the slightest hint of gray where the trace of lubricant had protected the inside of the barrel. Manop looked at her and nodded slightly. Then he unscrewed the firing pin assembly and took a stick with another scrap of silk rag wrapped around it. He probed inside the forward part of the bolt, looking for traces of the cosmoline that had been caked in there. Clean as well. Satisfied, he reassembled the rifle. When it was complete he was about to hand it back when he looked at the teak furniture. Looked again, then gazed sharply at Sirisoon.

"Treated it with linseed oil, Sergeant Major, then rubbed it with number twenty steel wool then applied more linseed oil."

Manop nodded slowly. "How did you know that? It isn't in the book."

"My father, Sergeant Major, he fought against the French in 1940. With the Queen's Cobra Division. We have the old Type 45 rifle at home, chambered for eight millimeter Siamese. Permission to take Nomenclature Test Sergeant Major?" Manop nodded. Sirisoon took a deep breath and pointed to the muzzle of the rifle. "Foresight Hood, Foresight, Foresight Hood Retaining Clip, Barrel, Cleaning Rod Half." The list went on as she worked her way down the rifle, pointing to and naming each part in turn. Eventually she came to the Lower Butt Plate Retaining Screw and stopped. Manop stared at her.

"You forgot the Magazine Plate Release Plunger Spring Cadet. Get three strips of canvas and tie your rifle to your leg tonight. Help you to remember in future." There was another swell of laughter around the room. Manop turned and pointed to one of the men. "You. Nomenclature Test in five minutes." The man went white. "The rest of you, look at the furniture on Cadet Sirisoon's rifle. See how it has a silk-like sheen? That is how it should look. It is satisfactory. In most armies the furniture on a rifle is birch or cheap laminated wood but Our King gives you a rifle with the best grade teak we can find. So make sure you earn that privilege by seeing to it that your rifle is satisfactory also. Dismissed Cadet Sirisoon." He tossed the rifle at her and she caught it neatly. Then he turned and went back to his room. But as he turned he gave her a slight acknowledging nod.

Office of Sir Martyn Sharpe, British Viceroy to India, New Delhi

"Well, we were expecting a damning report Sir Eric. Not quite this damning I admit though. Secretly, I must admit this report pleases me. The Commission of Inquiry did a splendid job, called the shots the way the evidence pointed and didn't pull any punches. If we're going to have an efficient modern government here, we must have a system where situations like this are investigated properly. We must, *must*, learn from our mistakes, not sweep them under the table and pretend they never happened."

There were times when Sir Eric Haohoa wished he had the Ambassador's ability to present one set of facial expressions while actually thinking something quite different. This was one of them. Sir Martyn's enthusiasm for open inquiries and learning from mistakes was all very well in theory but Sir Eric was a practical politician and could see the problems that reality tended to interject into such ideas.

There were those who objected to the path India was taking and the unfolding disaster at de Havilland (India) was ready-made ammunition for them. He leafed through the report issued by the Commission of Inquiry on Problems Experienced with Mosquito Aircraft. CIPEMA for short. They had certainly been thorough. If anything they could be criticized for being too thorough, they'd gone far beyond their official remit. They'd also suggested solutions to the problems they'd found, good workable solutions. Sir Eric sighed slightly, if the CIPEMA Report was anything to go by, the future for those who made a mess of Indian Government contracts would not be a pleasant one.

"They do commend your decision to ground the Mosquito, Sir Martyn. They also recommend a temporary solution that will keep the remaining fleet operational. Apparently, if the squadron maintenance units burn drainage holes in the lower wing panels, that will prevent the water build-up that caused the mid-air wing failures. Apparently burning the holes, rather than drilling them, prevents a rim of splinters forming inside and interrupting the water flow-out."

"Temporary though. We can't keep them in service like that. The Americans have heard something, their DEME people are hammering on the Air Ministry doors already. Offering us surplus B-27Es at give-away prices. More or less saying we can have them if we come to Russia and take them away."

"Very generous of them Sir Martyn. 'Disposal of Excess Military Equipment' indeed. We take their kind offer, kill off our own aircraft industry in the process and are stuck buying their spare parts for the next twenty years. I bet they didn't breath a word about giving us the spares as well."

"Not a word, Sir Eric, the matter appears never to have crossed their minds. The Australians are in a much better position than we are of course; they benefited greatly from Thwamap. They make the spares they need down there, the ones they need anyway. A glass of whisky?"

"Thank you. Thwamap, theThree-Way Military Assistance Program." Sir Eric rolled the words around his mouth then washed them down with whisky. Thwamap had funded much of Australia's industrial growth during the war years. A triangular relationship between the United States, Australia and Russia. America had bought war material made in Australia, given it to the Russians and charged the money against Russia's lend-Lease account. The arrangement had made Australia an alternate source of supply for American forces in Russia and the Pacific. In turn, that had enabled the Australians to re-equip their strangled industry. Now Australia was leveraging that industrial development into a peacetime industry structure. "If we get the B-27s, can the Australians supply us with spare parts for them?"

" I do not know, but I think we both know somebody who does."

"The Ambassador." Sir Eric looked both pensive. It seemed that everywhere one looked these days, there was a Thai businessman acting as an intermediary. Smoothing paths, calming troubled waters, providing the funding necessary to get mutually profitable deals off the ground. All scrupulously honest of course, it was just that the English language appeared to have been written with the specific intention of enabling Thai banks to make money out of brokering deals.

To make matters worse, nearly all the big trading houses from Hong Kong and Shanghai were moving to Bangkok now that the Japanese were consolidating their hold on China. Australia was too remote, India was too poor. Thailand was central, peaceful and its Government was determined to be hospitable to foreign investors. "That's something we'll have to explore later. In the meantime, what do we do with Sir Geoffrey de Havilland?"

"We will follow the recommendations of the CIPEMA Report. There is no doubt about his skills as a designer, he is probably one of the leading lights of his generation. The criticisms of the company are basically those of poor management and poor production engineering. The outline plan from CIPEMA is that we nationalize de Havilland (India). Sir Geoffrey can stay on as chief designer for one of its product streams. There's another man there who the report speaks well of. Chap called Folland. We can set him up as a second design stream.

"We'll tell Sir Geoffrey that we're taking the burden of running the company off his hands and bringing in production engineers to help him on that side of things. He'll go for it, its probably a lot better deal than he's expecting. CIPEMA have even given us a name for the new group. Hindustan Aviation. They recommend sixty percent of the shareholding be held by the Government of India, forty percent by the public.

"They are also suggesting that we have an external office to audit designs produced by all the aviation companies here. That's only Hindustan Aviation now of course. Others when they follow. They suggest we slow down on the various programs until that's done. The Hornet and Vampire fighters of course but also the Comet."

"The Comet as well?"

"Especially the Comet. Heaven knows we need that aircraft. The ground transport network is terrible, you know that. It takes days of hard travel to get from one city to another, even by train. If we can establish an air travel system, it will help immensely. We've made a start with the Australian-built Dakotas and Lodestars but a jet airliner will put us ahead in that market. It may even become the standard for the whole region. The last thing we need is for the thing to start its career by falling out of the sky."

Sir Eric nodded. The plan would play. Despite the collapse of communism in Russia, there were still a lot of people who believed in state-run and centrally planned economies and many of them were prominent in the Indian National Party. On the other hand, those looking to invest money in a country saw nationalization as barely better than outright theft. In fact, some did see it as outright theft. Given the loss of confidence resulting from the Mosquito program though, a sixty-forty split would satisfy both. State control, getting the company onto a sound financial and technical footing and offering the prospect of reverting to wholly private ownership later. As Cabinet Secretary, one of Sir Eric's responsibilities was to maneuver legislation through Parliament. This one wouldn't cause that many problems.

"I do have some good news Sir Martyn. I've heard from the directors of one of the new companies setting up. Bharat Ordnance. They've concluded the license agreement with the Swiss Oerlikon Company, allowing them to build Oerlikon's line of 20 millimeter and 30 millimeter guns here.

"Apparently, Oerlikon are launching a new range of guns, incorporating the lessons of the war. Which, of course, they are in a position to know since they industriously sold their guns to both sides. Anyway, the Swiss are sending out a team of their engineers to help set up the machinery and get everything in order. Apparently, they're going to stay for at least three or four years, until their Indian opposite numbers have been fully trained. They were quite insistent on that by all accounts, something about maintaining the integrity of the Oerlikon reputation."

"Hmmm. Switzerland is right next to Germany. I don't suppose their engineers desire to put distance between themselves and that radioactive wasteland has anything to do with their decision?"

"I believe it just might Sir Martyn, it just might."

Flight Line, Ramenskoye Test and Evaluation Establishment, Moscow, Russia

"That looks familiar." The drab brown bomber was small to eyes used to ten-engined intercontinental giants. Four propeller engines on the leading edge of the wings, a nose smooth and without a raised canopy. It was almost, but not quite, familiar. "Its a B-29!"

Guards-Colonel Aleksandr Pokryshkin shook his head. "No my friend. It is a Tupolev Four. This one belongs to Long Range Naval Aviation. See?" He pointed at the tall fin, half way up the rectangular red white and blue Russian tricolor had a black anchor superimposed over it. Looking at the tail, Colonel Dedmon could see that it was differently-shaped from the B-29. Taller. Pokryshkin laughed. "Boeing designed an improved design for the B-29. First they called it the B-29D then when SAC refused to buy a version of the B-29, they renamed it the B-50. SAC still didn't want it but for us it was perfect. We don't have engines powerful enough for a bomber like your *Texan Lady* but we had for this. So Gospodin Tupolev went to Boeing and got a license to build your B-50 and here it is. The Tu-4. We made some changes of course."

It was a challenge. Spot them. Dedmon looked over the airframe carefully. "The tail's different of course, taller. And the engine mounts are different as well. That'll be your engines. What have you got in her?"

"Shevetsov Ash-73TKs. Rated at 2,400 horsepower." Dedmon and his crew exchanged glances. Only a fraction more power than the B-29 had. Barely half that delivered by the R-4360 engines on *Texan Lady*.

"Guns. You've got different guns. 20 millimeter cannon?"

"23 millimeter Nudelman-Rikter. Twelve. Much better than the Brownings and even better than *Texan Lady's* 20 millimeter guns. But that is not the most important thing. Look underneath him."

Dedmon was flummoxed for a second, he was so used to calling aircraft "she" that the male pronoun threw him. Then what he saw under the Tu-4 knocked his breath from him. A long cylinder, gracefully curving to a point at the front, swelling to maximum a quarter of the way along its length, then tapering to a nozzle at the back. Trapezoidal wings, the tips cut sharply back, tail the same. And under the wing roots, two fat, open-ended cylinders with pointed nose-cones. It was painted white and it looked evil. "Whoa, this is something new. May I ask what this little beauty is?"

"We call it Sopka. Formally it is the Kh-1 anti-ship missile. We fire it from about 20,000 feet and steer it by radio control. All the bomb-aimer has to do is keep it on the line of sight between himself and the target. The rocket fires first and gets it up to speed then the ramjets take over. We are giving the first twenty off the production line to your Navy so they can assess it."

Dedmon reached out and ran his hand over the sleek nose. "Nuclear warhead here?" That would be American supplied, he thought.

"That is not the warhead, that is the rocket fuel tank. The warhead is in the middle. It is a shaped charge, one that can penetrate two meters of armor. And when it does it blasts the burning rocket fuel deep into the target. Rocket fuel, Grazhdanin Robert. Contains its own oxidizer so nothing can put the fires out. Not water not foam, nothing."

Dedmon winced, now he knew why the missile looked so evil. The memory of the burning *Shiloh* slipping beneath the waves came to his mind. The ugly picture was erased by the howl of a fighter flying overhead. He looked up, a straight-winged bird, looking like the Yak-15s and 17s but different. Weirdly different. For all the world, the jet fighter circling overhead looked like a racing car. Cockpit well back, a huge long nose in front of it.

"That is our Yak-23." Pokryshkin explained. "Our airframe, American engine. Much faster than the Yak-17. See that man over there." He pointed to a distinguished-looking figure standing beside a camera stage. "That is Aleksandr Sergeyevich Yakovlev himself. The test pilots have been complaining about the undercarriage on the Yak-23. The fighter lands almost 80 kilometers per hour faster than the Yak-17 and they say the wheels are too weak and the hydraulics not strong enough to lock them down. Aleksandr Sergeyevich will have none of it. He will not admit that he may have underestimated the stress of landing the new aircraft. And Yakovlev fighters have always been cursed with weak undercarriages."

The Yak 23 was approaching for its landing. The Americans were exchanging worried glances, their Russian friend was right, the undercarriage didn't look right. The Yak touched the end of the runway, bounced once and then all hell broke loose. The undercarriage collapsed in a shower of sparks and the fighter was sliding on its belly, starting a slow rotation to the left as it did. Even through the sound of its jet, they could hear the shrieking of tortured metal as the hard runway surface ground the airframe away. Then there was a dull whoomf as the fuel tanks exploded, engulfing the aircraft in orange flame.

Dedmon and his crew broke into a run, heading for the crash, knowing there was little they could do to help but wanting to try anyway. Even as the burning jet continued down the runway, leaving a trail of fire behind it, the cockpit opened. Incredibly, despite the sea of flames and the still-spinning wreckage, a figure leapt out of the cockpit, ran along the wing and jumped off. Immediately ground crew were around him, blasting him with fire extinguishers and throwing dirt over him.

By the time the Yak had come to a halt, it was a hundred yards down the runway and had stopped in a greasy black and orange pyre of smoke and flame. The pilot got up, slowly and shakily, shouting something.

"Is he all right?" Dedmon asked.

"Oh yes. But he is very angry. He is an old friend of mine, Captain Viktor Bubnov. A man with a very hot temper. I fear it has just boiled over. He is suggesting that Gospodin Designer Yakovlev initiate a maternally incestuous relationship. Now, he is alleging that the Gospodin Designer is of German ancestry. Oh."

The other side of the runway, the pilot in the singed flight suit had stopped shouting and was advancing on the Chief designer with definite menace. Suddenly, Yakovlev's nerve broke and he fled, hotly pursued by his nemesis. He tried to shelter behind the camera stand but Bubnov was following him, swinging kicks at his plump backside. Yakovlev had obviously decided that halting was a bad move and was frantically running away from the furious pilot. After their fifth circuit of the camera stand, the ground crew grabbed Bubnov and started calming him down. Yakovlev kept running for a few meters then stopped, sobbing for breath. Pokryshkin guessed that was further than the distinguised VIP had run in thirty years.

Beside him Major Clancy was looking exceptionally pleased. "I must remember that next time we're down at the Convair plant. You know, I think I really like Russia."

Part Two - Hammer

Chapter One
Raised

"Why, Maisie luv, you look beautiful. Really."

Maisie McMullen beamed with delight. She'd taken the South African bonuses her husband had earned, five of them in a six-day week, combined them with a few pennies she'd managed to save and her clothing ration coupons and bought herself a new dress. But it wasn't the dress that made the difference, it was the glow that shone from inside. For the first time in years there was hope of things getting better. She'd paid off the slate at the grocers and made a start at the butchers and the greengrocer. Soon, they'd be out of debt, something that a few weeks ago would have seemed a remote, unlikely dream. Somehow, Wallsend seemed to have become a less grimy, less depressing place over the last few days. Work in the shipyard meant life brought back into the community.

"We've got a few pennies left after paying the rent, Maisie." John McMullen could hardly believe it, the rent paid on a Fridays and it wasn't due until next week. Their landlord had been patient during the bad years, not that he'd had much choice. If he'd evicted one set of tenants for being late, their replacements wouldn't have been any better off. Still, he'd put up with late payment when times were bad. Now they were changing, McMullen took a stiff-necked pride in paying early. "How would you like to go down the pub? Been a long time since we went down to The Foundry together."

Maisie McMullen's beam got even bigger. It had, indeed, been a long time since they'd been out for an evening. The lean times, then the danger from the American Navy carrier strikes, all had made people stay at home. "That's a wonderful idea. I'll get my coat."

As McMullen closed the door of their home behind them, he realized his wife had been right about getting her coat, even old and worn as it was. McMullen privately promised himself that he'd swing a good hammer next week and get her a new coat even if he had to go down the corner to get it. There was an unseasonable chill in the air, even at the end of August, the air had a bite to it that shouldn't be there. Just wasn't right. Damned Yanks dropping atom bombs on everybody.

McMullen looked up. Early evening, the sky was clear but high up, so high and so faint it could hardly be seen, was a faint streaking of gray. When the sun set, it would catch that thin shroud and turn it into a spectacular display of color, everything from the faintest of pinks to the deepest, most intense scarlets. It had been more than a year since The Big One and every one of those days had seen sunsets so spectacular that they made the eyes water.

It had been the fires, according to the radio. The atom bombing in Germany had burned the cities, all of them, to ash but it had done something else as well. It had started forest fires across the country and, without anybody to put them out, they'd burned for weeks. The smoke had been driven so high that it couldn't come down and that was the cause of the sunsets and the unseasonable chill. Or so the radio said. Stood to reason, McMullen thought. It was the Yanks fault. It hadn't been fair how they'd ended the war like that, never given the Germans a chance. Just flew the bombers over and blew their country out of existence. That wasn't fighting fair.

He took his wife's arm and they walked down the street, together, greeting neighbors as they passed. That was something that came hard, five years of living with the Gestapo watching every move had left people reluctant to say anything they didn't have to. Only now were the old habits coming back. McMullen made himself a private bet that at least one of the people they were greeting as neighbors had been an informer.

Still, best forgotten now. Old Winnie, now Prime Minister Churchill again, had been right on that. Obsession with revenge lead to - Germany. Wallsend had nothing to be ashamed of, it might have had its informers and its Nazi sympathizers but it had also had its resistance. McMullen had been surprised when they'd come out into the open after the German surrender and he'd seen who they were and how many of them. Now, they were the town council and their leader was the Mayor.

"Here we are luv." They'd reached The Foundry and McMullen held the door to the Saloon Bar open for his wife. Carpet on the floor, padded seats and booths down a wall. If he'd been on his own, he'd have gone to the Public Bar where the floor was bare wood and sawdust and the seats were simple stools. No decent woman went into the Public Bar. A man with his wife went to the Saloon Bar. Maisie had taken off her coat, catching the envious glances at her dress from the other women.

McMullen seated her in a booth and collected two halves of beer. Another thing that had changed. Once a man wouldn't dare order a half pint of beer. Men drank full pints and to do less invited ridicule that could last for weeks. Only, now, rationing meant that a pint cost a point so a man who went to the pub with his wife split their rationed pint into two halves, dividing it between them.

"Here's to us luv." They chinked their glasses and drank. The beer was thin, watery stuff, a far cry from the rich foaming brown that they'd had years before. But it was beer and this was their first night out in years. They spoke of small things, of stories of experiences in the shops and down the corner. McMullen told his wife the funny stories of the yard, of the tricks played on apprentices. Especially the 'prentice who they'd sent to the stores for a "long weight". Maisie McMullen had chuckled at that, sitting erect in her seat and sipping at her beer. After a while, they'd got their ration book out and started adding up the numbers to see if they could afford 'the other half".

"Hey, Johnno, don't worry about that let me get it for you." The thick South African accent made the name sound like 'Yunno'.

"Thank you Mister...." To his embarrassment, McMullen realized he didn't know the man's name.

"Piet. Piet van der Haan. Please, this round on me, I have a visitor's ration card and you deserve a beer. Never seen a man swing a better hammer. And this is your lady wife?"

Maisie McMullen flushed slightly. Her husband looked up at van der Haan proudly. "Aye Sir. That she is. My wife Maisie. And we both thank you for a beer."

"On its way." Van der Haan waved and the barman started to ready the drinks. "But not so much of the sir Johnno. Not the way for two good Union men speak to each other is it?"

"You're Union? I thought you were with the bosses."

Van der Haan laughed, then paused to pay for the beers and have the points taken off his ration card. "Since when would a bossman know who was swinging a good hammer? Been a Union man all my life. Work the Simonstown yard."

"Which Union Brother? Boilermakers?"

"Shipbuilders. We only have one Union per yard in the Republic. Everybody who works in a shipyard is a Shipbuilder. Except the kaffirs of course." Van der Haan saw the puzzled look. "Blackfellers. You know. They just fetch and carry so there's no need for a Union for them. But for the rest of us, we're all Shipbuilders. Stops the bossmen playing one Union off against the others you see."

"Does your wife mind you being away, Mister van der Haan?" Maisie McMullen's voice was tentative, as if she wasn't sure she should be interrupting when the men were speaking.

"Call me Piet please. She's not happy about me coming here at all. Down in the Republic, we hear bad things about Europe. How the bombing made everybody sick and all. Tell you, haven't felt quite right since I came here either. Still, the bossmen had to pay a big bonus for us to come here so its worth it. Look forward to getting back though, that's the truth. Lord knows how I miss home."

They chatted on, exchanging stories about the occupation and life in the Republic of South Africa, and McMullen insisted on ordering another round. Eventually they parted, van der Haan back to

70

his hotel, the McMullens to their home. As they walked down the street, Maisie McMullen had a smug smile on her face because she had noticed something her husband had not. Their affable South African friend carried a gun under his jacket.

Headquarters, Second Karelian Front, Riga, "The Baltic Gallery"

The long lines of tanks and artillery had grown even thicker, denser, the cannon barrels seeming to bristle at the sky like some great steel porcupine defying the gods that lived beyond the clouds. Rows upon rows of them. Field Marshal Rommel hardly noticed. The professional part of his mind noted what he saw and even jabbed him into awareness when they passed something new, a long-range rocket battery. A bit like the German A-4 but a pointed cylinder instead of the A-4s graceful bullet shape. But, for the rest of the drive his mind was far away, churning over what he had learned. Or, rather, what he had been made to learn.

It had sounded so simple. Pick out a couple of units, ones that had no great crimes to stain their reputation, ones where the soldiers had just done their duty and deserved to find refuge where they could. He'd picked out some likely candidates and drawn their files to check them. Then, he'd been horrified by what he'd found. He'd checked others and found the same. There were no blameless units, there were no units without great crimes to stain their reputation. There were no honest, simple soldiers who had just done their duty.

Like most Wehrmacht officers, Erwin Rommel had convinced himself that the stories of vileness, of atrocities, of horror were all the work of others, the SS and the even more foul groups that followed them. The last 48 hours had shattered that comforting delusion. There were no clean, blameless units that had just done their duty. For the first time, he'd seen the truth of what the war on the Eastern Front had been like. It didn't help, it wasn't a comfort, to point to the Russians, or the Canadians or the Americans and say that they too had done the same. They had, but that was no excuse. It was their problem and their consciences would have to carry that burden. As he sat in his staff car, Erwin Rommel felt the vileness clinging to him and he believed he would never be clean again.

At the Russian headquarters, he saw the Russian infantry that surrounded it staring at him with cold, all-encompassing hatred. He'd seen it before, on his first visit, but then he'd dismissed it as the aftermath of war. It was a terrible feeling to understand how that hatred had been earned, to know that it was deserved. It was a relief to get inside where Konstantin Rokossovsky, ever the urbane and genial cavalryman, was waiting for him.

"Field Marshal Rommel, I have good news for you. The Swedes are prepared to take an initial five thousand of your men as refugees. They are even sending a ship, one of their Baltic ferries, to collect them. Finland and Norway are speaking of taking five thousand each also but we have no confirmation of that yet. Now, what white have you got that you can offer me?"

Rommel reached into his briefcase and took out three files. "My white is the 21st Panzer Division. They spend much of the war on occupation duty in France. As a panzer unit, they were used mostly for assaults and for counter-attacks, they took no part in anti-partisan operations and I can find few accusations against them. I suggest we start with the tank regiment first and then the artillery regiment. Then, if the five thousand are not yet filled, the two panzergrenadier regiments. The 21st is an old unit, regular Wehrmacht and they received fewer replacements than most."

That was something Rommel had noticed, the units that had received the most replacements, the ones filled with the brain-washed fanatics from the Hitler Jugend, were the ones that had the records bad enough to turn his stomach. Across the table Rokossovsky nodded. He spoke to one of the Russian women who left, glaring at Rommel as she did. "I understand why you hate us now."

Rokossovsky looked at him. "You do German? And why do we hate you?"

"I have seen what we did, even in the words of our own reports and statements. There can be no forgiveness for us. I do not expect any."

"German, that is war. It is not a game, it is horror incarnate and unimaginable. Perhaps we had forgotten that and it took General LeMay to remind us, but we do not hate you for war. Do you want to know why we hate you?" Rommel nodded.

"Because you were so rich, you had so much. We had nothing. The men in the rifle divisions, the Frontniki, are peasants from collective farms. They were so poor, for them to have nothing was an improvement. Yet you, who had everything, came to our country and took what little we had and that which you could not take you destroyed.

"Two starving peasants fighting for a piece of bread can fight desperately and cruelly, they can rip with their teeth and gouge eyes but they fight with desperation, not hatred. But a starving peasant with a crust of bread who sees a rich capitalist rob him of his bread, take a small bite and throw the rest down a sewer has a heart filled with the blackest hatred imaginable."

For a moment Rokossovsky's gracious demeanor slipped and Rommel saw the same blaze of loathing in his eyes. "There are many in Russia who strongly oppose letting any of the German soldiers return. They believe you should all be turned into slave labor, Zhukov's mules they call it, to be worked to death repairing the damage you have caused. President Zhukov does not agree with them. It would be very wise to ensure that he does not change his mind. Thank you Katya."

A Russian woman had brought out a pile of files. Rokossovsky took the one labeled 21st Panzer Division and read it quietly. The silence in the wooden building was oppressive, while Rokossovsky read, absorbing the contents of the file, Rommel mulling over what he had been told, the woman soldier staring at the German in the hope that the fury of her gaze might bring about his death.

"Your white is acceptable German. As we discussed earlier, 5,000 of the enlisted men and non-commissioned officers up to the rank of Sergeant will be released to Sweden. The exceptions are the men on a list I have here. As their units disband, their equipment will be handed over to us, and their senior NCOs and officers will surrender themselves for investigation. I cannot speak for the NKVD and would not wish to do so but it is my opinion that the majority of those men will not have much to fear. Now we have my black. There is a unit we want more than any other. The Dirlwanger Brigade. An anti-partisan unit with a record that would make the devil himself weep for their victims."

Rommel nodded. In his studies, he'd seen that unit's record and he guessed that it would be high on the list of Russian demands. "You may have them with my blessing. Of course, some may be dead when we deliver them. You will have no objection to that?"

"As the Americans say Field Marshal. Wanted, dead or alive. As they come. But if you do kill any, deliver their bodies. We demand an accounting for that unit."

"Marshal. There is something I must say. In the Wehrmacht we believed we had kept our hands clean of the worst of this war. That the things spoken of in whispers were the doing of the SS and units like Dirlwangers. I cannot believe that any longer. Our hands are as stained as any; we believed otherwise because we wanted to and denied what our own eyes told us. The ultimate responsibility for what happened in Army Group Vistula is mine. I accept that responsibility and am prepared to, no, I insist on, being judged accordingly."

"You will be, Field Marshal Rommel. But speaking for myself, brought up as a Polish Catholic, I will say realization of guilt is the first step towards redemption. And this war has caused enough guilt for all of us to share."

Rommel relaxed. It was true, confession did ease the soul. He felt the crushing weight that had been squeezing his spirit out of him lift slightly. "Marshal, may I ask a personal favor? My family lived in Mannheim. Is it possible to find out from the Red Cross if any have survived?"

"I will ask, Erwin, I will ask. But I counsel you to drive any hope from your heart. The Americans know destruction well and practice it with skill and efficiency. For them, destruction is just a job, something to be done as quickly and as completely as possible. I believe Mannheim is in the center of the Ruhr industrial belt. If that is so, there will be nothing left. Nothing at all."

HMS Xena, At Sea, Off Rotterdam

"Trim's on Sir. Ready to dive." The Outside Wrecker, who trusted officers about as far as he could carry the submarine's main batteries, ran his eyes over the array of valves. What should be shut was shut and what should be open, which wasn't much, was open. All was right with the world.

"Take her down. 100 feet. Then watch the gauge. I want this boat so finely balanced she moves when a fish swims under us." Commander Fox thought for a second. "Sonar, keep yours ears open. If we hear revolutions anywhere near us, I want to know about it pronto. No matter what else is happening." Fox reflected that too many submarines had been run down by surface ships because the officer of the watch had been fixated on getting the trim right.

"Swampy, I think we're over your undersea river now. I propose to get trimmed at 100 feet then we'll start taking depth soundings. Once we're over the old river bed, I'll put a tiny negative trim on her and we should settle down slowly. If you're theory is right and there's a fresh water stream down there, we should be able to sit on the interface between fresh and salt and let the flow carry us." Fox glanced around the control room. "I want an honest answer, Swampy. Is the contamination down here enough to hurt us? Just how bad is it? I do have hopes of a litter of little Foxes you know."

"Honestly, the water pollution isn't as bad as we feared. Its short-lived and the contamination is fading as fast as its spreading. Its the heavy stuff that's the worry and the problem is chemical toxicity as much as anything else. The figures I got so far indicate that the contaminated area is at about ten times background. Everything's radioactive you know, its a question of how much more so than normal. We're safe inside *Xena* although I wouldn't like to make a living swimming in the waters around here. Six months ago it was a little over eight times background. So my guess is that the initial surge of contamination is over. The amount coming down is nasty but its doing little more than keep up the levels as they fade from decay."

"How soon can we eat the fish?" Fox knew the North Sea fisheries were desperately needed to help feed the population of the UK. Britain was so desperately short of food that the fisheries would be worth their weight in gold – if only the fish was safe to eat. Which, going by experience to date, it was not.

"That's a harder question. One of the contaminants is an iodine product that the fish preferentially absorb. We're going to have to catch some fish samples and take readings. If we can organize that, it would be a big help. But, my guess is that it could be a very, very long time before we see North Sea fish again. Now, lets try and find my undersea river."

Grenade Pits, Chulachomklao Military Academy, Bangkok, Thailand

"That's not good enough. Nowhere near good enough. You must do better."

That could be the motto of the day, thought Officer Cadet Sirisoon Chandrapa na Ayuthya. Nowhere near good enough, she would have to do better. The day had started on the rifle ranges, shooting their Mausers for the first time. She'd laid down on the firing line and then felt the thumps as Sergeant Major Manop had kicked her legs into the approved firing position, none too gently she'd noted. It hadn't made matters any better when she'd noted that the "approved" position gave a much steadier hold on the heavy rifle.

She'd dropped a round into the receiver closed the bolt, taken careful aim and fired. The rifle had kicked savagely back into her shoulder and she'd seen stars as her erect thumb had jammed into her eye. Manop had laughed at her and explained why it was better to do things properly. The bullet had missed the targets completely of course, only the gods knew where it had gone. She'd tried again, keeping her thumb down and the rifle tucked into her shoulder. That shot had hurt less, but it was still a complete miss.

"You're snatching at the trigger. That pulls the rifle down and to the left. Squeeze the trigger, don't pull it. Equal pressure throughout the hand. Now try a clip of five."

She had taken the stripper clip, thumbed the rounds into the chamber and started firing. No sign of the stick with a red circle on the end that marked the position of a hit. After the fifth shot had thrown up a spray of dirt from the embankment in front of the targets, a stick had appeared but it had a white flag on it, being waved in the traditional 'surrender' gesture. She'd laughed despite the sting. Behind her Manop had quietly picked up the telephone to the target spotters. "Cut it out boys. Its her first day on the range. None of the others has done any better."

She'd fired off fifty rounds, the last few actually hitting the white target although scattered all over it. Then she'd taken her position behind the firing line while the next group of cadets started their shoots. Even with her little experience it had been easy to spot the mistakes they'd made and realize how much she had to learn. Then, they'd returned their rifles to the racks and set out to the grenade pits.

Once into the secluded area, they'd each been given a red-painted dummy grenade to throw. Up the range was a white line that marked the minimum acceptable range for a grenade throw. The cadets had thrown their dummy grenades then looked to see how they had done. There were a cluster of red blobs around the white line - and four well short of it. Nobody needed to be told who had made the short throws.

Beneath his impassive expression, Sergeant Major Manop was a deeply worried man. The four women cadets were studying harder than any of their coursemates, indeed harder than any he could remember. Their scores on tests and trials were high, well above average, and were particularly good in tasks that needed attention to details. Their equipment was clean and well-maintained. The problem was they were nowhere near the physical standards required. In fact, in virtually every task or exercise that required sheer physical strength, the women were coming out at the bottom. Not just by a small margin either, they were far short of the standards required and the specified physical training wasn't going to make up for that.

The instructors had discussed the matter at length. One had taken a day's leave to go to Bangkok and consult with the martial arts experts and fitness professionals down there. He'd come back with a revised training schedule and some insights into what the problems were. It wasn't just that the women were weaker, it was that their strength was all in the wrong places. It sounded trite, but women were different and the Army-specified training regime didn't allow for that.

The instructors were giving up their off-duty hours in the evening to give the women extra tuition using the exercises that the experts recommended but Manop wasn't even sure if that was a good idea. Even if an intense effort got the women up to the minimum acceptable standard, they wouldn't be able to maintain it once they left the Academy. Then, their lack of strength would catch up with them. Still, that might not matter. The Army was recruiting women to serve as secretarial and administrative staff, freeing up men for the combat elements. They probably wouldn't need the fitness training. As long as they could get through here....

He looked at Officer-Cadet Sirisoon waiting on him. "Cadet, did you ever do sports in your school? If so, any that involve throwing things?"

"Yes, Sergeant Major. Basketball and discus."

"Show me how you throw things your way."

Sirisoon picked up a practice grenade, took a deep breath and threw it 'her way'. Manop watched intently, it was a completely different set of actions using the whole body with different muscle movements and motions. When he checked the throw, it was a lot better, not nearly good enough but a lot better. Right, he thought, we have something to build on.

"You four women stay here." He went to the loudspeaker system. "Live grenade throw, Repeat live throw. All personnel clear the grenade pits move behind the protective berm. Instructors, inspect the pit line, ensure it is clear. Signal when confirmed then take cover yourselves. This will be a short throw. Right, You four, take cover in the bottom of the pit. You'll see why."

Once the clearances were in, Manop took a live grenade, pulled the pin then tossed it to where the women's practice grenades had landed. It actually took a mental effort to throw a grenade that close in. He dropped into cover. A second or two later, there was a deafening explosion and the sound of fragments flying overhead. Mud dropped into the pit. The women looked at him, wide-eyed.

"If you had been standing up when that went off, you would all now be dead. You must, repeat must, learn how to throw grenades to a safe distance. There is no alternative to that as you must now understand. It is literally a matter of life and death. If you do not pass here, no matter how well you do elsewhere, you will be washed out."

He reached into his sack and pulled out four grenades, red-painted but with a white H on them. "I want you to come here for one hour every evening and practice throwing using these. Don't worry about doing it the way the book says, it doesn't work for you. Cadet Sirisoon, show the others how you threw just now. Don't worry about using this range, there are always staff here so just tell them I sent you. Understand?"

The women nodded and Manop handed out the dummy grenades. They were heavier, half as heavy again, as the normal practice grenades. The logic was obvious, get used to throwing something heavy and the lighter practice grenades would come easily. Or so Manop hoped.

Flight Deck B-36H "Texan Lady", Main Runway, Sheremetevo Airbase, Russia

"Pre-flight checks completed. Preliminary checklist completed." Major Clancy was reading from the multi-page list on his clip-board. He actually knew it by heart but SAC regulations stated the list had to be read, not repeated. "Engineering reports fuel and oil pressure normal for all systems."

"Acknowledged." Colonel Dedmon turned *Texan Lady* on to the main runway at Sheremetevo, her brakes squealing with the sharp turn. The Germans had built Sheremetevo for fighters; the runways were long and wide enough but some of the turns were tight for the giant B-36s. Behind him, an JRB-36K, *Dixie Cupcake* was following him. She'd only arrived the previous evening, the deployment of a new K-ship was a sign of how important this mission was.

"Start jets one, two, three four."

"Starting jets. Engine flaps closed. Windows, doors and hatches all closed."

"Bombardier Compartment here. Secured and ready for take-off."

"Engineering Compartment here. Secured and ready for take-off."

"Aft Compartment here. Secured and ready for take-off."

"All crew, stand by for take-off under normal power. Engineering execute Vandenburg Shuffle. This will not, repeat not, be a maximum-performance take-off."

"Thank heavens for that. Those give me a terrible ache in all the frames down my left side." The female voice had a definitely relieved note to it. Dedmon shook his head. One day, he promised himself, he'd get to the bottom of that voice.

"Power stabilized at normal settings. Jets one hundred percent power." There was a pause as *Texan Lady* shimmied from side to side as her engines were run up and down. "Vandenburg Shuffle completed. All engines in forward thrust.

"Autopilot off. Nosewheel steering off. Lets go guys."

Texan Lady surged forward, not the berserk dash of a combat take-off but still something that made the sheer power of the aircraft obvious. She picked up speed as the engines animated her bulk, accelerating her down the long runway, past the buildings that housed the maintenance and repair units and the barracks that housed the base personnel. There was another building, new and well-separated from the main part of the airfield. A building that looked like a fortress, because that was what it was. Guarded by a battalion of troops, it was where the SAC kept a forward-deployed stockpile of nuclear weapons.

Then, the pitch of the engines dropped as the wheels lifted clear and she was back in her element, in the sky again after more than two weeks on the ground. TDY in Russia was a good experience but it was good to be going home, even if they were going back the long way. Next stop Honolulu, a thirty seven hour flight away. Of course, there was a job to be done first. Instinctively, Dedmon glanced back over his shoulder. Behind him, *Dixie Cupcake* was running down the runway, nose lifted in the first stages of rotation. She'd be with them for the first part of the flight, then once her job was done, she'd be peeling off to land at the huge air base complex around Anadyr. On the taxiway, *Barbie Doll* and *Sixth Crew Member* were waiting their turn to take off.

Theoretically it was called an "Open Skies Navigation Exercise". The name came from a new doctrine the United States had started to enforce over the last year. Open Skies. It explicitly stated that SAC's bombers could fly where they wanted, when they wanted and would do so. It was all wrapped up in political niceties of course. The information that was gathered on such flights would be made available to all as a friendly gesture, as a confidence building measure that would allow countries to know what was going on around them.

The stated idea was that countries would know what their neighbors were deploying in the border regions so that wars would not be started over groundless fears. Open Skies would allow countries to live in peace, not in fear that their neighbors were planning a secret attack. In reality the message was much simpler, 'we go where we want, you can't stop us and you'd be stupid to try. So make the best of it. We're here and we're watching. And, yes. We're carrying **them**.'

Dixie Cupcake was uniquely well-equipped for missions like this. Her number two and three bomb bays contained cameras, the like of which had never been seen before. They had a focal length of 240 inches and produced negatives that were 18 inches wide and 36 inches tall. Each camera was angled sideways so that it could photograph deep into the territory on either side of it. The aircraft carried enough film to monitor a thousand miles of border and, from 50,000 feet, the resolution was good enough to pick up a golfball. Even the film was new and unprecedented, Kodak had developed a special fine grain emulsion so that detail would not be lost.

Those cameras were the real reason for the flight today. The Russians were desperately worried that the Japanese were planning a strike across the border to try and seize the rich industrial areas that were growing up along the Trans-Siberian Railway. On the face of it, the worries were well justified. Geography and the demands of material supply had dictated that the new industrial plants be built along the railway route and that made them dangerously close to the border.

The war between the Japanese and China was winding down at last. Most of China had been occupied, precariously for certain, but occupied and was being 'pacified' in the traditional Japanese manner. There was still some resistance in the more remote areas but the war was essentially done. That left a large, battle-hardened Japanese force in China with little to do. They'd already tried to come north once, back in 1939, and now the possibility they might try again was too strong to be ignored.

Today, *Dixie Cupcake's* massive cameras would reveal just what forces the Japanese had deployed behind their border and, based on that, what the threat level really was. That would, in turn, determine how the Russians would react. If there was a threat, they were not inclined to wait for the other side to strike first.

"How many of these do you think we're going to do?" With the take-off over, Major Clancy was relaxing in the co-pilot's seat.

"Deployments to Russia? Or Open Skies exercises? Either way the answer will be the same. Depends who wins the election in November. Dewey's sold on both, Truman on neither." Dedmon thought carefully. "The Democrats really don't approve of the way things are going. They want to see a much more, a more international approach to things. Truman will reflect that no matter what his own opinions are. Republicans are much more isolationist, they like the idea of us staying out of things and acting only in our own interest. President Dewey got away with a lot because there was a war on. Don't count on that to continue. So is forward basing in Russia and Open Skies more appealing to the Democrats who want us out there "interacting" as they call it? Or more in the Republican line of staying out of everything unless we have to drop a hammer on somebody who threatens us? You tell me."

"Whoever wins, they're inheriting a basket of trouble, that's for sure. We have a lot of unfinished business with Japan. Have you read Sam Morison's new book, 'The Unfought War'?"

"Not yet. Bought it and meant to bring it over with me but forgot. Any good? His history of the North West Passage was great."

"I'd say 'Unfought War' is interesting rather than great. He thinks the Japanese were going to go to war in December 1941 but backed off at the last minute when we reinforced the Philippines and sold all that stuff to the Indians. He makes a pretty convincing case of it, it really does seem like the Japanese were planning hits on the Philippines and Malaya but called them off because the odds against success swung that little bit too far.

"The trouble is, he ruins the whole case by saying the Japanese were sending their aircraft carriers to attack the fleet in Pearl Harbor.

He claims it was the extra maritime surveillance units the Navy sent out to Hawaii that made them cancel the Pearl Harbor raid he says they had in mind. Too much recon to get them in, so that left the Philippines and Malaya operations in the cold."

"Yeah, right. Like anybody would be so damned stupid as to try and hit Pearl. And it had to be the navy who fouled up the Japanese plans didn't it? The bombers and fighters we sent to the Philippines had nothing to do with it nor did the Thais screwing over that Japanese division. That was back in December '41 wasn't it? Ole Sam's a great historian and a good writer but he needs to pedal the inter service rivalry back a bit. As for his opinions on international things, well, his book on the Washington Treaty negotiations was pretty dire. More or less said the rest of the world was out to get us and pulled it off."

Dedmon paused for a second. " Tell you something Phil, one thing a lot of people are going to be thinking. We dropped the hammer on Germany because they had no idea what was about to happen. They'd written nukes off as impossible and they just didn't believe anybody would come in as high and as fast as we did. How long before somebody gets to be able to pull the same trick on us? Pull something on us we can't defend against?"

Headquarters, Army Group Vistula, Riga, "The Baltic Gallery"

"You filthy treacherous, mother-humping pig dog!"

Rommel lifted an eyebrow slightly. He'd expected something much more fluent and original out of the highly intelligent Skorzeny. That was a disappointingly pedestrian string of insults. The Russian woman soldier on the cross-roads that morning had done much better. The women controlling traffic didn't blow whistles to give orders, they fired their PPSH sub-machineguns in the air. One of the Russian trucks had ignored her and tried to drive past. She'd emptied the entire drum magazine of her submachine gun into the windscreen and followed it with a magnificent tirade of highly imaginative obscenities. The officer in the truck had jumped out and run away to hide in the bushes. "A day in the life of the Russian Army." Konstantin Rokossovsky had said, a chuckle in his cultured voice. He'd promoted the woman soldier in the spot and left orders that the officer in hiding was to be found and shot. Marshal of the Russian Army Konstantin

Rokossovsky was a cultured and genial man but he was also a Russian officer and had no time for those who ran under fire.

"You sold my men out to get your own to safety!" Rommel's eyebrow lifted a little more. Really, Skorzeny should learn to think with his brains, not his balls. Time for a lesson in strategy.

"General Skorzeny. You did a staff officer's course. What did it teach you about priorities?"

"Mission. Men. Self. Of course. But..."

"And what is our mission?"

That knocked the wind out of Skorzeny's sails. He'd worked himself up to a point where he was in a fine fury. Now he had a contradiction to solve. "Well, our orders...."

"Are to surrender. So that brings us to our second priority. Our men. We owe our duty now to the men we command. We must both, both of us, work to save as many of our men as we can. And, of course the civilians, the women and the children here. You know what will happen to the women if the Russian soldiers break through don't you? But we now, both of us, have to plan and scheme to save our men. As many of them as we can. Some of them, like Dirlwanger's murderers are far beyond saving. At most we can use them as sacrifices to save others. Make their miserable lives worth something at any rate. You might think of using your men to hand them over, or their survivors over to the Russians. Might make them look upon you with a little less loathing."

"Use my men to....." Skorzeny was spluttering with affronted rage at the idea.

"Right. We may be called upon to make the greatest sacrifice of all. To go down in history as the men who sold out Army Group Vistula and die with nobody knowing that we did it to save the lives of the men who served us so well." Rommel sighed, theatrically. Out of the corner of his eye he watched Skorzeny. The appeal to gott-und-dammerung romanticism had struck home. The SS General was thinking at last.

"Disarm and surrender the Dirlwanger Brigade. Then use your troops to hand them over. Who knows what the Russians will do then? The only excuse they accept is that somebody had joined the Partisans. Perhaps handing Dirlwanger's butchers over will seem like that." Rommel stopped speaking, leaving Skorzeny to chew the problem over. He'd planted a seed, he decided to wait and see what happened to it. After all, there was enough night soil between Skorzeny's ears, something had to be able to grow there.

Flight Deck B-36H "Texan Lady", 50,500 feet over the Russian-Chinese Border

"Entering hostile airspace now." The voice from the bombardier section in the nose had a slightly tense note to it. This was the first time *Texan Lady* had been in hostile airspace since The Big One more than a year before. The flight plan here was very different from the Russian reconnaissance mission a few days before. There, the Russians had used a quirk in the border to create a plausible "navigation error". The B-36s hadn't bothered with subterfuge, they'd flown straight to the border, crossed it without a shred of pretense and would swing parallel to it almost a hundred miles inside Japanese-occupied China.

The three B-36 bombers were flying in a loose Hometown, two thousand feet below the lone RB-36 whose cameras were already turning, recording every detail of the ground below.

"Does this mean I'm going to get shot again?" The female voice had a distinctly dubious note to it. Phil Clancy patted his control stick.

"Don't worry, *Texan Lady*, we're far above any defense the Japanese can put up. We'll be OK."

"That's what you all said the last time."

Dedmon raised his eyebrows. They were used to the odd comments coming over the intercom now and then but that was the first time they'd actually had what amounted to a conversation. He shot a glance at Clancy, grinning in the co-pilot's seat. "That's new. Never had an answer before."

"Ever talked to other pilots about our voice Bob?" Dedmon shook his head, he'd always looked on it as being a bit of private crew business. "I mentioned it to a few guys, jokingly you know? All of them laughed, but about a quarter of them were faking it. Some looked real shifty. My guess is we're not the only crew that has this and the shifty-looking ones talk back. So I thought I'd try it."

"Electronics Pit here. We're picking up ground based radars from inside China. Japanese air surveillance radars. Two types, range and bearing and a height-finder. Guess the crew of that one must be doing double-takes about now. We're in evasion mode?"

"Sure thing Dirk. Revs and spacing all set as per specs. They won't get an accurate fix on us." Phil, take her up to 51,500. Just to ease *Texan Lady's* mind. Tell *Dixie Cupcake* to make the appropriate change as well if her cameras won't object. We'd better do it now, this high, it'll take at least a quarter of an hour to make the climb.

Dedmon relaxed in his seat as the engine notes changed with the shift from level flight to climb. Technically, according to regs, they should all be in partial pressure suits but none of the bomber crews bothered. Most of them didn't even carry the suits. If pressurization went, they'd all pass out almost instantly without them but if that happened, they'd have far more to worry about than just being unconscious. One day, General LeMay would get around to reinforcing the pressure suit regulations but, now, they were politely ignored.

From up here, the ground had lost most of its individuality to a human eye. It needed the cameras to make sense of what lay below. Far below them, isolated clouds posed like islands on a strangely colored sea. It was very different to the packed terrain of Europe they'd flown over a year before. And, Dedmon reminded himself, this time if the mission went right, they wouldn't have to end up destroying everything. They had a couple of lessons for the Japanese today. If they learned the first one, there would be no need to proceed to the second.

"We're being painted. Fire control radars. Anti-aircraft type." The voice from the electronics pit was calm, matter-of-fact.

"Roger. All Hometown aircraft, evasive action, no need to make it extreme. Follow my lead unless they get real close."

The anti-aircraft fire didn't. The black bursts were way below them and scattered all over the place. Even if they'd been at the right altitude, they were too scattered. None of them would have come close.

"Hey, guys, we have the altitude of the bursts at 32,000 and 36,000 feet." The voice from *Dixie Cupcake* sounded almost amused. "The Eyes in the Sky believe they are 130mm and 100mm guns. No sign of the 150mms we've heard about. Not that it would matter much."

"*Dixie*, thank the Eyes for us. We can expect to see some fighters soon. Got the New Thing loaded?"

"Sure have *Texan Lady*. Locked and loaded, ready to go."

Clancy looked down at the black flowers far below them. "That's pretty pathetic. Why do they even bother."

"Might be pathetic Phil but its better than anything we can do. You know how many heavy anti-aircraft guns are operational back home? One battalion of 90mm guns at Camp Roberts in California. There are probably more anti-aircraft guns firing at us now than the US even has. We've got a bit of light stuff around the cities on the East Coast, left over from the V-1 attacks, but heavy stuff? We're as wide open as Germany was. As for why do they bother, they're trying. Just as our guys would try under the same circumstances and hoping against hope they get lucky. They don't know they don't want to get lucky of course."

And that was the truth. That would be Lesson Two. Lesson One was "You can't touch us". Lesson Two was "OK, so you could touch us. You really didn't want to do that." The mission orders for that eventuality were in Dedmon's document pouch. Today, the flight tactics were different from The Big One. Then, only one aircraft had been loaded with a nuclear device. Now, all three bombers were carrying, in this case, two devices each. If one of the four B-36s was shot down, the rest would proceed to a point in Japan and laydown on a series of targets. Four in Tokyo, two in Yokohama. Open skies. SAC goes where it wants, when it wants.

"Bombardier Compartment here. We're picking up fighters, way below us, no threat. From performance, we think they're Kendras. That'll mean they top out at about 39,000. Guess is they were out anyway and just vectored in because they were available."

"Agree. Keep an eye on them though. They may have those guided air-to-air things we saw over Berlin."

The formation carried on, swimming serenely through the azure blue of the skies high over China. Far below them, the countryside was smudged by brown. A town with its haze of smoke and dust. Once again, the sky far below them erupted into a crazy pattern of black blobs. Scattered and far, far below them. No threat. That was the pattern for hours as the B-36s flew along the Russo-Chinese border.

"*Barbie Doll* here. We have two formations coming in. One very fast, estimated speed 600 miles per hour. Designating Bandit-One, provisional identification Layla. Other is much slower but is climbing steadily. Can't be sure but we have them as certainly piston engined. Designation is Bandit-Two, our guess is Fran."

"Thank you, *Barbie Doll*. Well, let's see if Herr Tank's reputation survived his very timely demise."

There was a snort of laughter around the flight deck. The Japanese Layla was a version of the German Ta-183, a swept-wing German jet that had "been on the verge of entering service" for two years before The Big One. Quite a few of the newer Japanese aircraft showed a lot of German influence, obviously there had been a pretty rapid flow of information from the Nazis to the Japanese. Probably bribes to get the Japanese to attack Russia from the east. Some of the aircraft were pretty good, Technical Air Intelligence had suggested that the Japanese designers were quite a bit smarter than their German equivalents. Once the Germans had pointed them in the right direction, they'd taken the ball and run with it. The Flying Tigers had confirmed that; they'd found the Kendra was a little bit faster, flew a bit higher and turned quite a bit tighter than its German ancestor. Better armed too.

So was the Layla the threat that the Ta-183 had conspicuously failed to be? Probably not, it still had the two problems that Tank, in his alleged wisdom, had failed to correct. It was horribly underpowered, had barely more than 2,000 pounds of thrust, and it had swept wings. They looked great and aerodynamics showed they would be immensely valuable at speeds approaching 700 mph and above but the Ta-183 was 100mph short of that regime. At those speeds, swept wings had very poor handling characteristics but gave no real benefits. A few 183s, probably service test models, had been encountered over the Volga and they'd been shot out of the sky by the straight-winged American F-74s and F-80s.

Now, if the Japanese had cracked the engine problem and had put more power into the design, it might be a problem. Dedmon watched below then caught sight of the contrails below them. They'd caught the sun and turned an orangey-yellow. At least 10,000 feet below them, that would fit he thought. If it was anything like the German original, Layla would top out around 41,000 feet and would be really struggling anywhere over 30,000.

"*Dixie Cupcake* here. Confirm Bandit-One is four Layla type fighters. They're leveling out, touch over 42,000 feet, speed barely 300 mph. The Eyes say at least one pilot is having difficulty holding his bird, he's snaking badly. If he stalls out, he'd better leave. Bandit Two is a single aircraft, still coming in. Confirm its Fran. It's just possible we might have a problem here."

Cockpit, Tachikawa Ki-94-II Five-Two, 48,000 feet over the Chinese Border.

He wasn't going to make it. For all the performance boosts and weight reductions, his aircraft just didn't have it in her. Her nose was pointed up still and her propeller was clawing at the thin air surrounding her, but she'd given all she had. The airspeed was virtually at nil, the fighter hanging on its prop, the controls mushy and useless.

Lieutenant Nishimura cursed, fluently in a mixture of Russian and English. Japanese was a particularly poor language for insults, Russian was so much better and English gave so much room for the imagination. His K-94 was a dedicated high altitude fighter, the best

Japan could produce. It had a turbocharged radial engine that was boosted until the metal alloys screamed for mercy. The design had first flown in 1945 and the test pilots had got it up to 42,000 feet. That had seemed splendid but there was no real need for such altitudes, or so it seemed. Then the Americans had flown over the German defenses and suddenly the Ki-94-II was needed more than any other aircraft.

The aircraft had been stripped down, all its armor gone, its battery of 30mm cannon replaced by a pair of 7.7mm machineguns. It had a single radio to allow it to be vectored to its target. Nishimura had left his parachute back at base to save a few pounds more when the message had come that four of the American giants were crossing the border. Three Ki-94s had taken off but two had turned back when their engines failed. His own would have to be replaced after this flight, the grimly-abused radials had only a few hours life each. And for all that, the American bombers were still out of reach. He could see them, a triangle of three far above him and a single aircraft higher still. Trailing their white ribbons behind them while they serenely cruising past him as his fighter hung helplessly on its prop.

Flight Deck B-36H "Texan Lady", 51,500 feet over the Russian-Chinese Border

"*Dixie Cupcake* here. We have Bandit-Two topped out at 48,400 feet. He's hanging there, isn't going anywhere but too mule-headed to give up."

"Read you *Dixie Cupcake*. Have you got the New Thing dialed in?"

"Sure have *Texan Lady*. Our electronics pit got him locked in nicely. We'll let him have it now."

Cockpit, Tachikawa Ki-94-II Five-Two, 48,000 feet over the Chinese Border.

It was no good, they were out of reach. For all his efforts, for all the hard work, the Americans were still out of reach. Then Nishimura became aware of something strange, the faint mush of static on his radio had suddenly increased in volume.

"YEEE - HA - HA - HA, HOOOH - HOOH - HAAA - HEEE HAHA."

The coyote laughter familiar to the world from hundreds of Walt Disney and Hanna-Barbera cartoons almost split his ears. He knew immediately what must have happened, the Americans had listened to his radio and isolated the fighter control frequency. Now they were transmitting a tape cut from one of their cartoons on his frequency. It went on and on, a mocking peel of hyena laughter than cut through his brain.

Enraged at the insult, Nishimura stroked the button that fired his machineguns, watching in furious wrath as the tracers arced through the air far, far short of their targets. But, even the featherlight recoil of the 7.7s was enough to upset the delicate balance that held his fighter in its place. It spun out, falling from the air as its wings and propeller frantically tried to grab enough air to regain stability.

It took Nishimura almost 20,000 feet to get his fighter back under control and for every one of those feet the vicious, derisive, mocking laughter tore at his ears. Low on fuel, his spirit crushed, Nishimura took his fighter back to its base.

Flight Deck B-36H "Texan Lady", 51,500 feet over the Sea of Japan

"Right guys, fun's almost over. *Dixie Cupcake*, you set for Anadyr?"

"Roger that *Texan Lady*. We'll be heading north now. There's a Guard Fighter unit waiting to escort us in once we start to drop." That was why they were off to Anadyr, Dedmon thought. The nearest base capable of taking a B-36 was Khabarovsk but that was too close to the Chinese border. Seeing a B-36 dropping down to land might just be too much temptation for the Japanese. So *Dixie Cupcake* would be flying far to the north and she'd have a regiment of Russian fighters to protect her once she started her descent. The three B-36s were off to Honolulu , they'd be overflying Japan then facing the long, long haul over the Pacific before landfall in Hawaii. Then, four days there and another long haul back to Maine. It suddenly occurred to Dedmon that when he landed back at Kozlowski, he'd have flown completely around the world.

Home of Retired Admiral Isoruku Yamamoto, Nagasaki, Japan.

"When I was in America, there was a strange story." Yamamoto looked at the figures that were sharing tea with him. They were bristling with rage at the casual way the Americans had ignored Japan's claim to control its airspace. Everybody had seen the contrails high, high in the sky as the American bombers had overflown the country on their way from somewhere to somewhere else. Open skies they'd called it and today, they'd made their point. The officers with him looked slightly confused. Since his retirement, Yamamoto had become something of an elder statesman in Japan, an advisor, using the prestige that age brought in this country to stop the young being carried away with enthusiasm. Disastrously carried away.

"American children all have puppies as their pets. When they go to school in their yellow schoolbuses they must leave their puppy behind for the day. All the puppy sees is their friend being taken away by this big yellow thing. Some just wait miserably for their friend to come back but the braver, more spirited puppies chase the schoolbus in an effort to rescue their human friend. Of course they always fail and must wait miserably like the rest. But, one day, a puppy, by great and valiant effort, caught the schoolbus and sank his teeth into its rear. Then he faced the question he hadn't thought of. He'd caught the schoolbus, *what was he going to do with it?*.

"Ask yourself, like that puppy, if you'd intercepted a B-36, *what would you have done with it?*"

"Shot it down of course!" The officer looked around triumphantly. Yamamoto was pleased to see that the expressions of the rest ranged from doubtful to dubious with a couple of downright scepticals.

"And then the Americans would have bombed us like they bombed Germany. You know Germany don't you? That black, smoking, radioactive hole in the middle of Europe. You want our Japan to end up like that? The Americans sent us a message today. They overflew our country, with their nuclear-armed bombers and did nothing. They told us that if we do nothing to stop them, they would do nothing to us."

"But we did everything in our power to stop them. We threw our best and our latest at them and they ignored it."

"And in doing so, you told them everything there was to know about what our latest and best equipment could do to threaten them. Now they know exactly what our defenses can do. It is better that we do nothing and let them think we cannot stop them than try and prove to them we cannot. After all, what did we lose today? Other than a little pride?"

The officers looked around, each hoping somebody else would answer. Eventually, one took the plunge. "But now they know exactly what forces we have along the border."

"And that matters because? We do not plan to attack Russia do we?" The officers shook their heads, The Japanese Army was redeploying away from that border. Far away. "Now the Russians know we do not have any intention of attacking them. They will not attack us, they have their plates filled with recovering western Russia after the occupation. The only reason they would have attacked us was fear that we would attack them and their desire to pre-empt any such attack. Now that fear has gone, we can expect peace on the border and that allows us to carry on with our plans elsewhere. And we have the Americans and their Open Skies to thank for that."

Reconnaissance and Intelligence Center, Khabarovsk

"My God, look at these pictures!"

Colonel Yvegeni Valerin looked at the film under his stereoscopic viewers. There was no doubt about it, the incredible pictures were too accurate, too detailed. The Japanese Army had gone from the frontier, just leaving a thin screen of border troops. The film went deep into China, and the story was the same. The Japanese Army had gone, all that was left was an occupation force, enough to keep the population in order and control minor incidents. Nowhere near enough to launch an attack. Valerin felt a great weight lift from his mind. Khabarovsk and the rest of the Siberian industrial heartland was safe. Of course that left just one small question unanswered.

If the Japanese Army wasn't here, where was it?

Chapter Two
Poised

Chulachomklao Military Academy, Bangkok, Thailand

"They're building a bridge."

The truck had been sitting for almost a quarter of an hour before Officer-Cadet Sirisoon had looked out. The old bridge was being taken down and replaced by a new concrete one. Part of the program of rebuilding the country that was seeing the old structures removed and new ones put in their place. Concrete bridges instead of wood, blacktop roads instead of dirt. Roads and railways instead of canals but she didn't think so much of that one. Canals were part of her country, it was hard to imagine what it would be like without them.

The new bridge was half-built, one span was in place, linking an abutment on the side with a pier in the middle of the river. Now, the workmen were building the other abutment and, when it was finished, the big mobile crane on the eight- by eight truck would swing the second span into place. That would be a long time yet, the little Army column, two jeeps and a truck, would have to use the temporary bridge.

She dropped the canvas back into place. In the back of the truck were eight cadets, the four women and four men. The women were bored, the men unhappy and resentful. This was an exercise, at a guess, one that would probably need the strength of eight men. Whichever sadistic instructor was in charge had put all the women cadets onto the same team. In the men's eyes, that put the entire team at a grave disadvantage in the muscle power department. In the highly competitive environment of Chulachomklao, that was cause enough for resentment.

The truck jerked and started to roll forward. Obviously, the temporary bridge was available for use again. The cadets heard the creaking of timber under the wheels, then the slurping noise as the wheels spun in the mud the other side. Then they were heading down the road, the truck bouncing on the now-unimproved surface. Through the back of the canvas cover, Sirisoon saw a small village pass, a few houses, a temple, a small store, then they were off down a track through the countryside again. Twenty minutes after they'd crossed the river, they stopped and Sergeant Major Manop banged the tailgate of the truck with his stick. "Out, everybody out."

They were in a patch of rough ground with a few trees and some scrub bushes. Best to keep away from those, that's where slithery friends would be sheltering from the sun. On one side of the trail was a large, a very large, block of concrete. Far too heavy to be shifted by a team even of eight men. Manop looked at the cadets and grinned. "Very well, we have a small task for you. Your instructor here had a keen desire to see this block of concrete on the other side of the trail. And since you are all so fond of him I volunteered you to move it. Its a bit heavy but its only about forty meters. We'll leave you a jeep with a radio, call in when you've finished." His grin grew positively evil as he climbed into the other jeep and followed the truck away.

Sirisoon watched them disappear then looked at the block. At a guess, it weighed well over a tonne, possibly two. There were various objects lying around. The test was obvious, use the objects to move the block. She took inventory; some logs, big, old, very hard. Seasoned until they were like iron. A jeep. Hmm, left unobtrusively in the back of the jeep was a length of towing chain and a set of tools. Quite a few spades.

OK, she thought, the answer is easy. Dig the ground out from under the block, sliding the logs under as rollers. Start at the front so the block is always supported. Then, once the ground was dug away and the block was on the logs, use the jeep to tow it over. As each log passed out behind the block, take it and put it back in front. With all the digging, fetching and carrying, it would be a very long, very hard, very dirty job. Dangerous too, if the logs moved while somebody was digging under the block, it could crush them. For all that, easy.

There had to be a catch.

She looked again. The ground sloped away and the slope was downhill to where the block had to go. THAT was the catch. Once the block was on the logs, the slope would mean it could roll. The jeep wasn't there to tow it, it was a brake, to stop the block rolling too fast. Idly she wondered how many teams had failed to spot that and written their jeep off when the block went out of control and plowed into it. Another thing, if it was used to hold the block from the start, that would make everything much safer.

She looked again at the cement monstrosity taunting them. One ring set in the concrete side, pointing away from where the block had to go. That was a hint for those with the wits to see it. Then she looked on top. Four more rings. Obviously, something like that had to be there, the Army had to have an easy way to move the block around. Suddenly Sirisoon's face broke out into a grin whose evil matched that of Sergeant Major Manop.

Behind her, the four men were arguing while the other women just stood and watched. Time to take charge. If nobody did, they'd be here all day and do nothing. She pointed to the men in turn. "You, you, you and you. Pick a comfortable piece of grass and lie down on it. Catch up on some sleep. Rest of you come with me. I'll explain on the way." Without waiting for questions she got into the jeep and started it up.

Bridge construction site, near Chulachomklao Military Academy, Bangkok, Thailand

The workmen like construction workers all over the world, erupted into whistles and cheers as the jeep pulled up. Four women got out, wearing shorts and white T-shirts, the fronts tied up in a knot. The women blew kisses at their admirers and made a bee-line for the site manager. One sat on his desk with her legs crossed, another on his lap. A third was already massaging his neck while the fourth, the one obviously in charge, was speaking earnestly to him. A conversation that was mysteriously assisted by some bottles of beer that had appeared from the back of the jeep. As it happened the little village store stocked Kloster beer. A good beer that was not so easy to get up-country. The conversation seemed quite animated and, after some more beer appeared, friendly. Eventually, the site foreman nodded.

It wasn't just the beer or the persuasive presence of the women. The foreman was an old soldier himself who couldn't resist helping to put one over on a bunch of officers. And he had daughters of his own and thought the instructors had played a dirty trick, putting all the women on one team. Serve them right to have it all blow up in their faces. Anyway, he wouldn't be needing the crane until afternoon and a little practice for the crew was helpful. Stop them getting bored.

"Hey, guys. Take the crane, go with these ladies and do what they ask. Get back here as soon as you've finished."

The four women made deep and respectful Wais to their benefactor, then got back into their jeep and headed off for the exercise site. Followed by an eight-by-eight cross-country truck fitted with a heavy-duty crane.

Tactical exercise site, near Chulachomklao Military Academy, Bangkok, Thailand

The four men had given up and were relaxing on the grass. They'd worked out what had to be done but also realized that their team just didn't have the muscle power to do it. Since they'd inevitably fail the test, there was no point in working themselves into exhaustion trying. Just take the hit of a failed exercise. And blame it on the women.

They were well into the process of alternately comprehensively trashing the female cadets and then speculating on the chances of persuading them to be affectionate during the wait for the exercise to end when they heard the engine noise. A few seconds later, the jeep appeared, followed by something that looked strangely like a very large, powerful, mobile crane. Awed, bewildered and a little nervous, they watched the crane halt by the block. There was a whine as the steadying jacks lowered into position , then a rattle as the chains unwound from their drum. The crane crew clambered on top of the block and secured four hooks to the rings up there.

Then they waved everybody away. Sirisoon guessed why. If one of those chains broke it would lash across the exercise site like a steel whip. Anybody in its way wouldn't stand a chance of survival. They'd be lucky if they were just killed. A heavy steel chain with that much energy behind it would pulp a human body beyond recognition. The crew took cover behind their crane-truck, the cadets joined them at the double-time.

Once the crane crew were convinced everybody was safe, the driver started throwing switches. To the awed amazement of the rest of the team, the whines and rattles turned to a deep-throated roar as the crane powered up. The block stayed put for a second, held down briefly by suction, then it lifted smoothly into the air. The crane rocked as the jib swung the block over the road and dropped it half-way to its resting place. The crew repositioned the crane, then took the block the rest of the way.

Within ten minutes, the job was done, the crane was on its way back to the bridge-building site and the team of cadets was looking at the block resting in the final, specified position. Officer-Cadet Sirisoon got back into her jeep, nobody daring to dispute that it was hers, and picked up the radio.

Training Center, Chulachomklao Military Academy, Bangkok, Thailand

"Officer-Cadet Sirisoon reporting Sir. Tactical exercise concluded."

The training officer's face clouded over. It was not the place of cadets to make joke reports, especially when on tactical evolutions and he explained that in great detail to the impertinent young woman abusing the radio communications system.

His wrath knew no bounds when she insisted on making her report official. It was ridiculous, impossible. The record for this particular exercise was six and a half hours and this woman was claiming her team had managed it in barely more than one! Absurd. He'd expose this quickly enough. Then may the gods help her.

"Operator. Patch through to Sergeant Major Manop."

There was a hiss and crackle on the line. "Manop-Actual Sir. I think you'd better get down here Sir. I assume they've called in already?"

Tactical exercise site, near Chulachomklao Military Academy, Bangkok, Thailand

It had taken half an hour to get to the exercise site. When the training officer reached the area, there could be no doubts about the facts of the matter. The block of concrete had been moved, according to orders. It was exactly where it was supposed to be. And that was quite impossible. Not only that, the cadets should be filthy dirty and exhausted. That was part of the point, to see how they behaved when under that sort of stress. Only they were clean, fresh and neat, the women sitting watching him with condescending smiles on their faces. The men didn't look nearly so happy.

There had to be something else and the evidence should be here. It was obvious they hadn't done it the way they were supposed to so how? The training officer looked at the tracks on the dirt road. A big, heavy truck had been here. He started to look around, what else was here that didn't belong?

Sirisoon watched him inspecting the ground. Behind him, Manop was standing trying desperately not to laugh. Suddenly it clicked into place, Sirisoon cursed herself for missing it. Of course, the Army wouldn't just leave them here. Somebody would be watching to see how they behaved and how they handled the situation. And, she suddenly realized, watching to see who took command of the little group. One of the purposes of the test was to see who were the leaders and who were the followers. It was a bit of a shock for her to realize that she had taken charge of the situation. That made her a leader. She hadn't thought of it that way before.

The training officer had found a depressed square in the ground, where one of the jack arms had dug in as the block swung across. With that as a reference, the tracks made sense. In fact it all made sense now, even to the laughter as he had passed back through the building site on his way down here. The one with the crane. The one where the workmen had all started laughing when they had seen him driving past.

"Sirisoon, you didn't." It was a flat statement, made out of hope that his conclusion was wrong yet with a distinct note of not wanting to know the answer.

"Didn't what Sir?"

"Explain yourself. How did you persuade the construction team to loan you their crane?"

"I discussed our need with the site foreman Sir, displaying officer-like qualities of persuasion, logic and exerting a commanding presence Sir." The training officer just stared at her. "And I stuck my tongue in his ear."

Manop couldn't hold it any longer and his suppressed snort of laughter echoed around the exercise area. The training officer spun around to stare at him as well and he struggled to get his face back under control.

"And, Sir I would like to claim, on behalf of my team, the Academy record for this particular exercise."

"But you didn't do it the way you were supposed to." The training officer knew that was a mistake as soon as he'd said it. He'd been wrong-footed by a group of cadets, and that was an experience he hadn't had before. The instructor looked at the four unhappy men on the team and felt a touch of sympathy for them. If this story got around, and it would, it was too good not to spread like wildfire, they would be laughing stocks.

"Sir, we were given no orders on how to do the job, just to get it done. And we did. Oh, and Sir we bought some beer as well for the construction team. Will the Academy reimburse us for that expense?"

The training officer looked as if he was about to have a stroke. Then, he shook his head. "Your new record will be officially listed as such in the Academy archives. As the result achieved by the team commanded by Officer-Cadet Sirisoon. And next year we will change to rules to stipulate the task be performed using resources at the site only. As for the beer, cadet, take a word of unofficial - and friendly - advice. Don't push your luck. Some things are better left undiscussed. A good officer knows when enough is enough"

100

"Lieutenant James Ladone to see Admiral Cunningham by appointment." The Admiral's Doggie nodded briefly and motioned Ladone to take a seat. A few minutes later the intercom buzzed.

"The Admiral will see you now Lieutenant."

Sir Andrew Cunningham was sitting behind his desk. He looked up as Ladone entered. "Have you made your decision yet Lieutenant?"

"Sir, I request permission to transfer to the Royal Indian Navy." Under the terms of the Imperial Gift, every Royal Navy officer was entitled to settle down anywhere in any of the countries that had accepted the gift. It had been the only fair way. After the Great Escape, the Navy had been scattered all over the world. Done well too, very well for a fleet without a real home. Some had found themselves in highly agreeable circumstances, some in very much less pleasant ones. A few had found themselves in something that was a close approach to hell and and a few others had found themselves somewhere far worse than hell. In Archangel. No, allowing people to choose had been the only fair way and the Royal Navy would take them where they wanted to go. For Ladone, who had thought long and hard over his decision, he was where he wanted to be.

"Britain not good enough for you then Lieutenant?"

"Its not that Sir, but its true there's nothing left for me there. My brother was killed on *Barham,* my sister was with the Resistance when the Germans killed her. All I know is being a Navy officer and Britain won't have much of a Navy, not now."

"Why not go to Australia then? The Aussies are building up a Navy and be with our own kind there?"

"Everybody wants Australia. They'll have more Navy personnel than they can swallow. But Sir..."

"So what's wrong with South Africa?"

"Sir." Ladone's voice was one of almost-despair. "Its not like that. I don't want to stay here because I ruled out everywhere else. I want to stay here, its my first choice not my last."

Cunningham softened and unbent slightly. "Then you'd better tell me why?"

"Sir, I've been here for three years now. This was a great country once and it can be again. It's happening, Sir and I want to be part of it. India, Sir, it gets into your blood and steals your heart. Oh I miss England, I always will but India's my home now. I belong here. Its sounds foolish Sir, but I love this country, its sights, its smells, its colors everything about it. I love the people here. Even the poorest have a sort of dignity about them. This country can be great again Sir and I want to help it. And the only way I can do that is to help them build their Navy."

Cunningham looked at the young Lieutenant. "You love the people here. One in particular I'll be bound." Ladone went bright red and looked at the floor. "Very well, you've made your choice. Your transfer to the Indian Navy is granted. Effective immediately. And its any help to you in what will be a difficult time, I made the same decision. For much the same reasons. Except the young lady of course."

Ladone left *Renown* in something of a daze. Behind him, the three battlecruisers of the Indian Navy's, his Navy's now, Flying Squadron were at anchor. Tomorrow, he'd be back on board *Repulse* doing what he had been doing for the last year. Only he'd be doing it as an Indian Naval Officer. Which brought him to his next duty of the day.

The house was large and well-built. In a city where grinding poverty was the norm, it was a mark of prosperity. He rang the doorbell and the Door Boy answered. The "boy" was a Mahratta and doubled as a bodyguard. "Please tell Doctor Gohill that Lieutenant Ladone of the Royal *Indian* Navy would be most grateful for a few minutes of his time."

The door boy let him in and took him to the parlor to wait. On the way, he passed Doctor Gohill's eldest daughter Indira. She had looked at him with a trace of fear and apprehension in her eyes. He smiled slightly and nodded. The eyes turned bright and shiny with happiness. The first reward of a hard decision. He'd met Indira Gohill a few months earlier and had started a gentle courtship. One watched by a bevy of relatives and some particularly large door boys all determined to see that the needs of propriety were met. After a while, Doctor Gohill had made it clear that, while his attentions were welcomed, he would not consider his daughter leaving India. That hadn't been the deciding factor but it had been a weighty one. Then, he heard steps approaching the parlor and Doctor Gohill entered. Ladone snapped to attention.

"Doctor Gohill Sir. Lieutenant James Ladone, Royal *Indian* Navy. I request permission to ask your daughter Indira for her hand in marriage." He thought he was fouling it up already, stumbling out with it like that. But the Doctor smiled.

"I think you will have a great future in our Navy Lieutenant. In fact I am very sure you will. You have my blessing if my daughter will accept you. You'd better ask her yourself." The stern face relaxed and a smile broke out. Indira Gohill stepped out from behind her father.

"Indira, please will you do me the honor, the very great honor, of consenting to be my wife?" Now he was sure he was fouling it up, he'd had a proper speech worked out but it had all gone and he'd just stumbled out with the question.

"Oh yes Jim. Oh *very, very* yes."

HMS Xena, At Sea, Off Rotterdam

Xena nosed gently, very gently, onto the mud. In the control room, there were some subdued grimaces but not many. After so many test dives it was what they had come to expect.

"Sorry, Swampy. It's about as definite as we're going to get. We can try a few more dives if you like but I can't see it changing the picture. There's no fresh water layer down here. We came down so gently that last time, we would have bounced off any change like that. We've looked hard but what we're looking for just isn't here."

"I know Robert. I'd guessed it was the case a couple of dives ago but I wanted to make certain. Damn it, the theory sounded right, we all were so sure. There should have been a layer down here. There's one in the Dardanelles and something similar off Gibraltar. Why not here?"

Fox shook his head. He'd taken Doctor Swamphen to the right place and they'd dived all over the area. Their high-frequency mine avoidance sonar was mapping the seabed around them and it showed the valley and river banks that had been the course of the Rhine before the North Sea had come in and flooded the plain. Once he'd even caught sight of what may have been the remains of a riverside village. Perhaps not though, the mine sonar wasn't designed for mapping and its readings were ambiguous to say the least. He'd marked the spot on the charts nevertheless, perhaps one day people with better equipment could come back and have another look.

"So, where does this leave us Swampy?"

"Well, with an opportunity of course. People don't win Nobel prizes by proving theories right, they get them for proving them wrong and coming up with better ones. That's science, we're always checking theories and discarding one's that don't fit the evidence. In this case, it comes back to what I was saying before we left, the whole undersea world is unimaginably complex and we're just getting a handle on how complex it is. We've been trying to predict the weather for how many years now? And we've got it right how often? Then SAC take their bombers up higher than anybody has ever done before and they've started to find a whole group of things up there that we didn't even suspect. Same with us down here. We haven't reached the point yet when we know how little we know."

"Very good, that's all very interesting, but what about this contamination we've been sampling. Now there isn't an undersea river down here, is that good or bad?"

Swamphen looked thoughtful for a few moments. "A bit of both I'd say. We were hoping that the river running under the sea would sweep the contamination out to the Atlantic where it would be so dispersed it wouldn't matter. Now, unless there is something else down here we don't know about - and there almost certainly is - that's gone out the window. The good news is that the spread of contamination is going to be much more limited; I'd guess this finger here" he tapped the chart on the table "has reached about as far as it's going to go. The bad news is that the degree of contamination in the affected areas is going to get a lot worse than we thought before it starts to subside. The really bad news is that, without that river, the North Sea is a closed system. What goes in, doesn't come out. The undersea Rhine we all thought was down here would have acted like a sewer, it would have spread contamination around a bit but flushed it out of the system as well. Without it, nothing's going to leave until it decays."

"And how long will that be?"

Swamphen looked thoughtful again. "Based on the figures we have so far, I'd say the degree of contamination is going to increase for at least ten years. Then, it'll start to fade. Fifty years perhaps before the centers of the contaminated areas are safe? Even during that time, sailing over them will be safe enough. Sailing through them, well, don't do it too often. Do you like Herring Robert?"

"Not particularly, no. Too oily, gives me the runs."

"That's OK then. You won't miss the North Sea and Baltic herring fisheries. They're gone. And the fishing industry they supported. The fishermen will have to convert to deep sea or find other employment. And speaking of the Baltic, that's a whole other question. When the Americans took out the Baltic ports and shipyards, they exploded their atom bombs in contact with the ground."

"I thought that's what all bombs did."

"Not these new ones. When it comes to most targets, apparently its more effective to explode them, initiate them in Nuke-talk, over the targets. High enough so the fireball doesn't touch the ground. However, where the target has a lot of really strong structures, like graving docks and U-boat pens, then they drop the atom bomb so it lands on the target before it explodes.

"The problem is that creates a huge plume of really vicious radioactivity, fallout its called, and that's been spreading along the coast. Contaminating the water like there's no tomorrow, Which, for the fishing industry up there, there isn't. The whole Baltic is seriously

105

contaminated, the Swedes and Norwegians are creating hell about it. The Finns would, only they appear to believe that if they make noises, the entire Russian Army will occupy the country and rape it clean. A not unrealistic assessment by the way. The Danes have just abandoned their Baltic coast although I think they are being pessimistic. As far as we know, the main water movement is west to east. Unfortunately as we've just proved, we know virtually nothing. Robert, what are your orders?"

"Basically, to take you where you want to go and do what you want to do as long as I don't hazard the boat or her crew in the process. To do as much training as I can and get this boat properly worked-up in the process."

"Can we go to the Baltic?"

"From what you've said, that comes under the heading of hazarding the crew."

Swamphen nodded. Faced with the knowledge of what the Americans had done to the Baltic and how little they knew about the movements of water, Fox's fears were reasonable. "How about this. We make course for the Skagerrak, taking readings all the way up. If my guess is right, contamination should drop quickly as we head north and then pick up again. When it gets to the same levels we have here, we turn around and give it up. Sound fair?"

"Fair enough." Fox's voice betrayed his reservations. He'd already decided that he would be looking at rate of increase as well as absolute levels, and if he didn't like what he was seeing, they would get out of the area. Then he had an ugly thought, if they were both this worried about contamination while still in the North Sea, just what were the levels in the Baltic like?

The Oval Office, the White House, Washington D.C.

"Senator Joseph Kennedy to see you Sir."

President Dewey cursed beneath his breath. The election was only months away and, according to the polls and the commentators, it was too close to call. Although Harry Truman was the face of the Democrats in this campaign, the reality was that Kennedy and his clique was taking over behind the scenes. One of the issues that Kennedy's clique of Democrats was driving hard was PoW/MIA. Prisoners of War and Missing in Action. The problem was that there were all too many of the second group and all too few of the first were being found. Kennedy and his supporters were spending their time attacking the administration for "not bringing the boys home" and "forgetting the prisoners".

Those accusations made Dewey's stomach knot with anger. How dare this bombastic SoB throw accusations like that around. When he'd been the Ambassador in the U.K., Kennedy had been in deep with Halifax and his Cliveden set. It was a level bet he *knew* what Halifax had been planning. Dammit, back then Kennedy had been close to being a Nazi supporter himself. That had only changed when.....

"Joe, its good to see you again. What can I do for you." Dewey's welcoming voice echoed in the expanse of the office.

"You can find my boy." Dewey's words had been friendly if insincere. Kennedy's were loaded with hate and totally sincere. Dewey was old-school politician, and whatever the differences in position, politicians kept their opposition professional, not personal. Participants in the give and take of politics didn't allow political differences to interfere with personal relationships. Truman was old school as well, he and Dewey were friends beneath their rivalry.

Kennedy and his clique were different. For them it was politics was personal and political differences were best solved by destroying everybody who did not agree with them. There was no give or take and solution by compromise for them. If they won, they took everything, if they lost they destroyed as much as they could to make their opponent's victory as barren as possible.

"Joe, Strategic Air Command have looked into this in depth. Joseph's B-29 exploded in mid-air when an Me-262 put a full salvo of R4Ms into it. The plane blew up Joe, it reached the ground in thousands of pieces. Nobody bailed out, there were no parachutes seen leaving the explosion and nobody could have survived the blast. I've got the whole report here. You can have a copy."

"They're lying. They're covering up the truth. There were parachutes seen."

"Joe, Joe. Nobody has any reason to try and cover anything up. Why should they? When Joseph's bomber went down, there were sixteen, sixteen other B-29s being shot out of the sky. Over a hundred bombers went down that day. It was a massacre, remember, one of the worst defeats the USAF ever suffered. There were almost twelve hundred men on those aircraft. About three hundred managed to bail out and were taken prisoner. Two of them survived to be rescued by SEALs. Two. The Germans killed the rest. Starved them, worked them to death as slaves, experimented on them or just gassed them in their death factories."

"That's another lie, the Germans signed the Hague and Geneva Conventions."

"Yes, they did. And they ignored them. Our SEALs have been going all over Europe trying to locate surviving prisoners of war and bring them home. You know how much luck they've been having. Your election campaign is repeating the numbers often enough."

"My boy's alive. I know it."

Suddenly, Dewey's temper broke. He'd had enough of this bombastic arrogant man with his bullying and hectoring. Dammit, America had fought a revolution to get rid of people who thought they were royalty and believed that gave them the right to trample everybody else. That revolution had sent George the Third scampering home. It was time to do the same to Joseph P Kennedy. He reached into his desk and pulled out a file. A thick one filled with depositions and pictures.

"Not a chance Joe. Not a chance. Ever hear of Novo-Alexandrovsk?" Kennedy tried to speak but Dewey rode him down. The authority of the Presidency made that work, even with Joseph P Kennedy.

"When the Germans broke through to the White Sea west of Archangel'sk, one of their flanking thrusts cut off a large part of the 23rd Infantry Division and a regiment of the 25th. Eighteen thousand Americans were taken prisoner and were sent to a prisoner of war camp at Novo-Alexandrovsk. Prisoner of war camp? No huts, no shelter, not even trees or bushes, just bare ground surrounded by barbed wire. And this was in a North Russian winter when the temperature was more than twenty below. The only provisions for feeding them were twelve cauldrons, holding enough for a hundred men each. The Germans boiled water in them and threw in a few hunks of rotten horseflesh. When the guards gave the order to come forward, the first 1,200 men would be fed. The rest would miss out. If anybody ran, sub-machine-gunners shot them down and their bodies left on the ground. Less than seven hundred survived, we're pretty certain they did because they were the living who ate the dead. That's right Joe, Americans starved into cannibalism by the people you say signed the Geneva Convention.

"Your boy went down in 1945. If he beat one-in-ten million odds and did bail out, you think he survived two years like that?. Here's some figures for you. The Germans took 7.6 million Russian soldiers prisoner. So far, the Russians have recovered fewer than one and a half million alive. Statistically, their soldiers stood a better chance of survival as front line infantrymen than they did as German PoWs. Ours are a little bit better, we've recovered just over 150,000 PoWs out of the 400,000 we knew were taken prisoner. We lost almost one and a third million men in Russia. Want to bet how many of those were killed after they'd been captured? We'll know, sooner or later.

"I'm sorry for your loss Joe, I really am. Joseph was a good kid, a brave kid who could have shirked his duty but stepped up to the mark instead. That's the hell of it, the good and the brave are always the ones who get killed. But he's gone Joe, just like one and a third million other kids. That's a loss that will hurt our whole nation for a generation or more. We have to honor his memory and we have to carry on for them."

"You're lying. He's not gone. He's out there somewhere and nobody can be bothered to look for him. Your precious SAC, its all their fault. They sent him in those damned bombers." Kennedy spun out of his seat and stormed out of the room.

Dewey sighed and spun in his chair, staring at the wall. Kennedy probably didn't know how revealing those last words were. When Joseph had volunteered for the Air Force, it had been the Army

Air Force then, his father had first tried to stop him, then had tried to get him into a safe posting. His son had fought that, and partially succeeded. He'd got himself into the bomber program. His father had won the other part of the battle, or so he'd thought. He'd bought into Boeing's propaganda about the B-29 and assumed the groups were safe compared with the fighter and light bomber units.

Of course, Joe Kennedy hadn't known about the B-36, he'd too many Nazi connections to be briefed on that. Then the B-29 groups had been slaughtered and he'd learned his son was dead. In maneuvering to get that posting for him, he'd as good as killed his own son and that was chewing away at his soul.

Dewey spun his chair again and sighed. For all his blustering and thuggish rudeness, Kennedy had a point. Intelligence was always presented by those who had an agenda. Sometimes it was done deliberately, sometimes unconsciously, but the agenda always distorted the message. What was needed was an outside agency, one that wasn't owned by any of the competing political and military power groups in Washington. One that was independent and could give the Presidency advice from its own perspective. Dewey stared at the wall some more, the idea germinating in his mind. Then, when he'd explored its possibilities, he picked up the phone on his desk.

"Find Harry Truman and ask him to see me will you? Tell him I have an idea I want to bounce off him."

Saloon Bar, The Foundry Public House, Wallsend, Tyneside, UK

"Johnno, Missus McMullen. Good to see you again. May I buy you a beer?" Piet van der Haan was his usual jocular self.

"Only if you let us buy you the second half, brother."

"Its a deal. Hey, have I got something to show you. Just arrived today." The men picked up their beers, McMullen carrying his wife's for her, and went over to a table. They 'cheers'd' and drank down some of the weak brew. "D'ya think its getting a bit better. Seems to have a bit more body to it?"

"Mebbe. Mebbe. Its about time things got a bit better here. Perhaps its just having good company."

"Aye. Hey look here. Got some pictures of my family. Just came in the post. My youngest's birthday party. He's two now, already getting some muscle on him. Look, that's him, Maartie. That's my daughter Emily and my eldest, Jan. That's my wife Paula. My father and my mother, my grandfather and grandmother, we call them oom-pa and oom-ma. Here, if you look at this one, that's the yard out back of our place."

"Oh its lovely Piet." Maisie McMullen looked enviously at the children. Plump and healthy. There weren't so many children in Wallsend, she couldn't think of one of her friends who'd got pregnant, not since the war's end. Not since the atom-bombing. And the older children were thin and half-starved. "Is it yours? Or do you rent like us?"

"Its mine, Mrs McMullen. The family has a farm out in the veldt and we go there often. Big family you see and like all Boer families, its one for all and all for one. Farm folk know it does the kids good to get out of the city, get good country air into their lungs. Jan, he's already got an eye with a rifle. Dropped his first buck just before I came. You see our party roast. Perhaps he got it for us. He's the man of the house while I'm here you see. His job to hunt."

McMullen looked enviously at the loaded table. More meat there than people had here in a month or more. "You always eat like this brother?'

"Oh no, this is a party. A big roast like that is for company. We set a good table, proud to tell you that, but this is special. We've even got our own wine, tell you something give us a few years and we'll give the French and Italians a run for their money."

Piet van der Haan flipped through the rest of the pictures. They really were all of his family but had been very carefully chosen. Nothing too ostentatious, just a reasonably prosperous family enjoying a special party. Something people could relate to, could perhaps remember themselves from better times. He watched Maisie McMullen looking at the pictures of the children, tears forming in her eyes and, for a moment, he felt thoroughly ashamed of himself. Then, he recalled the reason why he was here. The Republic was desperately short of skilled, white, workers. If the McMullens emigrated, left this bleak, ruined country, they'd be much better off. And the Republic needed them.

Maisie McMullen dabbed her eyes. "You have a beautiful home Piet. Its lovely. I'd love to see it really I would."

"You can you know Mrs McMullen." The faces of the couple with him were disbelieving. "Haven't you heard about the assisted passage scheme? For people who have skills the Republic of South Africa needs, there are special provisions. The Government will pay your fare out. There is a provision, if you leave after less than five years, you'll have to repay it but after that time, the debt is forgiven. And the way you swing a hammer, Johnno my boy, you'll have your own home by then. Shipbuilder is one of the highest priorities we have."

Maisie McMullen stared at him. "Piet, why do you carry a gun?"

For a second he was flustered. "We heard there was a lot of lawlessness out here, people being robbed of their ration cards for the Black Market. So I brought the family Browning. Turns out the information was wrong of course but I'm stuck with it now. Can't leave it unattended."

Maisie McMullen smiled understandingly. She knew van der Haan was lying. And now she had seen him lying, she knew everything else he had said was true.

Chapter Three
Falling

Chulachomklao Military Academy, Bangkok, Thailand

Four sheets of paper were pinned to the notice board, each with twenty five names on it. The system was simple and brutal. All the candidates who had made it to the end of the course were graded, a mixture of examinations, course work and the results of the tactical evolutions. Those whose grades did not meet the statutory minimum were failed. The brutal bit was that only a maximum of one hundred candidates were allowed to graduate from each class. If more than one hundred had exceeded that statutory minimum grade, only the top one hundred passed; the rest were failed as surely as those who had not made the minimum.

The four sheets were unofficially known as quarters. It was well-known that those who graduated from Chulachomklao in the top quarter were the high-flyers, the ones who would be sought out for prestige postings, groomed for the top ranks. Those in the bottom quarter were forever doomed to be the hewers of wood and the drawers of water, spending their careers in the backwaters of the Army. Officer Cadet Sirisoon Chandrapa na Ayuthya ran her eye down the list of names in the First Quarter. As she'd expected, hers was conspicuous by its absence. First Quarter had been too much to hope for and, being honest with herself, she guessed that she wouldn't find herself in the Second Quarter.

Honesty was appropriate, her name wasn't in the Second Quarter either. She started to read the Third Quarter, a knot forming in her stomach as her eye went down the list. When she reached the bottom, the knot felt like a lead ball. Reluctantly, she forced herself to look at the Fourth Quarter. That didn't take so long, her name was second from the top. She'd come 77th out of 100. The lump faded back to a knot. Whatever else had happened, whatever would happen in the future, she was now Second Lieutenant Sirisoon Chandrapa na Ayuthya.

Then she ran her eye down the rest of the list. 88th, 92nd and 99th. All four women had graduated, that was the good news, They were all in the Fourth Quarter, that was the bad news. Hewers of wood and drawers of water. No chance of getting the high ranks or the really good postings. She'd never thought that would matter to her but now she found it did. It mattered very much.

She heard a sniff behind her. Doi, the girl who had come 99th, was staring at her name as if it was a poisonous snake. "We didn't do that badly did we?? She whispered when she saw Sirisoon looking at her.

"It's not that bad. We've graduated, more than thirty of the men didn't. They failed. We passed. The rest of it is up to us now." She tried to sound encouraging but wasn't making a very good job of it.

"Ladies, would you please come to my office?" Sergeant Major (First Class) Manop Patmastana had been watching the candidates receiving their results. The process of evaluation at Chulachomklao never ended and how the candidates reacted on receiving their results, good or bad, was sometimes as important as the results themselves. Triumph could test character as sternly as defeat. The reaction of one cadet in First Quarter had already caused a black mark to be placed against his name.

Sirisoon looked around the office, one she had never been in before and that she had privately thought of as being the Holy of Holies. It was simple, spartan although she was amused to note that the Sergeant Major had a bigger desk than any of the officers and two telephones compared to their one.

"I wanted to speak with you four before the Passing Out ceremony. You've already graduated from the Academy but you haven't yet been commissioned. That gives us a very brief moment when we can talk frankly with each other. We'll never have this opportunity again.

"Firstly I want you to know that the Instructors were all very impressed by the way you conducted yourselves here. You had a difficult time, we know that, and you did well. Much better than those lists you were looking at suggest. I know you are all disappointed that you were Fourth Quarter. Had those results been based on your academic work and your attention to your duties, you would have graduated much higher.

"Soldiering is not academic work, it is much more than that. Unfortunately for you, most of the extra involves sheer physical strength and that is what pulled all four of you down to the Fourth Quarter. Frankly, you are not strong enough for front-line soldiering and you never will be. You were far, far below the required minimums when you came here and you are only just barely above them now. One of you only qualified literally by a heartbeat, by a fraction of a second. Don't get me wrong, I and every other instructor here, have been very impressed by the way you worked around the problems caused by your lack of physical strength. Sirisoon, that stunt with the crane will go down into Academy history. But don't ever forget you never solved the problems caused by your physique, you worked around them.

"That's impressive but you didn't solve them. And you can't. Sorry, there's no nice way to put it. Throughout your careers, you are going to have to face those problems and, one day, they're going to hit you somewhere you can't work around them. When we heard women were coming to the Academy, we had to make a decision. Do we expect you to meet the same standards as the men or do we set standards that are within the reach of more women? We settled on a policy of adopting the same standards for women as were already established for men.

"Why? Because we are soldiers and the physical requirements are set by the nature of our work. They are what we need to be to do our jobs. Artillery rounds don't get lighter because a woman lifts them, kilometers don't get shorter because a woman marches them. Bullets do not travel more slowly because they are about to strike a woman. So I beg you, in the future, never forget that you worked around physical problems, you didn't solve them. And try never to be caught in a position where strength is your only way out.

"Another thing. I watched you checking your names on the lists. You're disappointed to be Fourth Quarter. Don't be. Your academic and study records are exemplary. You won't be posted to infantry, artillery, cavalry or armor units, you'll be going to the administrative parts of the Army. Judge Advocate General, Pay Corps, Medical, whatever. It's your academic and job performance that people will be looking at, not your graduation position. That only becomes important when you're up for promotion to General and I don't think that will concern you.

"I wish you the best in your careers when you leave here. I believe that we will probably meet again; the Army is recruiting more women for its administrative sections and I do not doubt we will have women instructors here soon. In the meantime, I hope fortune attends you and the gods smile upon you wherever you serve."

Hindustan Shipyard, Mazagon, India

"And so, I declare this new shipyard, a symbol of India's growing industrial might, open. May the yard prosper and the ships built here have long and honorable careers."

Sir Martyn Sharpe reached forward with the golden scissors and cut the white ribbon across the gate of the shipyard. The ends of the tape was on spring-loaded reels so that they retracted across the road once the cut was made.

"And to mark this auspicious occasion, it is my great pleasure to announce that the Indian Government is proud to place the first order at this new shipyard. We have today signed an order with Hindustan Shipyards for a pair of new destroyers, the first major warships to be built in India for more than a hundred and fifty years.

"Then, the great Indian master shipwright, Jamsetjee Bomanjee designed and built some of the finest wooden warships in the world. Such was his skill and talent that he solved the problem of building ships out of teak, making the Bombay Dockyard a dominating presence in the wooden shipbuilding world. I call upon Hindustan Shipyards today to honor the memory of Jamsetjee Bomanjee by making the two destroyers we will build here the envy of the world's navies!"

There was a thunderous roar of applause from the crowd. The new president of Hindustan Shipyards rose to reply. Sir Martyn went through the motions of listening attentively but he didn't have to. Copies of the speeches to be made here had been circulated around all the primary guests. It didn't do to have unpleasant surprises on public occasions. As usual, what was important here was not what was being said but what had been carefully left out. The new destroyers for example, magnificent ships, good looking and larger than any current rivals. Yet for all his speeches, Sir Martyn reflected, they were about as Indian as the ships received from the Royal Navy as India's Imperial Gift. They were designed by Gibbs and Cox, the American Naval Architects, were armed with American guns and powered by American engines.

It wouldn't always be that way of course. One of the terms of the deal negotiated with Gibbs and Cox had been that the Americans would set up a design office in India and train Indian staff to design their own ships. Yet even that meant that the staff they trained would be indoctrinated in American ways and do things in the American style.

Sir Martyn suppressed a shudder. Doing things in the American Style meant The Big One and a whole country reduced to a smoking, blasted ruin. The pacifist movement in India, something that had almost vanished after Ghandi's "accident," had reappeared once the full enormity of what the Americans had done to Germany became apparent. They had little power in a political sense, not yet and the way the Indian political machine was constructed meant that they probably never would have. But they did have a sort of moral authority and they did have the ability to cause trouble. There had been some here, protests against the construction of "tools of death". Again, not enough to cause problems, just enough to cause embarrassment.

Only they had caused one problem, not a public but a private one. The truth was, Sir Martyn was not entirely convinced they were wrong. He'd seen the pictures that had come out of Germany, seen the film of the mushroom clouds rising over the cities, seen the images of charred bodies littering the burned-out streets.

Looking at the crowd cheering the Company President as he promised jobs and money and education, in fact promised a future, Sir Martyn wondered if these people understood that the shipyard here had made their town a target for a nuclear attack. He pictured the huge mushroom cloud rising over Mazagon and its effects on these people. Were the Ghandi-ites so wrong? Could India go any other way? If it came to it, could he order Indian forces to do to an enemy what the Americans had done to Germany?

Was it too late to do anything else? Buried in the news about the opening of the shipyard was something else. The cancellation of the Mosquito light bomber program and its replacement by a large purchase of American B-27 bombers and RB-27 reconnaissance aircraft. On the other hand the new Hindustan Hornet was being ordered into full production and another batch of Ostrich attack aircraft had been ordered from Australia so the dependence on America was mitigated a little.

The country was still heading down the American road though and Sir Martyn felt his concern deepening that prospect. Not least because of the oh-so-secret program that had been started in an oh-so-secret research facility tucked away in the depths of India. A program that would send the Ghandi-ites screaming mad.

"And so every effort must and will be made to make these new destroyers a fitting tribute to India's glorious naval heritage!"

The new President finished speaking and, again, a tide of cheering met his words. There was another point that troubled him. Suppose India didn't follow the American road, and rejected the solutions America had chosen? Implicitly that would mean India would be relying on the Americans to defend the country against a nuclear attack. And wasn't relying on another country to do what India was too 'moral' to do for itself even more reprehensible?

Sir Martyn sighed, gently and silently, and once again his mind's eye saw a mushroom cloud rising over Mazagon. And his mind's eye also saw a female face with a friendly, polite smile on it. And Sir Martyn knew there was one politician in Asia at least who wouldn't hesitate in the slightest to use nuclear weapons against people she considered to be the enemies of her country.

Halmstad, Sweden

The ferry Captain made a mess of it. A stray cross-current caught him unawares and swung the bow for just enough time to send in crunching into the timbers that lined the ferry bay. Fortunately, the timbers were there to absorb the blows from just such an accident and the only damage done was to the paintwork and the Captain's pride. There would be beers to be bought before his professional fellows allowed him to forget it. It was a pity the voyage had to end on a sour note, it had gone pretty well to date. They'd avoided the declared minefields easily, they hadn't run into the undeclared minefields and they'd stayed well clear of the off-limits areas along the German coast. Those areas were growing every time he made the trip and on every trip there were scientists taking water and mud samples. Every trip, the expressions on the faces of those scientists grew grimmer.

Still, they were safely back home, docked and the bow doors open. The passengers were streaming off, uncertainly, being directed by port authority police and red cross workers. In times past, the ferry had carried the usual mix, tourists going to visit the sights of Germany, traders, businessmen, truckloads of goods and supplies. Now, the load was German soldiers, released by the Russians and sent into what amounted to exile. Was it exile to be sent away from one's own country when that country didn't exist any more? The ferry Captain had heard the stories of what Germany was like now and he'd read Major Lup's story of his unit's calvary into the center of Duren just hours after the Americans had destroyed the city and everybody in it. Nothing left of Germany, nothing at all. A whole country wiped from the earth.

Down on the deck of the ferry, Matthias Schook found himself being carried along with the body of the crowd. There were almost a thousand passengers on the ferry, one small portion of the stream of demobilized soldiers being evacuated from the pocket of land held by Army Group Vistula. He was one of the lucky ones. His unit had been amongst the first to surrender to the Russians. There had been rumors that they would all be shot, that all that awaited them was a mass execution and an unmarked mass grave.

Some had even suggested that they mutiny against their orders and try to fight their way out but cooler heads had prevailed. Field

Marshal Rommel had ordered the surrender and he wouldn't send men to a pointless death they had argued. See what the Field Marshal has planned. How many times has the situation been hopeless and the Field Marshal has got us out? We can trust him.

So the men had surrendered and been taken to a camp in the forest. Their officers and most of their NCOs had been taken away then the NKVD had come in and taken those whose names were on lists they held. Curiously, Schook had noted, those who had spoken in favor of mutiny and a gallant escape attempt or fighting to the last round were the ones whose names were on the lists. The rest had been interviewed, the questions casual but pointed and then taken to Riga where they'd been put on ferries. Some were going to Denmark, some to Sweden, some to Norway. A few men had asked if they could go back to Germany; they'd been told that would be their decision later but first, they had to go to refugee camps.

So here they were. As expected, being divided up into alphabetical order by family name. It was a long wait, but eventually Schook stepped into the tent for the S group. An official was sitting behind a trestle table, tired and slightly irritable. It had been a long day and showed no sign of ending yet.

"You are Schook? Please remove your uniform and other clothing and place them in the container to be burned. Keep any personal property of course. Then go over there for a medical examination. After that, you may select some civilian clothes to get you started and you will be introduced to the people with whom you will be staying. But first, show me your arms please."

Schook frowned slightly and stretched out his arms. The official looked carefully then turned them over and checked again. "What are you looking for Sir?" Schook couldn't help asking.

"Tattoos of your blood group."

"But only the SS have those."

"Exactly. You would be surprised how many members of the SS turn up with identification papers of Heer soldiers. We presume they killed the original owners. Doesn't matter, when we find them, we send them back to the Russians. The Ivans didn't know about the tattoos at first; they do now of course."

"Sir, may I ask what happened to those who were taken away?"

"As far as we know most have been taken to Russian cities where they have been put to work repairing the damage they caused. We believe that some, the hard cases, have been sent to the gold mines in Kolymya. There are rumors that those against whom the Russians make the most serious allegations are being sent to the uranium mines at Aksu. The Russians will be staging war crimes trials soon for the most senior ranks. Now, move along please."

The medical inspection was routine and was followed by a delousing. It was actually the second since the surrender, the evacuees and their uniforms had been deloused before getting on to the ferry out. Still, Schook couldn't blame the Swedes for being careful. Then, he was sent through to the clothing section. There was a list up on the wall, each man was entitled to three sets of underwear, two shirts, two pairs of trousers, one suit and one overcoat. A gift from the Swedish Government to help the evacuees get back on their feet. Once he'd picked up his clothes and dressed, Schook was sent though to the next stage, meeting the people with whom he'd be living.

The couple looked prosperous and well-fed. As Schook emerged from the clothing section, they stepped forward, smiling hand outstretched. Schook almost saluted out of sheer instinct then stopped himself and seized the outstretched hand.

"Herr Schook? I am Sven Gundersen and this is my wife Helga. We would like you to stay with us until you get back on your feet." Gundersen looked at the young man in front of them with his haunted eyes. He'd been worried about his wife until now; food rations in Sweden were short because the Baltic fisheries were out of business. The fishing boats had the long trip out of the Baltic into the Arctic - and a lot of the fishermen were giving up because they were getting sick. He'd thought Helga was looking pale on the restricted diet, now, compared with this young man, she was the epitome of bouncing good health.

"Tomorrow we will take you to the town hall where you can look through the job vacancies here. There are many of those so you shouldn't have trouble. What did you do before you became a soldier?"

Schook thought for a second, it was so long, 'before becoming a soldier' seemed like a different world. He had to work hard to remember. "I was an apprentice carpenter."

The Swedish couple spoke quickly; then the man turned back to him. "Helga's cousin owns a small carpentry shop in town. Makes and repairs furniture. He is looking for an assistant. Perhaps you might like to speak with him. He will not pay as well as a big company but if one is a small fish, perhaps it is better to be in a small pond, yes?"

"Yes. I would be very pleased to meet your wife's cousin. Please thank your wife for her concern." Schook caught sight of himself in a window. Talking about getting a job. My God he thought to himself. I'm a civilian again. At last.

Administrative Building, Nevada Test and Experimental Area

"I would like to welcome you all to this facility. We are starting early today, once the sun comes up, the temperature rises very quickly and briefings can be quite uncomfortable. I will start by introducing the participants to this First Air Defense Exercise Series." Colonel Pico looked around at the room. There was another reason why the meeting was being held so early but they'd come to that later. Or, rather, it would come to them. "Most of you are already known to each other but we'll do the formalities nonetheless.

"Firstly, I would like to welcome Colonel Francis Gabreski of the 56th Fighter Wing and his F-74B Furys. Also with us is Colonel Joseph McConnell of the 51st Fighter Wing with their F-80G Shooting Stars. Take a bow, gentlemen, please. Modesty does not become fighter pilots." There were a series of cheers and some war-whoops from the assembled pilots.

"I would also like to extend a warm welcome to Guards-Colonel Aleksandr Pokryshkin and the MiG-9s of the Fourth Guards

Fighter Division." There was a burst of cheering and some of the nearer fighter pilots clapped the Russian on the back.

"The piston-engined fraternity is not forgotten. A big hand please for Colonel Robert Johnson of the 352nd Fighter Wing and Colonel James Jabara of the 4th Fighter Wing who have brought their F-72D Thunderstorms to the party. We would also like to welcome Major Dominic Gentile of the 479th Fighter Wing whose F-63G Kingcobras always add a certain level of style to any event.

"We would not like it to be thought that we have anything against the twin-engined community so to carry the flag for the multiply-screwed we have Major Manuel Fernandez with his F-58A Chain Lightnings and Major George Davis with that rarest of fighters, the F-71A Stormbird. In fact, I think the eight F-71s George brought with him are the only serviceable fighters of that type left. One of the questions we'll be investigating over the next two weeks will be whether we should recommend production of that aircraft be resumed. Finally, we have Colonel George Preddy and his F-65G Tigercat night fighters to help make sure nobody gets any sleep.

"To meet with this array of talent, we have some guests from Strategic Air Command." There was low growl. The tactical aviation groups in Russia resented the way SAC had got the credit for ending the war. This whole series of exercises had started life because of that ill-feeling.

"General Tibbets has brought the B-36Hs of the 100th Bomb Group while General Lucas has contributed the RB-36s of the 305th Strategic Reconnaissance Wing. There will also be detachments of KB-36 tankers and GB-36 fighter carriers participating. In additional, Kapitan Ivan Mayolev has brought a detachment of the Tu-4s from the Russian Navy's Third Long Range Naval Aviation Regiment."

Colonel Pico looked at the room. Mention of the Tu-4s had caused confusion, everybody knew the Tupolev was only an improved version of the B-29 and everybody knew what happened when B-29s met fighters.

After getting back from the Big One, he'd laid awake for nights on end, his mind filled with the images of the mushroom clouds rising over German cities and, when sleep had finally come, dreams filled with montages of similar clouds rising over American cities. The B-36 might be slow by fighter standards but it could fly higher than any of them. That's what had made The Big One work. There had been nothing the Germans could do to stop the bombers. Now, the same applied to America. If an enemy came at them with a fleet of B-36s, there would be nothing in America to stop them.

The Imperial Japanese Navy was known to be developing a B-36-like aircraft, Air Intelligence had code-named it "Frank" and if the Navy was developing such an aircraft, the Army could not be far behind. The B-36 had shown that such aircraft could be built and even given the more careful observers vital clues on how they could be built. And when they were built, there was nothing America could do to stop them.

"A word on the aims and organization of these exercises. We will be flying air problems during the day. These will all be quite simple, there will be assigned targets within the range area. Bombers from SAC will attempt to penetrate the defenses and strike those targets with simulated nuclear weapons. Your job, gentlemen, is to stop them. Any way you can. Once the exercise is completed and everybody is back here, we will be holding detailed debriefing sessions to assess what happened and how. By the way, General Tibbets has offered to carry any of you who wish to ride a B-36 on these exercises so you can see things from the bomber perspective. I urge you all to take advantage of that offer.

"Then, in the evenings there will be a series of presentations on new defense technologies and products. Tomorrow night will be the first, a team from Douglas, Raytheon and Bell Telephones will be here to talk about a new anti-aircraft missile system we are developing. The night after, Artem Mikoyan and a team from his design bureau will be here to tell us about their new MiG-15 fighter. Colonel Gabreski?"

"You mentioned missiles? Any ground-based anti-aircraft units here?"

"Indeed. The targets will be surrounded by the 90mm anti-aircraft guns from Camp Roberts and we've got some new 120mms direct from the manufacturers. In addition, we have some captured German 127mms and even some Wasserfall missiles to try out.

"One of the things we're evaluating here is the air defense system that will tie all these bits together. Most of you've read the reports on that German system, NAIADS. It looks like it was the tactical coordination provided by that system gave the Germans the edge needed to crucify the B-29 raids. For all that, we're not too impressed with NAIADS. Its a very Teutonic system, its reporting paths rigidly hierarchical and very strictly defined. That spells a fragile system to us, one that can be easily disrupted.

"We want to do better. That raises a question of how. The communications net we're defining is quite different in structure from NAIADS. The German system was, is, a tree with information flowing in defined paths from the branches to the roots then orders flowing back in the opposite direction. Break those paths anywhere and the information doesn't flow. We are designing a system that's more like a network a mass of interconnections. Break it at any one place and the information flows around the break.

"That begs a question, what do we control and how. One of the purposes of our work the next few weeks is to determine how defensive fighters can best be utilized within such a network. As most of you who served in Russia are aware, the Russians use fighters very differently from us. Their interceptors work under tight ground control, being vectored to their targets by ground stations. Our Russian friends have brought their own controllers with them and we will be comparing their doctrine with our own system. Some of you will be flying under Russian controllers, some of the MiG pilots will be flying under ours. We'll see what works."

There was a rumble of dissent at that. Pico looked at the gathering grimly. "Let me make one thing clear. This is not the World Series. This is a post-graduate course in air defense. It doesn't matter who 'wins' and who 'loses'. We're not defending 'our way' against 'their way' or 'TAC' against 'SAC'. We're trying to find what works and what does not. We all win if we learn, we all lose if we do not."

Pico glanced at the clock. He'd been stalling for time although nobody else was aware of it. Now, it was just about ready to go. "Our task here is to find out how to defend America against the sort of attack that we launched against Germany. If we fail, if we let our own limited rivalries defeat that greater aim.."

A brilliant light suddenly shone through the tightly-shuttered windows, strong enough to cast shadows on the walls and dazzle eyes accommodated to the low light levels previously in the briefing hall. A few seconds later the earth under the pilot's feet started to shake as the ground wave reached them, then they heard the building creaking and the roar of the explosion. The phone rang and Pico picked it up. He listened for a second then gave a curt acknowledgment. Walking across the room, he opened the shutters, exposing a view across the desert. The sun had still to rise but in its place was a glowing mushroom cloud rising over the Yucca Flats test site.

"That, gentlemen, is a test shot of our latest Mark Five nuclear device. The estimated yield is 81 kilotons, in other words, its explosive power is equal to the detonation of 81,000 tons of standard TNT. It weighs only 3,150 pounds a third of the weight of the devices we dropped on Germany but it is more than twice as powerful. I should know, I dropped twelve of our older devices on Berlin." And may God have mercy on me for that Pico thought silently. "As I was saying, if we fail, if we lose, if we do not find a way to stop modern bombers from penetrating our defenses, one day we will see fireballs like that rising over American - and Russian - cities."

The fighter pilots looked horrified at the evil glowing red cloud, twisting and changing as it rose in the pre-dawn gloom. It was the first time any of them had seen a nuclear explosion in its true awful reality and the sight stunned them into silence. Pictures in a magazine were one thing, film in a cinema was another. Neither could compete with the reality of the glare, the shaking, the crushing roar or the numbing sight of that evil, twisting cloud.

"Just to remind you of that fact, it has been decided that this series of air defense exercises will be designated 'Red Sun'".

Aboard MV "Union Castle", Southampton, UK.

"Here you are, Sir, Ma'am. Your cabin for our voyage. If you need anything, just dial 9 on the telephone and a steward will be here immediately."

It was a spartan cabin, two beds, a minimum of furniture. Just enough to keep a couple of immigrants on the Assisted Passage

126

Scheme reasonably comfortable for the voyage to South Africa. "Well, Maisie luv. We're off now and that's no mistake."

His wife nodded. It had been a hard couple of months. After they'd learned about the Assisted Passage Scheme, they'd talked long and seriously far into the night. It had been an eye-opening discussion, one in which they'd covered far more than just the possibility of leaving the UK.

Maisie McMullen had learned just how depressed and frustrated her husband was, no matter how good he was at his job, no matter how well he worked, he could never be more than he was now and would always be in the position of finding himself without a job at a few minutes notice.

He, in turn, learned how desperately tired and exhausted his wife was, struggling to keep a home running in the face of rationing, debts and never knowing whether there would be money coming in next week. And there was the grayness, the dank, futility of struggling to keep going in a bankrupt post-occupation Britain.

They hadn't decided to emigrate then, in fact they'd never made that decision. John McMullen had sought his friend out and got more information on the APS and on prospects in South Africa. Piet van der Haan had warned him that the material from the South African Government was rosily optimistic, that it presented the best of all possible cases in the best of all possible worlds. It wasn't untrue, just very glossy.

The three of them had spent a fun evening in the pub going over the material while van der Haan pointed out parts where the "official" line was unduly enthusiastic. "You'll have to work hard Johnno, no hiding that. But everything's there for a man who's prepared to make the effort." Somehow, without anybody making a decision, they'd met a South African embassy official who'd helped them fill out the paperwork applying for places on the APS. McMullen had shown him his work chits from the Yard and the official had done a double-take at the number of all-passed bonuses he'd received. They'd been approved in record time.

That wasn't what had decided the issue though. It was the yard itself. Work on the cruisers was going well but there was an issue boiling away below the surface. The next ships to be built there would be two new X-class submarines. Welded. Experts from Canadian Vickers were coming over to train the workforce in welding techniques and that was the problems. The Steelworkers Union and the Boilermaker's Union both claimed that welding as a job for their members and their members alone.

The yard management had protested, there were enough jobs for both but their appeal had fallen on deaf ears. The Steelworkers demanded that welding was a job for steelworkers, the Boilermakers demanded that welding was a job for boilermakers. And both threatened to take it to a strike. A strike meant the yard stopped, work stopped, money stopped. Without saying anything, the McMullens decided to leave before it came to that.

They'd sold up, told their landlord they were leaving. They'd got good money for their furniture and the other stuff they'd not wanted to take with them. It had been good, prewar stuff and the town was still flush with money from the yard work. The implications of the impending labor dispute hadn't begun to sink home yet and when they'd started to sell, there'd been queues around the block. They'd had some hostility from those who saw them as cutting and running, others had been envious of their decision. Others had asked them about the possibility of following the McMullen example. Despite the varied reactions, they'd ended the sale with a healthy nest-egg to get them started. One that had impressed van der Haan when he'd helped them fill out the currency transfer papers.

"Johnno, with this, you could start up your own business. Way you swing a hammer, you could do well."

"What, me join the bosses Brother?" McMullen's voice had been guarded.

"One thing to join the bosses brother, quite another to be your own boss. Stand on your own feet, be beholden' to none. That's what the Republic's all about in the end. White men standing tall, proud, on their own feet. Look, there's lots of riveting done on things other than ships. You set up a metal working shop, you do two things. One is get yourself work when there's nothing in the yards and you also can extend a helpin' hand to those who have just arrived and need a start. That's what the Union's all about so I've always thought. Give a helping hand to our brothers who need it. Get them started and on the right track."

Again, they'd never made the decision but by the time they'd handed the keys of what had been their home back and got on the train for Southampton, McMullen knew he'd be starting his own metal working company as soon as he'd got established. He'd got an employment contract already, a year's work at the Simonstown Naval base, helping refit and repair the South African Navy's Imperial Gift. Something he'd never had before and he and his wife still wondered at it. A contract that said, as long as he did his job and didn't engage in misconduct (defined in the contract), he had a year's wages coming, guaranteed. All at Shipbuilder's Union approved rates.

"Look at this John." Maisie McMullen handed over a sheet. It was a welcome letter "from the Captain" although the signature was obviously stamped and McMullen doubted whether the Captain had ever read it. It bid them welcome on board and gave them the ship's schedule. There were the menus for the meals next day and they were asked to select what they wanted to eat in advance so that the galleys could minimize wastage. There was information on emergencies, what to do if they were sick, what would happen if there was a collision or fire, how to abandon ship in an emergency. And there was a long list of courses held on board, about South African history, current events in the Republic, how to speak Afrikaans, cooking in South Africa, many, many things. Suddenly, the McMullens realized that they were indeed leaving everything they'd ever known behind them. As if to emphasize the point, the siren on the ship blasted.

"Come on luv, that's the ship getting ready to leave. Let's go up on deck and wave good-bye to the old country."

Office of Sir Martyn Sharpe, Chief of Staff to the President, New Delhi, India

"How does the new title sound?" Sir Eric Haohoa grinned at his friend as he planted the barbed question. He savored the taste of the vintage scotch whisky, usually only served when The Ambassador was visiting. But, today was special.

"Still getting used to it. Its going to be hard for a while, getting everything set up. How is it your end?"

"Fairing well. We've inherited a good network of human assets. Not much on the technical side and we're terribly short of funds but, we've a good intelligence base to work from. We'll manage. Given time."

"Given time. That's the crunch isn't it. Will we get it. What are the Japanese up to?"

"As far as we can gather, they're still trying to consolidate their hold on China. They hold most of the main areas no, they've pushed the Chinese Government back to the more remote areas. You heard the Flying Tigers had to pull out?" Sir Martyn nodded. The American Volunteer group in China had been a thorn in the Japanese side for almost a decade. Started off flying antique P-40s and eventually ended up in F-74s, all paid for by the Chinese Government of course and the pilots themselves were disowned by the Americans - although most of them seemed to rejoin the American armed forces with remarkably little difficulty after they left China. But, the last airfields capable of handling jets had gone so the Tigers had blown up their aircraft and left.

"The Japanese are expanding their army at an alarming speed. In late 1942 their Army had a total of 538,000 men active in 48 divisions. They had two divisions each in Japan, Indochina and Korea plus three Imperial Guard divisions in Japan, 12 divisions in Manchuria and 27 divisions in China. This has now risen to a total of 145 divisions, with over 5 million men. At least 55 of those divisions, with 2 million men, have been formed in China over the last year. In addition to the regular divisions, there's a large number of independent brigades, mostly light infantry and some motorized units.

"General Auchinleck believes that to get that rate of expansion they must be stripping their existing units of skilled cadres and filling up the ranks with Chinese conscripts. Disposition is much as we might expect. Japan still has its three Imperial Guard divisions and two regular Army divisions. Korea and Indochina two regular divisions each. China, now has 134 divisions. The oddity is Manchuria. There used to be twelve divisions up there, now there are four.

"That must ease the Russian mind considerably. Especially after the Americans pulled that border overflight."

Sir Eric laughed. "Indeed so. The Japanese went ballistic of course but they seem to be getting used to it. Didn't even murmur about the last couple. By the way, did you see those pictures the Americans took of Bengal during the floods? They were an immense help to us in getting the relief efforts mounted.

"Anyway, the Russians may be happy but it seems like there are at least eight divisions of Japanese troops missing and we've completely lost track of them. There are four independent armored brigades missing as well. That's a powerful little army loose somewhere. The Army is expanding its air force as well, not as fast but steadily and they're bringing in a lot of new types. Mostly jet fighters and bombers which raises a fuel question of course. They have the same problem getting jet fuel as everybody else.

"The big loser over the last few years has been the Navy. They're the ones paying the bill for China. They finished their earlier fleet expansion program, all four of those battleship monsters, four repeat Shokaku carriers, five repeat Taihos. Gives them twelve modern carriers. Their air groups are pretty grim though. A lot of their fighter units are still flying Zeros and we can count the naval jet units on the fingers of one thumb. Land-based aircraft aren't much better although they do have some jets. Reports are they're still flying those big Mitsubishi twin engined torpedo bombers, George, I think the Americans call them

"But for the rest? A few heavy cruisers and they're building a new class of destroyers using the Agano light cruiser as a base. For the rest of it, its not just that new construction has slowed right down to a crawl, they're going through the rest of the fleet with an ax. Just in the last two years, all the old armored cruisers went, not that they were worth much anyway, all those old three- and four-funnel light cruisers have gone, all their pre-Fubuki class destroyers and we aren't seeing much of their older big destroyers either. Three of their oldest carriers went last year, including the two big ones, *Akagi* and *Kaga*. Got some jeep carriers built on merchant ship hulls though.

"And now we get this. They've just pulled their six oldest battleships from service. Scrapped five of them, made the sixth into a 'Museum of Japanese Naval Art and Science'. Damn pretentious name. Those old battleships aren't much of a loss in power terms but it shows the Navy is on the bottom of the pecking list now."

Sir Martyn looked at the Cabinet Secretary and tried to resist but the historian's instincts got the better of him. "Just as a matter of interest, Eric, which battleship did they preserve?"

Sir Eric Haohoa grimaced. "I'm not sure. Didn't notice, anyway they're all just names really. It'll be in here somewhere. " He thumbed through the intelligence briefing. "Battleships scrapped........ Ah yes, here we are. Battleship preserved as museum. *Fuso.*"

Chapter Four
Striking

First Army Circle Headquarters, Ban Masdit, Recovered Provinces, Thailand

"Reporting for duty Sir."

"Settled into your quarters yet, Lieutenant?"

"Yes indeed Sir. And they are much better than I had expected. A private bath is a luxury I didn't expect out here."

"In the Wild East you mean? As a matter of fact, the army bases out here are much better than the ones back home. They've all been built in the last six years you see and they've all incorporated new ideas." And, thought General Songkitti, the most objectionable of those new ideas was women in the Army. "You'll have noticed the men have smaller barracks, more like large rooms really, and more privacy. Officers have small private quarters and about a quarter of them have separate bathrooms. Yours is one of those."

"I don't ask for special treatment Sir."

"And you won't get it. Get off your high horse, Lieutenant. It's a matter of simple fact that nobody wants a woman wandering around the barracks looking for a vacant bath. The decision to give you quarters with a bath was taken on purely common-sense grounds. It's better for good order and discipline. Now, that being settled, how is your office and workload? Sit down and give me your honest opinion on where we stand."

Second Lieutenant Sirisoon Chandrapa na Ayuthya sat in the chair opposite her General's desk. She had, what would be under any other circumstances, a plum assignment. Administrative aide to the Chief of Staff of First Area Army. That meant she was responsible for maintaining all the paperwork and routine managerial tasks of the headquarters, making sure that her general didn't have to worry over who had filled in which particular bureaucratic nightmare. A good administrative aid would be their General's protégé, rising with him from post to post, having their careers gently directed from one important job to the next until, one day, they wore stars and sat behind a desk, sizing up a young Lieutenant who might, or might not, have what it took. Only stuck out here on the frontier far from the centers of power back home, there was nowhere to go.

In any case, it wasn't going to happen in her case. Because she was a she and the Army was a boy's club and she didn't belong there. She'd be tolerated and used but she'd never become a protégé, never have her career directed inexorably upwards. If she was going to move up the ranks, she would have to claw her way up. She'd never realized it would matter to her so much. She'd joined the Army for an education that her family couldn't afford. At Chulachomklao, she'd discovered something that surprised her, she liked being a soldier.

"Sir, the administrative side of this organization is a mess. It looks like every piece of paperwork has been dumped in what is now my office and left there. I'm having it sorted through now, I expect to find the surrender document from the French Army any time now, the 1868 one of course, we already have the later one. I've obtained some filing cabinets and we'll be pulling double shifts until everything is sorted out."

Songkitti smiled to himself at the 'we' then leaned forward. "So what do you think our problems are going to be?"

"I think we have two Sir, one internal, the other external. The internal one stems from what's going on here. This area was a wreck when we pushed the French out and moved in ourselves. The farms were half derelict and none were self-supporting. The farmers, the ones left anyway, were virtually starving. They grew nothing but rice and had to buy everything else from the government store. All at government-fixed prices. Just a form of slavery really. We're trying to rebuild those farms and get people to come out here and kick-start the agricultural sector.

"We're also trying to get the local farmers to stand on their own feet, that's a tough one because they've had the spirit hammered out of them. They don't even complain and when farmers don't complain, that's a real problem. The criminal thing is the soil here is rich, this area should be a rice bowl. Now, with hard work, we can get it back to the 14th century. The government is sending a mass of aid through various agencies, fertilizer and farm equipment, seed, livestock, investment money. That's a lot of wealth going through a poor area. My guess is that much of the stuff coming in is going astray. Lot of petty banditry and the odd truck hijacking around here?"

Songkitti nodded. "Exactly so. We have some troops here we are using as guards for truck convoys. You'll need to work out some schedules and a better system of truck convoying."

"Troops sir, that brings us to the external problem. The Japanese. They never liked it when we took everything west of the Mekong and they don't like it now. They tried to call an early end to the war while we were still within sight of our own border and when the King's Ambassador refused, they didn't like that. They tried to force us to stop and they didn't like it when she beat them. Now, their China campaign is winding down, they must be thinking of how much they don't like us. Sir, when I was given the tour around here yesterday, the border troops looked awfully thin."

Songkitti sighed. This Lieutenant had spotted it right away. Man or woman, Chulachomklao turned them out well. "Lieutenant, I have two infantry divisions, the 9th and the 11th, scattered all over the recovered provinces. From the South China Sea to the Lao highlands. I can spread them along the border and what will that achieve?"

"Nothing Sir. They'll be spread too thin. Defeated in detail."

"Very good. So, they have to be held back as a counter-attack force. But that leaves the border almost bare. Smugglers' paradise of course. The border defenses have to buy time until we can concentrate 9th and 11th, then organize a counter-attack. All that's along there to do that are the villagers, we've distributed arms of course. The old-fashioned Type 45 rifles and other stuff we had before we re-equipped with German arms. And the stuff we took from the French. Mostly Berthier rifles and Chauchat machine-guns. No heavy stuff, the villagers couldn't use it even if we gave it to them. And there are Border Patrol Police mobile units."

"Mobile units Sir?"

"On bicycles." Songkitti looked embarrassed. An old military principle. If a unit had nothing to fight with, give them a flamboyant name. "I doubt if they can hold more than a few hours at most.

"So another thing I want you to do. The roads here run back to the Tonle Sap and Battambang. If the Japanese break through and get onto those they can overrun our whole position. Leaves the roads to Bangkok wide open and all that's there to stop them are the two Cavalry divisions in the strategic reserve. I want you to make up a plan to block the roads around here. We have landmines, some ours, some we captured from the French. How many, we don't know, its never been inventoried. Find out. And try to work out how we can commandeer trucks to turn into roadblocks. That's enough to be going on with. Dismissed."

Sirisoon went back to her office and rejoined the effort to restore some semblance of order to the Army's administration. Hours later, she returned to her quarters for some sleep. On her mind was the thin line of Border Patrol Police and armed villagers along the border with Japanese Indochina. Before sleeping, she took her Mauser out of its rack on the wall and carefully cleaned it.

HMS Xena, At Sea, Off Jutland

Despite the fact that *Xena* had never been out of the North Sea since she'd left Rosyth, she had all the appearance of a submarine that had been on patrol too long. Beards were growing unkempt and the food had descended from the monotonous to the indescribably boring. She had spent the last few days probing around the entrance to the Skagerrak and trying to establish the pattern of contamination coming out of the Baltic. They had the answer to that now and it wasn't good.

"No way, Swampy, no way at all I'm taking this boat in there. Baltic's out, through the narrows anyway and with the Kiel Canal gone, there's no other way."

"Robert, the contamination readings are lower than they were around Rotterdam."

"Agree. They are here. But look at the gradients. The way they rise as we head towards the narrows, we could get into trouble between readings. There's something flushing the muck out of the water and its all coming out here."

"The winter." Swamphen's voice was thoughtful. "It was a really bad winter, all over Europe and Scandinavia. Worst on record. Snowfall was two or three times the average. The climatologists haven't agreed why yet. Some say it was the bombing, some say just a normal fluctuation. Some say the next ice age is overdue and this is just the first sign of it. That's true by the way, the next ice age is overdue and the global temperature trends all show the planet is cooling. Global cooling is a problem and the bombing may have pushed us over the edge.

"Doesn't change what happened last winter though. A lot of snow, far more than the average, and its all melting. Most of that water goes into the Baltic and its flushing the contamination towards the North Sea. I bet if we go really deep around here, there's a freshwater stream down below that's almost glowing in the dark."

"Just like the underwater Rhine, Swampy?" Swamphen grimaced, the absence of that phenomenon had been a blow for him. He'd been so sure it was down there. "Anyway, its that glowing in the dark bit that's worrying me. I'm starting to be concerned about the effect radiation is having on the pressure hull. Embrittlement and all that."

Swamphen was surprised by the reference. Most scientists had a picture of Royal Navy officers as being very well educated in their professional sphere but with limited knowledge outside that. It wasn't so, he'd found that out often enough. As a group, they knew a lot about a lot and if they didn't know something, they knew how to find out about it. Swamphen guessed that Fox had been reading up on the effects of radiation on metals. How he'd discovered where to get the information onboard a submarine was a good question.

"It shouldn't be a problem, not at these levels. Look, we've got all these readings from the south of the Skagerrak, how about heading south and west then swinging around and taking readings from the north and west? That'll give us an idea of the shape of the contaminated area out here, then we can head for home. We've enough bad news to keep everybody in the vapors for weeks as it is."

Fox quickly ran through the fuel and food status in his mind. "Very well, we'll do that. We've got another ten days out so we can do this properly and still get home. But, no matter what those readings are, I'm not taking *Xena* into the Baltic. If anybody goes there, it'll be a surface ship. It's too hot for a submarine, literally and metaphorically."

Headquarters, Second Karelian Front, Riga, "The Baltic Gallery"

There were strangers present at today's meeting. That was unusual, unique in fact. Usually it was just him and Rokossovsky. And the Russian aides of course, like the one who had escorted him in, the one wearing her beret on the back of her head. Rommel understood the code now. A woman soldier wearing her beret on the back of her head was a "campaign wife' of a senior officer. If she wore her beret squarely on top of her head, she was unattached - and available.

"Erwin, I would like to introduce you to the representatives of Norway, Sweden and Denmark. Their governments have asked that they be allowed to attend today's meeting since our discussions will affect a large number of their nationals."

"The Nordland SS Division?"

"Exactly. Three mechanized regiments, one comprised mostly of Danish volunteers, one of Norwegians and one of Swedes. Not a unit with a bad reputation as SS units go. Which means of course that it stinks in the nostrils of civilized people."

Rommel sighed to himself. There would have been a time when he would have risen in the defense of the German armed forces but those days had long gone. He'd learned too much, seen too much of what he had closed his eyes to before.

For all that, he'd done quite well. Most of the Ninth Army was out and those that the Russians had detained had been sent to "Mild Regime" camps. That meant working in the destroyed Russian cities, clearing rubble and rebuilding the ruins so people could live there. Some of the prisoners had written back, saying that the Russians had told them they could leave once the city they were working on was repaired. It was fair enough in a way, he supposed.

Skorzeny had even managed to get some of his SS troops into the Mild Regime camps. There'd been no possibility of getting them released of course but he'd taken the units the Russians were likely to have had least objection and used them to force the handover of the ones they hated the most. The first such unit to pay the price for the release of others had been Dirlwanger's 36th Independent Motorized Brigade. When Rokossovsky had looked in the back of the trucks carrying their bodies his reply had a grim gallows humor to it. "Ah, some good Germans," he'd said. But he had upgraded the status of the troops who'd put down Dirlwanger's rebellion from "Severe" to "Mild" Regime.

"Erwin, first of all, before all that. I have had a reply from the Red Cross. It appears Mannheim was south of the worst area of attack but it was not spared. The Americans dropped a single atomic bomb on the city. One of their more powerful ones. I have a list of the known survivors for you. There are none with your family name but perhaps you may recognize some of them. I regret to tell you, it is not a long list, only a few hundred out of many tens of thousands."

Rommel took the list, reluctantly almost as if seeing what he had feared as words on a page would make its reality final.

"President Goering has attached a message for you. He wishes it to be known that he commends your conduct here and views with favor our efforts to find a just solution to the surrender of Army Group Vistula. He asks, however, that no persons be returned to Germany in the short term since there are no facilities to care for them and the available resources are strained to fed the population there already. He asks you and your men to be patient and to wait until there is a country you can return to."

"Quite." The two Army commanders laughed quietly with eachother. They both knew what Der Dicke really had in mind. His authority and that of the new German Government was still very weak. Weak enough for large bodies of organized men to find the possibility of a power-grab too tempting. Better to get the state established first, then bring the men back. "Thank you Konstantin, it was kind of you to make this happen. Now, the Nordland Division."

"The Nordland SS Division."

Rommel swore quietly under his breath, he'd hoped he'd get away with that. If he could establish a mindset where the Nordland were regarded as an extension of the Heer rather than the SS he might have reached better terms for them.

"It is our position that these men are still citizens of our countries and should be returned to us. It is for us to try any who are accused of war crimes." It was the Swedish representative who spoke. Rommel had noted that Sweden had been particularly generous when accepting demobilized soldiers as refugees. He'd guessed there would be a price for that generosity and it looked like the bill was about to be presented. He winced at the thought.

The Russians had won the war on the Eastern Front and they were prickly about their rights and status as the winners. Rommel had played on that, appealing to their pride to get as many of his men out as he could. If the Swedes tried to throw their weight around, they'd be cutting their own throats. Idly, Rommel wondered how long it would take the Russians to occupy Sweden. Judging by the amount of equipment within a few miles of this headquarters, not long. Even less if the Americans helped their Russian ally along by using their hellburners to blast a path through the Swedish defenses. The Swedes were playing a dangerous game and Rommel didn't think they understood just how dangerous.

"I would like to point out that, although the men for this unit are now represented by independent Governments, they were recruited while the areas in question were under German military occupation. In fact, the majority of these men were recruited in the period 1945 to 1947 when the SS was conscripting its troops rather than seeking volunteers."

"That is true of Norway and Denmark. But not of Sweden." Rokossovsky leaned back in his seat, eyeing the Swede in much the same way a hungry wolf might eye a particularly succulent sheep.

Rommel took over smoothly, before the Swede could have a chance to reply and turn cutting his own throat into radical decapitation. "A very sound point, Konstantin. The Nordland SS Division represents two quite different cases. The Danish and Norwegian regiments are mostly composed of conscripts, taken from their homes, almost at gunpoint and certainly regardless of their opinions on the matter. The Swedish Regiment is entirely composed of volunteers, not just volunteers but volunteers who went to great lengths and personal expense to reach our territory so they could enlist."

"I take your point Erwin. You are right here. We have two very different cases and we must temper our judgment according to those circumstances."

Opposite them, the Norwegian was nodding thoughtfully. He'd guessed where this was going and could see advantages for his people. The Dane was about to speak but suddenly changed his mind, Rokossovsky guessed that, under the table, a Norwegian boot had sharply kicked a Danish ankle.

"However, the case revolves around their induction to service rather than their national origin. I do not see the relevance of that for the crimes of which this unit is accused, a weighty and shameful list, were all committed on Russian territory. I am prepared to accept that they were conscripted at gunpoint and by threats to their families as some small mitigation. But for those who volunteered? I think there can be no mitigation and certainly we will not allow any others to claim jurisdiction." The Norwegian and Danish delegates were speaking quietly. Rokossovsky gave them his best Russian General's glare. "There is one meeting here and one meeting only. If you have something to say, say it for all to hear."

"My apologies Marshal." The Danish delegate was obviously now the spokesmen of the pair. "I have a suggestion that may quickly resolve our problem at least. The Norwegian and Danish Governments will concede your claims to jurisdiction over our nationals in the German armed forces. We also concede that the conduct of the unit in which they formed a part was such that criminal punishment is in

141

order. We suggest, however, that instead of trying to separate out the bad from the not-so-bad, you treat the unit as a whole and sentence the two regiments as a whole to Mild Regime work rebuilding your cities.

"In return for our concession on these points we request that representatives of our government be allowed to remain in contact with these prisoners, that the prisoners be allowed to contact their families back home on a regular basis, say, two letters a month? And that their work be considered a substitute for any demand for reparations Russia may ask of us. Our men will work much better if they feel their efforts are of direct benefit to their country."

Rokossovsky nodded slowly. It was a good compromise, one that gave Russia what it needed the most. Absolute jurisdiction over the prisoners, unaffected by the demands of any other nation. Given the witches brew of nationalities in the SS units, that was the one thing President Zhukov demanded above all others. Crimes against Russia and the Russians must be punished by the Russians. Otherwise there was no guarantee they would be punished at all. "Very well I accept these arrangements. Erwin, you will draft the orders for the two regiments in question to surrender to the designated Russian forces?"

"Very well. Noon tomorrow be acceptable?" Rokossovsky nodded.

"This arrangement is unacceptable to us. We must demand that all Swedish nationals be repatriated to us without delay. If you accuse any of crimes then it is for you to present your evidence to our prosecutors who will pursue the matter. If they feel the evidence warrants it."

Rommel and Rokossovsky locked eyes over the table. It was going to be a long, hard day.

Part Three - Necessity

Chapter One
Demands

Operations Center, Laum Mwuak Airfield, Thai/Japanese Indochina Border

"Have you seen these latest exchanges? And the last Japanese reply?" Flight Lieutenant Usah Chainam ruffled through the papers in his hands and pulled out the last flimsy. "And if we do not receive a positive response to our proposals, things will proceed from that point."

"I think that's a threat." Wing Commander Luang Chumsai's voice was thoughtful. "And the Japanese have a long history of starting things without advance warning. If the book from that American historian is right, they were even planning to do the same to the Americans back in '41."

"Might have saved the world a lot of trouble if they had." Usah's voice was equally thoughtful. Both men were running the situation around Laum Mwuak around in their heads and calculating forces and dispositions. "Then the Americans would have turned Japan into a smoking hole as well. Some sort of large-scale incursion across the border? Won't be a full-scale, the Americans won't stand for it. They've made it quite clear what'll happen to anybody who starts launching wars of conquest."

Luang's face was expressionless, his fingers drumming his desk. The peace agreement with the French in May 1941 had stipulated that the border between Thailand and French Indochina ran along the Mekong river from the Chinese highlands in the north to the sea. Then French Indochina had become Japanese Indochina and problems had started to emerge. One of them was the Mekong Delta.

The original interpretation of the agreement was that the border ran through the largest of the arms of that delta, splitting the area neatly in half and putting Saigon on the border. Now, the Japanese were claiming it ran along the southernmost arm of the delta. They had another claim, an even more outrageous one. Under international law, when a river was stipulated as marking a border, the actual frontier ran along the median line down the center of the river. The Japanese were claiming that the border wasn't just the Thai bank, it was the westernmost extreme of the watershed that fed the river. A claim that , if allowed, would put most of the Recovered Provinces and a big chunk of Northern Thailand into Japanese hands. It was, in fact, the same land-grab the French had carried out in the forty years from 1868 onwards.

"Order an alert. For the next seven days, pilots and ground crews are to sleep near their aircraft. Park the aircraft on the runways, ready for immediate takeoff. Pilot Officer Somsri's airfield defense company is to man a full perimeter. We're too close to the border here to take chances, if the Japanese do try something, this airfield is the prime target."

The airfield, Luang thought sadly, not the aircraft on it. Khong Bin Noi Thi Haa was supposed to have three squadrons, two of fighters, one of dive bombers. One of the fighter squadrons was at Don Muang, converting from its old Curtiss Hawk IIs to the new F-80 fighters the Government had just bought. The fighter squadron here had twelve single-seat Curtiss Hawk IIIs and the dive bomber squadron a dozen two-seater Vought Corsairs. Both of the old biplanes had done well against the French back in 1941 but types were horribly obsolete now. Military re-equipment programs had been on life support for years now while the Government poured money into building the country's infrastructure. Decisions like that were a gamble and this one looked like coming up on the short end.

"I want a detachment, ten men with a machine-gun, over by Ta Luak. Their job is to hold the back door open. Get everybody who isn't on the perimeter or with the aircraft, that includes the families, digging fortifications around the golf course. That'll be our last redoubt, if we can't hold the perimeter, we'll fall back, burning the base as we go and make our last stand there. If we can't hold the golf course, any survivors can try and get out through the jungle. Oh, and send a message to the police, warn them as well."

"You think its that bad?"

"I think its worse. But that's the best we can do."

Police Station, Laum Mwuak Village, Thai/Japanese Indochina Border

Why anybody had suddenly decided to post a guard was beyond Police Private Songwon. The other nineteen police officers assigned to this area were all safely asleep which was where all civilized people should be at 0400. He paced around and blew into his hands, everybody who didn't live here assumed that it was hot all the time but that was a sad mistake. The pre-dawn chill could be enough to make the bones ache. Then he stopped, he had heard the sound of gunfire from around the town hall and the telegraph office. Was it anything to worry about? Probably not, it was nearing the Loi Krathong festivities, it was amazing how people could interpret floating a bunch of flowers down a river as firing guns into the air but they did. Then, Songwon knew he was wrong for there were shadowy shapes moving through the darkness towards the police station.

As he watched, one of them became less shadowy, resolving itself into a Japanese soldier walking up to the front door of the police station, waving a piece of paper at Songwon. The policeman was confused, bewildered, could not understand what or why Japanese soldiers were trying to give him orders. In any case, he didn't read or understand Japanese so it didn't really matter. He had orders to let nobody into the police station, so his duty was obvious. He refused to let the soldier in.

That's when the aggravated soldier made a fatal mistake. In Thailand striking somebody in the face is a deadly insult and the Thai police were notoriously sensitive about their dignity at the best of times. When the soldier hit Songwon, the police private was infuriated and appalled that anybody would take such liberties. Instinctively he did two things, he took a step back and he dropped his Lee-Enfield rifle to an approximation of the "guard" position. Sensing he'd gained an advantage, the Japanese soldier took a step forward and literally walked onto the point of the leveled bayonet.

Songwon was shocked by how easily the long triangular bayonet slid through the Japanese body. Less than a kilogram of pressure, he thought remembering a long-ago lesson on using his bayonet. That's all it took to run a man through with a pig-sticker. The Japanese made a little sigh and crumpled as if he was an inflated balloon and somebody had let all the air out. As he slumped around the bayonet, Songwon remembered something else from the long-forgotten lessons. He pulled the trigger, the recoil from the shot yanking the bayonet out of the body. The Japanese immediately responded by opening fire on the police station. Songwon took a horrified look at what had started and dived for cover.

To a man, the sleeping policemen inside the station thought that a thunderstorm had started when the hail of gunfire hit their building. The sergeant in charge took a careful look through a window and saw no lightning in the sky but a fair equivalent of it along the treeline a hundred meters or so away. He also saw a single figure break cover and sprint for the barracks door. It opened briefly and Songwon dived through. "Japanese" he gasped, "the Japanese are attacking the town."

The Police Sergeant grasped that situation immediately. "Take seven men, get out through the cellar and run for the airbase. Warn them, tell them the Japanese are coming. We'll hold here." Not for long he thought grimly. They had six rifles, two Lee-Enfields, from a batch the Army had purchased for next-to-nothing from the British Army after WW1, the rest were the old Type 45s. A quick glance added a shotgun and that left the rest of the police with their revolvers. Not much to fight an army with. Still, the six riflemen were at the windows trying to return fire. No point in firing revolvers yet, anyway the volume of incoming fire made the defense seem puny. Over his shoulder, the Sergeant saw Songwon and six others scrambling down through the hatch in the floor. The cellar was long and thin, it surfaced some way away from the station. They should make it, the Sergeant thought, just as long as the ones left behind could buy some time.

To the slight surprise of the Sergeant, he and the twelve men left in the police station bought twenty minutes. That's how long it took for the firefight to reach the point where the Japanese had worked close enough to throw hand grenades into the building. As Songwon and his group eased out through the jungle, they heard the explosions that silencing the defenders' firing. They didn't see the invaders enter the building, but they did hear the screams as the Japanese took their time finishing off the wounded policemen with their knives and bayonets.

Cookhouse, Laum Mwuak Airfield, Thai/Japanese Indochina Border

If there was a plum assignment when pulling a night alert, this had to be it. Guarding the cookhouse while a friendly cook prepared breakfast for the base. Chief Cook was a friendly, motherly woman who saw it as her duty to ensure "the boys" guarding her cookhouse were properly fed. Breakfast in an hour or so time would be noodle soup with meatballs and "her boys" had already had a bowl each, filled with tasty vegetables and meatballs fresh from the oven.

There was history behind Chief Cook's concern for the Air Force guards. She'd been born Thai and free but when she'd been a young girl, the French had stolen the province she came from and they'd treated the occupants like they'd treated the rest of their Indochinese subjects - as serfs. Then, in 1941, the Royal Thai Army had come and liberated them. Chief Cook remembered her first sight of the young men in jungle green uniforms with their strangely-shaped helmets who'd made her Thai again. Assistant Cook was young, Cambodian and couldn't remember a time before the French. Not the brightest of girls, all she knew was that life had become much better since the French had gone.

Airman Ronna Phakasad didn't know the history, all he did know was that the cook had looked after them almost unnervingly well. There was an advantage to being part of the guard unit on an air base, machine guns were hardly in short supply. There were so many that there was a joke in the guard company that the only soldiers who didn't have thirty-caliber Browning machine guns were the ones who had the fifty-calibers. They were aircraft guns, true, and their mountings were improvised but they were still there and they could pour out lead. They'd need to.

Ronna's little command had eight men, two two-man machinegun crews with a .30 Browning each and four men with the MP40 machine pistols Lopburi made under license. He reckoned that if everything dropped in the pot, he'd need them. This building was designated as a strongpoint that covered the entry to the base and a line of trees that offered quick access to the flight line beside the east-west 1,000 meter runway. That meant he was guarding the Corsair divebombers that needed the longer runway to get off. Over the other side of the base, the Hawk IIIs were parked beside the 800 meter north-south runway. They were somebody else's responsibility.

The eastern sky was just beginning to redden with the dawn when Ronna saw a pair of headlights coming up the road towards the main gates. Erratic, unsteadily driven, as if the driver was drunk - or something worse. Ronna patted the gunner for the Browning covering the gate and pointed at the approaching vehicle. The gunner said nothing but heaved the cocking handle of the machine gun back. The vehicle continued to approach until it was under the lights by the entrance barrier. Ronna took his binoculars and looked hard. "Don't shoot, they're our policemen!"

"How do you know boss?"

"Some of them are still wearing their pajamas."

That, the machinegunner thought, was unsettling on so many levels

Main Gate, Laum Mwuak Airfield, Thai/Japanese Indochina Border

"Sir, you got to help us! The rest of the men are in the police station, the Japanese are slaughtering everybody". Private Songwon was distraught, barely intelligible, thought Sergeant Nikorn Phwuangphairoch, who commanded the 20-men detachment in charge of holding the gates, the guardhouse and the rest of the approach to the accommodation areas. He'd placed his men inside the guardhouse itself and in foxholes along the side of the road.

Nikorn had already called in the arrival of the policemen and asked to mount a rescue mission to the police station. The request had been curtly refused, it was obviously far too late to save anybody down there. The base doctor had arrived almost immediately and tried to treat the men by the truck. They'd pushed him away, telling him they were unhurt. Then they'd told him their commander, Police Lieutenant Sangob Pornmanonth, was in the back of the truck.

"He was living at his house sir, with his family. It was on the way here we'd stolen this truck you see, so we stopped to pick him and his family up. But the Japanese had got there first. Our Lieutenant was in the garden by the door and his family were, it was dreadful, horrible, they were all dead even the children. The Lieutenant's alive just, please help him Sir. The telegraph station's gone, the town hall as well. We heard firing from the railway station. All over. The Japanese are on foot, they're a few minutes behind us."

Nikorn tried to descramble the valuable information from the man. The town was gone, captured, no doubt about that. And the Japanese were coming up the road, fast. Nobody should ever underestimate just how fast the Japanese infantry could move on foot. A few minutes was the best they could hope for. As he turned to send a message to the operations center the doctor jumped down from the truck, his face frozen, his eyes sick. "Regret to tell you Sergeant, Police Lieutenant Sangob has died from the wounds inflicted on him by the Japanese at his home. Nothing anybody could do, wounds like that."

Nikron nodded. "Suggest you get back to the Operations Center. " He dropped his voice "and tell the Wing Commander what you saw here. We must get the families out. Rest of you, get ready, they're coming. You, the policeman who drove that truck. Get it out of the way. Burn it if that's the only way to stop the Japs using it."

Operations Center, Laum Mwuak Airfield, Thai/Japanese Indochina Border

"You were right Sir, we're coming under attack. The Japanese are in Laum Mwuak already. They've taken the police station, we know that, and we think they've taken the town hall and the railway. The telegraph also."

"Get a message out to Phnom Penh and Bangkok."

"Telegraph's down Sir, that's why we think the Japanese got there. Radio, its atmospherics, we can't get through."

"Right. If the Japanese are coming through the town, they'll hit us from that side. That means the Hawks are the nearest aircraft to

151

their attack. Get them up and out now. Get them to the Kong Bin Noi Thi Saam base at Phnom Penh. They've got Ostrichs there. We're going to need some help."

He stopped as the sound firing erupted from the perimeter by the residential area. The rapid hammering noise of the Brownings, the duller crack of the Mausers and a lighter crackle. Japanese Arisakas.

"We're going to need a lot of help."

Flight Line, Laum Mwuak Airfield, Thai/Japanese Indochina Border

The violence of the attack was unexpected. What seemed like a whole battalion of Japanese troops had swarmed out of the treeline and charged across the cleared area. They'd come under a crossfire from the machine guns in the Guardhouse and the Cookhouse but that hadn't stopped them.. They'd left bodies behind on the grass, that was certain, but not enough. They'd blown the wire and only a barrage of point-blank fire form the machine pistols of the troops in the residential area had finally stopped them.

Then, the Japanese had opened up on the flight line with the small mortars they carried. Two of the Hawk IIIs were already burning, their fabric skins had already gone and their structure was outlined in the pre-dawn darkness as a glowing blueprint of fire.

Down the line, Pilot Officer Maen Prasongdi was first to get his aircraft moving, swerving out of the parking lot and down the runway. His move caught the Japanese by surprise, they hadn't expected the pilots to be waiting in their aircraft and their fire went wild. Maen got off the runway, clawed for altitude then swung his aircraft around for a strafing pass. His twin .30s started hammering as his nose lined up with the Japanese troops pinned by the crossfire outside the residential area. They were firing back and he felt the thuds as bullets tore into the fabric of his aircraft. Then, his Hawk lurched as the four 60 kilogram bombs dropped free and he was clear, trailing smoke but out and heading for Phnom Penh and the Ostrichs

Flight Sergeant Phrom Shuwong never got that far. Following Maen down the runway, he caught all the fire aimed at his aircraft plus most of the bullets aimed at his leader. His Hawk III was badly damaged before it even left the runway and as he climbed out, those on the ground saw his body jerking in the cockpit. Airborne for less than a few seconds, his Hawk III stalled out and spun into the ground.

Behind him, Sergeant Jamnien Wariyakun never even got off the ground. Raked by bullets, his tires blew as he made his run. The Hawk III swerved off the runway, then its wingtip caught the grass and it ground-looped, disintegrating as it spun across the grass and exploded. To the amazement of everybody, Jamnien actually managed to jump clear as the aircraft flew apart and tried to run for cover. He made about ten steps before Japanese fire cut him down.

Perhaps the spectacle distracted the Japanese because Flight Sergeant Sanit Rohityothin actually made it into the air. Like his leader, he swung around, trying to strafe the approaching Japanese. He was too low, and too slow. The groundfire got him as he started his run and his Hawk was burning before it started its dive into the ground.

Flight Sergeant Kab Khamsiri was still trying to start his engine when he and the plane next to his were rushed by Japanese troops. They'd used a drainage ditch for cover and had got through the first defense line to get loose into the fighter park. Their bullets raked both aircraft, killing Kab in his cockpit and severely wounding Flight Sergeant Phorn Chalermsuk.

The Japanese might have been better advised to take a closer look at the aircraft on the flight line, or perhaps brush up on their aircraft recognition because they missed an important fact. The aircraft they passed on their way to attack the two Hawks wasn't a fighter at all. The old biplane was a Corsair ground attack aircraft, manned by Flying Officer Suan Sukhserm, with Airman Somphong Naelbanthad as his rear gunner. The Japanese rushing past were a target Somphong couldn't resist. His twin .30 machineguns raked the group, mowing them down as the Corsair turned out of the flightline onto the runway. Somphong kept firing, his machine guns stitching the area where the Japanese were firing on the escaping aircraft. He pinned them down just long enough for the Corsair to get off the ground. Over the racket of the engine and the hammering of his machine guns he could have sworn he could hear the cheers from the airmen fighting in the residential area and around the guardhouse. Behind them, the fighter parking area was a sea of black smoke and burning aircraft.

The black smoke was clearly visible over the roofs of the residential area buildings, lit by the sun edging over the eastern horizon. That residential area was quickly turning into a death-trap for the advancing Japanese. The Thai airmen with their machine pistols were in their element, fighting room to room. They knew the ground, it was, quite literally their homes, and they were making the Japanese pay for every meter. Automatic fire was the key, even the new semi-automatic Arisakas couldn't match the fire from those machine pistols at close range.

Major Kisoyoshi Utsunomiya had already worked out what to do about it. The residential area was a hornet's nest but it was untenable if he could get his people around its flanks. The thing that stood in his way were the two strong points off to his left, what was obviously a guard house and another building beyond that. Both hadn't been fully engaged yet and the streams of machine gun fire from them were pinning down his flank. Take those two strongpoints out and he'd have a clear path through the hangars, cutting the whole residential area off. Time to take down the strongpoints.

"Follow me!" He leapt up swinging his sword, his flag-carrier unfurling the great Rising Sun beside him. As his men got up to advance on the Guardhouse, he heard the sound of an aircraft engine. That's when he realized his mistake. The first pilots to try and take off had been fighter pilots, full of courage and urge to fight but untrained in the ways of ground attack. They'd turned too early and been shot down. The Corsair crew were ground attack specialists, they were wily, they'd got clear, built up speed and come in when they judged the moment right.

Now the Corsair was sweeping over his men, its forward .50 caliber machineguns spewing tracer into their ranks, the tail gunner spraying the infantry as they passed. Beneath them, a line of explosions marked the 60 kilogram bombs dropping clear. Utsunomiya cursed, the attack was perfectly timed, it had broken the momentum of his move and revealed his plan. The guardhouse would be expecting to become the center of attention.

Then, as the Corsair swept overhead, Utsunomiya saw something he thought was long past. For perhaps the last time in modern warfare, a old biplane with an open cockpit was flying over a battlefield with its pilot's white silk scarf streaming in the wind behind him. As the Corsair vanished behind the treeline on its way to Phnom Penh, Utsunomiya carefully and very precisely saluted its crew.

Phnom Penh South Airfield, Recovered Provinces, Thailand

The flight line was boiling with activity. Each of the twelve Ostriches lined up by the main runway had a group of men feeding their charge with the supplies it needed to fight. One group was feeding belts of .50 Browning ammunition into the tanks supplying the wing guns, another was beside the fuselage, lifting up belts of the big 23mm V-YA cannon rounds into the armored bathtub that protected the aircraft's crew. Other groups were hanging rockets on the rails under the wings or fitting bombs to the fuselage and inner-wing hardpoints. Yet more men were by the fuel bowsers, feeding aviation gasoline into the aircraft's self-sealing tanks.

For all the activity, the sound of an aircraft engine brought a standstill. The base was so used to the hearty roar of twin Pratt and Whitney R-2800s that the little Wright R-1820 sounded puny. Then, the aircraft itself came over the treeline, instantly recognized as a Hawk III. That meant it had to be from Laum Mwuak, the wing there was the only one still operating the old Curtiss biplane. The trail of black smoke and the unsteadiness of its flight were eloquent of an aircraft and pilot in serious trouble. Underneath the staggering fighter, the sound of its engine was drowned out by the sirens of a rescue truck and an ambulance racing out to be on hand when it landed.

The pilot nearly brought his aircraft in unharmed. Almost, but not quite. He put it down too hard and wiped the undercarriage off on touchdown. The Hawk slid on its belly down the runway, the ambulance and crash truck driving recklessly to keep up with it. As it came to a halt and started to burn, the crash truck had its foam hose ready and doused the wreck. It took only a few seconds to get the pilot out of the cockpit and even less time for the ambulance paramedic to make his decision. "Get him to the infirmary. Now."

"No, wait." Maen's voice was weak but urgent. "Laum Mwuak, the Japanese are attacking it, Ground troops. They're holding up there but they need help. Get help to them."

The word spread faster than possible and the aircrew waiting by their planes stared at the control tower, waiting for the signal. It came just as fast as it took a man to run up the control tower steps and speak to the Squadron commander. A red flare arcing into the sky. "Get ready for immediate take off." Then, there was a sound like a barrage of gunfire as the ground crews started closing the hatches and access points on the waiting Ostrichs.

"First flight, get to Laum Mwuak. Identify the positions held by our people and give them support. Can't tell you exactly what to do, you'll know when you get there. Second Flight. The Japanese have crossed the border in strength. There's a regiment of the 9th Division moving up to block the enemy's advance. Contact the 9ths forward controllers, set up a cab rank using Channel Five and support them. Whatever they need. The other Ostrich squadron will be joining you. As for fighter cover." There was a derisive laugh from the Ostrich crews, their Australian-built ground attack aircraft were almost 70 miles an hour faster than the Hawk 75N fighters that were supposed to cover them. "Escort yourselves. The fighters will be on free chase. Now GO!"

The ground crews were already turning the propellers by hand, distributing the oil that would have built up in the lower cylinders overnight. Before they could fire the starters, another biplane came in, swinging neatly into line and touching down on the runway. A Corsair. It taxied off the runway and its crew leapt from the aircraft, frantically looking for somebody to report to. The Squadron leader grabbed the pilot.

"You, I need a full report of what's happening, everything you've seen. At once. We've got to get word to Bangkok and to First Army Headquarters. Do you know how to fly an Ostrich?"

Flying Officer Suan took a careful look at the hulking beasts starting to taxi out onto the runway and shook his head. They were from a different age and he'd never before realized just how obsolete his old Corsair was.

"Time to learn" said the Squadron Leader. The rest of his words were drowned out as more R-2800s joined the roaring flightline and the first Ostriches started their take-off runs down the runway.

First Army Circle Headquarters, Ban Masdit, Recovered Provinces, Thailand

Despite the early hour and the new air conditioning system, General Songkitti was sweating. The picture from the front was threatening, worse than that, it looked like there was a military catastrophe in the making. There were reports of at least two Japanese infantry divisions and three independent regiments crossing the Mekong. No sightings of tanks yet and the Japanese weren't committing their aircraft. Trying to keep this on the level of a border incident he guessed. They'd penetrate to the watershed boundary they'd claimed was the correct line of the border then the follow up forces would go through the breach and spread sideways. Ten years ago, there would have been wild talk of an expanding torrent through a hole in the front, loose in the rear areas, destroying everything in its path. Nobody believed that rubbish any more. Reality was bad enough. Then the phone rang and Songkitti picked it up, listening for a few minutes. He acknowledged the caller and hung up again.

"Good news Sir?" His aide's voice was tentative, perhaps afraid that if somebody mentioned good news, it would vanish.

"Supreme's on the ball. They're sending the Second Cavalry to reinforce us. Second Army will be turning one of its divisions through 180 degrees and taking over the Laotian frontier so we can pull the 11th Infantry down. That gives us two leg infantry divisions and a motorized division to fight with. The lead elements of the Second will be here tomorrow evening, we can have the 11th disengaged and down twelve to 24 hours later. The bad news is the intelligence people think there could be six more infantry divisions and four independent tank brigades waiting behind the Mekong. Apparently they went missing from Manchuria a few months ago and now, it looks like they've turned up here."

There was a gentle tap on the door and the clerk put his head around. "Lieutenant Sirisoon to see you sir."

Songkitti looked dourly at the female officer. "What do you want?"

"Sir, my desk is clear, all my present assignments are completed. In view of the current emergency, what are your orders?"

"Go back to your desk, hide under it if you like, that's probably a good idea, and keep out of the way."

Songkitti turned back to the map and stared again at the developing threat. The sparse information coming in suggested that the Japanese advance was shaped like a kidney, two lobes, parting at about 30 degrees. Fair bet one division in each lobe. They were splitting at a place called Laum Mwuak, there was an airfield there and the town was a minorly important road and rail junction. Nobody had heard from the airfield but the map was suggesting it was still holding out. Then..... Songkitti was suddenly aware Sirisoon was still waiting in front of his desk. "I told you to leave. Do you want me to have you dragged out by your hair?"

Sirisoon's eyes widened at the insult. Songkitti was an urbane and courteous man, for him to be so openly rude indicated how critical this situation was. "Sir, the Army recruited women officers so we could take over rear area jobs and free up men for the front. Let me do my job sir and make available another male officer for the front line."

Songkitti was just about to explode and say something unforgivable when his aide cut in. "Sir, we've got a pool of replacement infantry here, the ones we've been using to guard truck convoys. They're going to be badly needed but we can't send them up without an officer taking charge of them on the way. Perfect job I would have thought."

"Yes. Sirisoon, this is the situation. We're moving 2nd regiment, 9th infantry division up to here, to block this lobe of the Japanese advance. They're assembling now. That's a regiment taking on an entire Japanese division. Once they engage, the 29th is going to be chewed up, they'll need every replacement rifleman they can get. The Sergeants are organizing the unattached replacements into scratch platoons. There's one in the supply unit ready to go.

"Take command of it, take it up to the 29th assembly area here. Once the commander of the 29th releases you, return and take another platoon up." Songkitti scribbled orders onto his pad and handed them over. Sirisoon grabbed them and fled before he could change his mind.

In her office, Sirisoon grabbed her telephone and called the motor pool. "Sergeant, I need four trucks and a jeep outside the supply unit in ten minutes........ None available? Sergeant, my next task is to reconcile your equipment inventory against your requisitions. If I get my trucks, that job won't be started for weeks. If I don't, it'll start the moment I hang up and I will be in a very bad temper. I'm sure neither of us want me to be reconciling your inventories and supply vouchers while in a bad temper...... I thought not......... That's right, one jeep, four trucks, ten minutes. Thank you Sergeant." Sirisoon grinned to herself, that was an application of logistics her instructors had never thought of.

Ever since she'd seen the operations map, she'd kept a set of combat gear and her rifle in her office. She changed out of her regular uniform into the fatigues, reflecting quickly that anybody who came into her office now was going to get an unexpected eyeful. She took a quick look at herself in the window reflection as she left, webbing in place, fully armed, fully equipped. A very **militant** water lily she thought with smug satisfaction.

Supply Section Barracks, First Army Circle, Ban Masdit, Recovered Provinces, Thailand

Sergeant Yawd had worked wonders since everything had dropped in the pot. He'd got 43 men together, drawn a full platoon set of equipment for them, even down to the machine guns, the new rocket launchers and a radio. Even better, one of the men knew how to operate the radio and another had basic medical training. He had created a fully fledged infantry platoon out of nothing, all it needed was an officer. There was a bang as the door opened and "Men Attention! Officer on....... Ma'am?"

"Sergeant Yawd, by order of General Songkitti I am taking command of this unit and will be taking us to join the 29th Infantry Regiment. " She looked quickly around. "Men organized and properly armed. Good job Sergeant." Then she frowned for a second and pointed at one of the men. "Private Phom, you were the man who got that truck out of a ditch a few days back. That was well done. Glad to have you along. And you Private Voi, has your wife recovered?" The two men flushed slightly, one with pride at being praised in public, the other that this strange officer had taken the trouble to ask after his wife, recovering in base hospital after an appendix operation.

Sirisoon pulled the map out of her pocket. In the last ten minutes she'd pulled the list of names from records and noted two outstanding things she could "remember". Now, she had to keep things moving onwards so nobody would notice those were the only two things she knew about this group of men. "Sergeant, this is the assembly area here, I have to report to the Regimental Commander and he'll use us as he sees fit."

"Going to be a long march ma'am, take most of the day I think."

"Won't be a march at all Sergeant, I've organized some motor transport. One squad in each truck. Me, you, our radioman and medic in the jeep. What's our weapons section got?"

"Two MG34s on tripod's Ma'am and three RPG-2 teams. Rifle squads got an MG-34 each and a couple of Mausers fitted for rifle grenades. Rest have straight rifles. NCOs and weapons crews have these" He lifted his MP40 machine pistol. I got one for our officer but you brought your rifle."

"Give it to the medic, the Japanese don't respect the Red Cross. Sergeant, get the men mounted up, we've got to get moving."

Ban Phra Chuap, Recovered Provinces, Thailand.

The roads were jammed, truck convoys and marching infantry heading in one direction, refugees going in the other. The backwash of a nation at war, one that had been caught completely flat-footed. It had been hard enough getting her little convoy out of the base area, there were just too many vehicles, too little space. Once on the road, they'd made pretty good time given the circumstances. The villagers were out, guarding the road, helping the army trucks find their way from one village to the next. The police were out as well, helping keep traffic flowing and listening to the invitations to come and arrest the Japanese with weary patience. All in all, it was worse than it should have been but not as bad as it could be either.

By the time her jeep pulled into the 29th Regiment field HQ, Sirisoon was coated with a fine layer of laterite dust. She found the Command section and waited for a few minutes until the Regimental commander was ready to see her. "Lieutenant Sirisoon, Sir. Ordered to bring up reinforcements for you. Awaiting your orders sir." The Colonel took the message and read it with relief. He had too much front to cover, too few units to do it. Reinforcements to be used at his discretion. A fully organized infantry platoon. Better, much better than nothing.

"Sirisoon, I'm attaching your platoon to 1st Company, 2nd Battalion. 219th battalion is forming up along here," his hand moved on the map "and 1st Company is here. Report to the Company Commander for your orders. When you get there, send your trucks back here, I need them." Suddenly he peered at the Lieutenant in front of him. "You're a woman!"

"From birth Sir." The Colonel shuddered and looked like he wanted to say something, then changed his mind. He had an understrength regiment fighting a reinforced division and anything was better than nothing.

Sirisoon took a deep breath and climbed back into the jeep. "They're not breaking us up. We're being attached to one of the infantry companies. Not far, back on the road, about two klicks down, break right. Another two or three klicks. Then we have to send our trucks back."

The little convoy swung back out onto the main road and set off to the designated assembly area. As they approached the main turn, Yawd looked at his new officer a bit diffidently. "Ma'am, we're going to be the newbies in an established company. You know what that means don't you?"

"We'll get the dirty jobs and be the ones who draw fire? Yes, I know that. The only thing we can do about it is to make sure we all get to be veterans fast so we can send some other poor schleps out to draw fire."

Yawd laughed, relaxing slightly "Ma'am, I like the way you think."

Another headquarters area, another group of officers studying maps. Sirisoon got out of her jeep and reported in. Another set of raised eyebrows, another acceptance on grounds that anything was better than nothing. In the back of her mind was a grim determination, one day, *one day*, people would take her assignment as a welcome bonus, not an affliction that had to be tolerated. And if she got there over a pile of dead Japanese, so much the better.

"Sirisoon." The voice snapped her out of her reverie. "Get your people together, we need to find out where the Japanese are and in what strength. I want you to be our spearpoint. Advance down the road to Tong Klao, its about five klicks that way. We think the Japanese have that village already. You should meet them half way. You've got a radioman? Well done. Cabrank frequency is channel five, our net is channel seven. Call in when you make contact."

Sirisoon saluted and walked back to her men, already debussing from their trucks. Behind her the Company Sergeant Major spoke quietly to the commander. "Bit of a rotten thing to do sir."

"Somebody has to do the dirty jobs. We can send a bunch of repple newbies lead by a woman or one of our seasoned platoons. Which would you rather lose?"

The sergeant major sighed. Put like that, there really was no argument. Pity though, that young lieutenant seemed quite capable. For a woman of course.

Back at the trucks, Sirisoon called her NCO's together. "We have an advance to contact. That usually means advance until they shoot us. I don't want that, bullet holes are out of fashion this year. First section, I want you way out on the left flank, second section halfway out. Third section right flank, the other side of the road. Command group and weapons section to the right of the road but between it and third. Everybody keep off that road, if the enemy have pre-registered anything that will be it. We'll move cross country for about a kilometer, fast as we can then take it slow with overwatch. The Japanese love outflanking people so First Section, keep your eyes open. The odds are pretty good if we do run into a flanker, they'll do it from their right, our left."

"Why's that ma'am?"

"Because most people are right handed and the right is their strong hand so they instinctively think of doing things with their right.

I'm hoping we won't run into a Jap who's a leftie but even if we do, it might not matter. They're conformists all of them, kids who are naturally left-handed get beaten until they use their right. So I'm betting if we run into a flanker, it'll be on our left and First, you can flank the flankers. Important thing. Everybody. If we run into small groups, keep the machine guns quiet. Rifles only. There's our militia out there and they have rifles only. I want everybody to think we're militia until they learn the horrible truth. I want to get some good ground and chew the enemy up on it before they know who and what we are. Clear everybody?"

There was a murmur of agreement.

"Right. Let's get out there. And lets do things to them that we most certainly do not want done to us."

Administrative Building, Nevada Test and Experimental Area

"We've got the wrong aircraft. That's all there is to it." The voice was loaded with frustration and anger. Not to mention fear. The trials had been going on for two weeks now and, from the fighter pilot's view, they had been a complete failure. Nothing, but nothing, they had been able to do had even got them close to the B-36s. To make matters worse, some sadist organizing the exercises had designated each evolution after an American city. Today's had been "Mission Springfield" and, like all the rest, the question wasn't whether the fighters could defend the target but how badly they would fail and how close the B-36 Hometown would get to dropping its device on the aiming point. The answers had been disastrously badly and five hundred feet. If this had been the real world, Springfield would be history. The thick atmosphere of misery and futility could be cut with a knife.

"What do you mean Francis?" Gabreski's F-74s were the highest flying of all the American fighters in the exercise. They could get up to over 48,000 feet, agonizingly close to the B-36s cruising serenely over their heads, but not quite close enough. And, to make matters worse, it took almost 20 minutes to reach that altitude. The B-36s had seen them coming and changed course just enough to preclude any possibility of an intercept.

163

"Four thousand pounds of thrust just doesn't hack it. We need power, much more power." By the time the F-74s had got up to their service ceiling, their engines were pushing out less than 600 pounds of thrust. "And we need swept wings."

"There's a possible answer to that. North American is sending over a prototype, the XF-86A, for testing. Should be here in a day or so. Got the J-47 engine, same as the B-36s, and swept wings. North American is claiming 49,000 feet and getting there in 15 minutes. Artem, is there any chance of getting some MiG-15s over here?"

Across the room, the Russian designer shook his head. He spoke slowly and the interpreter paused a little before relaying his words. "The Chief Designer says that he is very sorry but it is quite impossible. We have a serious problem with the aircraft and it is proving difficult to solve. At 1,000 kilometers per hour, the aircraft drops a wing and stalls. Goes into a ... mmmmm .... a flat spin? And crashes. Already we have lost three aircraft to this. He says that if they could get a MiG-15 here they would but it just cannot be done. We will be visiting North American soon and perhaps they can help."

Mikoyan spoke again and again the interpreter paused before answering. "The Chief Designer also says that perhaps this would not help anyway. The problem is not swept wings, they give extra speed but they are less efficient at giving lift. So there is a penalty in altitude to pay. The key is wings and engine power. For high altitude the aircraft needs much power and wings with lift. After all, he says, that is why the B-36 can fly so high. Big wings and much power."

"Navy aircraft then." Joseph McConnell spoke from a corner of the room. His F-80Gs were actually 30 miles per hour faster than the F-74s at low altitude but their performance bled off quickly with altitude and they ran out of climb 3,000 feet below the newer fighter. "Navy birds have lower wing loadings than ours, they have to in order to land on a carrier. Perhaps we should call in the Navy?" There was a groan around the room, quickly stifled.

"It's worth trying, the latest model Banshee gets up to 48,500 and can do it in ten minutes. The Panthers are a bit worse in both departments. But, stripping them down might give us some capability."

"Why do we worry about this? It's not as if anybody can copy the B-36 yet." George Davis's voice was aggrieved and combative. His Stormbirds had shown up badly, so much so they'd been withdrawn to be rebuilt. The idea had been good, the Stormbird had a 75mm cannon in its nose and the operational concept had been to get it up as high as it could and then use it as a sky-fired anti-aircraft gun. The problem was they'd run out of altitude at 37,500 feet and that just wasn't high enough to make the idea work. The F-71s were having every possible ounce of weight stripped out of them to see if that would make the idea feasible.

"We wish that was true. Only, it isn't. The Japanese Navy are working on a long-range heavy bomber, the Frank. We don't know its performance details but it's B-36 size. We have to assume that its got the same altitude capability. You see, the Japanese Navy are building two German designs, the Heinkel He-274 and the He-277. The Germans gave up on them back in '44 when they ditched their heavy bomber effort in favor of fighters and ground support but the Japanese Navy has both in service, the 277 in quite large numbers.

"The 274, the CADS code name is Dick, can get up to 47,000 feet, the 277 to 49,000. That one's the Eric according to CADS. They haven't got the range to worry us yet; the Dick is strictly a medium-range bomber radius is around 600 miles tops. Eric's at the bottom of the heavy bomber range capability, operational radius about a thousand miles. So, neither aircraft is a threat to us yet but we have to recognize the possibility that the Japanese will apply the technology from the two German aircraft to their own long-range bomber. Then we have a very real threat to the American mainland.

"How long will that take? We don't know. But, how long did the Germans think they had before we flew over their defenses and blew them into the history books?"

"Guys, I've had a thought." Colonel Pico stopped and looked at McConnell. "Our fighters can't get up high enough to stop a B-36, but there's one aircraft that can."

"Go on Joe, you can't leave it there."

"I used to be a bombardier before I got into flight school. The only aircraft that can get up high enough to fight a B-36 is another B-

36. So why don't we intercept the inbound high altitude bombers with B-36s and drop atomic bombs on them?"

There was a profound silence. Eventually, Pico looked around the room. "Will *somebody, please* think of a reason why that isn't a good idea? Anybody, please?"

Approaches to HM Submarine Base, Faslane, UK

The rain was savage, lashing across *Xena's* sail in an almost horizontal sheet, driving into the men's eyes and streaming off the superstructure around them. It had long since penetrated the towel Commander Fox wore around his neck and was now soaking under his oilskin and into his shirt and vest. He had a megaphone held over his face, reversed so the wide end covered his eyes and he could look out of the narrow end through the torrent that would otherwise have blinded him.

"Approaching the cleared channel now. Swampy, is this rain hot?" It was a question that wouldn't have occurred to Fox a few weeks earlier.

Across the bridge, trying to shelter behind the periscope stays, Swamphen shook his head. "Last year might have been a little above background but the winter washed all that muck out of the air. This'll be clean." Swamphen spoke confidently, apparently in sure knowledge of the theoretical basis of his statement. In fact, he'd been worried enough by the rainstorm to take a few Geiger counter readings. To his relief, he'd found the rain was wet, not hot.

"Buoy coming up on to starboard right. Prepare for hard starboard helm. Don't cut that buoy too fine. " The buoy marked the grave of *Unlimited*, sunk a few months before. She'd strayed out of the cleared channel somehow and been mined. Nine months after the war had ended. About half her crew had got out, the bodies of the rest had been recovered by divers.

These were still dangerous waters, for three years the Americans and the Germans had played a little game around here, the same one they'd played off all the ports in Europe. Who could lay the largest number of mines off the ports with bonus points for the most complex fusing. Magnetic, acoustic, pressure, magnetic-acoustic, all fitted with counters. Antenna mines, even, now and then, a good old contact mine. There were thousands off this port alone, hundreds of thousands around the UK, millions around Europe.

The newer ones couldn't be swept at all, there was only one way to get rid of them. They had to be found, one at a time, a diver had to go down, place a demolition charge against the mine and then retreat to a safe distance. It took about an hour in all, not very long really. Some humorist had calculated that it would take a diver, working 24 hours a day, 365 days a year, a full 6,000 years to clear all the mines around Europe. And a lot of the mines were booby-trapped, cunningly enough for the divers to get danger pay and be refused life insurance.

"Mines Robert?"

"Damned things. I'm not that confident even in this safe channel. They drift, and some have thirty or forty-hit counters. Watch it helm., the water's always ebbing here, even when the tide is in flood."

"Could be worse Robert. The Americans have enough atomic bombs now that they're thinking of other ways to use them. Nuclear mines is one. Lay one in the seaway of a port, let the first ship to find it wipe the harbor out. The tidal wave and contamination from an underwater burst would be horrible."

"Damn, Swampy, haven't they done enough damage? Thank God, we're out the rain at last."

Xena had slipped under the stepped overhang that protected the caisson to the concrete submarine pen. The sail crew straightened up, now without the rain beating down on them. Fox ordered full astern, slipping his submarine neatly into place inside the basin. Cables snaked across the water and were made fast. "Finished with main engines and steering." The shore party were already warping *Xena* in to where the dockside crews were waiting to take her over. It was a sign of the times that the waiting dockies included a man with a Geiger counter to check the hull for radioactive contamination.

Submarine Bunker, Faslane, UK

"Julia darling! Been waiting long?" It had taken Fox a couple of hours to finish off the job of handing *Xena* over to the portside watch. Now, he had a few hours for his family. Julia took a careful sniff and decided the first of those hours would be spent getting him into a bath. Like all submariners after a longish deployment, Fox was ripe. A mixture of foul air, slightly off food, diesel fuel and a shortage of water all made for an eye-watering cocktail,

"Not long Robert, I saw her coming in and I've been a Navy wife long enough to know the drill." Unconsciously Julia had used the word "her" edge-uppermost. Secretly, she looked on her husband's command the way she would look upon a woman she suspected, but wasn't *quite* sure was his mistress. "How was it out there?"

Fox looked around. "Dreadful. The southern end of the North Sea and the Baltic Approaches, they're, oh I don't know what word to use. So foul nobody would want to go there. The North Sea will be a mess for years and the Baltic must be even worse, we couldn't even get in there. The only bright side, for us anyway, is that the filth coming out of the Baltic is staying well to the east. Water around here is cleaner. Anyway, that's for later. How are you settling in. House all right?"

Julia pulled a face. House was a nice word for it. Faslane had been heavily bombed and while the American fighter-bombers were accurate, they weren't that accurate. Still, it was better than Portsmouth. The stories were that Pompey had been hit so hard it looked like the surface of the moon. According to legend, the few people left lived in holes in the ground there and were fortunate to call them home. Up here, there were houses and work building replacements had started. Cheap, quickly-thrown together replacements that were barely more than a pre-fabricated wooden shack. Designed for a lifetime of five years, to give people walls and a roof until something better could be built.

"Its not the house Robert, its, ohh, now I don't know the word for it. Its the whole thing about living here. The people here hate us, did you know that? Wives aren't supposed to go outside the base area, its not safe. I can understand why." She waved her hand in front of herself. "These clothes aren't new but I bought them in America and they're so much better than anything people have here. We're the ones who left and lived in 'luxury' in America while people here suffered. Nobody spits on us but we get the feeling they'd like to."

Fox's face tightened although he didn't say anything. His arm gathered his wife just a touch more protectively to him.

"Something else you should know Robert." Julia was now Mrs Captain, advising her husband of things he ought to know about the families of his crew. "There's a lot of women around here selling themselves. I know its always been like that around naval bases but this is different. Its not the women you'd expect to do that, its also the ones you never thought would. The ones before the war we'd have called respectable married women. And some of them are mixed up with pretty ugly people. There's already been cases of sailors being knifed after going out with one of them."

"Julia, would you like to get away from here. I don't mean for a trip, I mean get away, never come back?"

"Can we?"

"That's a yes isn't it? You remember Jimmy Forrester? He ended the war in Australia, driving *Clyde* one of the old River class boats. The Australians loved them and they're building up a submarine arm out there. Jimmy elected to stay under the Imperial Gift and they've made him flotilla commander. They're short of submarine drivers, most of the gang had ties to Canada and elected to go there. Jimmy says, if we elect to go out under the Imperial Gift, he'll see that I get a boat for sure. Probably one of the modernized T-boats to start with."

"Does the Gift apply to us, we're here?"

"I don't think it was intended to but the way the agreement is worded, any Royal Navy officer can elect to settle in any country that accepts the Gift. Australia's going to be no picnic. They're broke out there and the end of the war flipped them into recession but they're a better bet for the future than here. They've got food and a future."

Julia nodded. Secretly, she'd been dreading living in the gray, hopelessness of Faslane. At least in Australia they'd have something to build. And Robert would still be able to play with his boats.

Office of Sir Martyn Sharpe, Chief of Staff to the President, New Delhi, India

"Sir Martyn, have you heard the news?"

Sir Martyn Sharpe lifted up his head. He'd heard the news from Thailand a few minutes before and he'd been weighing its consequences. As far as he could see, none of them would be good. "We need to talk to Sir Gregory Locock. And, of course, The Ambassador although I suspect she may be too busy to speak with us right now. Eric, the situation hasn't really changed since 1941. Thailand's still our forward line of defense. Singapore and Malaya can only be defended on the Mekong, if we lose that, we lose almost everything."

"I didn't mean that Sir Martyn, although God knows, that situation is bad enough. I meant the news from South Africa. They're out."

"Out?"

"Of the Commonwealth. Their government made the announcement a few minutes ago, the Embassy there wired us the news immediately. There's a lot of diplomatic diarrhea but essentially, they're resigning their membership of the Commonwealth and pulling out of all the agreements that are part of that arrangement. The withdrawal is going to be absolute in six months."

"We knew it was coming. They've expanded north and absorbed Rhodesia, Nyasaland, the old German and Portuguese colonies. And we virtually gave them Madagascar. They've become a pretty big force now, regionally at least, and old memories die hard. They still remember the turn of the century and the wars against the British. Anyway, I couldn't see the British tolerating the system they're bringing in over there very long. I think the Boers decided they would resign before they were kicked out."

"Seems a bit, I don't know, heartless somehow. Leaving now."

"Eric, we're on our way out as well. Two years, perhaps three at the outside. Australia, I don't know, they might stay in, but we've

170

got to leave. You know how strong nationalist feeling is here. They don't want to be under a British thumb any longer and the Nationalists see being a part of the Commonwealth as being under the British thumb. I can't blame them for that.

"At the moment, we can trade off being a member of the Commonwealth for a long, slow phased transfer of government. We can train our successors, we can establish the system that runs this country the way it should be run. But to do that we have to give the appearance of casting off the British link and that means we too must leave the Commonwealth.

"Anyway, the Commonwealth is going to be pretty irrelevant to us now. Perhaps, if Halifax hadn't thrown in the towel and left England to be occupied, it might have been different. Who knows? But when the Germans occupied Britain, they kicked the center out of the Commonwealth, broke it apart and nothing can put it back together again. We have to look to ourselves now, and our future lies here, in the East. This news from Thailand just confirms that. If the Japanese get away with this they'll turn Thailand into one of their protectorates, an occupied colony, just like they tried back in '41."

Sir Eric nodded. "The trouble is that the Japanese got China and Hong Kong, but Madam Ambassador filched the crown jewels while they weren't looking. Jardine and Matheson, Swires, Hutchinson-Whampoa, Hongkong and Shanghai Banking Corporation, you name it. They're all in Bangkok now. Economic power in the Far East is in the hands of the great Chinese trading companies, always has been. The smart Europeans knew that and rode the Dragon's back.

"Now the Dragon has a new lair and its making itself very comfortable, thank you. All the network of business contacts, family, personal, professional, all of them, have moved to Bangkok. They've nowhere else to go. If the Japanese get their hands on all that, within twenty years, they'll be the dominant economic power in Asia. That's why they're staging this whole thing."

"Exactly. The Great Houses went to Bangkok because it offered stability and the resources of a reasonably large country. If that stability goes, they'll try to run again, though heaven knows where to. But Thailand will be left in the lurch and that means our defense in depth goes. I must speak with The Ambassador as soon as our

Embassy in Bangkok can arrange a conference. Whether we like it or not, our fate's linked to Thailand - and to Australia come to that. The question is, what do we do about it?"

Chapter Two
Options

Headquarters Section, Japanese 2nd Battalion, 143 Division

They'd finally taken the road that joined the Guardhouse to the residential area. That had split the defense here into two parts, the two fortified buildings over on his left and the residential hell-hole on his right. He'd finally managed to storm the line of foxholes along the road and he'd been expecting to fight it out with the bayonet as their occupants defended them to the last. But, when he and his men had finally taken them, they were empty except for the dead and there were few of those. The occupants had fallen back before he'd got there and were now blazing away with their accursed machine guns from a new line. It would all have to be done again. But first, the flank of the Guardhouse was exposed and that could be taken out.

Major Kisoyoshi Utsunomiya had brought up the tools he needed to do the job. His battalion had been heavily reinforced for the job, its gun company had six 75mm infantry support guns instead of the usual two and all his men had been given the new Type 8 semi-automatic carbines. In fact, his command had the 143rd division's entire allocation of those marvelous rifles. It was lucky they did for the hail of fire they had put out was the only thing keeping his casualties within tolerable limits. As it was, he was way behind schedule. This base was supposed to have fallen easily, to have been seized by a coup-de-main before the invasion proper even started. But it hadn't, they'd been waiting for him and now the entire 143rd division was backed up on the road behind him. Perhaps that was an exaggeration, the troops would have been filtering through countryside to by-pass the base but they'd need the road cleared soon . The 75s would do it.

The building shook as the first shell plowed into the wall facing the residential area. Sergeant Nikorn Phwuangphairoch had guessed it would be coming, the studies of how the Japanese fought in China had been compulsory reading for a long time. They relied heavily on artillery brought forward and fired over open sights at strong points.

Sergeant Nikorn wasn't quite certain whether the guardhouse counted as a strongpoint but doubtless the Japanese thought of it as being one. It wasn't really designed that way but he'd strengthened the walls with sandbags and mounted machine guns in the windows. Now, the air inside was thick with dust, with acrid ammonia-tinged smoke from the cordite and the coppery smell of blood. He'd started holding the building with eight men, the other twelve had been in the foxholes along the road. They'd been driven back but were still covering his flanks with fire.

"Who's hurt?" There was a brief pause while the men inside peered through the gloom and the rancid smoke to make a check. They didn't get to answer because another shell and another crumped into the walls, filling the air still further. Men pulled their neck-clothes over their noses to try and keep out the dust. Nikorn grabbed the phone and cranked the handle. "Operations, Guardhouse. We're under artillery fire here. We need help."

"On its way. Keep your heads down." The voice at the other end was completely emotionless.

"They want us to hit the north end of the field. Up here by the Guardhouse and the personnel quarters. The defense company is holding both but the road between the has fallen." Flight Sergeant Kusol Chale had swung his seat around and was getting the ground situation on the radio, leaving his 20mm gun unmanned. On paper at least, the Ostrich had accommodation for a third crew member if needed, on a jump seat between the pilot and gunner. The Thai crews believed the Australians had bred a special species of airmen to occupy that seat, one 45 centimeters tall with their head between their legs and arms two meters long. None of the aircraft in the flight had ever flown with more than two crewmen on board.

Flight Lieutenant Phol Thongpricha nodded and looked down. The Ostrich had one vital characteristic for a ground attack aircraft, the pilot sat well forward and his vision downwards was excellent. He could see the square of the guardhouse, even the puffs of smoke around it that marked the start of an artillery barrage. The Japanese thought that a few guns firing over open sights constituted infantry support. They were about to learn differently. He banked left, rolling the Ostrich over into a long dive. Behind him, Djiap-Two followed the maneuver, then Djiap-Three and the rest of the flight. One plane after another, their silver skins gleaming in the sun as they formed a long line heading downwards.

The Ostrich was a big plane but Phol was flying it gently, making tiny adjustments as he lined the nose up on the area in front of the Guardhouse. There were two gun buttons on his control column, one fired the six .50 caliber machine guns in the wings, the other the four 23mm cannon under the nose. He'd decided to use only the .50s on this run, the 23mms were primarily anti-tank guns with a secondary air-to-air role. Against infantry, the fast-firing M-3 Brownings were the weapon of choice. Those and the six 250 kilogram bombs he had hanging under his belly.

Beneath him he could see the figures moving forward, seeming to stop and look up at the aircraft descending upon them. Off in front of him were the blotches of the field guns, sandbags piled in front to give the gunners a modicum of protection as they served their pieces. Even as he watched there was a belch of white smoke from one and an almost simultaneous black explosion on the Guardhouse. Still holding out then. Another slight adjustment on the controls and the nose of the diving Ostrich centered on the nearest of the field guns. Six of them, that was unusual; a Japanese infantry battalion usually only had two. Didn't matter, as he pulled out, his gunfire would rake along the line.

"Two, follow me down onto the guns, three and four hit the infantry." Some of the men on the ground were kneeling, firing back with their rifles. If ever there was a forlorn hope, shooting at an Ostrich with a rifle was it. Phol almost imagined he could hear a 'ting' as a rifle bullet bounced off his armored belly, the belly that had a double layer of armor that could stop a 20mm shell cold.

Then, he squeezed the trigger on his control column and heard the roar as his wing guns poured fire at the men below. Poured fire literally, the usual allocation was one tracer round in five but the Ostriches had every other round tracer. A red sheet poured from the wings, washing over the guns below him. His thumb depressed and held the bomb release switch. He felt the thumps as each 250 kilogram bomb was released. One, two, three, four, five, six. A stick right across the field guns or so he hoped. Then Phol pulled back the control column easing the Ostrich out of its wild dive. That wasn't as easy as it sounded, the Ostrich was nose-heavy and more than one of its pilots had become so fixated by the targets on the ground, they'd left pulling out too late and flown straight into the ground.

Phol made it, his heavy aircraft skimming a few tens of feet over the grass. In the mirror behind him he could see the boiling black and red cloud from his bombs and those of Djiap-Two. Then Djiap-Two burst out of the cloud, it's silver skin stained from the explosions but safe and racing across the airfield after him. Ahead was a road, and as every good ground attack pilot knew, roads meant targets. This one led to the village. If the airfield was holding the first wave of the attack, there was a good chance the follow-up units were backed up there.

He was right, a group of trucks escorted by a foolish-looking armored car with a cylindrical turret. Phol shifted his grip slightly, adjusted the flight path - and as the pipper in his sight touched the armored car, squeezed the trigger of his 23mm guns. Those guns had been designed to stop a German tank, slicing through its thin topsides and into its fuel and engines. Penetration equivalent to 25 millimeters of hardened armor steel at 400 meters.

The armored car didn't have anything like that level of protection. It was designed to frighten Chinese infantry and was proof against rifle fire, no more. The first few shots landed short but the rest marched into the archaic-looking vehicle and tore it apart. As the shells from the V-Ya cannon ripped into the plating, there was in a spectacular display of instantaneous destruction. The whole vehicle was thrown backwards, the turret with its short-barreled gun flew into the air, the wheels were torn from the body, some burning, some spinning, one rolling down the road towards the trucks.

Even as the armored car was chopped apart, Phol was lifting the nose, just enough to walk the stream of fire into the trucks. More black clouds of smoke and flame, the Ostriches bursting through them as Djiap-One and Djiap-Two ran past the village and started to turn and climb away, ready for another pass at the troops attacking the airfield.

Headquarters Section, Japanese 2nd Battalion, 143 Division

What had happened was something totally outside his experience. His head was fuzzy, shaken, the thoughts in it disjointed and dispersed. They just wouldn't come together. Although he didn't know it, he was staggering in the clouds of dust and rolling black shroud of smoke. To Major Utsunomiya, air support was a small light bomber like a Ki-51 or Ki-71 that turned up from a nearby landing strip, dropped a few hand-grenade sized bombs then watched as the Chinese panicked and left their positions.

The silver monsters that had roared across the battlefield, spewing death and destruction beneath them, the yellow tigers painted on their tail fins snarling defiance, they were something from a different universe. Utsunomiya had heard Germans talking about ground attack aircraft on the Eastern Front, the Russian Sturmoviks, the American Jabos, the Australian Ostriches. He'd heard the stories of cannon fire, of bombs and rockets, of the American's frightful jellygas but he hadn't understood them, not until now.

Overhead, he saw the sunlight flashing off the silver paint as the aircraft climbed away, doubtless getting ready for another pass. Over the trees, from where the village sat, a column of black smoke rose. Burning trucks. Utsunomiya had guessed that the soldiers waiting for the way forward to be cleared would have been amusing themselves with the village girls. The Ostriches had probably been the worst form of coitus interruptus imaginable. The irreverent thought shocked Utsunomiya's mind back into military gear. If his men were in the open, the Ostriches would slaughter them all. They had to get into cover and the only way to do that was to take the Guardhouse ahead of them. Almost by remote control, he swung his sword over his head and pointed it at the building. "Charge! Follow me!"

The machine gun in the Guardhouse seemed puny, pathetic, after the Ostriches. Utsunomiya couldn't believe it had pinned him and his men down for so long. The guns had knocked most of one wall down, just leaving a pile of masonry rubble. Utsunomiya leapt up it, his feet scrabbling for a second as the broken bricks rolled and fell but he was up and over. In front of him a Sergeant was trying to point one of the machine pistols at him. Too late, the katana swung and Utsunomiya saw the man's left arm fall as the sword lopped it off. Then he swung again and the man's head fell from his body. Another soldier was in the cloud of dust and he fell as one of the Arisakas pumped half a dozen rounds into him. The Ostriches had failed; the Guardhouse was secure.

Cookhouse, Laum Mwuak Airfield, Thai/Japanese Indochina Border

"We're next. You'd better get out of here while you can, mother." Airman Ronna Phakasad saw the Rising Sun flag flutter up over the Guardhouse. The air strike had been vicious but not vicious enough. Whatever else the Japanese were, cowardly they were not. They'd pushed on and taken the building while the aircraft came around for another pass. That took courage and skill.

"And leave my nice kitchen for those animals? I think not young man. This is where I..." The rest of the words were cut off as a crash shook the building and dust filled the air. Somehow, the surviving Japanese gunners had got at least one of their pieces back into action and were firing on the cookhouse. There was a crackle of automatic fire outside; the Japanese infantry were pushing inwards. Ronna grabbed his Browning and started firing short bursts, chopping down the figures as they came towards him. Then, a series of loud pops as 50mm mortar shells dropped down on top of the men outside. The Japanese knee mortars. Ronna fired again moving methodically from left to right. He never made the full swing for a 75mm shell hit squarely onto the firing port.

Chief Cook opened her eyes and saw the nice young Airman who'd been so grateful for his bowl of soup, lying on the floor. Dead, may his spirit be rewarded by a propitious rebirth, she thought. Assistant Cook was lying across the room, a splinter almost a meter long sticking in her chest. The strange angle of her neck told Chief Cook all she needed to know about her late assistant.

Almost without thinking, Chief Cook took the kerosene container from the rack and started pouring it on the floor. As the

178

container glugged empty, she dragged herself across the to the gas stove and opened the valve on the propane cylinder as wide as it would go. The gas hissed into the room, making her choke but it was all ready now. She got out the battery-powered lighter one of the airmen had bought her after she'd burned her thumb lighting her stove with a match and got ready. Then, even above her coughing from the gas that was rapidly filling the room, she heard the crash as the Japanese broke down the door. And she even thought she heard the click as the end of the lighter burst out into flame.

Operations Center, Laum Mwuak Airfield, Thai/Japanese Indochina Border

"Whoa, look at that. The Japanese won't be eating anything there!" The explosion that blasted the cookhouse was spectacular even by the standards of the airstrike a few minutes earlier. Still, the defenders there might have taken some Japanese down with them but the Cookhouse had still fallen.

"Order Cabrank to hit the Guardhouse. Take out what's left of it. The residency is gone, we can't hold it any longer. Call the commander there and tell him to fall back. Burn the place as he goes."

"Sir, the Clubhouse?" The Clubhouse was also the wing museum, filled with their trophies from the war with France. Parts of aircraft shot down, pictures of victories, a wall covered with the signatures of pilots.

"Burn it. Tell Cabrank to hit anything and everything short of the Golf Course. We'll fall back there. They've still got their rockets?"

"Yes Sir. The big ones, the 132s"

"That will do. Lord be praised, the Ozwalds do like to put big warheads on everything. The Ostriches have to buy us time to regroup around the Golf Course. Are the families out?"

"On their way, out the back door. We're holding that open, there's been some skirmishing in the hills but nothing serious. They're taking as many of the wounded with them as they can." The ground shook as one of the Ostriches roared overhead, then an ear-ripping

179

scream as it fired a salvo of RS-132 rockets into a group of Japanese trying to outflank the residential area. "How long can we hold Sir?"

"At least to dusk. We've got to hold until dusk."

On the Road to Tong Klao, Recovered Provinces, Thailand

"It's the Army. Lord be praised, the Army is here." The policeman's voice was remote, even, almost distant. His eyes were the same way, haunted, as if they were focused on something a thousand meters away that only he could see. His uniform, light green rather than the Thai Army's dark jungle green, was torn and dirty, stained with sweat and the red laterite dust. The policeman had only his pistol but with him were half a dozen villagers, some carrying old Type 45 rifles, one had a thick-barreled flintlock musket.

"How far behind you are they? How long have we got? And are there any more of your people out there?"

"No more, there were, but the Japanese got them. A few minutes no more. They move so fast, never seen men move so fast through the scrub. Every time we set up, they flanked us, drove us out."

"Very good. Corporal, get your men to the rear, you've done more than anybody could have possibly hoped. I have to ask, did you actually use that flintlock?"

The policeman's eyes flicked into focus "Oh yes, we did that. The Japanese thought it was a field gun, it created so much smoke when we fired it. We bluffed them three or four times with it before they realized what it was."

Sirisoon nodded. That was the theme tune for today. Make use of whatever came to hand and pray it would hold just long enough. "Go on, get back, get your people something to eat and drink. Sergeant, this is good ground, we'll hold here. Third section out on the right, second section and us here, First, back there and on our left. Give first both the weapons section MG34s, one rocket launcher to each section."

"Both machine guns on the left ma'am?"

"Both. You heard, the Japanese are in a flanking mood. I want them to try it and walk into three MG34s. Say again, nobody fires anything but rifles until I say otherwise. When I give the word, Second section drops back to there, halfway between first and third. That way we'll get their main body in an L-shaped ambush. Now move."

Underneath the German-style coal-scuttle helmet, sweat was rapidly turning Sirisoons hair into a tangled, sodden mass. Lesson one she thought. American-style crew-cut hair. It would send her mother mad of course. But there was a reason why Thai women of old had cut their hair short and Sirisoon had just relearned it. Then she saw something in the grass up ahead. Figures moving forward up ahead. A skirmish line, moving cautiously but as a unit. Not fire-and-movement, all the men moving together. Risky but a price paid for speed. Move fast enough, keep the enemy off balance and one could get away with taking chances. Only, this time, they hadn't moved quite fast enough. Then she saw a flash of light, reflecting off glass. Binoculars? Eyeglasses? Something like that.

As she watched, she saw the figures moving forward, some half crouched, others kneeling. One of them did have binoculars. You're mine, she thought and centered the hooded foresight of her rifle on his chest, about six inches below his neck. And the foresight blade evenly spaced between the leaves of the rear sight, its top level with the top of each leaf. Safety catch over to the left. Gentle, gentle pressure, an even squeeze throughout her hand and - it was a surprise when the heavy Mauser kicked into her shoulder. She could see the puff of dust from the man's jacket as he was flipped backwards. Then the stutter of rifle fire along the line as her men followed her lead and opened fire on the point unit of the Japanese advance.

There had been ten Japanese in the unit but only a handful got a chance to return fire. The Mausers took them down fast, one after another. Those who survived the initial shots tried to fire back at the figures who were lying in wait for them but they never got an even break. Sirisoon worked the bolt on her rifle, blessing the silk-smooth Mauser action that was so different from the sticky, heavy bolt on her father's Mannlicher and picked herself a second man. She fired, he went down although she wasn't sure whether she'd hit him or he'd just dived for cover. She hadn't watched because after her second shot, she'd rolled away from her first position. Fire one shot, she thought, they know you're there. Fire a second and they'll know where you are. She could hear a *wheet, wheet* noise as the Japanese return fire sliced through the grass but the time she'd got into position to fire again, it had stopped.

"Get back, everybody stay down and get back to the fall-back position. Now. Fast. Move, move, move."

Her HQ section and Second obeyed her, crawling back through the grass to the line she'd picked. About 70 meters behind the first and in a shallow ditch. Now, her three sections were in a diagonal line, third advanced, second the center, first refused.

"Why are we running away? We were winning." She heard a soldier whispering. Almost as if the Japanese were answering him, there was a whistle and a line of explosions marked their old positions. Japanese, 50mm knee mortars. Actually, more like grenade throwers but still deadly. She counted the patterns, the shells were landing in threes, so three mortars then. That made sense. Probably a company operating as six ten-man squads, three with a Type 99 light machine gun, three with knee mortars. A point squad that was now in the great void. And an HQ section. Her quick mental inventory was interrupted by a metallic smack as Sergeant Yawd smacked a coal-scuttle helmet over its owners eyes.

"Now do you see why we pulled back so fast duck-lover? Get it into your head, our officer knows what she's doing."

I do so hope so, Sirisoon thought, Lord Buddha help me, I do so hope so.

The ditch was perfect, zig-zagged with deep depressions ideally suited to her machine guns and rocket launchers. It was so perfect, she couldn't help but wonder whether it had been dug as part of border defenses back in '41. Even if it hadn't, it was doing its job now. The Japanese mortar barrage was falling short anyway, concentrating on the positions her unit had been in a few minutes earlier. But still, the ditch was protecting her men from overs and stray fragments.

The barrage seemed to go on and on, for hours. In fact, Lieutenant Sirisoon knew that it was lasting just long enough to pin her unit down while the Japanese commander moved the bulk of his unit around to flank her. Any second now, those men would be in position, the mortar fire would lift and they'd attack. It would be the standard way of doing it, a frontal attack to pin her, a flank attack to role her up and envelope her. Even as she thought the words, the mortar fire ceased and there were screams of orders, the Japanese clearly drifting across the momentarily-silent battle field.

Then they broke cover. Two infantry groups, five riflemen each, a three-man gun group with a Type 99 machine gun, another three man gun group with a 50mm mortar. Smaller than she'd thought. Assuming this was a third of the total force, the attack was being carried out on platoon size. And that meant there were two more platoons just like this one following it up. "Kep, when I say, take the machine gun group out first, then the mortar crew. Then as needed." The MG34 gunner nodded. He settled himself slightly, the muzzle of his machine gun covering the advancing Japanese machine gun group.

Sirisoon watched as the charging Japanese neared her original position seventy meters in front of her. The Japanese Type 99 machine gun was first cousin to the British Bren gun, no match for her MG34s but it was still most of the enemy's firepower. Now there was yelling on her left, the Japanese flanking force had bounced off and was making its move. Her head felt weird, it was almost as if she had left her body and was floating above the battlefield, she could see herself and her platoon in its lightning-flash formation lying in the grass, the Japanese charging her center and left. The key was her left, that had to be where the Japanese main body was. When her instincts told her they had reached the right position, it was as if she'd fallen out of the sky, back into her own body.

The Japanese in front had reached her original position. They'd jumped at her position, attempting to take it with the bayonet - and found it deserted. They'd hesitated, confused for a second, and in that moment Sirisoon smacked her machine gunner between the shoulder blades. "Now!" There was a ripping noise, the characteristic high rate of fire of the German-designed machine gun and the Japanese Type 99 crew were cut down almost instantly. A brief pause, so brief it could hardly be registered then another ripping burst at the mortar crew. Then a stutter of rifle fire as her men opened up, the dull thump of the Mausers complementing the sawing noise of the MG34 as her unit's fire dominated the killing zone in front of her. She took aim herself, picking one man and squeezing off a shot, then another.

She had no idea whether she had hit him or not for, once again, her mind had left her body and was looking down on the battlefield from above. She could see the three machine guns on her left crucifying the Japanese flanking force. Cutting them down, stacking their bodies like cordwood, the machine guns eliminating the crew-served weapons first, then shooting down the riflemen.

The Japanese had made a terrible mistake, they hadn't expected machine guns and now it was the machine guns that were doing the killing. The rifles, at best, were holding the enemy up until the MG34s could kill them. In front of her center, the Japanese pinning force was already destroyed, its men reduced to isolated pockets, pinned down by rifle fire until they could be taken out by the MG34. Off to her right, her remaining section lay quietly waiting for the signal to spring their own special trap on the enemy. As she looked down, her mind's eye saw what would happen next, as surely as if it had already happened and she was writing the report on it the next day.

The Japanese had charged riflemen and met machine guns. The platoon dying in the killing zone in front of her would never make that mistake again but there were two more platoons following it and she knew exactly what they were going to do. She also knew exactly what to do about it. Her mind snapped back into her body again and she quickly wrote on a pad what she wanted first section to do. Then gave it to her runner to take over to the sergeant commanding first.

Headquarters Section, First Company 2nd Battalion, 324th Division

He'd recognized his mistake as soon as he'd heard the vicious rasping noise. He'd thought this had been just another group of militia, another motley crew of the civilians and policemen who'd been harassing his company all day. Not skilled enough to do much damage or cause casualties but their mere presence had slowed him up. Frustration had made him think these were more of the same. He'd ignored the different sound of the rifles, ignored the change from the wild fire of armed civilians to the disciplined barrage of aimed rifle shots. He'd even ignored the fact that they'd taken out his lead squad. He'd willfully ignored all that, because they had to be just more militia. Because if they weren't, it would mean that rag-tag circus of civilians and policemen had held him up long enough for the enemy regular army to arrive.

The sound of the machine guns stripped that excuse away. No doubt left now, Captain Nagashino knew he was facing regular troops, line infantry. It was worse than that. He could tell from the volume of fire being poured out, from where that volume was coming from, that the enemy commander had guessed his move and been one jump ahead of him. He'd been expecting the flanking attack and moved the mass of his defense over to prepare for it. The flanking force that should have enveloped the enemy unit and rolled it up had walked straight into a prepared defense and were being cut down.

Well, that meant the strength of the force was out on the left. Convenient. Like most Japanese company, Nagashino's headquarters unit was small. He simply didn't have the command control resources to do anything elaborate but elaborate wasn't necessary. The enemy commander had anticipated his flanking move and countered it but in doing so, his front had been left dangerously weak. It had taken them time to cut down his pinning force. One really good push, that's all it would need and his company would break through that thin line and take the flank force from the rear. He issued the orders, second platoon to charge, third platoon to follow it in support and smash the enemy. After most of the day fighting militia who melted away when threatened, it was a relief to have an enemy who stood and fought.

Headquarters Section, Point Platoon, 219th Infantry Regiment

"Grenadiers, rifle grenades ready. Here they come." Just as she'd seen, the Japanese were launching a sledgehammer blow at her front, aiming to crush her through sheer weight of numbers and roll up her unit. The Japanese were screaming, some were firing from the hip as they ran across the killing zone, others just trying to close with the bayonet. This time, all six squads were charging her position, three Type 99s, three 50mm mortars, more than 30 riflemen against her single machine gun, nine rifles and two submachine guns. Only third section out on her right remained uncommitted. That was angled at 45 degrees to her line so the Japanese were charging into a deadly crossfire. It was light though, very light.

185

"Fire!" the two grenade launchers coughed and a split second later there were the explosions of the grenades in the Japanese charge. It was a first blow and a signal. She hadn't told her machine gunner what to do next, he knew the drill already. His first burst cut down one of the machine gun crews, then the whole left of the charging Japanese platoon appeared to crumple as third section opened up on it. Two rifle grenades took down one of the remaining Type 99 crews, a burst of machinegun fire killed a mortar crew. Then, the other two Japanese 50mm crews went to ground. She knew what had to happen next, the whistle of descending mortar rounds, the explosions in her lines, not safely in front of them.

A flash of sunlight off something, she took aim and fired. A despairing click, her rifle was dry. A quick fumble with one of the six pouches on her webbing and a box of rounds slid into her hand. It was a moment's work to thumb the stripper clip of five rounds but even in that time, the Japanese were much closer. Took aim again and fired, the man dropping in a heap.

Next to her, one of her riflemen was fumbling with his pouches, the box was stuck, wouldn't come out. Sirisoon flipped him one of her stripper clips and he thumbed it home safely. There was a lighter rattle now, the 9mm submachine guns carried by Sergeant Yawd and the number twos on the RPG and machinegun crews. It was interrupted by the heavy crash of the inbound 50mm mortar rounds and the smaller explosions of the outbound rifle grenades.

More screams, more yelling and another Japanese line burst out of its position up ahead and charged. This one had something new, a small group, just two men, one waving a sword, the other carrying a flag. This was the main push, the first wave had bled her and pinned her men down. Now its survivors, firing from no more than 20 or 30 meters in front of her position, would keep up the fire while the fresh platoon charged through them and overran her. And, despite the L-shaped ambush and the bodies in the killing zone, she wouldn't be able to stop them.

Once again, she had the weird feeling of her mind leaving her body. She could see her men, now some of the figures broken and still, the rest pouring fire into the killing zone. Through it, the Japanese assault moving inexorably towards her line, threatening to overwhelm it with its numbers. And she could also see something else, her first section with its extra machine guns moving forward, swinging like a door on its hinge point, the joint with her second section.

In a few seconds, just a few seconds, those guns would be enveloping the Japanese from the left and both their flanks would be over-reached. It was as if she was looking down on the battle at the exercise tables of Chulachomklao and she could hear the dry voice of the instructor. "Well done Cadet Sirisoon. You're outnumbered four to one, you're outgunned, you've taken casualties and now you're attacking the enemy. An unconventional solution. A trifle *over-aggressive* don't you think?"

Her shoulder felt stiff, while her mind had been viewing the action from above, her body had been operating the bolt on her rifle, squeezing off round after round. She had no idea who she'd hit or how many, only that the line advancing on her position was closing fast and the machine gun out on her right flank had been silenced. Hit by a mortar round probably. "Fix bayonets" her voice carrying and being relayed as she and her men drew the silver, 30 centimeter-long sawbacks and clicked them into place. And the Japanese seemed to wait for them to do it, but not from choice. For there was a roar as the two tripod-mounted MG-34s opened up from the long grass, enfilading the line of Japanese infantry, cutting them down, sending them tumbling over as the twin streams of tracer raked the formation.

Surprise was total. It shouldn't have been, it was just another infantry section opening fire but it was the last straw, the Japanese were already in a crossfire and had assumed this was as bad as it could get. Now, they'd been hit by a much greater density of fire from the flank they'd thought they held. Surprise is in the mind of an enemy and Sirisoon saw the Japanese advance stagger with bewilderment, its men crumpling as they tried to get their minds around what had happened. What shouldn't have happened but had. Then a voice echoed in Sirisoon's head, not her instructors but an Englishman. A man speaking in English with the accent she'd heard in films about the English aristocracy. She didn't speak enough English to know what the words meant but she knew what they were saying. "Now! Now's your time!"

And she was on her feet, the rest of her platoon with her, closing in from the front and both flanks. The Japanese didn't break, Japanese infantry never did, but they were stunned by the sudden development. For years they'd fought Chinese who usually didn't hold and if they did rarely counter attacked. And never fought it out with the bayonet. They took time to react to the unprecedented thing that was happening and by the time they did, it was too late. Sirisoon saw one of them coming at her, his Arisaka leveled. She batted it out of line and lunged, her sawback slicing into the man's midriff. Twist and pull, the sawback ripping the man open. Behind her, Yawd cut down another Japanese with his MP40 before he could blindside her.

Then, it was over. The Japanese were down and her men held the field. What was left of them anyway. "Keep the men moving forward, don't stop. Find out how many we've lost. Radio Sergeant, we have to report contact." Her voice was distant, level, her eyes scanning for any sign of resistance. There was a quick crackle of MP40 fire and her head jerked round. A Japanese casualty had raised his head and one of her men had shot him. Yawd caught her look.

"Can't do it ma'am. These are Japanese. They don't surrender. Try to take a prisoner, they'll explode a grenade in your face or squeeze off one last shot." Sirisoon nodded. Ahead, her men had already retaken their original position and were forming a skirmish line, advancing by bounds. At her feet lay an officer, his chest half-torn away by a machine gun. "Ma'am, his sword. Pick up his sword, its yours by right."

She shook her head. "Haven't time. We've got to move forward, keep pushing."

"Ma'am. You *really need* to capture his sword. The men need to see you do it."

She got the message and picked it up. It was a genuine katana, not one of the cheap stamped imitations so many officers carried. The scabbard lay not far away. She picked up that as well. Then she held it over her head, flashing in the afternoon sun. Those of her men who saw it cheered and the one's who hadn't heard the noise and looked, then added their voices.

"Radio, Ma'am. And the butcher's bill. Nine dead, six wounded. Few more got scratches but they won't admit it."

"Thank you Sergeant. Ken, patch me though on Channel Seven." She waited until the channel was clear. "1219, this is Sirisoon-Actual. We have made contact with the enemy. Infantry formation in company strength. We have defeated them and are pushing forward, advancing on Tong Klao. Request resupply of ammunition and any replacements if you have them. We have nine dead here, six wounded need evacuation. Enemy casualties, in excess of one hundred."

There was a long pause then the familiar voice from HQ 1219 broke it. "Received and understood. Advance to Tong Klao and hold. Be warned, we have reports of enemy armor in the area. We will resupply you in Tong Klao."

Back at company headquarters, the company commander shut down the channel. "Well Sergeant Major, what do you make of that?"

"I think the Japanese chose the wrong time of the month to invade Sir."

Headquarters Section, Japanese 2nd Battalion, 143 Division

The setting sun stained the Rising Sun flying over the golf course bright red. Major Kisoyoshi Utsunomiya stared around at the airfield that had finally fallen to his men. The gathering gloom was punctuated by the reddened skeletons of the buildings that had been burned down. He couldn't see that well, one half of his face was covered by a bandage where a fragment from a rocket had torn him. He knew what the Doctor knew but wouldn't tell him, that eye would never see again.

But the golf course had fallen at last. The enemy rearguard had held until the last, buying time for the rest to escape. They had darkness on their side now, the Japanese prided themselves that their infantry owned the night but catching a retreating enemy on their own turf was not part of that. Anyway, he didn't have the men left. He'd started with more than 700, now 391 were dead and a couple of hundred more badly wounded. It had been the airstrikes that had done the real damage. The ground troops had fought bravely but they weren't professional infantry. It was those damned invincible Ostriches that had done it with their bombs and rockets and guns.

"Sir! A trophy! They left the flag in the hole."

An infantryman was pulling the flag from the 18th hole on the golf course, a long pole with a Thai flag on one end. Utsunomiya frowned, golf course markers didn't normally have national flags on them. Then his mind went into overdrive and he screamed out a despairing "No!" It was too late. The anti-personnel mine hidden under the green threw its ball a meter into the air before it exploded, spraying fragments in a vicious arc. Utsunomiya felt the thump in his legs as some of the metal cubes struck home. His fourth wound of the day, he thought grimly. Then he felt resentful. Surely there was a rule against booby-trapping a golf course?

First Army Circle Headquarters, Ban Masdit, Recovered Provinces, Thailand

"Sir, Its General Chaovalit. From Ninth Forward Command."

General Songkitti grabbed the phone from his aide. "Van. Can you hold?"

The phone crackled a little before the voice came through. "Yes."

"Lord be praised for that. Can you hold the line unassisted for another day? Our plot shows two Japanese divisions have crossed."

"I know. Believe me, I know. But we've got all four regiments on the line now. 19th and 29th are holding the line and even pushed the Japanese back a little. 39th and 49th took longer to move up but they were in position by sunset. If Laum Mwuak hadn't held out as long as it had......." Songkitti bit his lip. The news from Laum Mwuak had been grim. The airfield captured, the airfield defense company, 120 men, wiped out to the last man. At least half the other air force personnel gone. The rest trying to take their families out through the jungle. Chaovalit was still speaking. "And the aircraft of course. We couldn't have done anything without them. But we've the whole division on the line now and based on today, yes, I can buy you tomorrow."

Songkitti's eyes were on the map. There was a thin line of blue pins now, marking the kidney-shaped bulge of the Japanese

190

incursion. 16 kilometers deep at its thickest. Five at the thinnest by Laum Mwuak. Tomorrow was the critical day. The Second Cavalry was arriving in Phnom Penh overnight, they'd be forming up to the east of the Japanese kidney. And to its west, 11th Infantry was also slowly moving up. If 9th could hold for that one day, he'd be able to counter attack north and south, cut the Japanese force south of the Mekong off and envelope it. Today had been close run, all too close. The militia had held just long enough, Laum Mwuak had held just long enough, the Ostriches had done just enough damage and together they'd bought enough time for the 9th to come on line. Now, if he had one more day, he could start to put this right.

"I don't know if we'll have air support tomorrow. We had air superiority all day today, I don't know why. Can't guarantee we'll have it tomorrow. Anything else I can send you?"

"Replacements, always replacements. And if you've got any more officers like that woman you sent to 29th, get them up here. Prad thought you were mad sending a woman but she's been out there kicking butt and taking names all afternoon."

"I'll shake some more personnel loose. And some 150s. Thanks Van." Songkitti hung up and turned to his aide. "You hear that? That's the one I threatened to have dragged out of here by her hair. You think she'll hold a grudge?"

"Don't they always, Sir?"

Chapter Three
Solutions

Flight Deck B-36H "Texan Lady", 50,150 feet over the Nevada Test and Experimental Area

"Alex, did you hear what the 509th Composite pulled yesterday on Mannie Fernandez's Chain Lightnings?"

"I missed the briefings last night. Chief Designer Mikoyan was advising us on his visit to North American. But I have heard Major Fernandez was not in a happy mood. Also that his aircraft did not perform well."

"They did as well as any I suppose. But the 305th were scheduled to do their pre-raid penetration only the 509th played a wild-card. They put one of their GB-36s, *Guardian Angel* up there instead of a Recon Rat. When Mannie's F-58s came up to play, the GB-36 crew waited until the fighters had topped out then dropped their Goblins on them. Mannie's birds were at 43,000, hanging on their props, and the Goblins just shot them up while the 58's were struggling not to stall and spin out. Camera gun shots are a sight to behold. All six down, then *Guardian Angel* swept down picked up her fighters and climbed up again. Mannie wasn't happy about that, says in a real strike there would have been more fighters around to prevent the pick up. Right too I suppose."

"*Guardian Angel*, isn't she one of the ones that saved your ass over France." Major Clancy was riding in the pilot's seat with Colonel Dedmon in the aircraft commander's position and Guards-Colonel Aleksandr Pokryshkin as co-pilot.

"That's right. Trynn Allen's bird. *Guardian Angel, Sweet Caroline* and *Golden Girl* aren't allowed to buy their own beer any time they come up to Kozlowski. Not when they pulled our nuts out of the fire after some crazy fighter jock, no offense Alex, blew our port wing to hell. He missed with his rockets but got lucky with cannonfire. We were losing altitude and there were long-wing Messerschmitts waiting for us. Then those three turned up and blew the reception committee away for us.

"Blohm und Voss, not Messerschmitts. It was originally a Messerschmitt but Blohm und Voss took it over when Messerschmitt pigged up the design work." Pokryshkin spoke absently as he got used to the feel of the B-36. "There are a couple at Ramenskoye, our designers are looking them over."

"Boss, we're picking up a contact. Single fighter burning sky, 660 miles per hour. Climbing fast as well. Much faster than anything we've picked up to date. Whoa, 7,600 feet per minute."

"That must be the North American XF-86A. They told us it would be joining the exercise today. It is 50 kilometers faster than our MiG-15 but the Aluminum Rabbit climbs faster. I do not think we should worry though. Both aircraft will run out of climb some distance below us."

"Thank's Alex. Any word on the problems with the MiG-15? Argus, keep an eye on that contact alert us when it crossed 40,000 feet."

"Chief Designer Mikoyan said the designers at North American were most helpful. They say that with swept wings it is essential to build them a different way. We built them the old way, with the spars and frames first then covering them with skin. Build the wing from the inside out but that is not accurate enough any more. North American have special jigs where they lay the skin first then apply the frames and spars to the wing skin. Build the wing from the outside in. Chief Designer Mikoyan is sending that back to Russia today and our factories will try the new method. In exchange we have given them North American information on our cannons for fighters. Our friend down there still has .50 machine guns. Not good enough.

Strange. Your XF-86 can fly but not shoot, our MiG-15 can shoot but not fly."

"Crossing 40,000 now. Rate of climb slowing right down. Losing a lot of speed. He's leveled off, trying to build up speed again, 600 miles per hour. OK, he's climbing but a lot slower."

"Running out of power. He must be down to less than a thousand pounds of thrust by now." Clancy altered course slightly, extending the distance between the climbing fighter and *Texan Lady's* serene progress across the Nevada sky. Aft, the twin 20mm guns in the tail moved slightly, John-Paul Martin making sure they hadn't frozen up in the intense cold outside.

"Still climbing, very slow now. Guess is he'll level off at around 48 to 49. You were right up there, he isn't going to make it."

"And that's the best we have."

Texan Lady continued her stately turn in the sky over the test range. About 3,000 feet below them, the XF-86 was wallowing as the pilot fought to reach the silver giant overhead without stalling. A hard job, the gap between his stalling speed and his maximum speed was less than a couple of miles per hour. Helplessly, the pilot watched the B-36 turning away from him and separating.

"Phil, I'm taking over for a few minutes." Dedmon dropped down and slid into the pilot's seat. "Crew, preparing for descent. Argus, altitude and position on that fighter?"

"2,500 feet below, off to around 8 o'clock. He's trying to turn with us but he can't make it. He'll stall if he pulls the bank needed."

"Thank's. Let me know immediately if anything changes." Dedmon could hear the little groans and squeaks in his aircraft's structure as she dropped down to 49,500 feet. He could see the XF-86 now, off to his left, essentially just hanging in the air, its thrust barely adequate to hold the aircraft in position. The pilot was trying to turn but he had neither the lift nor the control authority to manage anything more than a gentle drift. Then, Dedmon lost sight of the fighter as *Texan Lady* continued her own starboard turn.

Mentally, he held the position in his mind, visualizing the relative locations of the two aircraft. At the right second, he looked over his right shoulder and saw the XF-86 swimming back into view. As he watched, it seemed to creep forward, moving towards the front of the bomber's bubble cockpit. The fighter pilot had leveled off now and was trying to accelerate away from the bomber that was slowly but surely getting into his six o'clock.

"OK guys, here we go." The XF-86 was now directly in front of them, still accelerating in an attempt to gain separation from the threatening giant behind. "Piston engines full power, jets likewise. Alex, jets lose power up here, our turbocharged radials don't. Not as much anyway." Dedmon was watching closely, he was trying to make a point, not cause an accident. "Power down five on turners, keep burners at maximum."

The distance between the XF-86 and the B-36 had dropped to a couple of hundred yards, the fighter looking for all the world like a pilotfish ahead of a whale. The fighter pilot was trying to turn now, making the gentle banks to port and starboard that were all aerodynamics allowed, in an attempt to throw the bomber off his tail but it was futile. *Texan Lady* easily matched him turn for turn, chasing the XF-86 around the sky.

"*Texan Lady* this is Sabre-one. I concede. Drop back will you." The fighter pilot's voice was aggrieved and resentful. Dedmon grinned nastily and edged *Texan Lady* a little closer to the persecuted fighter.

"*Texan Lady*, back off will you." There was a distinct edge of panic in the pilot's voice now. Viewed objectively, Dedmon couldn't blame him, *Texan Lady* must be filling the sky behind him. And fighter pilots weren't used to being chased around the sky by bombers.

"Ride Him Cowboy." The female voice echoed through the intercom system. Pokryshkin raised his eyebrows curiously.

"We have a crewmember who does a very good female impersonation. Don't know who." Dedmon's voice was tense also, his eyes never left the fighter in front of them.

"*Texan Lady*, this is range control. Break away from that fighter now."

"Sorry Ground Control, repeat please, your message broke up."

"There he goes Bob." The ailerons on the XF-86 were visibly shaking. Suddenly, the pilot must have banked a little too far and his lift dropped below the critical point. The XF-86 stalled and dropped away in a savage spin.

"Right, full military power, all engines, turning and burning. We've got some altitude to get back."

It took twenty minutes to regain the altitude lost in the persecution of the fighter pilot. Then, *Texan Lady* finished her scheduled flight plan and set course for her temporary duty base. A few minutes into their descent, Ground Control came back on the air. "*Texan Lady*, this is Range Control. For your information, the XF-86 recovered at 22,000 feet and landed safely. "The voice took on an ominous tone. "And General LeMay wants to see the cockpit crew in his office, immediately on landing."

General LeMay's Office. Nevada Test and Experimental Area

"Yabama Mat. You put the accent on the wrong syllable." LeMay's eyes bulged in astonishment. Nobody had ever interrupted one of his tirades before, let alone to correct his pronunciation. Before he could resume his verbal incineration of *Texan Lady's* crew, Pokryshkin carried smoothly on. "And, if you will excuse me for saying so Sir, you wouldn't want to do that to my mother anyway. You've never met my mother, she's a sweet old lady but one day she was gathering wood in the forests and she was surprised by an amorous black bear, one that was feeling the needs of springtime as it were. The bear was about to have his way with her when he saw her face and he had to put a bag over her head first."

Dedmon felt an insane desire to laugh. Nobody, but nobody, had ever done this in Curtis LeMay's office before. Pokryshkin was standing to attention in from of the general's desk with a perfectly serious expression on his face, respectful, and simply attempting to give his General the information he needed.

LeMay turned away slightly for a second and put a drop of something in each eye. That was something known in SAC but never mentioned. General LeMay had bilateral Bell's Palsy, his face was being slowly paralyzed. It was in its early stages yet, the attacks rare and short-lived but they were slowly increasing in frequency and severity. One day, they would cease to be attacks and the general's face would be permanently paralyzed.

"Just what were you playing at?" LeMay's voice rasped with barely-suppressed fury. "You were endangering a multi-million dollar aircraft and seventeen lives with that showboating."

Before Dedmon could speak, Pokryshkin cut in again, still smoothly and elegantly. "General LeMay sir, you aren't a fighter pilot. I am, and I see things with a fighter pilot's eyes. To us, Sir, bombers are prey, things to be hunted and killed. That is all bombers are, prey to be hunted and killed. Sitting in *Texan Lady* this morning, I saw that this has not changed. The B-36 is prey and the fighters are hunting it. Now, the B-36 has advantages in the altitude that it flies at and its ability to turn at those altitudes. It has escaped the hunters by going where the hunters cannot go. Like a cat chased by dogs, it has found a tree and climbed up it. Now your B-36s are sitting on a branch of that tree looking down at the dogs below. But it is only a question of time before a bigger, stronger, faster, dog comes along and can jump up to where the cat sits."

General LeMay's furious anger had faded and he was listening to the Russian with professional attention. "Guards-Colonel, we have the B-60 coming. A jet-engined version of the B-36. Not quite so much range but faster and higher flying. Beyond that we have the B-52, faster and higher-flying still."

"Yes General, and so the cat moves to a higher branch. And still the dogs will catch it one day. And when it does, the cat will be torn apart. General, when we hunt bombers we have only one thing to think about at a time. First to find the bomber. Then to reach the bomber. Then to kill the bomber.

"Radar has solved the problem of finding the bomber. Oh I know how good your radio-electronic warfare equipment is but radar will still tell the fighters the bomber is coming and roughly where it is. Reaching the bomber is something we are working on now. We will solve that too. If the XF-86 and the MiG-15 don't achieve this, then the next generation will. Already we have an advanced MiG-15 on the drawing boards. Two years, perhaps three and the MiG-17 will be here at Red Sun. Killing the bomber? Once we have reached it that is easy. We have heavy cannon, we have rockets, already both our countries are working on practical air-to-air missiles. And through all this, the bomber just sits there, a passive target to be hunted.

"Over the last few weeks, the fighters have failed again and again but they are still the hunters and the B-36 is still the hunted, passive, waiting to be killed. Today, for the first time, it was different. A bomber attacked the fighter. Look at the films in the cameras. The pilot of the XF-86 didn't know what to do. He panicked because this had never happened to him before. Bombers do not attack fighters, only today one did. His reaction was the same as a tiger who has just been bitten by a rabbit. He thought, this cannot be happening. Sitting where I was, I could see that the solution to his problem was simple, all he had to do was dive away, pick up speed and come back after us before we could have climbed to safety. He did not think of doing that. Because that would have been a fighter conceding victory in a dogfight to a bomber and he could not do it.

"Sir, if the bomber has the ability to attack the fighters, that complicates the task of the fighter very greatly. The fighter pilot must not only think of attacking the bomber, he must think of defending himself as well. The GB-36 and the F-85 are steps in that direction but there are bigger and better ones to be made."

"Guards-Colonel, we built a version of the B29 as an escort bomber. The YB-41, we doubled its armament, gave it multiple quad-fifties. Some even had twin or quad 20mms. The Germans got them all. Shot them all down. Every one of them."

"I know the YB-41 General. I saw some of them go down. For all their extra guns, they were just prey. A bit tougher, a bit harder to kill but still prey. They were passive and they died. I believe the key is an active defense. A bomber that can take the fight to the fighters. Your strategic reconnaissance B-36s map enemy defenses, why should they not attack them as well?"

"How can a bomber take the fight to the fighters." LeMay's voice was a bullying derisive sneer. "Loaded down with fuel and bombs, how can it. You were lucky today, you had a fighter that was almost helpless. How can a bomber have the performance to fight a fighter?"

"It can't General. So we build the performance into the weapon, not the aircraft."

LeMay's expression didn't change, it couldn't. Bell's Palsy saw to that. But if he had been able to, his jaw would have dropped open. It was an elegant concept, one that would solve problems far into the future. Build performance into the weapons. Arm the bombers with the new air-to-air missiles. Use the strategic reconnaissance aircraft to blast a path through the defenses so the bombers would have a clear ride. It wasn't just elegant, it was brilliant.

Red Sun had been designed to develop fighter defenses against bombers like the B-36 yet it looked like the first big lesson was one that would greatly increase the threat, not develop a counter to it. His mind started to gallop ahead. The new strategic reconnaissance aircraft would have to be fast, relatively agile, flexible so it could counter whatever unknowns a defense could throw at it. Something that could trick the enemy into engaging it, then destroy whatever the enemy threw up A real hustler of an aircraft. Then, he put that idea away for another time when he had an opportunity to think.

The Russian was still standing in front of him, his expression still one of polite helpfulness. "Guards-Colonel, you have made your point. And *Texan Lady* made hers. Tell me, Pokryshkin, just what does it take to intimidate you Russians?"

Pokryshkin returned the baleful stare, glare for glare. "General, Sir, you really never have met my mother have you?"

General LeMay shook his head. "Dismissed,. Get out the whole lot of you before I change my mind and bust you all to Airman Basic."

Outside, Dedmon sighed and relaxed against the wall. "Alex, thank you. I thought we were doomed for sure."

Pokryshkin did his best to look solemn and dutiful. "If necessary, it is the duty of the fighter to die in the defense of the bombers they are sworn to protect." Then his face broke into a grin. "Besides, communism did my country immense harm but it had one great virtue. The threat of facing an NKVD interrogator taught every good Russian to think on his feet."

Dedmon chuckled, more with relief than anything else. "Come on Alex, I'll buy you a beer or six. I have to ask though, did your mother really have a run-in with an amorous bear."

"In a way. She was attacked by a bear once but there was no harm done. She punched it out." Pokryshkin looked at the Americans sideways, to see if they'd fall for it.

"Uh huh." Dedmon's voice was skeptical. "Tell us about it. Over beers."

Portsmouth Naval Base, Great Britain.

"Oh no! Not her too!" Commander Fox had been let through the main gate of Portsmouth Royal Naval Dockyard and had walked along the wide road leading up to the base's administrative area. In a way, he'd been pleasantly surprised by the city. The stories had been that it had been bombed to a flat ruin, the few remaining people living in wooden-covered holes in the ground. It hadn't been that bad, not quite. The buildings had been shot up, strafed, bombed, rocketed, but enough of them survived to make the city livable. It was even a shadow of its former self, the Pompey of old, the sailors dream and the Master-at-Arms nightmare was still there. Getting off the train and walking down to the road that lead to the base, he'd felt quite cheered. Then, he'd turned the corner to see this.

Victory was still sitting in her concrete basin but her masts were down and there was a blackened hole almost dead amidships. Even from a distance, Fox could see where fire had curled out through the gunports and licked at her sides. Almost without wanting to, almost not wanting to, Fox broke into a run. The other side of the ship was as bad as he'd feared. It must have been one of the big rockets, the ones the Americans called Tiny Tim. It had blown out almost a third of the ship's side and sprayed the wood fragments over half the yard. A gaping, savage exit wound surrounded by the black infection of fire.

"Why her? She wasn't of any war value. Why did they have to do for her as well?" Fox's voice was anguished, almost a wail, carrying around the dockyard. It caused people to stop and look and that motion caused Fox to compose himself. By the time he had managed it, one of the workmen had come over to him.

"Now don't you take on so Sir. She's not as bad hurt as she looks, honest. We'll get her fixed up again."

"What happened.... sorry, I don't know your name."

"It's Thomas, Sir. It was Americans, one of them bent-wing bastards. Corsairs. Wasn't his fault either really. They were hitting the storage buildings down the way. Couple of old destroyers were tied up down there and they were going for them as well. The Huns had flak all around of course and they'd put a twin-30 on the building over there, that one Sir. You can still see the hole where it was. It got the Yank as he came over the rooftop from the river. He must have been hit just as he fired 'cos his nose dropped and one of the rockets hit the old girl. She burned Sir, but some of the mates, well we got hoses and sand on her and we put it out before she went up proper. If you want to see the one that done it, the wreck's still down there a bit. Burned out of course. Pilot rode it in."

Fox shook his head. It seemed so pointless, it hadn't even been done deliberately. If it had, if there had been a reason for it, even if it had been for the sheer joy of destruction, perhaps it would have seemed a little less cruel. But for the old girl to get gutted like that, by accident, by a pilot aiming at something else and a flak crew trying to stop him, it was a wanton act of fate.

Without even sensing it he thanked Thomas and wandered away, drifting towards the river that lay the other side of the line of warehouses. Then, looking across the river, he saw where the stories of the destruction of Portsmouth had come from. Pompey had survived, just, but Gosport hadn't. Where Gosport had been was a flattened desert, only relieved by the square structure of the great German submarine bunker. Twice the size of the one at Faslane, a bombproof structure for two dozen U-boats and the stores needed to keep them running.

The workman had followed him. "Aye, a grim sight isn't it. Yanks did that too, last day of the war. Same time as they atom bombed Germany near enough. At least two dozen of them big bastards they say, flying so high nobody could see them. Dropped a thousand tons of bombs in a minute so they say. One minute it was all there, just the way it had been, the next it had all gone. Could feel the ground shaking all over Pompey. Us, Huns, U-boat crews, their folks, our folks, everybody just gone. There's nothing left over there now. Only that damned concrete tomb right in the middle. Smashed Gosport to hell the Yanks did but the U-boat pens survived."

Thomas looked as if he wanted to curse somebody but didn't know who. The Americans perhaps who'd brought such destruction? Or the Germans who'd brought the American bombers down on Gosport? Or Halifax who'd brought in the Germans? Or the politicians who'd brought in Halifax? Or the people whose votes had brought in those politicians. In the final analysis, had the people of Gosport brought the B-36s down on their own heads? Surely that couldn't be right or fair. Just who was to blame? Or was nobody to blame, was the whole nightmare just the results of blind chance and evil fate?

Fox sat on a concrete bollard, looking over the gray, stained river towards the moonlike plain where Gosport had been. Sitting in the concrete bunker was HMS *Thule*, shortly to become HMAS *Thule*. A modernized, streamlined T-boat that would be his command the moment he signed his transfer to the Australian Navy. He'd take her out and Julia would follow on one of the liners and they'd meet up again out there. Somewhere fresh where they could make a new start, build a future. He'd come down to Portsmouth for no other reason than to sign those papers and look at *Thule*

Fox felt the breeze freshen slightly and he caught a slight hint of burned timber. He felt it was from *Victory* but probably it wasn't. There were enough burned buildings around here to make up the numbers. There was something else on the breeze, a smell of fresh timber. He turned around and saw a cart was unloading wood, good English oak, beside *Victory*. Some was being carried inside and he could hear the sounds of saws and hammers. Even as he watched, damaged timber was carried out and lengths of new wood carried in to replace it.

It occurred to him that *Victory* was a good allegory for England itself. Smashed, broken, burned, wrecked by friends and enemies alike. Yet still, despite all the odds, despite all the hardship, people were at work putting the pieces back together again. Rebuilding what could be rebuilt, replacing what could be replaced, making do where neither was possible. Making the best of what they had left.

He couldn't leave, Fox thought, it would be deserting. But he had his own life, he'd survived eight years of a war that had killed most of his class-mates. Wasn't that enough? And Julia deserved a proper life, one where she could have some of the things she deserved. Including a future and a family. Fox sat, staring alternately at the ruins of Gosport and the slow work on *Victory*, the arguments surging backwards and forwards in his mind. As soon as he made a decision, one way or the other, the losers retreated, regathered and surged back, swinging him the other way.

Fox sat on his bollard, unaware of the hours that were passing and the soft gray dusk that was slowly closing in on him. A lonely figure, torn by his indecision and the weight that was pressing down on him. Britain or Australia? When night fell, he was still sitting there, his face in his hands, and still he had not made his decision.

Headquarters, Second Karelian Front, Riga, "The Baltic Gallery"

"Vodka!" Rokossovsky's voice held a quiet air of desperation.

"Lord God Yes, for the love of mercy, Vodka!" Rommel's voice shared the desperation and added a touch of incredulity. Across the table from him, Rokossovsky banged the surface with his fist. Two of his women came in with a bottle of real vodka, not the home-brew that seemed to appear every time a Russian Army unit halted for a few minutes. One moved slightly faster than the other and got her glass in front of the Russian first.

"Thank you Anya." Rokossovsky looked at the other girl then at Rommel. The girl shook her head and his hand dropped to his pistol holster. The girl shrugged and sat by Rommel, pouring him a glass of the clear liquid. Rommel understood the silent conversation as if it had been spoken in German. "Sit with the German and pour his drinks." "Over my dead body." "That can be arranged." "Oh, all right then."

"Erwin, let us drink to insanity. There is so much of it in the world."

"To insanity, Konstantin. Yours, ours and most especially, theirs." Both men burst out laughing, the tension released. Neither of them was in any doubt who 'they' were. They touched glasses and drained the contents, the two girls refilling them as soon as they touched the table.

"Four governments, four different sets of boundaries, every one of them claiming to be the only true representative of the Polish people. This set want the pre-1939 borders, that set want some that haven't been seen since the 17th Century. We should have known this would happen Erwin, we both have Polish troops in our armies."

"Yes my friend. And if we give mine to that lot, every one of them will be dead by dusk. And if we give yours to those maniacs down there, all of yours will be the same. They'll probably kill everybody. I wonder who they hate more, you, us or each other?"

Rokossovsky thought for a moment. "They all hate you more than they hate each other. Two of the four hate us more than they hate the other two, the remainder hate the others more than they hate us. And its not just us. You heard the Czechs and the Slovaks are at each other's throats? Their threats are words only, now, but words will become reality in time unless somebody stops it. So what are we to do?"

Rommel shrugged, he'd done better than he'd expected. He had succeeded in buying the freedom for some of his men by accepting the fate of others. Using the deaths of the bad to buy the lives of the not so bad. After five years fighting on the Eastern Front, he'd gained the reputation of the man who could pull the unexpected out of nothing but this maze was beyond him. Rokossovsky was grinning broadly. Rommel knew he was missing something.

"Erwin, if all our men will die, yours, mine, no matter which of the four we hand them over to, what do we do?"

"Find somebody else of course. But who? We've sent so many people out that there are few people left who'll take more. The South Africans have offered refuge but we're still running short of places."

"Erwin, if one doesn't want any of the four horses in a race to win the solution is obvious. Bring a fifth horse."

"Not another Polish Government, Konstantin?"

"And why not? All the Polish troops on both sides know that they'll get massacred if they get released to one of the existing juntas. But, we bring in a fifth government, one that's been carefully prepared and knows that its chance of survival depends upon it exploiting all those men, the ones from your Polish divisions, the ones from ours, then we've got a chance. Its a tripod, the fifth government depends on the troops for its survival yet, independently, the two sets of troops don't quite have the strength to do the job. Together, the three parts will have the strength to put down the other four governments but each part, the government and the two sets of troops know that if one side lets the tripod down, they'll all go down. Anyway, its better that way, a balance of power is good in a situation like this."

Rommel shook his head. It was a brilliant scheme, risky but brilliant. If it worked it could set up a stable Poland quickly. The four pretender governments would have no chance against the combined forces of the Polish troops released from the German and Russian armies. Fighting together, restoring order to the country instead of enduring a never-ending four-sided civil war, might just heal some old wounds. "Konstantin, that's brilliant. Of course, your fifth government will give you the borders in Eastern Europe you want."

"Of course."

"I'd guessed that. Who thought of this scheme? Zhukov?"

"No, his predecessor."

"STALIN! He's dead." Then a horrible thought struck Rommel. "He *is* dead isn't he?"

Rokossovsky looked as if he was going to say something and had quickly changed his mind. "I think so; you're in a better position to know than I am. You commanded the troops that made the final assault on Moscow. Did you ever find his body? The story is he died fighting as a private soldier. But there are rumors......"

"We looked, we never found any bodies that looked like his. But you know street fighting, most of the dead were hard to recognize. The stories were all the same though, then and for years afterwards, he died fighting as an infantryman. We've always assumed that was the case."

"So do those of us who don't know for sure and those that do say nothing. But Stalin anticipated this situation and set the scheme in motion. We have governments trained for the countries that are strategically essential to us. The original set were communist of course, they met with accidents or resigned. The ones we have now are, how shall we say, more national, in outlook but will still see things our way."

"Konstantin, this Government you're sending to Poland. Will all the troops you're releasing to it be Polish?"

Rokossovsky's grin became positively feral. "That, Erwin, would be telling."

Manager's Office, Simonstown Branch of the Bank of Pretoria, South Africa.

"Now, how can I help you, Mister McMullen."

John McMullen started. To him, bankers had been far-off figures, remote entities that dealt with others. To be addressed politely by one was a strange and disquieting feeling.

"Well, its like this. My missus and I have just got off the boat from England and we've got this draft from the Government. They said I had to see a bank so it could be converted into real money again."

That part had made McMullen nervous. He'd given the Embassy in London all his English money and been told there would be a draft for the South African equivalent waiting for him. He'd been worried about that, how was he to know that he would see it again. The memories of his bonuses paid promptly without argument had swayed him and he'd accepted the deal. Sure enough, when he and his wife had landed, the draft had been waiting for him.

"Ah yes. Of course. We handle many of these for our new residents. How are you settling in?"

"Pretty well, thanks. We have a place in the new arrivals hostel while we look for a place of our own. And I started work Monday. At the shipyard."

"Good, good. Thinking of buying a place? Very wise. Right Mister McMullen, I have your draft here. Its made out in Sovereigns of course. The financial section of the Embassy in London converted the money you gave them into sovereigns for us. We'll check that of course. Then we'll convert your sovereigns into rand for you and you will have your money. You know, you've timed your trip just right. There were some currency movements while you were at sea and I think you've probably made a pretty penny on the exchanges."

"Sovereigns? What are they? How did they get into this." McMullen's voice was suspicious and a little alarmed. The comment about buying a house had caught him off-guard. When he'd said find a place of their own, he'd meant rent one. That's what he'd always done. The idea of actually owning a house was strange.

The bank manager sighed, Inaudibly and invisibly but still sighed. That was the trouble with immigrants, especially the ones from England. They just weren't familiar with banking and how money moved around.

"Mister McMullen, when England made its agreement with Germany in 1940, they effectively dropped out the Commonwealth. They were still there in name, but the rest of the Commonwealth wouldn't talk to them. The problem was that before the war, the pound was the standard currency in the Commonwealth. Essentially, all the Commonwealth countries formed a pool and negotiated currency movements as a block. Gave them much greater strength in the market you see. And the Germans moving into England kicked the center out of that system. Nobody would touch the pound and nobody knew what a rupee or a rand was. The currencies went into a tailspin. Their value went to almost nothing.

"So the Commonwealth countries got together and created a new pool currency. The sovereign. Backed by South African gold and diamonds. Its the standard currency of all the ex-Empire countries now, Commonwealth and non-Commonwealth alike. To move currencies from one country to another, the local currency is converted to sovereigns at source then the sovereigns converted to the new local currency at destination. The sovereign pool negotiates the value of the sovereign against the U.S. dollar as a block, then they negotiate the rates of exchange of their individual currencies against the sovereign individually. Its not the best possible system but it works and setting that up in the middle of the war was hard enough."

While he'd been speaking, the bank manager had been looking up numbers and cranking an adding machine.

"Right, well, since you started your journey, currencies have moved because we left the Commonwealth and because of the fighting in Thailand. You got more sovereigns for your pounds as a result, and quite a few more rand for your sovereigns. It looks like you made around 15 percent on the deal while you were at sea."

"What? But I didn't do anything. It can't be right."

"Actually you did, you just didn't know it. You invested your money and made a profit on the investment. Actually, it was a safe deal because the Government guarantees your money. If the currency movements had gone the other way, they'd have made good the loss."

"Well, shouldn't they get the profit then? Don't seem fair."

"Mister McMullen, let me give you a word of financial advice. Never even think about giving the Government any more money than you absolutely have to. Now, what are your plans?"

"We're going to get a place of our own, said that, then I want to start up a metal working shop. I'm a riveter see, made a friend at the yard who's a welder and he's got a mate who's a steelworker. We set up together we can do jobbing metalwork, cover us for the times there's no work at the yard."

"Getting your own house first, then starting a business eh. Good plan. Get bricks and mortar of your own first, then start up the business. You've got a good down payment on a house here, and with a steady job, there'll be no problem giving you a mortgage for the rest.

Then, once you're a property owner, the bank will see no problem in lending you the money for a start up. Very wise planning Mister McMullen, lot of people would have gone the other way, set up the business first and thought about a house later. That's not nearly so good from a planning perspective. Got a house in mind yet?"

"No Sir. Not yet."

"We've got a good property department here. Bring your wife in and you can look through the books. Buy a property we're brokering and you'll save a lot on fees.

"Now, in the meantime, might I suggest you put your money in a deposit account so it can work for you while you're looking? Our Golden Opportunity account can pay you three and a half percent and you can withdraw the money any time you like. Alternatively there's our Diamond Stake scheme. You promise to leave the money with us for six months and we'll pay you five and a half percent. All figures for a full year of course. By the way, I'm not Sir. Call me Mike. And you're John?"

"Aye, John. Well thank's Mike. The Golden Opportunity sounds good. Can I see my money?"

"Come with me." As he lead McMullen down to the vault, the manager grinned to himself. They all asked that and the bank had a pile of gold sovereigns they showed to the people who made the request. It was so much simpler than trying to explain paper deposits and reserve movements.

"There you are John. Soon as you sign the papers, it'll start to work for you."

"Got just one question Mike. How many people have you told that pile of coins belongs to them? Not complaining, just asking."

Changi Airport, Singapore

Runway lighting was a wonderful thing for sure. It had already taken Sir Martyn Sharpe's Lockheed Constellation seven and a half hours to cover the 2,500 miles from New Delhi to Singapore. A few years earlier, they would have had to wait overnight at a waypoint to avoid landing in darkness. No, that wasn't true, a few years earlier, he wouldn't have been able to make the trip at all. The war had brought about some startling changes in airliners. Well, American airliners anyway. Now, there was the Constellation for speed and the Cloudliner for range. Sir Martyn blessed Air India's decision to get the Constellation first, it was over eighty miles an hour faster than the Cloudliner, cruising at 330 miles per hour instead of the Cloudliner's 250. That speed difference took nearly three hours off the trip.

Out in the night, another set of navigation lights were twinkling. That would be Sir Gregory Locock's aircraft coming in. This meeting had been hurriedly arranged when the news of the fighting had broken out. Despite the war and some emergency cable laying, communications weren't as good as they could be, in fact they were pretty grim. That was something that would have to be addressed. This was something that should have been discussed directly before staging a meeting but the inadequate cable network just didn't allow it. Still, one thing had worked in their favor. Sir Greg had been in Darwin on a visit when the decision to stage an emergency summit meeting was made. That had put him only six and a half hours out from Singapore.

Now, after the exhausting flights and the flurry of cable messages, the meeting was about to start. Out in the midnight sky, Sir Gregory's aircraft was making its final approach, undoubtedly the pilot listening to the instructions from ground control. The runway lights started flashing, then the Australian aircraft touched down. Another Constellation, this one in the colors of the Royal Australian Air Force. The graceful airliner turned off the runway and headed for the parking stands where Sir Martyn's Connie was already being refueled.

"Sir Gregory, its good to see you again. How was your flight?" It had only taken a few minutes for Sir Gregory Locock to reach the airport terminal building. "I see you have a Connie as well?"

"Indeed so. A very good aircraft indeed Martyn, very good. A far superior machine to the old Handley Page Hercules we flew in back before the war. Hundred miles an hour, remember? We called it the built-in headwind. Now, there was reported to be turbulence in the Netherl.... in Indonesia...... so we just flew over it."

"There always seems to be turbulence in Indonesia these days. With the transitionary authorities trying to hold power in Jakarta and BUPKIS...."

"Ah yes, the Bahasa Ummah Partai Karya Indonesia Sejahtera." Sir Gregory rolled the polysyllabic words around his mouth with pleasure. "Who would ever have thought they would end up as the leading local light."

"After the Jakarta riots back in '46 I think it was fairly inevitable Greg. Once the Dutch went down in 1940, their rule out here was a rapidly-depleting resource. No fresh-faced young Dutchmen coming off the boat to replenish the ranks so they had to recruit replacements locally.

"American oil purchases for Russia kept them going economically, or at least the oil-producing areas but the rest of the country got hit by recession. Set virtually everybody at eachother's throats. Once the riots started in Jakarta, they spread all over the place. Old story. Family Bing has a feud with family Ching so they whip up a local riot and burn their house down. The Dutch couldn't control it no matter how much they wanted to.

"Damn it, we've still got troops in Bali and Lombok and you've got how many in Timor? We could all use them elsewhere. BUPKIS were just the guys who moved fastest, that's all. And they had the money from somewhere."

"Guess where." Greg's voice was dry.

"Directly? From the Chinese Great House trading companies of course. Indirectly?" Sir Martyn theatrically shaded his eyes and looked northwards towards Thailand. "BUPKIS is going to take over, we know it, they know it, the Dutch know it. The Dutch are just trying to hold out the for the best deal they can get. That stunt somebody pulled with the forged Constitutional Conference agenda didn't help. Compared with the problems that caused, everything else fades into insignificance."

"Not for us it doesn't. The eastern end of the island chain is Christian and they don't want to be part of a Moslem country. Very strongly, they don't want that. They want to break away and frankly I don't blame them. The Javanese don't want them to, they have ideas about re-establishing one of the old empires in the area. Without somebody stepping in from outside, there's going to be hell to pay. We've had gentle requests already from, eerrr, interested parties to establish a protectorate over an independent Moluccan state there."

"The Dutch?"

"Couldn't say. But probably, through intermediaries. The Dutch tried to get some sort of privileged status for their people but BUPKIS wouldn't hear of it. So now, they're trying to strike deals with the smaller islands, trying to buy themselves a haven. Timor and the Moluccas are Christian so I'd guess they tried there first. Your Hindus are a tolerant lot so that was probably choice two. But all the islands are at each others throats. You know that."

"And that's not so very far away from where the Huks are playing up in the Philippines. Damn it Greg, when the Germans took Britain out, the lifted the cork on the bottle of every regional issue out here. Now we've got this so called "border incident" blowing up in our faces. We've got pressure on us as well on the Indonesian thing. Bali and a few of the smaller islands are Hindu and the extreme nationalists want us to take them over. Or establish a "protectorate" as you so elegantly put it."

"I know. We've got a problem there we're going to have to talk about. But you're right about the whole situation here melting down. Martyn, you're not helping the situation you know. Everybody knows India's pulling out of the Commonwealth sooner or later. We're staying in, its the one thing that's holding this place together at the moment. Anyway, I don't think Australians will accept pulling out. Too much to lose, nothing much to gain by doing it. Seems like it would be stabbing the old country in the back as well. Anyway, the old Commonwealth's pretty much of a spent force. Won't much longer, once India's out, the Commonwealth's just a shell, out here at any rate."

"We've got to get out Greg. Look, the Hindu nationalists want power yesterday and, to be honest about it, they can make a pretty good case. Amritsar and all that. Only there isn't a class of top-level administrators yet. The lower-grade civil servants we've got are as good as we'll find but they just don't have the experience for running things at the top. There's got to be a phased handover, we've got to keep running things while we train our replacements. Thank God the Indian National Congress understood the problems."

Sir Martyn was quiet for a moment. Getting the INC to understand that an immediate handover of power in June 1940 was impossible had probably been his finest achievement. The INC had entered discussions wanting all the administration transferred to their hands and wanted it done immediately. He'd explained the problems to them, lead them carefully through the maze of economic, strategic and political hazards that bedevilled India in this crisis. He'd shown them how few solutions really offered themselves and how the very survival of India as an independent country was at stake.

The leader of the INC, Nehru, was many things but a fool he wasn't and he, like Sir Martyn, had India's best interests at heart. He couldn't have been more different from Sir Martyn in political outlook but he also had the strength of character to realize that it would need all their combined strengths and skills to weather the situation. As their discussions had continued they'd both realized that their different political beliefs had one common factor. They both loved India and wanted to see it great again. That realization had lead Nehru to accept that there had to be an interim stage, a gradual transition of power. But he'd also made it clear that power would change hands, sooner rather than later.

"Leaving the Commonwealth is the sort of political gesture that will allow us to do that. Publicly severing ties with Britain and the Commonwealth will give them enough to keep the INCs supporters quiet while we make sure the handover of the administration is smooth. Time, Greg, that's what we need and we're buying it. If we rush this transition, if we just pack up and hand everything over, there'll be civil war. The Moslems will pull out, try to set up their own state and they'll try and drive the Hindus out. With fire and sword and, believe me, there'll be plenty of both. The Hindus will hit back at the Moslems and there'll be hundreds of thousands of dead by the time its all over. And India will be split. We've got to avoid that, Greg, and leaving the Commonwealth is a small price to pay."

"For you, perhaps, for us is a disaster. We've got to have some sort of regional organization out here and if its not the Commonwealth, what is it going to be? What the devil........"

The lights in the airport building had flipped out. From the darkness outside, Sir Martyn guessed that the runway lights he'd admired earlier had also gone out. Almost simultaneously there was a roar overhead, two aircraft, perhaps more, flying very low overhead.

"What's happening, are we under attack? Surely the Japanese couldn't be thinking of....." Sir Greg was interrupted by two more low-flying aircraft. Sir Martyn chanced a look outside. Just turning off the runway was the dark, shadowy shape of a B-27, it's navigation lights out and its somber gray paint merging in with the background. Looking behind it, he could see two more shapes making their final approaches.

"No, Greg. We're not under attack. I think our old friend is making an uncharacteristically dramatic arrival."

He was right. As soon as the aircraft had landed, the lights came back on and the B-27 and the fighters were tucked away on the hard stand. It took only a few minutes before a familiar figure arrived in the lounge.

"Sir Martyn, Sir Gregory. I am pleased to see you. My apologies if our arrival caused disturbance but the Japanese had night-fighters up, Mitsubishi Ki-83 Ingas, and we had to fly down from Bangkok without lights."

"It is always a pleasure to see you Madam Ambassador. I trust you were not exposed to any danger?"

"No more than usual. One of the Ingas was a little too close but my Tigercat escorts got it. Japanese radar is still not very good and their night-fighters are very poor. I have four Tigercats patrolling overhead so it is unlikely that we will be disturbed. I would suggest that when you leave here, you head south as long as you can to get well clear before turning for home. I suspect Japanese aircraft will be very active tomorrow. We had air superiority all over the battlefield today, the Japanese will try and change that tomorrow."

"How does the battle go, Madam Ambassador? I was in Darwin and the only reports I have are very outdated."

"The Japanese crossed at dawn. Two full infantry divisions. All we had along the border was militia. Civilians armed with shotguns and gunpowder muskets against trained infantrymen." She sighed. In reality it hadn't been quite that bad but it had been desperately close.

"They held the line just long enough for us to move a full infantry division up but they suffered terribly. If it hadn't been for the Ostriches flying close support, we would have been in desperate straits. But they did hold. In the east they stopped the Japanese advance, in the west we even pushed them back a bit. There's armor in that bulge somewhere but the Japanese haven't committed it yet.

"We think they're organized as four corps, each with two infantry divisions and an independent armored brigade. So far, they've probed with one of those corps. Depending on what happens to it, the others may cross or try to grind us up along the river. We've got to end it quickly, there's no way we can fight a long, drawn-out engagement against the whole Japanese Army."

Sir Gregory nodded sympathetically. "I understand how concerned you must be. We, too, are stuck with an unwanted and apparently unending troop commitment, in our case peacekeeping in Timor and the Moluccas. We even have a request from some of the interested parties to take that area under our wing and form it into an Australian Protectorate. We would like nothing more than for BUPKIS to agree to that arrangement and allow the Christian east to go their own way."

Although no trace of it showed on her face, the Ambassador felt an enormous surge of relief pass through her. As the news of the fighting had come in, she'd known that the one chance of her country surviving the Japanese assault was to get help from the allies she's spent two years cultivating. All day, she'd had the dreaded thought in the back of her mind, that it had all been for nothing. That Australia and India would leave her in the lurch to deal with the Japanese by herself. Now, Sir Gregory had laid out a bargaining chip, she knew that would not be the case. They would help, all that they were negotiating was the price of that assistance.

"Sir Gregory, would you have any objections if I was to speak with the BUPKIS leaders on your behalf? I may have some small degree of influence with them and I am sure that the grave number of pressing concerns that they feel need urgent attention will make them agreeable to the suggestion of the Christian areas seceding. After all, they have the intention of establishing an Islamic state and a large Christian minority would be an embarrassment to them."

And if it isn't, she would make sure it soon would be, thought Sir Gregory. "Madam Ambassador, we would be most grateful for any efforts you may feel able to provide in this matter. Our nations may be recent friends but I feel that we have so much in common that we should stand more closely together. Our links are of friendship and mutual respect and we both benefit economically from them."

"Speaking of economics Madam Ambassador." Sir Martyn picked up the opening smoothly. "I wonder if I might take this opportunity of mentioning another small matter. As you doubtless have heard, India will soon be leaving the Commonwealth and this will have a serious impact on the international strength of the sovereign. The effects on our international trade could be most worrying if this was to escalate. We already have such close economic links,

"I was wondering if Thailand had given any thought to joining the sovereign pool? I know the baht is currently linked to the U.S. dollar but so much of your trade is with India and Australia that it would ease the formalities greatly. And, of course, the sight of a non-Commonwealth country joining the sovereign pool would built great international confidence in our new currency."

"It is strange you should mention that Sir Martyn. My Government has had exactly the same thoughts concerning the value of the baht and our international trading arrangements. There would be great advantages for us all in linking the value of the baht to that of the sovereign."

None of which of course had any relation to international confidence she thought. The great weakness of the sovereign pool as compared to the old Pound Sterling was that the latter had used the Lloyds communications system as its nerve center. That had meant the currency was responsive and could accommodate changes on an international basis swiftly and effectively. None of the existing sovereign pool countries had anything like that capability.

But, Thailand was now host to the great Chinese trading corporations. They had their own communications system, one that was, in its way, as effective and flexible as the old Lloyds net. It was a different sort of net, one that ran by extended family relationships and the sort of unqualified trust that could only go with ties of blood in a culture that took family relationships very seriously indeed. A different communication systems from Lloyds indeed, but one that was there and one that worked. On a regional basis at least.

With Thailand in the Sovereign Pool, that communications system would work for the pool as a whole. And that meant her country would control the communications for the whole pool. Once again, Suriyothai was amazed by westerner's lack of foresight.

"That is very gratifying news Madam Ambassador, very gratifying indeed. I am sure that this will be of the greatest benefit to us all."

"That is our most sincere wish Sir Martyn, indeed we had hoped to make the announcement already but this wretched border incident has delayed everything. As soon as it is concluded, the financial markets will be informed of the new arrangements."

"Madam Ambassador, I wonder if I may sound you out on an idea that has come to us." Sir Gregory's voice was thoughtful and tentative. "Before your dramatic arrival, Sir Martyn and I were exchanging opinions on the state of affairs in this part of the world. We found ourselves to be in agreement that the effective collapse of the British Commonwealth has left this region in a most dangerous, indeed I am forced to say a completely unacceptable, state of instability. There is a pressing, nay desperate, need for a new form of regional organization to take over the role of stabilizing relations.

"Madam Ambassador, Sir Martyn, I think that since the three of us have shown we have so many interests in common and we are so well attuned to each other's interest and priorities, we might well form the core of such a new regional stability-enhancing organization."

"What do you have in mind, Sir Gregory?"

"Nothing complex, such things are best kept simple. I had in mind a mutual defense pact between our three countries, one in which any attack by an outsider on one of the members would be considered an attack on all three. Should one member of the pact be attacked, the other two would automatically come to its aid."

"Greg, the problem is that even if we had such an alliance, the three of us together don't have the ability to counter Japan."

"No Martyn, we don't. But if the three of us stand together, any attack on one of us means a large-scale war breaking out. And that is one thing the Americans have made very clear they will not permit. We don't intend to attack anybody so that doesn't worry us. But it does mean that anybody who attacks one of us will be attacking all three and that is an event big enough to bring the wrath of the Americans down on their heads."

The three nodded their heads slowly, each measuring the probabilities inherent in the new arrangement. After a few minutes, Sir Gregory continued. "Madam Ambassador, there is one problem. We can't make this fly until the border incident presently in progress has been resolved. You must restore the border by your own efforts. Once that is done, we can prevent any follow-on attack. Can your country do that."

Suriyothai thought for a second, no more than that. "Yes. We are moving the forces into position. We can do that."

"Then we have an agreement. Only one decision left. What do we call this new organization. The Changi Pact?"

Sir Martyn snorted. "Greg, that sounds like a treatment for an unmentionable type of disease."

"Or its symptom. And the term pact is in disrepute these days." Suriyothai thought for a second. "How about the South East Asian Treaty Organization?"

Sir Martyn shook his head. "Too clumsy Madam. But you are right about Pact. Look, there are three of us. Why not call the new agreement The Triple Alliance?"

There was another measured nodding of heads in agreement. After some discussions thrashed out the remaining details, the ambassador took her leave. Simple prudence dictated she had to be back in Thailand before dawn. After she left, Sir Martyn stretched out his feet. "You know, Greg. I've got a feeling we just bullied that poor defenseless woman into accepting everything she ever wanted."

Chapter Four
Consequences

The rifle bolt wouldn't fit back in. The private was struggling with it but it just wouldn't slide into place. Lieutenant Sirisoon took the bolt from his hands and looked around. Fortunately what she needed was close by. A hard, flat surface. She hooked the cocking piece over it, took a breath then pushed down hard and twisted. The firing pin spring compressed and the cocking piece slid into place. She flipped the safety into the upright position and relaxed. The rest was easy. The bolt slid smoothly back into place.

"Soldier, you must make sure the rifle is cocked and the safety in the upright position before you remove the bolt. Otherwise you can't get it back in." She looked more closely at the soldier. He was the one who'd had trouble with his ammunition pouches that afternoon. "Let me see your pouches." The cardboard ammunition box was stuck to the leather. She levered it free. As she'd suspected, the leather was dry and hard, the surfaces rough as heavy-grade sandpaper. "Sergeant, a word if you please."

She and Sergeant Yawd walked away from the soldiers. "Sergeant, I don't have to say it do I?"

"No, Ell-tee. I let it slide. My fault. No excuses."

"Check around the barns, there may be some leather polish for the animal harnesses." The animals wouldn't need it, that was for certain. Tong Klao had owned three water buffalo. All were in the barns, dead, bayoneted and shot by the Japanese. "If so, get the inside of those pouches polished. If not, store the ammunition in them without the box, the rounds will rattle but at least they won't get stuck again. Meanwhile, I'll be away for a few minutes."

"Sure thing Ell-tee. Pak, over here. Go with our Ell-tee."

"Sergeant, that's..."

"Ell-tee, it'll be the same for everybody. Its night and the Japanese own the night. We've got a nice tight perimeter and we're ok inside it but as sure as death and taxes, there are Japanese infantry prowling around out there. Looking for people they can lift for tactical intelligence. Nobody goes anywhere alone. Not me not you. Nobody."

Sirisoon nodded and sought a patch of ground away from the bulk of the unit. Her business finished, she rejoined the platoon just as the pickets watching the road to the rear of Tong Klao sounded an alarm. A few seconds later she saw why. There was a truck convoy coming up the road, lights out. She'd placed two of her three RPG-2s covering that road, the third was covering the forward arc. Now, both of those RPGs would be trained on the trucks. To her relief they were the unmistakable shape of American six-by-sixes. Thai Army. Replacements. Then a chilling thought struck her, there might also be her replacement on board.

The trucks pulled into her perimeter, the machine guns and RPGs still covering them. Figures started jumping out, ten, fifteen, twenty, twenty five. Her heart leapt upwards, no officers. Precious few NCOs as well and those she could see were corporals. Another cheerful thing, she recognized the stubby 60 millimeter mortars and counted at least three more MG34 machine guns.

"Lieutenant. We need to talk." It was the company commander she'd met earlier that morning.

"Sir." They didn't exchange salutes, no point in making a sniper's job easier.

"Some bad news for you. We're getting reinforcements and replacements but we're desperately short of officers and NCOs. The few we're getting have to go to units that lost theirs. I'm going to have to ask you to stay out here a while longer. I know you're admin but you did a fine job this afternoon. Good news is I've brought you your replacements. I can take out your wounded and you'll be up to strength.

"In addition, I'm augmenting your unit. Some of the replacements we got included three machine gun crews, I've giving them to you and I'm also giving you one of my mortar sections, two 60mm mortar crews, detached from the company mortar battery. I don't know how you want to organize the additions, as a second weapons section, whatever. I'm boosting you for another reason as well. I want you to take point again tomorrow."

"Again Sir?"

"Yes, again. Look, I'll be honest. Today we put you out as point because you were expendable. A newbie replacement unit. Tomorrow, I want you out there because this unit has proved itself. You've proved yourself. General Chaovalit and General Songkitti have been told of your action this afternoon. I can tell you this, you and your platoon have been Mentioned in the Dispatches. Tomorrow is going to be critical and I want the best I've got out there."

"Thank you Sir. Thank you very much."

"Don't thank me, after tomorrow you might not be feeling so grateful. You're holed up here for the night?"

"Yes Sir."

"Wise move. The Japanese are too good at night fighting for us to chance anything. The whole division is hunkering down for the night, we'll start moving at dawn. I want you to push along this road here." The Company Commander got out a map covered with lines. "This is your map for tomorrow. See the phase lines? Its critical, say again critical, you do not charge past them. Get to each line, radio in and hold until you get permission to move to the next. I can't stress this strongly enough. Do not pass a phase line without getting clearance. Do you understand?"

"Yes Sir. Phased advance holding at each phase line until given clearance to move further."

"Good. As far as I know, you'll be engaging part of the same battalion you chewed on today. Our guess is they'll have tank support tomorrow. You won't. Nor will anybody else. We haven't got any tanks to support you with. By the way I hear you captured a sword and a battle flag?"

Sirisoon grinned and pulled the sword out from its scabbard over her back, handing it to the Company Commander hilt first. He looked at it and whistled. "It's a beauty. You want me to take care of it for you? I'll send it to General Songkitti for safe keeping. Sergeant Major? My pad please." The Sergeant Major handed him an order pad. The Company commander wrote out a quick description of the sword and scabbard and signed it. "Here, this will act as your receipt. Kick off, 0500 tomorrow. And well done Lieutenant."

The trucks pulled out, leaving her watching the road while the new arrivals milled around. "Sergeant Yawd?"

"Yes Ell-tee?"

"Assign the replacements, bring first section up to strength as top priority and then the rest. We have some reinforcements, including three extra machine gun crews. I want one assigned to each of our rifle sections, reorganize each section as two gun teams, an MG34 crew and four riflemen each. One grenade launcher to each team. We'll add our new mortars to the weapons section. Get the men as rested as possible. Tomorrow is going to be a long day. I want everybody up and in defense positions at 0330." She dropped her voice. "We're kicking off at dawn, 0500. If I was the Japanese commander out there, I'd guess that and try a pre-dawn spoiling attack. If he gets that idea, let's have a nice surprise waiting for him. I'll take first watch." Sergeant Yawd cleared his throat. "Sergeant?"

"Ell-tee, Guard tonight is Sergeant's work. You get some sleep. We'll wake you if anything starts."

Ostrich Djiap-One, over the Mekong River, Thai/Japanese Indochina Border

The Japanese engineers had used the night well. The wide, sluggish, muddy Mekong River already had two bridges across it at this point and there were probably others lower down. That was somebody else's business. The six Ostriches under Flight Lieutenant Phol Thongpricha had these as their target. First three aircraft would hit the bridge on the left, the others would hit the bridge on the right. With a little luck they'd get some of the armor the Japanese were reported to be bringing over the river.

"Take them down!" Djiap-One made a wing-over and started its long dive on the bridges below. He'd elected to make his approach along the length of the bridge, using the freshly-cut scar of the road as a marker and, hopefully planting the bombs and rockets along the bridge. It was a gamble but a calculated one. The errors in bombing were much more often those of range rather than deflection, a lengthwise run would mean multiple hits and massive damage. A crosswise run meant fewer hits, even at best. And there was always a chance of hitting the engineers as well.....

The big Ostrich started lurching as black puffs appeared all around it. Probably 75mms at a guess, Type 88s or Type 4s most likely. Probably the former, overnight the two divisions that had crossed the Mekong had been identified as the 143rd and 324th Infantry divisions, both Manchurian Army outfits. That meant they'd seen little fighting in China and the Japanese Army didn't send units replacements. They ran a unit into the ground then rebuilt it. So these divisions would be up to or beyond paper strength. The Japanese didn't re-equip units either. When a division was formed or rebuilt, it got what the factories were producing, for good or ill, and that was it. So the unattrited Manchurian Divisions would have a lot of men and equipment but little of it would be new. So probably Type 4s.

The bridge below was growing fast, stretched like a ribbon over the dirty brown of the Mekong. The pipper on the bomb sight built into the Ostrich's nose was just touching the roadway where it transitioned to the bridge. Phol held it there, watching the ribbon swell and widen underneath him. He was totally focused on his bridge now, ignoring the sounds and sights around him. Then, as the bridge raced towards him, he squeezed the bomb release. The two 500 kilogram bombs under his belly went first, followed by the four 250 kilogram weapons under his inner wings.

Then his nose seemed to race along the bridge as he pulled the nose up. Sure enough there were trucks and bulldozers on the

Indochina side of the river, the engineers that had put the bridge up over night. A pretty good engineering feat, thought Phol, and no good deed should ever go unpunished. He squeezed both firing buttons on his control stick and felt his Ostrich almost stop dead in midair as all ten guns opened up at once. The road in front of him vanished in a smoking cloud of red dust as the hail of 23mm and .50 caliber ammunition ripped up the laterite surface. And everything on it.

"Bridge is down. Both bridges down!" From the rear seat, Kusol Chale's words were almost a cheer. As he brought the Ostrich's nose around, Phol could see he was right, where the bridges had been was a boiling mass of black smoke, the shattered southern end of the wooden structures already sticking out. On the southern side, he could see more figures running around, vehicles trying to get clear. Including tanks, the squat, ugly little Japanese light tanks. They were a priority target and he started his dive towards them.

Again the lurch, marked this time by a shriek and screaming lines of fire as his eight RS-132 rockets leapt out in front of him. The tank laager seemed to vanish in the explosions but Phol had learned too much to assume that meant anything. Even the lightly-armored Japanese tanks needed direct hits to destroy them and the Russian-designed, Australian-made rockets just weren't that accurate. Time to go home, get another load.

"Laylas, Laylas!" Kusol's words slashed through the intercom. The gunner-observer spun his seat around on its mounting and shoved aft to man his 20mm gun. Behind the Ostrich formation, a group of shapes were diving on the ground attack aircraft, coming in fast, very fast. The swept wings immediately identified them. Kusol had been right, they were Japanese Army Laylas. More than 200 miles an hour faster than the Ostrich, fighters, not ground attack bombers. In other words, in any language, trouble.

"Laylas! Formation break up, everybody get down on the deck and run for it." Close to the ground, flying between the trees and down valleys, the Laylas couldn't use their speed. That way, the Ostriches stood a chance. Not for Djiap-Five though. The Laylas had closed dreadfully fast and three of them had concentrated on the extreme left hand aircraft. The rear gunners were all firing but their hand-held cannon just couldn't track fast enough to follow the Laylas and they hadn't saved Djiap-Five. It was going down in a long, gentle dive, both its engines trailing thick black smoke. Even as Phol watched, the dive steepened and ended in a rolling black and orange ball.

Then Phol heard the sound of Kusol's 20mm gun thudding. He pushed the nose down faster, trying to get into the safety of the treetops but they were far away and the Laylas were too fast. He felt Djiap-One lurching and shuddering as the 20mm guns on the Laylas ripped into its structure. If anything, the heavy armor on the Ostrich's belly made things worse, causing the fragments from the shells to bounce around inside, rather than exit through a thin skin. The control panel erupted into a sea of red and yellow warning lights an instant before Djiap-One rolled on its back and dived vertically into the ground.

F-72C Thunderstorm "Fan-Seven" 22,000 feet over the Mekong River, Thai/Japanese Indochina Border

It looked like the old P-47, that was for sure, but it wasn't. The Thunderstorm had an R-4360 engine rated at 3,450 horsepower, 1,150 more than the R-2800-63 in the P-47. It had contraprops to absorb all that extra power and, most importantly it had four 37mm cannons in its wings. Not the low-firing, low velocity M-4 that had armed the P-39 series but the later M-9, designed with all the experience of the brutal war in Russia and the combined skills of Russian and American armorers. Equally adapt at anti-tank and anti-aircraft worked, the M-9 had more than 50 percent greater muzzle energy than the M-4. That translated into range and hitting power. A lot more hitting power; there were few single-engined fighters that could take a hit from an M-9.

Yesterday, Squadron Leader Nual Hinshinant had been using his guns as ground attack weapons. The Japanese had crossed the Mekong and the Air Force had been thrown in to hold them while the Army moved up ground troops. Today was different. Early this morning, the Japanese Army Air Force had appeared in strength, creating chaos with the heavy Ostriches flying ground support for the troops. More than a dozen Ostriches had gone down said the reports, a lot more had been badly shot up. So now, the Thunderstorms were flying top cover, although what an F-72 could do against the jet-engined, swept wing Laylas, Nual couldn't guess. Third Wing was moving into Nakhon Phanom with its F-80s, perhaps they stood a better chance but even the F-80 was obsolete compared with the Layla.

A bright flash in the sun from up ahead. "Bogies, 1 o'clock high." The four Thunderstorms accelerated as the pilots applied power, climbing in an effort to gain altitude before they were spotted by the unknown enemy in the sky. They didn't manage it, not quite. Nual saw the lead fighter in the hostile formation, hostile because it was dark against the light sky and that meant it was painted gray and green, not the natural metal silver of the Thai fighters, change in shape and angle over. They'd almost made it though, the Thunderstorms might not have gained an altitude advantage but they'd denied it to the Japanese. The approach would be the classical start to a joust, head-on, balls to the wall, and then the first to lose their nerve broke right.

They almost collided head on in their stubborn determination not to be the one's to break. In the seconds as the two formations closed, Nual recognized his enemy. Gails, Ki-84 Hayate the Japanese Army called them. Radial engined, just like the Thunderstorm. Slower, but more agile, two nose-mounted 13mm machine guns, some carried a 20mm cannon in each wing, others replaced the single gun with a pair of 13mms. It was rumored some carried 20mm guns in the nose as well. The Japanese had never made much of standardization. Fast firing guns, to fill the sky with bullets but lacking the range and hitting power of the Thunderstorm's 37mms.

At the last second, Nual and his fighters broke right skidding away from the Japanese group. The Japanese didn't, not at once. They went upwards, the pilots hauling back on the stick, pouring in power from their engines, yanking the Gails upwards as if they were mounted on rubber bands stretching across the deep blue sky. Then, the Japanese formation broke, their leader arching over on his back, the rest bursting away as the Japanese pilots sought one-on-one combat with their opponents.

The unexpected maneuver had given the Japanese back the high bounce position, and their leader took full advantage of it. He was coming down on Nual in a beautiful pursuit curve, one calculated with all the expertise that the superbly-trained and exhaustively-experienced Japanese could manage. It let him pick the time and place to open fire on the clumsier Thunderstorm. The Japanese chose to close to point-blank range and threw a hailstorm of bullets at the swerving Thai fighter. He didn't try for accuracy in the swerving pass, but paddled his rudder backwards and forwards, filling the sky with bullets, saturating the area through which the Thunderstorm had to fly.

Almost by instinct, Nual looked at the Gail, counting the flashes, two on the nose, four in the wings. Six 13mm machine-guns. The Japanese had nailed him beautifully, he'd been outflown, outthought, outfought. There was only one way out and Nual took it, yanking back on the stick, slamming the controls over, pulling through the stream of fire in a crazy, tumbling maneuver that arced his heavy fighter up, out of the cone of fire and killing all his speed and energy in one crazy gyration. With all the speed and energy from his dive, the Japanese pilot couldn't match the insane aerobatics and he raced past, the pilot wondering how he could have missed.

He hadn't. Nual had felt a dull thump in his thigh, not a bullet because his leg still worked but something else. A fragment blown off the airframe? He jerked the stick over to the right and stamped a full right rudder, then swept the stick over to the left. The Thunderstorm went crazy from the opposing control inputs, spinning around its axis, tumbling in the sky, only the massive power of its big radial keeping it from stalling out completely. Nual felt himself bounce off the cockpit sides, the Thunderstorm was built for American pilots and its proportions were generous for Thais.

The Japanese was coming in again, his turn had been wide, dictated by speed, by gravity, by centrifugal forces. He was superb, forcing the combat to close range where his rapid-fire machine-guns had the advantage. Nual used tricks he'd never heard of, that nobody had thought of to keep out of the fierce attacks, each time gaining experience, gaining a little more of the measure of this terribly skilled adversary. His Thunderstorm lacked the agility to dodge and twist with his enemy but he had the speed and, given a chance, he could separate. Then the positions would change and his big 37s came into their own. Now, every time the Japanese set up for one of his slashing passes, Nual could lead his path of flight and a burst of 37mm shells would thump out. But it wasn't enough, the Japanese was a natural pilot, one for whom his fighter was an extension of his own limbs, his own thoughts and he would slip though the long-range bursts of fire with little damage and then the battle would change again, and Nual would once more be dodging the streams of machine-gun fire.

He had another problem, his fuel gauge was edging down slowly but surely into the red. The dogfight was a stalemate but only because his engine was at full power, gulping fuel. Sooner or later, he'd run out and the Thunderstorm would be a big, heavy, glider. Easy prey. Time for a last throw of the dice. The Gail was making another pass, the 13mm bullets surrounding the Thunderstorm. Then, the Japanese raced past him and Nual slammed full left rudder, stick over to the left, emergency power and full forward on the stick. As the Thunderstorm started to tumble, he reversed the rudder and stick and headed straight down, out of the fight in a whirling snap-dive. The Thunderstorm was big and it was heavy and it picked up speed fast in a dive. The Gail was following him down, the Japanese pilot grimly determined to catch the pilot who's nerve had clearly broken. *He was running from the battle. What sort of warrior was this?* Below him, the Thunderstorm had stopped receding and the two aircraft were holding position.

Then, the Thunderstorm started to grow in the Japanese pilot's sights, it had pulled out of its dive and was running straight and level. In his mirror, Nual could see the Gail following him down, a thin line of black smoke streaming from its exhaust as it tried to catch him up. Then, as he saw the bright flashes on the wings and nose of the Gail, he hauled back on the stick, throwing the aircraft in a vertical bank, reversing the turn as it started. The Japanese pilot tried to follow the turn but his speed was too great, in his determination to catch the Thunderstorm he'd let speed and energy and centrifugal force build up until they'd locked his aircraft on its course. Right past the nose of the Thunderstorm.

Nual took his time for the fight was over. His cannons thumped and the big shells struck home, one blowing the engine off its mounts, another smashing the fuel lines open, a third shredding the cockpit and everything in it. There were others as well but they didn't matter. The Gail was already exploding in mid-air. Nual pulled back, turning his aircraft away from the ball of fire that had once been the Japanese fighter.

Then, he looked around the sky, only to see it was empty. They'd gone, all of them, he was the only survivor. The score was four for three. Somehow, it didn't seem like a victory.

Short of Phase Line Execute, North of Tong Klao Village, Recovered
Provinces, Thailand

"How are your feet holding out?"

Private Kan's facial expression was a combination of relief and nervousness. He'd been one of two men who'd had trouble with their feet the day before, typical of garrison soldiers who'd spent to much time in barracks and not enough in the field. Not taking proper care of one's feet wasn't the worst sin an infantry man could commit, not quite, but it was certainly close.

"They're fine Ell-tee. *The stuff* worked fine but its gone and burned holes in my socks." A ripple of laughter swirled around the men in the group. The previous evening Sirisoon had noticed a couple of the men limping and made it her business to find out why. Then she'd produced a bottle of the Army's dreaded *stuff*, a lotion designed to cure the problems that afflicted soldier's feet. Like most army solutions, it was quick, violent and more than a little indiscriminate but also effective.

"You're lucky its only your socks. Had an Ell-tee once, stirred *the stuff* with his eating irons. Turned them green it did, then dissolved them. Had to spend the rest of the march eating with his fingers." Another ripple of laughter spread across the group. Sergeant Yawd smiled contentedly, a scratch platoon was settling down into a real team, even the repples who'd arrived the night before were finding their place. Of course, having an officer who knew what she was doing helped. Yawd stopped briefly, realizing the import of his casual thought.

"Sergeant, a word please." The two drifted away from the rest of the unit. "Company says we have to hold here. Hold if attacked but don't move forward to Phase Line Execute. Rest of the Company is on Phase Line Decimate two klicks behind us."

"What gives Ell-tee? What are the brass up to?" Sergeant Yawd looked at Sirisoon and saw the black pupil of her eyes contract almost to a dot. She was gone, her mind somewhere else. When she came back she would know exactly what was happening, why it was happening and what would happen next. A couple of the men had noticed it and there was a quiet whisper doing the rounds that their strange Ell-tee wasn't a human at all, that she was a pret, a ghostly spirit who had taken human form. One who could see the future and anticipate it.

That had come in eerily useful all morning. The Japanese Army Air Force had been up, over the battlefield with their light bombers. Mostly Harvs and Kens but there'd been reports of the new Oscar in other areas. Yesterday, it had been the Thai Air Force that had dominated the battlefield, today it had been absent and it had been the Japanese turn to lash at the ground troops with aircraft. Neither Harv nor Ken carried the devastating firepower of the Ostriches but they were there. The Ostriches weren't. Some of the Harvs had attacked Sirsoon's unit but she'd had a strange art of knowing when they were likely to appear and finding cover just in time.

"Its a converging advance, it has to be. We're pushing slowly forward and that's doing two things. One is its pulling the enemy forward onto us. The other is its making sure that the other limb of the advance doesn't crunch into us rather than the enemy. Standard drill for taking out a riverhead like this is to attack its flanks by the river. Pinch it off, surround it and destroy it. Has to be that, can't be anything else. Sergeant, do you see that, up by Execute?"

Phase Line Execute was the ridgeline up in front of them. The platoon was in front of the treeline, flanks extended to guard against one of the Japanese flanking moves. There was a long patch of level ground before the ridge rose, not high but enough to screen the ground the other side. As Yawd stared, he could see a faint trace of black smoke glistening in the morning sun. Could, just possibly be cooking fires but this was war and war wasn't that kind. That was diesel smoke and diesels meant. "Tanks."

"Tanks." Sirisoon said agreeably. "I wonder why they haven't attacked us yet. Must be waiting for something."

"Us to move forward? Catch us in the open?"

"Could be. They're in for a wait. Hold one." The radio had crackled with static for a second. Sirisoon held the headset to her ear, her eyes still fixed on the faint trace of smoke. "Received. Air raid warning get everybody down now. Nobody shoot, nobody move."

The radar, somewhere to the rear, had been right. There was a humming noise and a couple of the Japanese light bombers swept over. Harvs, Mitsubishi Ki-51s. There were a series of sharp cracks in the treeline as the 15 kilogram bombs went off. Lying down in the elephant grass, Sirisoon silently blessed the instructors who'd hammered home a basic lesson. Never set up in a treeline. If you want to fight close, set up inside the trees, if you want a clear field of fire, set up in front of the trees but never, ever set up on the treeline itself. Because that is where you'll be expected to set up.

More cracks, a bit closer, the Harvs were trying to get her unit to give their positions away. Then she thought again. They're not sure we're here at all. The rest of the company is behind us, they may be assuming that's the main body. More cracks, and a crackle of machine-gun fire. For a moment her heart stopped, had one of her men disobeyed and opened up on the aircraft that were taunting them? Then she relaxed, the machine-guns had been the heavy thump of the Japanese 13.2 millimeter, not the rasp of the MG-34. Cautiously sneaking a look, she saw the trace of smoke from over the ridge had thickened and turned into a distinct cloud.

"Here they come. On the word, mortars fire smoke. Machine-gunners spray the infantry, sieve them away from the tanks. I want those tanks blinded, when they come out of the smoke screen, RPG-2 gunners hit the center one. He'll be the platoon commander. Concentrate on him, take him down."

There was screaming and bugle calls from the ridge in front. Then, the Japanese swarmed over, a battle-flag flying in the center, the troops rolling forward in a khaki wave. Out in front of them were the tanks, three of them, light tanks. The Harvs were still circling overhead, waiting for her unit to reveal their position by opening fire. This, Sirisoon thought, was going to get bloody.

Ostrich Djiap-Eleven, over Phase Line Butcher, Thai/Japanese Indochina Border

"Cabrank, this is Cabrank. Am moving in support of Pony-Sirisoon." Flight Lieutenant Pondit frowned, that was right wasn't it. Pony was the code for a beefed-up infantry platoon, taking the point for the battalion. Sirisoon was the nickname of its commander. Thai names were so confusing to outsiders that they formed a perfect code system without any further assistance. But Sirisoon was a woman's name wasn't it? No matter, the call had come up the radio net with the speed and efficiency the Thais had perfected in the war with France seven years earlier.

Pony-Sirisoon was under attack by a combined tank-infantry-aircraft group. Now the Ostriches were streaking in to take out the enemy air cover and savage the ground units. If they lived long enough, early this morning the Japanese fighters had turned up in strength and the Ostrich units had been pummeled. The six aircraft in this formation were all that remained operational out of a full squadron.

"All aircraft, Buster." Buster was full throttle. Normally, Thai ground support aircraft flew in at medium altitude and dive-bombed their targets but with the air filling with Japanese fighters, that was suicidal. This time they were skimming through the treetops, the way they'd heard the American and Russian pilots had flown their Sturmoviks. Would it be enough when the Laylas arrived. The Ostriches had an escort now, that's why they'd been committed again. But the F-80E was an old straight winged design, could it protect them from the rakish, swept-wing Layla?

"Laylas, Laylas!" Pondit's gunner gave out the cry as he saw the shapes high overhead. Pondit dropped a little lower and fingered the Buddha amulet hanging around his neck. If ever he needed divine protection, it was now.

F-80E Taeng-Onn-One, over Phase Line Butcher, Thai/Japanese Indochina Border

"Laylas, Laylas. Take them out!" Flight Lieutenant Chan Nuat-Kheo shoved his throttle forward, pouring power into his J-33 engine. There were twelve Laylas in front of Taeng-Onn flight, angling down towards the Ostriches skimming through the treetops far below. An observer wouldn't have given Taeng-Onn much of a chance. They were outnumbered three to one, their aircraft looked old and antiquated compared to the swept-wing Laylas. And, objectively they were. The F-80E was an American cast off, replaced and now its replacements were being replaced. The F-80 had been in service since 1945 and three years was a long time to stay around. Yet appearances weren't everything and Chan had spoken to the American pilots who'd trained him at Luke Air Force Base. Veterans who'd flown over the Russian Front and had hacked the German jets out of the sky.

Because appearances weren't everything. The F-80E was a joy to fly, a legendary flying machine with all the power it could handle, smooth on the controls, light, agile and above all, responsive. There was nothing Chan could ask of his aircraft that it couldn't give. If the Americans were right, the Layla was treacherous and its pilots had to pay much more attention to simply flying their aircraft and that gave the Thai pilots a subtle but decisive edge right from the start.

The Japanese pilots saw them curving in from above, the classic top-cover position. The fighters swerved around, swinging to face the diving F-80s, then abruptly hauling up into a wicked climb, the low drag of their swept wings sending them skywards as if on elastic. The lead Japanese pilot swept up under the lead of the Thai finger-four and - it was gone. Chan had simply poured yet more power into his engine for that was another advantage the F-80 had. 2,450 kilograms of thrust, almost three times that of the Layla. He'd half-rolled and slammed his throttle all the way to the stops, blasting around in a tight curve that had the Layla floundering.

The Japanese fighter tried to follow him but now another factor cut in. The F-80s straight wings turned every scrap of air flow into lift, the fighter grabbing the sky as if it was a Siamese cat climbing the curtains. The Layla had swept wings and that meant a portion of its airflow was drifting spanwise, sucking the lift away from the aircraft. Already the Layla was shuddering on the edge of a stall. And the Layla was an unforgiving beast that wouldn't stand for that sort of treatment. It whipped out from its pilot's hands and fell into an uncontrollable spin. Chan was on it in a flash, his M-3 Browning machine-guns clipping out short, sharp bursts that flayed green and gray skin from the tumbling Layla. Then, the fragments turned to perspex before the jet gouted black and orange smoke.

Chan never watched it crash, he hauled back on the stick, climbing as fast as his J-33 would drive him. Up and over, into the maneuver that had been perfected by a German and still bore his name. The Immelman. His F-80 was in its element now, raw engine power dominating the sky as it always would. Another Layla was attempting to follow him up, a futile move because 900 kilograms of thrust couldn't compete with 2,450. Chan pointed his nose at the laboring fighter and his machine-guns snapped out a short burst. Hits flashed all over the Layla and bits chopped off as the Japanese pilot dropped out of the climb and dived away.

The Layla's cleaner airframe meant it picked up speed fast in a dive and, anyway, it had a good eighty kilometers per hour over the F-80E. The speed went up as Chan frantically tried to catch his prey. His mount was doing 980 kilometers per hour now, as fast as she'd go. At this speed, the shockwave from his nose was touching the wingtips and drag would mount enormously with every extra kilometer. The Layla didn't have that problem, the sweep on its wings kept it from picking up drag even as it pushed past a thousand kilometers per hour.

Then Chan saw that the Layla had another problem, a far worse one than just transonic drag. Even as he watched, the Layla's left wing dropped, savagely, viciously, flipping the plane into a deadly flat spin. For a brief second, the aircraft managed to hold together as it whirled in the air then the airframe gave up under aerodynamic loads it had never been meant to resist. Suddenly, the sky was full of fragments as the Layla just broke up in mid-air.

That was when Chan proved himself to be a fighter pilot. He actually wondered whether that could legitimately be considered a kill as his fighter arced up once more. Lights flashed around him as he streaked through a burst of fire from a Layla, then his wings went vertical and he hauled his F-80 around. Once again, a Layla pilot had the infuriating experience of having one of the silver fighters suddenly vanish from in front of him.

The two fighters were curving around, the Layla frantically trying to catch the jet that was exasperatingly out of reach. Then the Layla staggered under a long, deadly burst. Chan's wing man had seen the Layla drift into position and taken him out. The Japanese were warriors who fought one-on-one in individual conflict for honor and a warrior's virtue. The Thais had been trained by Americans and Russians who fought to kill their enemies and knew that the teamwork was the best, the proven, way to that end.

Black smoke, all over the sky. Green and gray shapes fighting the silver fish that darted and raced around them. In front of him one of the few surviving Laylas had gone into a steep climb. Chan almost laughed for even with swept wings a fighter has to run out of speed, out of energy, out of ideas. This trick was an old one, the Japanese was hoping Chan would follow him, then the Layla would do a tailslide and stand on his jet exhaust, paddling the rudder backwards and forwards while he chewed the F-80 to pieces with his cannon. Chan knew the answer to that maneuver and suddenly he was tired, sick and tired of the whole stupid business. He slammed out his speed brakes, feeling the fighter grumbling with the sudden drag as it slowed. Then he lifted his nose and sprayed the climbing Layla with killing fury, tearing it apart.

It was over, there were no green and gray fighters in the sky, only silver. Three F-80s looking intact, one was trailing black smoke. They couldn't have got all the Laylas, some must have broken away and been running for the border, probably desperately low on fuel. The F-80s were the same. But Phnon Penh airfield was only a few tens of kilometers away. They could glide it if they had to. Perhaps not but the base was only a few minutes flying time away while the Laylas had to go all the way back to Saigon or even Hanoi. It didn't matter, all that mattered was that the Ostriches were safe and clear to do their job.

Ostrich Djiap-Eleven, over Phase Line Decimate, Thai/Japanese Indochina Border

The radio had been filled with the chaos of combat, the fighter pilots overhead screaming at each other as they fought to keep the Laylas away from the Ostriches. At first, Pondit had believed they'd lose, that he and his Ostriches would be fighting to survive but their top-cover had scythed through the attacking Laylas, shooting some down and putting the rest to flight. He'd breathed a quick prayer of thanks and then got back down to his job.

Up ahead a pair of Japanese light bombers, Harvs or Kens, it was too far to see, were circling an area. That was the scene, the Japanese launching a company - level attack, trying to break out of the impending encirclement and the bombers were waiting for the Thai infantry to unmask so they could bomb and strafe the defenders. Only, this wasn't China. In China, the Japanese had never fought the Ostrich.

The Japanese aircraft were Harvs and they were no match for the twin-engined Ostrich. One didn't even see the charging aircraft until it was too late and the little bomber just fell apart as the sky filled

236

with cannon shells and machine gun bullets. Pondit's prey did spot him and tried to turn into him but it made no difference. The Harv's wing guns flashed and an opaque patch formed on the heavily armored screen in front of Pondit's face. Then he returned fire with all ten of his guns and the Harv wasn't there any more. Just shattered metal fragments falling to the ground.

In front, three green, crab-like shapes with little ants running with them Tanks with their infantry support. Pondit lifted his nose slightly and thumbed the rocket release, seeing the black trails streak out in front of his aircraft. Then, drop the nose again and let the enemy feel the lash of his 23mm cannon. They'd been designed to destroy tanks and the Japanese lights were no great challenge. Pondit had picked the one on the right and it was boiling black smoke as he flashed overhead.

Then, a long climbing curve and a bombing pass the way he'd been taught to do it. A long dive, dropping the bombs as late as he could. He felt the lurch as the six 250 kilogram bombs dropped then felt the kidney-crunching slam as they went off, throwing his Ostrich upwards with fragments from its own bombs peppering its belly. The Ostrich's armor was as much to protect it from itself as from the enemy. Below, the combination of explosions, blast and fragments should have held the enemy up, pinned them down, given the Thai troops down there a chance to inflict damage themselves.

"Sirisoon-Pony this is Cab Rank. We're hanging around until told differently. We've got more 132mm rockets, plenty of 23 mike-mike and point-fifty. So feel free to ask."

"Sirisoon-actual here. We'll remember that. Can you swing around and see if there is a follow up to this? We'll handle what's left down here."

Glory be, thought Pondit. That voice was unmistakably female. The world was going crazy. Then he thought for a second, his topcover had been named after the famous warrior Taeng-Onn hadn't it? Who'd died defending her village of Bangrachan against invaders? He found him hoping the owner of the voice on the radio would have better fortune than Taeng-Onn.

Sirisoon had been watching the Harvs wait for her unit to open fire. The word had been trembling on her lips when there had been a roar, a crushing cascade of sound that had seemed to flatten her ears to her head. The Harvs had just blown up, ripped apart as the Ostriches thundered across the sky. Then the roar of the engines had been drowned out by the screaming rocket salvos that had turned the sky dark before crashing into the enemy infantry.

Those explosions had been the loudest but it was the cannon fire that had been the most spectacular. One of the Japanese light tanks had seemed to melt as the hits flashed all over it, hammering its armor and setting it ablaze. Another was less spectacular but black smoke boiled from its engine compartment. The Ostriches turned up and away, out of the smoke that billowed form their first strike. Then they peeled over and dived on the approaching Japanese, bombs tumbling from their bellies and wings.

The thunder of the explosions was something Sirisoon could never have imagined. It surrounded her, pressing in on her, driving the air from her body and the feeling from her limbs. Dully, she heard the fragments flying overhead and her instructor's voice. "Close support is no use unless its close. Very close. So when you call for it, get down and stay down. Or you'll be as dead as the enemy."

Then it faded and she lifted her head. She knew the mathematics well enough. The standard close support weapon was a 250 kilogram bomb, equivalent to five rounds from a 150mm gun. Each Ostrich carried six and there had been six Ostriches. That meant the infantry company attacking them had just been hit by the equivalent of 180 heavy artillery shells. More than an artillery regiment could fire. Yet, mathematics hadn't conveyed the full impact of what had happened, the stunning, enveloping noise, the waves of pressure, the shaking of the ground. The Ostriches had dropped their bombs very close to the inner safety limit, the point at which they'd become as dangerous to friends as enemy. Very close support indeed.

And mathematics couldn't have told her the effect of the bombs. What had been a scene of beauty in the bright afternoon sun, green grass, blue sky, even the khaki of the Japanese infantry and the splotchy brown-green of their tanks had gone. A pall of black heavy smoke, shot with red and crimson, was boiling into the sky, turning the sun, dimly seen through the shroud, into a dull orange ball. The ground was invisible, no, that wasn't quite true, Sirisoon realized she could see the ground, it was just she couldn't see where the ground ended and the smoke began. Then, out of the chaos in front of her a tank, the only survivor of the three, emerged. White streaks of smoke streaked out from her positions. The RPG-2 wasn't that accurate and two of them missed but the third exploded square on the frontal armor.

Sirisoon was awed at the sight of more infantry, emerging from the smoke and dust of the bombs. The airstrike had been bad enough from her positions, out of the immediate danger area and dug in. What must it have been like in the midst of the bombing? And yet the Japanese infantry were coming on. The explosions from her 60 millimeter mortars yapped amongst them, the explosions seeming inconsequential after the earthquakes of the 250 kilogram bombs.

The tank was moving again, shrugging off three rifle grenades that hit it. Then the RPG gunners fired again, their launchers reloaded at last. One hit on the side of the turret, one over the top, another in the ground and yet it was that one, a miss, that stopped the tank at last. It broke a track and the tank spun to one side before stopping. The crew tried to bail out, obviously the tank was burning even if nobody could see it yet, but a burst from an MG34 cut them down.

The Japanese infantry was pinned down, they'd been relying on their armor to get them through and it had failed. China had done the Japanese Army no favors, she thought. They'd learned all the wrong lessons there. They'd learned that infantry wouldn't stand in front of tanks, that a few rounds of artillery would disperse a defense, that a few light bombs from an aircraft would cause panic. Above all, they'd learned, or thought they had, that fighting spirit was more important than weapons and in China that probably had been true. Only, this wasn't China and here relying on fighting spirit meant pitting flesh and blood against machine guns and explosives.

Time for another lesson. "Fix bayonets." Her order went out and there was a rattle as the long sawbacks were drawn and fixed in position. In China, the Japanese had viewed themselves the masters of bayonet fighting, a claim the Chinese had never contested. Now, the Japanese were finding themselves matched, bayonet for bayonet with an enemy who relished its use as much as they did. And had a much better bayonet, Sirisoon reflected smugly. "Attack! Follow me!"

The Thai platoon poured into the Japanese unit, throwing it back in confusion. Sirisoon fired once from the hip, dropping a Japanese sergeant, then engaged a private. She parried his thrust but that left her out of position for a thrust of her own so she kicked him in the groin instead. He victim doubled up and she thrust the bayonet into his shoulder, right where the neck started. Twist and pull, the sawback ripping the flesh as it was withdrawn. Another soldier coming in from the right, another parry and this time a superb thrust to the stomach. She was just withdrawing her sawback when there was a terrible blow in her side.

Sirisoon sprawled on the ground, her rifle out of reach. Over her, a Japanese soldier stood, bayonet poised for the downthrust. That's how it ends she thought. Like Taeng-Onn, knocked down then stabbed on the ground, over and over again. Just as her stomach muscles contracted to resist the killing blow, she saw the Japanese stagger and fall, red flowers on his chest where Yawd's MP-40 had sprayed him. A hand grabbed her shoulder and helped her up.

It was over, the Japanese were done. "Get me Channel Seven." There was a pause. "Sirisoon-Actual here. We stopped them. Permission to advance to Execute? Very Good Sir."

She looked around her unit was falling back into a skirmish line, ready to either hold or advance. "Forward, we have to take the ridgeline. Sergeant, casualty count, soon as you can. Medic, look after the wounded. And watch the Japanese, their dead might not want to stay dead."

First Army Circle Headquarters, Ban Masdit, Recovered Provinces, Thailand

"Damned politicians. Even Her. They're screwing around and its costing my boys." General Songkitti's aid looked surreptitiously around as if the King's Ambassador-Plenipotentiary would suddenly appear in the room, breathing fire. On the other hand, the general's frustration was understandable. He'd wanted to hold back until the 11th and Second Cavalry divisions were in place so he could launch a full strength counter-attack and destroy the Japanese invaders. Only, just after dawn, the word had come down from the Ambassador herself. 'Go today with what you've got. Feed the units in as they arrive.'

As a result, the two advances along the river were going much more slowly than they should have been. What was intended to be a massive pair of converging thrusts that would cut off the Japanese advance and encircle it was turning into a even push all along the front. The 12th Cavalry Regiment was moving slightly faster but that wasn't much. At best the push was at walking pace. The only bright spot was that the Japanese were falling steadily back and the area of their riverhead had shrunk dramatically. The 9th Division had advanced some ten kilometers in the same number of hours and their lead element should be in sight of the river soon. 211th Regiment was already on the river, pushing along its banks narrowing the frontage of river held by the Japanese and threatening their bridges.

Better news was that the Japanese fighter effort over the area had subsided at last. The sudden appearance of their fighters over the battle area early in the morning had been a disaster. They'd bled the ground attack units badly and only the commitment of Second Wing had restored the situation. In two days, the Air Force overall had taken a pounding. Fifth Wing had virtually gone, mostly destroyed on the ground at Laum Mwuak Airfield. Fourth Wing had lost about half its effectives, most of the losses being in the vital Ostrich squadrons. Third Wing, a pure fighter outfit with F-72s and F-80s had lost a couple of aircraft but was virtually unscathed otherwise. And it had decimated the vaunted Japanese Laylas in the air battles that morning. Still, with three wings out of seven involved, almost half the Air Force was committed to this one battle and about half of that had been lost. In two days.

Three divisions out of seven committed, three air wings out of seven already in the battle. Only the Navy wasn't being sucked into this "border incident" and they didn't really have much to offer. If the fighting spread, there simply wouldn't be enough in the way of available forces to counter it.

"Telephone Sir. On the scrambled line from Bangkok. The Ambassador herself."

Songkitti cursed and picked up his extension. What did she want now? To order him to lead a bayonet charge himself. Not that he wouldn't welcome the chance. "Songkitti, Your Excellency."

"Just out of curiosity, General, what did you just call me?" The contralto voice on the telephone was friendly and slightly amused. Which meant nothing at all of course.

"Errr, Your Excellency?"

"Never mind. Just be assured, I know how you feel. Been there myself. What's the situation on the ground?"

"End Game, Your Excellency. The Japanese are pulling back, recrossing the river to avoid being encircled. They're doing so slowly and fighting every inch of the way but they are pulling back. We should be on the river by nightfall. Lead elements of the Ninth have recaptured Laum Mwuak Airfield and rescued the surviving air force personnel who were trying to get out through the jungle. What worries me is the Japanese follow-up. They've got three times the force they committed yesterday already on scene and if that lot hits us, we can't stop them."

"You don't have to worry about that General. It won't happen. That's why I'm calling. At 2000 tonight our time, the Governments of Australia, India and Thailand will be announcing a new mutual defense pact by which an attack on any one of the three members will be considered an attack on them all. That's why you had to advance today and feed the reinforcements in piecemeal. This wouldn't have been possible if you and your men hadn't driven the Japanese back today."

"But, your Excellency, India has, what, 27 divisions? Australia two or three? Even all three of us cannot match the Japanese in sheer numbers. Even, if we could, it would take weeks to get those troops here. We'd still have to fight this Japanese force on our own and we're shot, we can't match them."

"And the Japanese cannot match the American bombers. For weeks now, the Americans have shown that nobody can stop their bombers. As part of their open skies policy, they've overflown Japan many times and the Japanese can do nothing to stop them. In fact, the Japanese have even less in the way of defense than Germany did. The

242

Americans have also made it very clear they will not tolerate any more major wars of aggression. The Japanese attack yesterday was a border incident, one beneath their attention. A major war involving all three of us will not be acceptable to them and they will act to end it. I know that, don't ask how, but I do. There will be no follow-up attack General, and if by chance there is, there will no longer be a Japan to threaten us."

"Thank the Lord, Your Excellency."

"No, thank the B-36. Good evening General." The phone cut off abruptly.

His aide came in, a long box in his hands and a bemused expression on his face. "General?"

"Her Excellency assures us there will be no follow-up Japanese attack. We've won this one, Kam, by the skin of our teeth but we've won it. Once the troops settle down for the night, keep them on full alert just in case. The next regiment of 11th to arrive,"

"The 411th sir?"

"That's the one. They'll do a sweep tomorrow, clean out our rear areas of any by-passed holdouts. That's all. We stay on our side of the river. Once the river line is held, pull the Second Cavalry out of the line. The Ninth as well provided things settle down. They're been mauled, they need to regroup and absorb replacements. What's in the box?"

"A Company Commander from the 29th sent it up Sir. By courier no less and for your personal attention. I don't know....... My God, its beautiful."

Songkitti had opened the box. Inside was a Japanese katana complete with scabbard. There was a note attached to it and he read it with rising eyebrows while his aide admired the sword. "According to the good Captain, this sword was captured from its original owner, in personal combat, by our fragrant and delightful Lieutenant Sirisoon who placed in his hands for safe keeping. He most respectfully asks that we hold it in trust, awaiting her return to reclaim it.

243

"This is the real thing Sir. 18th Century certainly, possibly 17th. Not a cheap imitation. Must have been a family heirloom once. I'll put it up on the wall of the Officer's Mess."

"No Kam, you won't. We'll put this into safe keeping as the Captain requests. When Sirisoon gets back, we'll return it to her and ask her if we can have it for display in the mess with a memorial that explains who captured it and how."

"Suppose she says no?"

"She won't. She wants more than anything else for us to accept her as a soldier. This way she gets a very obvious public symbol of acceptance and we get her sword legally. Everybody's happy. Now, get the orders out."

Text of a Press Statement Issued By The Foreign Office's of Australia, India And Thailand.

"Developments in the international situation as it affects the countries of the Far East have shown that the existing framework of relations is no longer functional and cannot be repaired to a status that best serves the interests of all the peoples of the region. This is well-illustrated by the current unrest in Indonesia and the southern Philippines and by the events of the last few days in Indo China. The Governments of Australia, India and Thailand therefore announce the formation of a new super-national identity to be known as The Triple Alliance.

"Under the terms of this agreement, the three principle members agree to a pact of mutual defense under which any attack by any party on any member of the Alliance shall be considered as an attack upon all three. Each member of the Triple Alliance has committed itself to the full support, with all its resources, of any of the other members that have come under attack. This is not an offensive alliance, it has as its purpose, purely the reduction of tension and maintenance of international peace.

"The members of the Triple Alliance also commit themselves to developing the economic stability and well-being of the region for the benefit of all its citizens. To this end, they have elected to adopt the sovereign as their common internal trading currency in the hope that this will promote both stability and investment."

Statement released by the State Department, Washington, D.C.

"The United States of America applauds the initiative taken by Australia, India and Thailand to form a regional structure that will both prevent international disturbances and enhance the prospects for peace, security and prosperity in the region. The United States looks forward to the opportunity for peaceful trade and diplomatic relations with all the countries in the region.

"In this spirit, the United States would like to offer its services as an honest broker to resolve the present conflict in accordance with the strict provisions of international law. The unfortunate events that have taken place along the Mekong River during the last few days are a sad reminder of how relatively minor problems can escalate out of all proportion and lead to the most dire of consequences. All good-willed peoples of the world wish for peace and mutual understanding and we hope that this event can be resolved in appreciation of this spirit. We propose an immediate cease-fire and a return to pre-hostilities positions on both sides as a preliminary to an inclusive conference that will address all the outstanding issues raised by the conflict."

Office of President Zhukov, Field Kremlin, Nizhny Novgorod, Russia

"Gospodin President, this announcement has just been received." Marshal Cherniakhovskii was carrying a sheaf of papers. Zhukov looked up at his deputy, his eyes bleary with tiredness even though it was only mid-morning. Too little sleep, too much work, too many problems. He couldn't understand why people wanted this job and wondered just how many of the world's leaders privately and secretly regretted the climb to the top. Some hadn't, some had positively relished the position but he was prepared to bet they were a minority. Zhukov knew that the load of being Russia's President was killing him. Only, he couldn't give it up, not until he had a successor who could take Russia the way it needed to go. He had a strong feeling Cherniakhovskii was that man.

"Have you read this?"

"Yes Gospodin President, but I don't see how it affects us."

"It does my friend, in many ways. Not least of which, a strong alliance to the south of Japan bars the route to any further expansion in that direction. We, the Americans and us, bar the way north. Japan is contained, still very powerful and very dangerous but it is contained."

"I do not see any great signs of strength in this Triple Alliance. It seems a very limited pact. Adequate for the purpose yes, but there is no great strength to it. All three countries together have forces that do not equal those of the Second Karelian Front and we have others as well."

"It will be a strong alliance because it has to be a strong alliance. The members have no choice but to make it so whether they wish it or not. Remember the saying of Catherine The Great. *'Strong alliances are like strong steel. They are not forged on a mattress of desire but on the anvil of necessity.'* It will take them time to realize that but, yes, it will be a strong alliance."

"And the Americans? Their talk of trade and offer of mediation?"

"President Dewey told me that America has a new policy now. They will not make war upon their enemies, they will simply destroy them. This is an announcement of that policy and contains a warning to Japan. They will back off this attack or they will be destroyed as thoroughly as Germany was. And there is nothing they can do to stop it. Now, the question is, how do we make ourselves felt in this 'mediation'?"

"Is it so necessary that we should?"

Zhukov looked affectionately at his deputy. Cherniakhovskii was one of the younger men he was grooming as his successor. This one showed initiative, asked questions, expressed his opinions, all attributes that would have got him killed a decade earlier. He shook himself, had Stalin's great purges been only a decade ago? It seemed like a lifetime. For far too many Russians it had been their lifetime.

"Indeed it is. Our greatest weakness is that we need the Americans. We need their nuclear firepower, we need their economic strength, their skills, their expertise. We need their endless cornucopia of weapons and the tools to make weapons. We need their knowledge of how to run an economy so that it produces enough to feed and cloth our people. We need the Americans, Russia has been so terribly hurt by this war that we cannot survive without them. But, they do not need us. We are useful to them certainly, but they do not need us. So we must never let them think they can do things alone.

"Every time they make a move, we must be there, helping them, supporting them. We must make ourselves so useful to them that usefulness become approximate to need. And, remember this, the Americans are generous to a fault and they hate to be under obligations. Offer them bread, they will return with meat and think nothing of it. If we aid them as much as it within our power to do so, they will return the aid tenfold."

"So the anvil of necessity drives us together as much as it does the Triple Alliance."

"Indeed it does. But also remember this. The Americans, for all their strength and power, need a friend in the world. That one friend will be a very privileged entity indeed, for the shadow of American power will make it seem many times stronger than it is. I tell you this. *To survive, Russia must be that friend.* So I ask again. How do we help the Americans?"

There was a long silence. Then, Cherniakhovskii tentatively, almost as if he was speaking to himself, broke it. "We could always offer to host the meeting. Neutral ground, away from the scene. Emphasizing that we are also independent, honest brokers. And we could add that the ruins of Moscow are fitting place for the conference since it would highlight the destruction of modern war."

Zhukov laughed, the barking growl that usually meant somebody's army was about to get destroyed. "In that case we should offer to hold the conference in Berlin. At least there, the radiation levels will ensure they reach agreement quickly before the delegates start to glow in the dark."

Cherniakhovskii joined in the laughter. "Shall I contact President Dewey then on your behalf? Advise him that we intend to make the offer of conference facilities to support his initiative."

A beam of pride spread across Zhukov's face. The young Marshal had got the message. "Yes indeed. Do that."

The Ambassador's Office, Supreme Command Headquarters, Bangkok, Thailand

The night had seemed infinite, eternal. It reminded her of another night, long ago, when she'd stood at another window watching the glow on the horizon as the old Capital of Ayuthya burned to the ground. A traitor had finally done what siege couldn't. The city had fallen and every man, woman and child had been killed. It had been under siege for 18 months before it fell but that didn't make her failure then any the less. Nor did the fact that it had taken two Burmese armies, each 100,000 strong to defeat Ayuthya's armies and besiege the capital. The capital had fallen, the country had been defeated and occupied.

She'd been outside, gathering new armies, mobilizing more troops until one night the glow on the horizon had told her it was too late. Then had followed more years, of guerrilla warfare, of resistance, then of a renewed war that had driven the Burmese out. She had feared that, once again, her country would be occupied and, once again, she would have to fight the invader from the jungle.

It almost seemed to her that the glow had returned, a rich, red glow lightening the eastern sky. It was dawn, not fire, and as she watched the sun lifted over the horizon and started its arc in the sky. She stood there, still, unmoving as dawn lit the city and slowly brought it to life. An uncertain, apprehensive life as people searched for news of the fighting on the Mekong. Then she moved, turning around as there was a knock on the door. A messenger.

She read the message, a brief communiqué from Tokyo accepting the offer of American mediation and the Russian offer of a location for the conference. Also, agreeing to the cease-fire, the few remaining troops on the south bank of the Mekong withdrawing over the river.

The crisis was over. There was no need to plan a new guerrilla war, no need to plan resistance in the countryside against the day the Japanese could be driven out. She walked to her office door and locked it. Then, she quietly sat at her desk and wept with relief.

The airfields were empty at last, six weeks of testing and evaluation had finally ended. Colonel Pico stopped typing and looked out of his office window at the runway, the glare from the concrete blinding in the mid-day sun. The lesson learned from the first Red Sun exercise was simple. Air defense had failed completely, the United States was as vulnerable to high-altitude nuclear bombers as Germany had been a year earlier. The B-36s had overflown the best fighters in the United States Air Force. They hadn't fought their way through the defenses, they'd simply ignored them. It was what he had feared, what his nightmares had warned him of. The United States could not defend itself against the sort of attack that had destroyed Germany.

His eyes returned to the paragraph he had just finished typing. "Present generations of fighters have proved incapable of reaching the altitudes routinely used by B-36-type aircraft for the penetration of hostile airspace. Only the German Go-229 fighter had any capability to reach these altitudes and its lack of maneuverability meant that it was unable to successfully engage the B-36. In any case, this type of aircraft is, as far as is known, now extinct and its deficiencies in other areas are such that we find it most unlikely that any nation would wish to copy it's layout. Field modifications to the types of fighters used during the Red Sun trials proved unsuccessful and the representatives of the aircraft companies attending cannot hold out any hope of future modifications improving the situation. New types of aircraft must be developed to provide a high-altitude intercept capability. Until then, the unexpected ascendancy of the turbocharged, piston-engined bomber is complete."

And wasn't that the truth, Pico thought. Artem Mikoyan had been quite explicit about it; even his vaunted new MiG-15 would only have a marginal capability against the Featherweight IV B-36H. He had an advanced version of the aircraft on the drawing board and the Russians had promised to get a prototype MiG-17 over to Nevada as soon as it left the factory. There was an engine development that could help, a thing called reheat. It was another combustion chamber at the rear of the engine where raw fuel was dumped into the jet and ignited. It was supposed to provide a surge of power at high altitude - at the expense of massive fuel consumption. Would it be enough? Mikoyan was gambling it would be with his MiG-17 and North American were doing the same with the XF-86D Sabredog. And would it stay enough? There were new versions of the B-36 coming and on the horizon was an all-jet derivative, the XB-60. That was due to fly in a couple of years time. Boeing was designing a rival, a more advanced bomber still, the XB-52. Were the fighters doomed to an everlastingly futile game of catch-up. And could anything help them?

"Existing ground based anti-aircraft defenses proved entirely ineffective. Existing anti-aircraft guns could not reach the altitudes flow by the B-36 and the proposed new 120mm gun is also ineffective against targets flying at that altitude. It is urgently advised that maximum effort be placed behind the development of the new Ajax missile."

The Russians had more to fear than the United States did. The Japanese were introducing two new bombers, derivatives of German designs, that were also high-altitude bombers. Pico chuckled to himself, one of them was a version of the He-274 and had been code-named Curt. A name that had been very hurriedly changed to Dick. There were legends about why that had happened. The Russians, their help had been invaluable here. They flew fighters a different way from the American pilots and their ground control techniques were different. Once again, Pico's eye fell on the relevant section of his report.

"Comparison of the American system of free-ranging fighters receiving operational information from ground control and the Russian system of fighters flying under strict course and speed directions from their fighter direction center has shown no clear advantage for either system. Each worked best under specific circumstances. In good weather and where the fighters were covering large areas, the American system worked best. In bad weather and in the point defense of high value targets, the Russian system proved superior.

"The considered opinion of the participants is that the command and control system eventually adopted by NORAD should be a combination of both systems, exploiting the best advantages of each. Further trials will be necessary to determine the exact nature of that combination."

The Russians had shown something else as well. Their Tu-4s had lumbered up to the range, within easy intercept parameters of the fighters. Only then, they'd turned away, leaving small shapes streaking through the sky towards the targets. Air-to surface missiles, stand-off weapons. Both the Americans and Russians had been working on them but the Russians had got theirs operational first. They'd been too fast for the piston-engined fighters to intercept and the jets had barely enough time to engage them.

Eventually, the answer had been George Preddy and his F-65G Tigercat night fighters. Their radar had allowed them to track the inbound stand-off missiles and plot an intercept. Not a high probability, the Tigercat was too slow for that, but a good possibility. With practice they had one chance in five. Which was more than they had against the B-36. Of course, that raised an ugly possibility, B-36s carrying stand-off missiles.

"The provision of search and target acquisition radars should be considered essential. The increasing speed of modern combat aircraft means that the old days of target acquisition by Mark One Eyeball are no longer viable. A modern radar is so essential to fighter combat that it should be an integral part of the aircraft's design."

Pico sighed again and rubbed his eyes. His last conclusion was the one he really hated. "Only one possible form of defense against high-flying heavy bombers appears practical until the new generations of fighters and anti-aircraft missiles enter service. It is most urgently recommended that at least one group of B-36 bombers be assigned to an air defense role and trained in the use of air-to-air bombing of enemy aircraft using nuclear weapons."

Damn, he thought, was this what the world had come to? The nightmares he'd had ever since looking back on the twelve mushroom clouds rising over Berlin seemed to crowd in on him. Air-to-air bombing with nuclear weapons was the least-worst option. The world really was going mad.

Headquarters, Second Karelian Front, Riga, "The Baltic Gallery"

"Well, we've done it Erwin. We've done the impossible." The map was empty, the last units of Army Group Vistula had surrendered. Oddly, quite a few of the problematic units, the ones that had been expected to cause the worst complications, had suddenly turned out to be 'Polish'. They'd been given a choice, join the new Polish Army supporting the Russian-sponsored government or dig uranium ore with wooden shovels. They'd joined the Polish Army.

With eyes wide open, for they knew what Rommel and Rokossovsky both knew. The units would get the dirty jobs, the suicidal attacks, be rammed into the fighting again and again until they were all gone. But, they would die on their feet, like men, not diseased troglodytes coughing their lungs out in the radioactive dust of a uranium mine. That was a deal worth making and they'd taken it. All but one. General Otto Skorzeny had shot himself the night after his last unit had surrendered to the Russians. Rommel thought of him with contempt. In the end, he hadn't had the courage to face responsibility for what he'd done. Physical courage, he'd had in plenty but not moral courage. Perhaps, Rommel fought, that was what had led Germany astray, too much physical courage, too much physical skill at fighting, not enough moral courage to ask why?

"Your General Staff was a remarkable organization Erwin, quite remarkable. Twice this century, it has taken on almost the whole world and nearly fought it to a standstill. And never once did one of its members ask 'Why are we taking on the whole world?' Never once."

Rommel shook his head helplessly. He'd learned too much over the months of negotiations to argue the point. It was redundant anyway, the General Staff were ashes floating somewhere in an incinerated Germany. "I can't disagree with you Konstantin. Looking back now, we started to go astray sometime in the 19th century, those damned unreadable philosophers everybody quotes and raves about but can't be bothered to study in full. They poisoned the minds of just enough people and the whole world had to pay."

"It did Erwin, but there is blame enough for more than just you Germans. The rest of Europe shares your guilt and is being punished now for its sins. They saw the cancer growing in its midst and they did nothing to cut it out. And we Russians have more blame than most to bear. We didn't just fail to cut the cancer out, we helped it grow and caught a bad case of the disease ourselves. Perhaps why we have been punished so terribly. I do not know. There are those in Russia who say that what has happened is God's punishment for our sin of omission. They may be right but such things are not our concern today. It is not the question of the blame of one people or one nation but that of one man. You, Erwin."

252

Rommel squared his shoulders and nodded sharply. It was what he had expected. From the first time his eyes had opened to what the German Army had done in Russia he had been certain of his fate. Now it had come and he felt a strange relief. "So, my trial will start?"

"Your trial is over Erwin. You have been on trial here every day since we first met. We have watched you, try to save your men yet also do what was right. You have not earned an acquittal but you have earned clemency." Rokossovsky looked pensive for a moment. "There is a bend in the Volga, where the war did not reach. The river surrounds it on three sides and the fourth is guarded by mountains. A place called Zhiguli. A very beautiful place. In that bend, secure and isolated from the rest of Russia are the dachas, the country homes, of retired Russian leaders. Marshals, politicians, scientists, others who have retired to private life. I have a dacha there and so does Zhukov, and Koniev and Malinski. So now do you and a few of your comrades. The ones who have earned clemency."

Rokossovsky stood and drew himself to attention. "Field Marshal Rommel, for your crimes against the Russian people you are here by sentenced to life imprisonment in Zhiguli. You will serve your sentence under house arrest."

He sat down again. "You will live there the same as us, the only difference being you will not be allowed to leave the town without an escort. Believe me, that is for your protection, it will be many years before a German accent will be tolerated in Russia. You will have to stay there with other retired Generals, yours and ours, drink tea and vodka, play chess and refight old battles. It's a dirty job Erwin, but somebody has to do it."

Rommel nodded. It wasn't as if he had anywhere else to go, the American bombers had seen to that. "Marshal Rokossovsky, I submit myself to the judgment of the Russian people." Then he too relaxed. "You say you have a dacha there as well? When will you be coming out?"

"Soon, Erwin, very soon. I have one campaign left and Poland to get straightened out. Then I too will retire to Zhiguli. All of us who fought this war are worn out, our time is done. It is for the younger men to take over now. And for God to guide them."

The Garden Hotel, London, U.K.

London was quiet, eerily so. There were few vehicles, most people walked, the luckier had bicycles. Animals had returned, for deliveries and transport and their leavings were once again a problem in the city. And Commander Robert Fox still had not made up his mind. He'd done right by the Australians, he'd checked *Thule* over from stem to stern. She'd been well modernized at Groton in Connecticut and was now pretty close to a Type XXI in performance. Her batteries were new and her sensor suite was first class. She was a good boat, in his heart he knew she was a better boat that his *Xena*. Was she still his *Xena*? He'd changed his mind half a dozen times on the long train trip up from Pompey.

The decision was logically inevitable, he knew it. Even with his fabled luck, the peace-time Royal Navy would have no place for him. It was shrinking almost hourly, its ships being sold for scrap as the Government frantically tried to raise money to pay its bills. There would soon be no commands for Commanders, there were too many officers and most would be beached. In Australia, he would have a command, a future. Yet he couldn't just leave the country, it would be deserting his post. The evening before he'd met Dr Swamphen for dinner and they'd talked far into the night. Swamphen was leaving, he was going to a place called Wood's Hole in America. Wouldn't say what he would be doing but said it was a sound, well-financed project.

He stretched out on the bed with its patched cover and sheets. The hotel served dinner but it was a fixed time and no choices. Still, it was worth waiting for. There was something else he was waiting for and it came sooner than he expected. The telephone rang and the operator's voice told him his long distance call was through.

"Robert Darling! How is your trip going."

"Julia, Very well, *Thule* is beautiful but Portsmouth's a wreck. Gosport's just gone. You remember our first married quarters? The whole street has vanished, its as if a giant child had just wiped it away with his hand. Even *Victory's* hurt. She got hit by a rocket, a big one." His voice petered away as he remembered the blackened wood and the smell of burning. The silence grew, heavily and expensively. Eventually Julia broke it.

"We're staying in England, aren't we?" They'd been married a long time and Fox recognized the tone of her voice, a wife desperately trying to bury her own bitter disappointment and support the decision her husband had made. Suddenly, the decision was made. He couldn't do it, not to her.

"Whatever are you talking about? I'm signing on for Australia in just a few minutes. The Embassy is just around the corner and they're waiting for me now. I just called to tell you to start packing. Why on earth would you think I would turn down a modernized T-boat?"

Fox could tell from Julia's voice she was crying with relief. "No, I suppose you couldn't. Robert, you go play with your boats and I'll have everything sorted out by the time you get back. A lot of it's still packed anyway. And don't consort with naughty women while you're down in London. I've heard about that city. Now run along before this telephone call bankrupts us."

Fox laughed and hung up the phone. He left his room and went down to reception, dropping off the key as he left.

"Dinner at six, Sir."

"Thank you, I'll be back by then. Just going for a walk."

The Australian Embassy was less than a mile away, he had plenty of time. Goodbye *Xena*, hello *Thule* he thought. Yes, he was leaving his post, but he had his wife and a future to think about. Britain would survive, it always had, always would. He glanced up and saw, high in the sky overhead, a wide contrail, red and white against the darkening sky. A silver point at its head, a B-36 probably on its way to Russia.

There was a fog coming down, barely more than a hint now but soon it would become the pearlescent gray that turned the London streets into a magical place, lit by the welcoming yellow of the shop lights. He'd miss London, always would but London, also would survive. It didn't need him, Julia did and it wasn't right to ask her to stay here. Australia would be their home now. Suddenly, he urgently wanted to get back to *Thule,* he'd heard there were some new tricks that could be done with the modernized T-boats and he wanted to try them out.

Radio Broadcast Studio, Washington D.C.

"My fellow Americans, I speak to you tonight, to advise you of the events that have taken place in recent weeks. Before I do that, I would like to speak about the events of 1939 and 1940. In those years, a single power, aggressive, over-mighty, convinced that its might gave it the right to rule by force every nation that could be made to submit, attacked the countries around it. Its neighbors prevaricated, made excuses, appeased the aggressor. Nobody resisted until it was too late and by the time they did, the aggressor had grown too strong for them. They were defeated and the war spread until it engulfed the whole world. Because of that war, a million and a half American boys will never come home again.

"This must never happen again.

"We have heard much in this campaign about international agreements and multi-national organizations and the need for America to maintain peace in the world community.

"In the end this will mean just one thing. More American boys will leave home never to return. More American mothers will grieve for their lost children, more American fathers will have nothing left of their sons but a folded flag and a memory. And so it will go on, far into the future. An endless sacrifice of the best we have.

"We must find a better way.

"That brings us back to where we started, to the events of the last few weeks. In that time, we have averted two wars without the loss of a single American life. The first was a war that could have started by mistake, by two nations who each believed the worst of eachother. Each believed the other was massing troops on the border to attack, each was tempted to strike first and gain the upper hand. Two nations in the street at High Noon, each waiting for the slightest move that would cause them to go for their guns.

"Under our Open Skies policy we flew reconnaissance aircraft along the border and took photographs, the best our technology could

256

provide. We gave those pictures to both sides, showing them that there were no troop concentrations, there were no plans on either side for an attack. The tension in that area faded away.

"This was the best way to end a war, not by sending large numbers of American boys to die in far-off lands but by removing the cause of the war before it ever started.

"We have also made it clear that we will not tolerate wars of aggression. A nation that tries to overrun and conquer its neighbors will face the wrath of American bombers. We will not tolerate the strong forcing the submission of the weak.

"Let us be clear about this. We do not rule the world. We do not say to others, this you will do, this is how you will live, this is who will rule you. We do not demand they love us, we do not even ask that they like us or agree with what we are or how we live. We merely say to them, live in peace and let others do the same. For if you want war you will be an enemy of America and America no longer makes war on its enemies, it destroys them.

"When a small war in a far-off land threatened to expand to a much larger conflict, just as the war in Europe expanded ten long years ago, we made that point clear. We simply reminded those responsible for starting that conflict of the motto of Strategic Air Command. 'Peace Is Our Profession.' We do not rule the world, we do not wish to and we will not make the attempt. We will just keep the peace.

"Tomorrow the American people have a choice. They can vote for a never ending commitment of American troops in far-off lands, fighting wars in sweaty jungles or the icy wastes, a policy that will send our sons back to the hell of Archangel. Or they can vote that Peace Is Our Profession and live behind the sword of Strategic Air Command and the shield of the oceans and our fighter defenses.

"Thank you and good night."

President Dewey leaned back from the microphone and stretched. Then he quietly left the radio broadcast room and made for his official limousine. The poll figures looked bad but there was only one poll that mattered. The one tomorrow.

The small convoy pulled to a halt in the street, dust swirling around the vehicles, a few curious dogs sniffing cautiously around to see who these new arrivals were. A jeep, five trucks. Sergeant Yawd leaned back in the rear seat "How did you get the transport Ell-tee?"

"Just told the motor pool sergeant that I knew all about his little sidelines and if we got transport, he'd have a week or two to get straightened out before we did an audit."

"What was he up to?"

"I don't know. I let him fill in the blanks for himself. Obviously there's something he doesn't want investigated. There usually is."

"What's going to happen to us Ell-tee? Back to truck guard duty?"

Sirisoon shook her head. They'd spent weeks garrisoning the river before being pulled back and replaced by a unit from the Eleventh. That was when she'd had her orders direct from General Songkitti in an envelope that included news that her sword had arrived and was in safe keeping for her. That had surprised her, privately she'd put her chance of getting it back at no more than 50:50. "We're being constituted as a ready alert platoon. There'll be one at each base from now on. The General says it's to make sure we don't get caught like this again." She looked at Yawd out of the corner of her eyes. "You're stuck with me as well. General says, too many junior officers got killed leading from the front to replace me. By the way, I've been meaning to ask. When did I stop being Ma'am and become Ell-tee?"

Yawd looked embarrassed. "Well, errr." He waved a hand in front of her. "Ma'am just came with the configuration so to speak. You earned the right to be our Ell-tee."

"Ah, so." The imitation Japanese made them both laugh. "Sergeant, the men have had a hard time. We've got two hours or so, let them wander around as they wish." Yawd cleared his throat. Sirisoon carried on smoothly. "Under the supervision of their corporals of course. Reassemble in two hours."

Yawd smiled contentedly. There was something very satisfying about seeing a young officer taking the first steps to becoming a good officer. "And you Ell-tee?"

"Got some personal things to get from the store over there."

Sirisoon set out for the village store, easy to pick out as it was the largest frontage. Yawd followed her and settled down in a chair by the door, happy to relax in the sun. Sirisoon went inside; there were indeed some personal things she needed to get.

The store was typical of its kind, an uneven wooden floor, dusty despite the owner's wife sweeping it twice a day. Goods piled around in no particular order, some new, some old, some valuable, some junk. She searched through the shelves before she found what she needed. The counter where the shopkeeper and his assistant stood was by the door. The assistant was a young girl, probably the shopkeeper's daughter for most stores like this were run by the family. Sirisoon went over to them to pay.

There was another woman there, a young mother with a child. Sirisoon put her purchases on the table and dug out the money to pay for them. As she did, she absent-mindedly shifted the rifle hanging over her shoulder and moved the sawback bayonet on her belt. The child ran past her, to his mother and Sirisoon looked down at him, smiling as she picked up her goods. The young boy made a choking noise and buried his face in her mother's skirts. The woman grabbed him and swung him around, putting herself between her child and the stranger who stood in the store. She glared at Sirisoon, trying to erect a visual barbed wire fence to protect her child. The young shop assistant was staring at Sirisoon, something close to horror on her face. Sirisoon picked up her purchases and left. As she stepped through the doors, she heard the voices from inside the store.

"Lord have mercy on us. Did you see her eyes? Real killer's eyes!"

"Shush, she'll hear you."

Outside, Sergeant Yawd fell in beside his officer his voice quiet and fraternal. "Welcome to the club, Ell-tee."

Nellis Air Force Base, Las Vegas, Nevada.

The crew slid into their accustomed places and started reading off the long check-list before take-off. The cockpit was hot, stiflingly so, and nobody on the flight deck wanted to delay getting off the ground and up into the cool air high above.

"It's hot out here." Major Clancy was running through the electronics list, reading it as per regulations.

"We'd better get used to it, we're going to be out here from now on."

"Confirmed then?"

"Yup. Just came through. The whole 100th is transferring from Kozlowski to Nellis. The base has got to be expanded to take us but as soon as it's done, we'll be basing out of Nevada. Facing west across the Pacific, not east across the Atlantic."

"We're staying here?" It was the voice they already associated with *Texan Lady* although Dedmon still privately believed it was somebody playing a joke. Or perhaps just his imagination. He talked to his aircraft, every pilot did, and it was quite possible he was imagining the responses. But then why did others hear what he heard?

"That's right. This is our new home."

"Oh good. It's nice sitting here in the sun. Maine is so cold makes my frames ache."

Clancy and Dedmon grinned at each other and shook their heads. Some things just defied a rational explanation. Time for a quick mission orders recap. "Profile mission everybody. We're going to hit Hawaii. We'll fly out at 40,000 feet, go to 43,000 for our bomb run then come home. Argus, radar only. No visuals."

"How long before the rest of the group comes down Bob?" Clancy put his clip-board into its holder and settled himself into his seat.

"At least six months. And that's assuming there's no change in the Administration. Did you get your vote in?"

"Of course. As long as that?"

"General LeMay came down to inspect the base and had one of his raging furies. Reportedly he made the base commander cry. Described the married quarters here as unfit even for a particularly slovenly breed of syphilitic cockroaches and is having the whole lot torn down. The group won't move down until the enlisted married quarters are ready. Iron-Ass says the officers can wait a little, they can afford to rent off-base."

There was a silence as Dedmon and Clancy waited nervously, glancing around to see if General LeMay was going to suddenly materialize in the cockpit. He didn't and they relaxed. "Enlisted getting their married quarters first. That's a break with tradition." Clancy's voice was thoughtful

"General LeMay," Dedmon reckoned they'd got away with one Iron-Ass, two would be pushing their luck "Says that we can't expect our ground crews to work the duty hours they have to while they're worried about their families. So they get priority for new living accommodation. I've seen the new quarters up at Offutt. Six-man rooms for the unmarried enlisted men, small studio apartments for the married couples. They're spartan but they look pretty good and they don't cost so much more than the old designs. I hear some of the enlisted men's wives have started calling the General 'Saint Curtis'."

"Yeah." Clancy's voice was disbelieving. "They don't have to work for him. Right, we've got tower clearance to taxi out. Hawaii here we come. For God, America and Saint Curtis!"

The McMullen Household, Simonstown, Republic of South Africa.

"Maisie? Where are you? Luv, I'd like you to meet Jorgie and Deke. Who are known to the world as the Management, workforce and administration of McMullen Metalworking Industries. We're bosses now."

"Its agreed? That's wonderful. Jorgie, Deke, John's said so much about you."

"Nothing too awful I hope." Maisie McMullen giggled and shook her head. "And John's told us all about you Maisie, said what a fine job you'd made of the house. Didn't do you justice though, this place is beautiful. John, your wife's got a real talent for doing a house. And for cooking too by the smell from the kitchen."

Maisie McMullen flushed. She'd bought a standing rib of beef for the dinner tonight and stared at it, not knowing what to do. For a decade, Britain had been at war and then suffered a miserable peace. Food had been in short supply and cooking large meals was a forgotten art. The joint she'd bought had been more meat than her family had seen in a three-month. She simply didn't know how to start cooking it. In fact, she realized, she didn't really know how to cook at all. Not with real food. She could turn the rations into meals, as good as any and better than most, but real food like this? Where was she supposed to start?

Fortunately, Jorgie and Deke's wives had turned up bring some contributions for the feast and they'd learned of the problem. So Maisie had sat at the table, watched and taken notes while the two South African women had taken over her kitchen and cooked the dinner. Not that the men would ever know that, as far as they would be concerned, Maisie had cooked this meal. She'd also made a private note to get cookery lessons as quickly as possible although she'd already noted how many white households had a black cook and domestic help.

The McMullens lead the way out where the meal was waiting. The party settled down and waited while grace was said, in Afrikaans and English. Then, as he carved the joint (clumsily and not too well but nobody remarked on the fact), he picked up on the business news. "Not only have we registered the company, we've got our first contract. Ammunition boxes for Denel. Its welding and metal-working so it fits just fine, I'm doing riveting down at the yard while Dirk and Jorgie can look after the boxes. Think we've got a good thing going here."

"We've got some more good news John." Maisie spoke a little diffidently, looking down at her plate.

"We have?" McMullen was curious.

"Not you John." Maisie McMullen put her hand on her stomach. "We've got some news. Just confirmed today."

It took a minute for the message to sink in, then the room erupted with cheers. The women patted Maisie on the pack and made clucking noises while the men took turns to pump McMullen's hand. After the fuss settled down, he finished serving the meat and watched the rest of the feast being passed around. Eventually his own plate was filled. Meat and vegetables, more than he'd thought he'd ever see served to a person. He sighed very happily.

"Good simple, solid grub, that's what I like."

Epilogue

The Oval Office, the White House, Washington D.C.

TRUMAN BEATS DEWEY!

"Did you see the headlines Sir?" The young woman behind the secretarial desk help up a copy of the Chicago Daily Tribune, the headline emblazoned across the from page in huge type.

"I did indeed honey. Half the country is laughing and the other half weeping. I hear Joe Kennedy swears he'll take the whole system to court. Anyway, the boss asked me to come around."

"Yes indeed Mister Stuyvesant. If you'll just take a seat for a few minutes. The President will call for you shortly."

It was actually a bit longer than that. Stuyvesant had a chance to read the whole of the Chicago Tribune article on Truman's defeat of President Dewey and speculate on just how many red faces there were in newspapers around the country this morning. Eventually, the phone rang and the receptionist spoke quietly. "If you'll come with me, Mister Stuyvesant, the President will see you now."

"Congratulations Mister President. A fine win, by seven and a half points according to the latest counts. Electoral College 342 to 189."

"Thank you, Philip. Harry Truman has already called me and conceded. In a fine, gentlemanly speech I might add. One that should be an example to everybody in this city. My new administration will make a point of finding him a post that honors his qualities. I must admit though, for the last few days, I was beginning to feel it would be I who would graciously concede. How could the press have got it so wrong?"

"Couple of things Sir. One was that they stopped polling too early, a week before the election. They assumed that people would have made their minds up by then and the picture wouldn't shift. They missed that there were two independent candidates who had a strong volume of support. People said they supported them anyway, but when push came to shove they wanted to make their vote count and went for one of the two primary candidates. Wallace's support came mostly from Democrats and what little he kept took support from them. Strom Thurmond's Dixiecrats are primarily Democrat as well but they are also the families of a lot of the boys who went to Russia and didn't come back. They don't want to see that happening again and they broke solidly for you Sir. Joe Kennedy's invectives against Strategic Air Command didn't help. The way that group saw things, it was the bombers that allowed the rest of the boys to come home."

"You said two things? And the other?"

"The press supported the Democrats Sir, most of it anyway. They saw what they wanted to see, not what was actually happening. Its a common thing, everybody does it, but this time it was worse than usual. Perhaps because of the way Joe Kennedy kept stirring things, I don't know. There's no harm in being part of a self-validating community as long as one remembers that's what it is. Only that got forgotten this time. The press experts assumed that people would vote the way they expected because they couldn't imagine them going any other way. My guess is, if they'd taken the second-preference votes of the independents and forecast using those, they'd have got pretty close."

President Dewey nodded. "How is your uncle doing Stuyvesant? I heard the shipyard shut down. Must have been a blow for him, he loved that yard."

"Indeed so Sir, but he knew its time was gone. The war showed that, it just couldn't build anything really useful, just a few PT boats. So he and the yard retired together. I believe he looks forward to living in retirement now."

"And well-deserved it is. He did well by this country, served with honor and made public service something to be respected. You'd do well to follow his example."

"I intend to Sir, my uncle and I were always very close. I sincerely wish to continue his work."

"Good. Stuyvesant ... or do you prefer to be called 'The Seer'?"

"The Seer Sir, if you have no objections. That means my Uncle's reputation and name will remain his alone."

"Odd code-name. How did you get it?"

"It's based on a time when I taught some people a lesson sir, one they didn't want to learn. But that was a long time ago." The Seer leaned forward a little expectantly. President Dewey had a pattern in meetings like this, a few minutes of harmless generalities then straight down to business.

"And you taught the Germans another. The whole world in fact. Seer, a few minutes ago you spoke of people only seeing what they want to see, not what really was there. Did you mean that?"

"Certainly sir. I'd say most problems people face come down to that."

"Hmmm. People, I don't know about that. Governments, its certainly true. Anyway, the way you people planned the destruction of Germany has been noticed and a lot of my colleagues have been thinking about its lessons. You, targeteers you called yourselves, were contracted to do a job and you did it. Fast, efficiently and without outside interference. That's a capability we want to keep. That's not true, we don't want to keep it, we want to exploit it and develop it.

"We are proposing that a new agency be started, the National Security Council. This will be a completely independent agency, outside the normal bureaucratic structure of Washington. It will be run by the same consortium of contractors who planned The Big One and its remit will be to provide independent and objective analyses of the threats facing the United States.

"The NSC will have the duty of calling the shots the way it sees them, without fear or favor. If I or my successors are wrong, it will be up to you to say so. If we are ignoring important things, tell us. You'll have full access to all intelligence and any other information you want. The contract under which the NSC will be run will stipulate your budget and your objectives. How you achieve those objectives is your business. That contract will run for ten years and be renewable at the end of each period. It will not be cancelable within that period. So no matter what you say or do, the NSC and its staff can't be fired.

"Seer, I want you to run the NSC. You will have the title of National Security Advisor and you will have full access to me at any time. Its a Cabinet-level post and you will be expected to attend cabinet meetings. Sorry about that. You accept?"

"Sir. It's an honor." The Seer grinned. "The Democrats are going to go ballistic."

"Some will. Not as many as you think. I talked this over with Harry Truman before the election. If his party had won, this plan would still have gone ahead, and you'd still have got the offer. If there's one thing the world's learning, its that we can't afford bad decisions any more."

Dewey looked through a file. "There's a US Army Corps of Engineers project for a new office building not far from here. Its been decided that building will be the headquarters of the National Security Council. Once the contracts are signed, go and see them and make sure the building is suited to your requirements. How will you get your staff?"

"We'll build on the core from the planning staff for The Big One Sir. I know many useful people we can bring in. We can draw on a widespread range of expertise, there's a lot of experience for us to make use of."

More than you can possibly know, thought the Seer although no sign of the reflection passed across his face.

"That's the advantage of a country like ours. There's always somebody who knows what we need to know, even if one has to look in all sorts of strange places to find them."

President Dewey's face was thoughtful. "You can start your new job now. We ran the election on a policy of no foreign entanglements, keeping ourselves to ourselves and only intervening when our vital national interests are at stake. And when we do, it is with our bombers, not by sending troops. Is that right?"

"Neo-Isolationism. In the short term, Sir, I think so. At the moment, our nuclear monopoly puts us top of the heap by a margin so large we can't measure it. We can destroy anybody we want to, and nobody can stop us. That won't last Sir, I give it five years, six at the most, before Japan gets its own nuclear weapons. Even then, they won't mess with us, it just isn't worth it for them.

"We're entering the Pax Americana Sir, the era when we keep the peace. We won't get thanked for it but its a good thing to do. How long will it last? That depends, the Pax Britannica lasted for almost a century but that was a different era. We don't rule the world, Sir, we don't want to and we couldn't even if we did. The Pax Americana just means that we'll stop anybody else who does want to be Emperor of the World. That should be good enough."

"The Pax Americana. " Dewey's voice was thoughtful. "I like the sound of that. NSC will generate a report exploring those ideas further. Make it your first priority."

The Seer left the office and left, picking his hat and coat up as he did. His car was waiting for him outside, its driver a young woman. Naturally a blonde, like most fair-haired girls, she'd dyed it dark brown. Looking like a German was not a tactful thing in an America that had only just ended the bloodiest war in human history.

"Inanna, take me our home in Georgetown. We've just got everything we wanted. I'll need to talk to Nefertiti on this one. I really ought to let Eldest know what's happening as well."

"He won't like it you know. You know what he thinks about interfering."

"I do and he's right. But we've got a new situation here, something we've never faced before. I don't think we've ever had weapons that can wipe the whole species out before. Anyway, we're not interfering, we're not going to tell people what to do. We're just going to try and stop everybody from making any serious mistakes while they follow their own plans.

"That's something that should have done that a long time ago and this country fought a civil war because of it. I think if Sam Grant had known that war could have been stopped and hadn't been, he'd have shot everybody on the spot."

The Seer was silent, seeing a picture of a meeting around a camp fire at three in the morning as the casualty results from Spotsylvania had come in, the image haunting his mind. Grant's words echoed in his mind complementing the image. "After this war is won, I hope to God that I never fight another one." Sam had been drunk enough to see too clearly and say things that were too true. Far too true. Would the Pax Americana mean that he could think the same, that he would never have to plan another war?

Inanna was chuckling as she edged the car through the roads to Georgetown. "Honey, do you find the idea of getting shot by a drunken general amusing?"

"Frankly boss, yes. Somehow you'd turn it into an advantage. That wasn't why I was laughing though. I was thinking about the phrase the Christians have in their Bible. 'When the end days come, Demons will walk the earth.' Does that make these the end days."

The Seer didn't join her laugh. "All too probably I'm afraid. Technology development is moving much faster than people's ability to control that technology. That was obvious even as early as the Civil War. Even then, technology had moved faster than the ability to understand its implications. They were still trying to fight rifled muskets with Napoleonic tactics. Damn it, Sam should never have tried that last assault at Cold Harbor and he nearly shot himself when he realized what he'd done.

"Now, its a thousand times worse. We planned The Big One as a horrible example to the world of what the power of modern

\pons really meant. Curt sees it the same way, just a different perspective. I don't think anybody has listened to either of us."

"So the prophets were right then? Could it be some mystics are right?"

"Oh come on Inanna." The Seer was slightly irritated. "In all the time we've been around, have you ever known a mystical prophet to be right? 'There will be accidents'. 'Important people will die'. 'There will be discontent.' 'Trade will be affected.' That's the best they can do. Vague generalizations that could mean anything and only mean something long after the event. Most of them were so far gone on hallucinogens that their minds were up in the clouds anyway."

"What are you going to do about Loki, Seer? He hates you for not telling him that The Big One was about to happen."

"I know, and it could have got him killed as well. Loki will get over it. Its not the first time he's lost people due to his own lack of foresight. There was the Morrigan business a few years back. I've heard that was connected with the way Odin vanished from circulation but I expect I'll get the truth of it eventually. He'll cool down in the end. Any word from Suriyothai yet?"

"None yet. I think she's still tied up with the Moscow Conference. The status of Saigon or something."

"We'll need to talk to her, Loki as well. Mostly Suriyothai though, it looks like she was right after all. We can't carry on wandering from country to country avoiding trouble. We've run out of places to wander to. My guess is, here we are and here we'll stay. Its a good country and these are good people, we should cast our lot in with them. Eldest won't like that either, he's never approved of Suriyothai's attachment to her homeland. I don't think we have a choice though. We have to join the Americans and that means doing the best we can for them."

"The Anvil of Necessity." Inanna's voice was thoughtful.

"That old Russian saying? Its true though. We have to stay with the Americans for both our sakes and necessity makes the alliance a strong one. I just pray that its strong enough. I don't know what's going to hit us eventually but something will and when it does it will be very, very nasty."

The two occupants of the car settled back in silence, contemplating the future. Unknown to either of them, the wire recorder concealed in the car hissed gently as it transcribed the silence onto its reels.

The End